AUGUST 17

PRAISE FOR *AUGUST 17*

'"What if" is a tantalizing question for those who are invested in the plot twists of subcontinental history. In S. Hareesh's rich political imagination, that question erupts into a genre-defying, history-smashing novel about a country that didn't happen. Jayasree Kalathil captures the wit and creativity of this novel in her expert translation. Ultimately, this is a novel about the fictional nature of nation states and their borders.'

– Shahnaz Habib,
author of *Airplane Mode*, and JCB Prize–winning translator of *Jasmine Days*

'The real and the imagined commingle in this brilliant, and superbly translated, novel. In the verve of alternate history, under layers of research and play and invention, one finds a vital jostling with the questions of what fiction can do and what fiction must do.'

– Tanuj Solanki,
author of *Diwali in Muzaffarnagar* and *Manjhi's Mayhem*

AUGUST 17

A NOVEL

S. HAREESH

Translated from the Malayalam by
JAYASREE KALATHIL

HARPERPERENNIAL

An Imprint of HarperCollins *Publishers*

First published in English in India by Harper Perennial 2026
An imprint of HarperCollins *Publishers*
HarperCollins *Publishers* India, Cyber City, Building 10-A, Gurugram,
Haryana – 122002, India
www.harpercollins.co.in

2 4 6 8 10 9 7 5 3 1

P-ISBN: 978-93-6989-155-9
E-ISBN: 978-93-6989-716-2

Typeset in 11/15.1 Scala Pro
by HarperCollins *Publishers* India Pvt. Ltd

Printed and bound at
Nutech Print Services Pvt. Ltd.

FSC
www.fsc.org
MIX
Paper | Supporting responsible forestry
FSC® C195953

This book is printed on FSC® certified paper
which ensures responsible forest management.

*

HarperCollins *Publishers*, Macken House, 39/40 Mayor Street Upper, Dublin 1,
D01 C9W8, Ireland

'Historical truth, for him, is not what has happened; it is what we judge to have happened.'

– Jorge Luis Borges, 'Pierre Menard, Author of the Quixote', translated by Anthony Bonner

AUTHOR'S NOTE

Many were the doubts and dilemmas in my mind when I sat down to write a novel based on the history of a small state in the southernmost corner of India. The most significant of these was how much people remembered or understood the events that form the backdrop to this novel and had taken place only three-quarters of a century ago. The histories of large nation states, geographical areas and of influential communities are readily accepted as 'world history' – the history of Europe, for example. Setting out to write a novel based on events from that history, a writer would surely find several easy and convenient routes into the story. They would not have to work too hard to convince the reader about the ingredients of their handiwork.

In the case of *August 17*, things are somewhat more complex. This is a novel that imagines what would have happened if the history of Thiruvithamkoor (Travancore) – an area at the southern tip of Kerala that was, before Independence, a sovereign country – had unfolded differently. Even those who live within its old boundaries, a substantial number of them, are not aware that such a country existed, nor have they heard about the most important and decisive moments in its history. Three-quarters of a century – indeed a short period of time, but enough to erase from memory the history of a country that had existed for several centuries.

And yet, there is one significant moment in the history of this country which, had it not happened, would have changed the destinies of the people living in this region now, and of India itself. This novel is about that moment. The novel imagines what would have happened if, in 1947, Thiruvithamkoor had not joined the Indian Union, and had instead retained its sovereignty and remained an independent nation. To give readers a general sense of the background, I will briefly describe certain things pertaining to the country. Remember, as you read on, that the novel deals with real and imagined histories, but this note is about its real – or, rather, publicly accepted – history.

The British ruled India mainly in two ways. Some places, such as the United Provinces that included present-day Uttar Pradesh, were under their direct rule. In other places, they held power indirectly by controlling the local kingdoms while also letting the native royal rulers retain self-governance. Thiruvithamkoor was one of these princely states alongside Gwalior, Mysore, Hyderabad and so on.

Geographically, Thiruvithamkoor was formed of the southern parts of present-day Kerala and Tamil Nadu. To the north of the country was another princely state, the kingdom of Kochi, and to the east the Madras Province of British India, which included the Malabar region and the northern districts of contemporary Kerala. The western and southern borders were marked by the Arabian Sea and the Indian Ocean respectively.

It was officially a Hindu nation. The majority of the population was Hindu, but there were substantial numbers of Christians and not an inconsiderable number of Muslims. Many were the educational institutions serving all these communities, partly also as a result of missionary work. Malayalam and Tamil were the main languages spoken. Thiruvananthapuram, Kollam and Alappuzha were the main cities. The Hindu Nair community and the Suriyani Christian community (also known as St Thomas Christians or Syriac Christians) enjoyed economic as well as political privilege. Although marginalized in the social order, the Ezhava community was well represented in the population. In governance, however, Brahmins from outside the country, especially from Mysore and

Tamil Nadu, had great prominence and held powerful positions. Leaders of the Kerala Renaissance, including Sree Narayana Guru, Mahatma Ayyankali and Mannath Padmanabhan, were natives of Thiruvithamkoor.

The architect of modern Thiruvithamkoor was Maharaja Marthanda Varma who ruled the kingdom from 1729 to 1758. He waged wars against the neighbouring lands, conquered them and attached them to Thiruvithamkoor, thus extending its boundaries. Marthanda Varma and his descendants accepted British imperialism, but Thiruvithamkoor continued to enjoy the right to govern itself.

It was considered that Thiruvithamkoor belonged to Sree Padmanabhan (Lord Vishnu), the titulary deity of the royal family, enshrined in the Padmanabhaswamy temple in Thiruvananthapuram, one of the richest temples in India. The belief is that the country belonged to Sree Padmanabhan and the king was his servant, a figurehead who ruled the land in his service. The Thiruvithamkoor royal family followed the matrilineal system of inheritance.

The few years before the British left India were a time of political turbulence in Thiruvithamkoor. The main political party was the Thiruvithamkoor State Congress, which could be seen as a subsidiary of the Indian National Congress. Equally active were the Thiruvithamkoor National Congress which supported royal rule and the Communist Party which opposed it. An important incident of the time was the Punnapra–Vayalar Samaram, an uprising primarily against the diwan Sir C.P. Ramaswami Iyer, a bloody people's struggle that ended in police shooting and the killing of over a hundred people.

When it was time for the British to leave, the princely states of India had two options before them: join either India or Pakistan, or retain sovereignty as independent nations. Like

Kashmir and Hyderabad, Thiruvithamkoor initially chose to remain independent, and a constitution in the American model was prepared by Sir C.P. Ramaswami Iyer. But revolts broke out across the country opposing this plan; a group of political activists attempted to assassinate the diwan. The attempt was unsuccessful, but having sustained stab wounds to his face, Sir C.P. left the country. Thiruvithamkoor decided to join the Indian Union after all, first becoming part of the Thirukochi state with the neighbouring kingdom of Kochi, and then, along with Malabar, forming the state of Kerala in 1956. The Tamil-speaking parts of Thiruvithamkoor, including places like Kanyakumari at the southern tip, became part of Tamil Nadu. The nation of Thiruvithamkoor ceased to exist. Still, from the viewpoint of the history buff, the southern parts of Kerala and Tamil Nadu are, even today, full of remnants of royal rule.

As a person born and brought up in a place that was part of the old Thiruvithamkoor, its history had made itself at home in my mind right from the time I began reading. My father was born as the citizen of a country that people have almost completely forgotten. Before him, for generations, we were Thiruvithamkoorians. But even before that, before 1750 to be precise, we were part of another country named Vadakkumkoor. Its southern border was within a few feet of our home. It was Marthanda Varma who forcefully annexed it to Thiruvithamkoor. I walk back and forth across that disappeared border several times a day, and that old country comes into my reverie every now and then, along with the thought that borders, all borders, are susceptible to being rubbed off at some future time.

Even after it became part of independent India, the people of Thiruvithamkoor retained their dedication to the royal family for a very long time. I grew up hearing stories about Marthanda Varma, his diwan Ramayyan Dalawa, Dharma Raja who succeeded his uncle Marthanda Varma to the throne, Raja Kesavadas, the diwan during Dharma Raja's reign, and many others. C.V. Raman Pillai (1858–1922), perhaps the most important novelist in Malayalam literature, wrote the historical trilogy, *Marthanda Varma*, *Dharmaraja* and *Ramaraja Bahadur*, based on these figures. In the process, this great writer mixed up beyond recognition historical facts and his own imagination in his readers' minds. History textbooks, even today, present events and stories he created from his imagination as facts!

The themes in this novel have been inside me from a young age, but the immediate persuasion to write it was the excessive nationalist fervour that has been growing all around us in the last few years. Nationalist sentiment, when excessive, is as problematic as religious sentiment. My father who was born a Thiruvithamkoorian and died an Indian and my ancestors who were people of Vadakkumkoor and before that people of some unknown country remind me every day of the transient nature of countries and borders. Had an important historical event taken a different route, I, too, would not have been Indian, would have, perhaps, been the citizen of a country in perpetual enmity with India. In essence, then, nationalism can be put on or taken off as easily as the clothes we wear; nothing inherently sentimental about it. As I was writing this novel, the concerns I have about the recent trajectories of Indian democracy were also at the surface of my mind. Thiruvithamkoor was a religious state. If it had continued in that way, it would have been a grave tragedy. I do not like the fact that the country I am part of is choosing to travel down religiously defined paths.

This novel is an attempt to reimagine a history that would be unfamiliar to most of its readers. I had concerns about the translatability of such a novel. The fact that Jayasree Kalathil took on the task gave me confidence – she has already done a brilliant job of taking my first novel, *Moustache*, and a collection of short stories, *Adam*, to English readers. Her translation of this novel underlines, once again, the fact that translation is a creative art independent of the original. One should not shower too much praise on those who are close to us, so I will just say 'thank you' to Jayasree.

– S. Hareesh
Neendoor, Kerala

TRANSLATOR'S NOTE

Critics and readers have called *August 17* historical fiction, speculative historical fiction, alternative history, parallel history, historical metafiction, and so on and so forth. In some sense, then, the book came with the burden of its engagement with history, one that was not all that familiar to me. I knew of many of the characters and their general role in the history of Kerala. But people of my generation were taught more about the various empires in India than the native, sovereign kingdoms that existed in the strip of land currently called Kerala.

Could I translate this novel without knowing the history of Thiruvithamkoor as intimately as Hareesh did or, at the very least, as much as an informed inhabitant of the region? Would I be able to take it across to readers who did not know anything at all about this history? As I began translating this novel, I let myself be troubled by these questions, stopped writing in order to read through a list of material that kept growing longer and longer, until the project was in danger of stalling. The answer came from conversations with Hareesh. In the preface to the Malayalam edition of *August 17*, Hareesh writes that all stories about human beings are prefaced or accompanied by history and politics, and that writers are not required to be faithful to 'actual' history but can treat it as raw material for creating fiction just as people and episodes from our lives are imagined differently to create stories and characters. As we discussed what this meant, I began to think about works of fiction based in history that I have enjoyed as a reader. I knew very little of French cultural and architectural history when I read and enjoyed Victor Hugo's Gothic historical classic

The Hunchback of Notre-Dame (translated by Frederic Shoberl), or of the Almoravid dynasty, the Crusades and the Reconquista while reading the historical metafiction *The History of the Siege of Lisbon* by José Saramago (translated by Giovanni Pontiero), or of the Anglo-Asante wars or the early colonial history of Ghana when reading *Homegoing,* Yaa Gyasi's generational historical saga.

The thing to remember then, I told myself, is that *August 17* is not history but fiction, and fiction that takes liberties with recorded history. Released thus from the burden of history, I could return to the story world that Hareesh had created. I thank him for these conversations, and for his patience, friendship and unwavering faith in me as his translator.

Translating this novel was also an opportunity to reread the works of Vaikom Muhammad Basheer. It went far beyond consulting the stories referenced in this novel to rediscovering the world our beloved Beypore Sultan had created. I thank my sister Sreeja Kalathil, a Basheer-lover herself, for gifting me the thick, two-volume edition of his collected works. Many people came to my rescue when I was stuck wondering how to take a word, an event, an idea from Malayalam over to English. My gratitude to all of them, especially to my friends E.V. Fathima, K.N. Sunandan, Karunakaran, Ashtamoorthy Desamangalam and Bindu Menon. As usual, Shefali Jha and Adley Siddiqi gave the first draft their critical consideration. I am grateful for their thoughtful feedback.

I am ever so grateful to our agents, the brilliant Ambar Sahil and Hemali Sodhi at A Suitable Agency. They championed this work and helped us find it a home with HarperCollins India.

And as always, I am mindful of my good fortune in working with an editor who personifies talent, patience (despite the many dropped deadlines) and grace. I am eternally grateful to Rahul Soni for being that person despite the pressures of his own writing.

– Jayasree Kalathil
Hampshire, England

PART I

I

Everyone knows that the history of modern Thiruvithamkoor begins with the first day of the month of Chingam in the year 1123 of the Malayalam calendar Kollavarsham – that is, 17 August 1947 CE – when Maharaja Sree Chithira Thirunal Balarama Varma hoisted the saffron flag emblazoned with the sinistral form of the divine conch at Kizhakkekotta fort in Thiruvananthapuram. Of course, our country existed long before that, its history extending well into the medieval kingdom of Venad and into the empire of the Cheras. Still, with its current borders defined by Maharaja Marthanda Varma in 1729, Thiruvithamkoor can be said to have enjoyed true sovereignty only for about seventy years, after which, for centuries, we were under the shadow of the British empire. When they decided to leave the subcontinent, it was generally assumed that we would surrender our identity and become part of India, one of the two nations that were being formed. But history had other plans for us. Thiruvithamkoor became a free, sovereign country.

This writer is not a historian. He is not experienced in the art of writing, nor does he have the linguistic skills required. Besides, the history of this part of the world has already been written by others. Then why bother, you might ask. I have an answer to that question. I was present to witness the historic event described above. I was standing, somewhat lost in my thoughts, at a little distance from the crowd, aware, of course, that what was unfolding before us was perhaps the most beautiful event of all times in the history of the great nation of Thiruvithamkoor. However, I was also distracted, unable to register fully the sights in front of me, as I was keenly aware of our enemies, both within and outside the country.

As the flag unfurled in the pleasant breeze of the Onam season and showered flower petals over the crowd, everyone had their eyes trained upwards. In that moment, I felt an inexplicable urge to glance at the bottom of the flagpole. I can't quite describe what I saw. When we witness something that entirely fulfils our lives, it is in our nature to doubt the experience later, to question its veracity. This, indeed, was such a moment! I realized that there was one other person who was not looking upwards at the fluttering flag. It was none other than the hero of the hour, Rao Bahadur Maharaja Sree Chithira Thirunal Balarama Varma. With his head cocked to the left, he was looking straight at me! Did it really happen? I am not sure. But I felt that moment stretching as long as a decade or two.

People like me are destined to have our mistakes discovered, even if it is at a later date, while the services we render go unrecognized and unvalued. And yet, there he was, the most important person of the land, gazing at me, telling me silently, 'You too have contributed to this moment.' My joy was so great that I could not even shed happy tears! I suppose we humans empty out and become hollow beings in moments of great doings.

I have tried reading the odd history book. And I have been amazed at how different people interpret the same things in completely different ways. Is there anything that we human beings agree on? Ten people write twenty different stories about what is in front of their own eyes. So, consider this the history of our country as witnessed by me alone. You will find here things that happened before and after our country became independent. Do not expect it to follow the conventions of history writing. This is just something I felt like writing down. You may think of it as an autobiography, or the biographies of several people I have met, or even a story. Also, do not expect that everything in here will be substantiated with evidence. People usually don't want that. Who knows what they want!

I shall begin.

2

I knew the man by sight, but the first time I met him in person was at the post office ground in Muhamma. Towards the end of 1939, I think it was. In those days, I went by the name of Bhasi. I had arrived a couple of days earlier, hitching a ride in a coconut boat from northern Paravoor to Thavanakkadavu, and then walking the rest of the way via Cherthala.

In those days, the whole place was a waterscape with isolated islets within it. Walk a few yards in any direction and the path would end at a canal or a dyke. One could jump across the smaller ones. But to cross the others, one had to wait for a boat passing by. That was dangerous. The obliging boatmen usually wanted you to fulfil their curiosity in return for a ride. Name, native place, caste, purpose of visit – they asked questions that dug deep, even into one's past life, as though they were on a mission not to let anyone live with even a little bit of privacy. Making up lies was an unavoidable part of my job. Except in the most crucial instances, I was careful not to fabricate too many stories or go into details. If I did, I would then have to remember all those details in case I ended up meeting the same person again and they cunningly asked the same questions. So, whenever my path was bisected by a canal, instead of waiting around for a boat to pass by, I would choose a direction and walk along the canal bank until I came to – and I invariably did – at least an old and decaying length of coconut tree laid across it. If you took care to step on it only with your big toes, imagined yourself to be entirely weightless, you might just make it across. If someone were to map my meandering journeys ... Ha! It would be quite amusing.

Except for a few hovels and ponds stinking with the coconut husks left to soak in the water to make coir, the place was full of tall coconut trees with their heads tapped for toddy. A stench rose from the rotting dried fish strewn around the trees as fertilizer. In between were huge mounds of silver sand, almost as high as the trees. They looked like mountaintops covered in snow, or at least as I imagined them to be. They blazed in the sunlight. Ignoring my burning feet, I climbed one of them like a child on a haystack. Covered in sugar-sand, I reached the top and looked over to the other side. Two women sat by a tiny channel of water bordered by verungu trees, plaiting coconut fronds. The younger one split the fronds and bent the leaves, and the one that looked like her mother finished the job, braiding them neatly and tightly. They raised their heads and looked at me as though wondering why anyone in their right mind would climb up to where not even grass sprouted. They did not seem perturbed by the sight. I climbed down quickly and walked towards them, hoping for a drink of kanjivellam. But when I got there, they had faded away into the sunlight.

I reached Muhamma by evening, lay down on a kalithattu, the resting place made of rough-hewn stones where folk sat chatting during the day, and slept for a while. When darkness fell, I walked eastwards, went to a Muslim household, and asked them for something to eat.

'Where are you from?' the householder asked as I ate the boiled tapioca they gave me.

'Ah, south,' I said, 'a bit away.'

'And where are you off to?'

'Oh, nowhere in specific. I deal in copra. I'm looking for coconut to buy in bulk at a reasonable price.'

As we continued chatting, I tried surreptitiously to wangle information about local activities of the State Congress from him.

'Pricks!' he said. 'All they've managed to do is get beaten up or shot to death. Like they can stand up to the Pattar, our esteemed Diwanji!'

'Still, Ikka, justice is on their side, no?' I tried prodding him, addressing him politely as older brother, wanting to know what he actually thought, but he ignored me, walked to the edge of the lake and sat down to urinate.

I went back to the kalithattu and spent the night there. The next day, I woke up early and wrote a short report of all that had happened. When I finished, I took out the government circular and read it carefully once again. This is what it said:

> *The government has been made aware that the State Congress is planning to hold assemblies in several locations in the country this month. It is hereby ordered that the pravruthyars in charge of the villages in these locations should round up fifteen rowdies in their respective jurisdictions, ply them with intoxicants such as toddy and arrack, and instruct them to go to the venues and disrupt the meetings in the following manner:*
>
> *1) Insinuate themselves into the crowd and cause a ruckus by pushing and shoving one another.*
>
> *2) Pelt gravel and stones into the crowd and create an atmosphere of disorder.*
>
> *3) Praise Amma Maharani, His Royal Majesty and Diwanji, shouting 'ki jai' to all three at the top of their voices.*
>
> *4) If the meeting still continues, run on to the stage and start a skirmish.*
>
> *5) Try to disrobe the speaker and the others on the stage by force.*

I spent the day wandering around the place pretending to be a coconut trader, meeting landowners and a man who ran a wholesale coconut depot to fix prices in advance. My meal was a plate of kanji at a Chovan's house in Kayippuram. The information I gathered from the people I met is summarized below.

As in most other places across the land, the Christians here supported the State Congress. However, the rich among them did not express their support openly. The poor too – Nairs, Chovans and Muslims alike – supported them. Regardless, lately there seemed to be increasing resentment among the rank and file towards leaders such as Pattom Thanu Pillai and T.M. Varghese. There was a considerable number of Thiruvithamkoor National Congress supporters among the Nairs, who, by the way, have more power socially. Taken as a whole, very few people held bad feelings towards the Maharaja or Amma Maharani. The majority would rise from their seats, their eyes lowered respectfully, at the mere mention of His Majesty. However, they had equal respect for people like Gandhi and Rajagopalachari. Hatred for the British was widespread. Local activities of the State Congress were being led by a man named Narayanapillah, a man with a school education. TNC did not seem to have any organized activities around here.

In the evening, I sat with a man from the Paravan community by the side of a canal and drank arrack. As a coconut picker, he knew every household and every person in the locality like the inside of his palm. Careful not to lose my head, I sipped the arrack and listened to him.

'My lot is pathetic, you know, if you think about it,' he said, referring to his occupation. 'There's nothing I haven't seen from the top of a coconut tree. But can I talk about it? No! They'll cut my head off! Some things I see, some things they show me...'

'Same with me,' I replied in a serious voice. 'The things I see as I wander around ... I forget them immediately. What else!'

Encouraged by my response, he began pouring out all the secrets he had witnessed. I have a lot of experience listening to such revelations and am quite capable of telling truths and lies apart, so I sat there with a smile on my face. Some people like revealing secrets. Others enjoy listening to them.

The next day was a Sunday. In the morning, the Paravan took me to Naduvathachan who was the pravruthyar, the village officer. He owned a three-acre coconut grove in Kalavoor. Agree on the price now and come back with a boat for the next harvest, said Naduvathachan who was a respectable man. I think he liked it when I said I would pay him on the same day I picked up the coconuts. At his command, the Paravan cut down a young coconut and gave it to me.

'Aren't you having one?' I asked, sitting on a branch of a cashew tree that bent almost to the ground.

'Hm! His Lordship won't even let the children have one!' said the Paravan reverentially.

'That's true!' Naduvathachan said. 'I don't mind if they eat a coconut at the time of harvest. Wasting it when it is still young – that I don't like.'

From our chit-chat, I soon deduced that the local leader of the State Congress, Narayanapillah, was the son of a sort-of sister of Naduvathachan. Nevertheless, as the pravruthyar of the land who looked after matters relating to its revenue, he tried to follow the instructions in the government circular. He had not succeeded in rounding up the required fifteen rowdies, but six or seven had been organized from the seaside villages around Arthunkal on the initiative of the parish priest there. A man named Bhaskaran had agreed to arrange the toddy and arrack for the rowdies. Still, Naduvathachan was hoping that the events tomorrow would end without creating too much havoc. If the police came, things would only get worse.

'Can't they mind their own business?' he said, his voice only a whisper even though there was no one around to overhear. 'What all they did last year ... and did they achieve anything? Some people got killed, that's all.'

'Really?' I said, acting surprised. 'I don't pay attention to such things. Work hard and have a bellyful of kanji. That's all I care about.'

Naduvathachan's face brightened. 'And you're absolutely right. Let them lose control of themselves and end up in jail. See what happened to that Akkamma and Kunju Pillah.'

I told him I had no idea who they were, and that put him in a better mood. I asked him why, when across the country the State Congress kept a low profile, they were getting ready for a public assembly. He had no real explanation.

'Making trouble, what else!' he said.

3

On the day of the assembly, I washed by the lake bright and early and set out towards the post office area. There was nothing special to see there. It was 10 a.m. by the time a couple of men arrived and began digging holes in the ground to put up the bamboo poles for the stage. Afraid that I would attract unnecessary attention if I loitered, I walked back to the lake and went to the jetty. A few people asked me who I was and where I was from. I brushed off their questions with some vague responses and hung around there, chewed a couple of paans. It was a perfect place to watch the goings-on. Small fishing boats bobbed peacefully on the placid lake in the gentle breeze that carried the slimy odour of fish. Canopied passenger boats plied back and forth. In my job, it is important to learn not to be suspicious about ordinary things and waste time investigating them, while at the same time be alert enough to notice even the slightest sign of something strange in the mundane. There are those among my kind who fail to understand this. They smell a conspiracy in everything they encounter and begin making assumptions that lead them astray from their goal. Doing this job, I have come to understand certain things. People conspire, of course, all the time, and put those conspiracies into action. But the more people and actions are involved in a conspiracy, the more the likelihood of unexpected developments. I have seen that these unexpected developments have a way of influencing the outcome in the end. So, the best thing to do is to follow what is in front of us and try to use it to our advantage. Throw in a bit of luck, and it will yield results beyond our expectations.

By noon, a crowded boat from Kumarakom arrived. People disembarked hurriedly, carrying bundles of rope, sacks of dry tapioca, and stacks of mats and baskets. The last to disembark, chatting with one another and in no obvious hurry, were two people clad in khaddar. Their clothes attracted some attention from onlookers. I decided to follow them at a safe distance. According to the information I had received, one of them was Chacko Joseph and the other was K.N. Bharathan. Chacko Joseph had served a nine-month prison term for making a treasonous public speech in Koothattukulam. Bharathan had also received a jail sentence – six months – for leading a procession in Changanassery. Both of them looked around thirty-five years of age. They caught up with a young man waiting outside in the lane and set out with him. I followed until, after half a mile south, they walked into Narayanapillah's house, at which point I turned back and went towards the Kanjikuzhi area. On the way, I stopped at a prosperous-looking house and asked for a glass of kanjivellam. The woman there gave me a plate of kanji with some gravy from a fish curry poured over it.

As the sun went down in the sky, young men began congregating at the Kanjikuzhi junction singly and in groups. All of them were dressed in khaddar, and some of them had white caps on. Soon, there were around thirty of them. A large number of people had already lined the street as though expecting some interesting event. Suddenly, one of the young men shouted in a throat-searing voice:

State Congress ki ... JAI!
Mahatma Gandhi ki ... JAI!

As people repeated the slogans, I moved behind a tree and took out the khaddar mundu, shirt and Gandhi cap I had brought along. I changed into them, tucked the clothes I was wearing into the crotch of a branch and stepped out. When the procession began moving forward, I joined it, not right at the front nor quite in the middle. I was careful not to do anything that would attract attention. Gradually, the slogans lost steam. Then, a young man with the voice of a child began singing:

Come, come, little brother
There's our battlefield
Today we are mere children
But tomorrow, citizens indeed
If we sneeze, comes the police
If we spit, the army it is
Pick up the pen, end up in jail
Meet up with friends, bullets hail
Let them kill us with their spears
Let our young blood flow like rivers
Come, come, little brother...

The song ended and the slogans picked up again. Women and children waited in the compounds all along the route to see the procession go by.

The crowd that awaited the procession at the post office ground was much larger than I had anticipated. Over five hundred people scrambling for space. I took off my cap and made small talk with some of them. Most were from neighbouring places. I did not get the sense that they had any motive other than listening to the speeches and joining in in the sloganeering. I even met a few people who did not know the difference between the State Congress and the TNC.

The programme began soon enough, and it was unplanned and chaotic, to say the least. Some people climbed up on the stage and began singing enthusiastically. Every now and then, slogans erupted from the audience. It happened suddenly. A commotion that seemed to alarm the crowd at the front of the stage and make them scatter. As people jostled and swung back and forth trying not to lose their footing, a space, like a circle with a sagging, ill-defined circumference, formed in the middle. Everyone wanted to have a look, even the ones who had, until then, been standing aside from the crowd by the periphery of the ground. It was clear from the noise that whatever was happening there made the people ecstatic or enraged. I squeezed myself through the heaving bodies, trying to get to a better vantage point.

In the middle of the circle was a man dressed only in a pair of blue-and-white underpants, swinging his arms, slapping his oiled thighs and shoulders, and yelling as though throwing out a challenge. He looked around the crowd and beckoned people, and they looked away, 'Not me,' 'Not me.' At any moment now, someone will jump into the circle, the crowd hoped collectively. I looked around but could not find anyone who might be capable of taking up his challenge. Suddenly, a realization flashed through my mind. This was the moment I had been waiting for, the opportunity that presented itself only once in a lifetime. In my job, there were many occasions when I needed to make decisions without waiting for orders from above. In fact, it was those occasions, their innate freedom and danger, that thrilled me. There was nothing like *that* kind of fulfilment.

It was on the last day of a meeting of the Congress in Madurai that a gusthi, a traditional wrestling match like the one about to unfold here, took place for the first time. Almost fifty State Congress workers went to Madurai for that meeting, including Kumbalath Shanku Pillai and Thazhava Keshavan. When the audience began to show signs of boredom listening to the long-winded speeches, they got on the stage and began wrestling with one another. The audience, made up entirely of proponents of non-violence, ahimsapremis, enjoyed it thoroughly, and clapped harder and longer than they had when the speechmakers derided the British. The hypocrisy! Those who preached that violence is a sin wallowing in the enjoyment of bodily harm as an artform! How long would they hide the violence in their hearts? Was there any reason that the hunger strikes spearheaded by their fox-like leader were successful other than the fact that the British masters were scared of the violence that would be unleashed if he died? Their non-violent tactics worked only because of the fear of the anticipated violence. We had seen their true colours in the revolts that took place when they were not successful.

The year 1114 of the Kollavarsham was marked by the agitations for Utharavada Bharanam – the demand that people be given voting rights and the right to form a 'responsible government'. Those were the days of huge meetings that brought together supporters and dissidents in large numbers in one place, not to mention the rowdies as stipulated in the government circular and the police who were there to arrest those who broke the law. Kumbalath and Thazhava had a different objective for the gusthi performances they put up at these meetings. As the atmosphere turned increasingly volatile, one of them, dressed for gusthi, would step into the middle of the crowd, slap his muscles and lay down the gauntlet. Watching the crowd's unbridled joy, one would be forgiven for thinking that he was challenging the diwan Sir C.P. Ramaswami Iyer himself or the British. In a little while, the other one, pretending to be just another spectator, would step out of the crowd to accept the challenge. The crowd would welcome him as though he were their sworn enemy. A show-fight lasting at least half an hour would follow as though it were an intense hand-to-hand combat. Several times, the challenger would pretend that he was about to lose, keeping the spectators on the knife-edge of suspense, until, invariably, he would win the match. And the foolish crowd would bay in victory as though the honourable Diwanji had been defeated right in front of their eyes. Kumbalath and Thazhava knew that their performance would have the psychological effect of energizing their supporters and disheartening their enemies. But no one had expected a gusthi to take place in this smallish meeting here in Muhamma. The presence of prominent leaders like Kumbalath Shanku Pillai and Thazhava Keshavan was usually announced beforehand.

I watched the gusthikkaaran carefully. He was not one of the better-known leaders. Average skin tone, average height, a somewhat thick lower lip, a small moustache. His hairline had begun to recede, but he could not be more than a few years over thirty. Trying to recall where I had seen him before, I took off my shirt and handed it to the man standing next to me, pulled the ends of my mundu between my legs and tucked it at the back. The man who took my shirt raised his arms and bellowed. Immediately, the people closest to me pulled away and another circle formed around me. In the energy of the cheering crowd, I walked as though my feet were not quite touching the ground and stood in front of the gusthikkaaran. The crowd whistled and shouted as we stood face to face and circled one another slowly as is done before commencing a match. I felt my feet sinking in the sandy soil, the type of soil that made one lose one's footing. He looked deep into my eyes and spoke loudly, and I had the futile thought that we could not continue like this for long and that I was somewhat responsible for fulfilling the expectations of the spectators. Pulling my feet off the sand, I lunged forward, put my arms around his neck and tried to push him to the ground. The crowd heaved back in fright, and as our arms tightened around each other, heaved forward again. His strategy was to lock his legs around mine to pull me down. But I stood firm. Time stopped for a while, and then a man who had appointed himself as the referee pulled us apart. By then, the spectators, these ahimsapremis, were beside themselves and began shouting, 'Finish him off!', 'Break his neck!', and so on. We circled one another again. This time, it was his turn. Flexing his muscles, he bided his time, then rushing at me crouching, he caught hold of my waist. For a split second, I found myself being pushed back, but locked my arms around his neck and head, and began applying pressure. Suddenly, I felt a weightlessness, and in the next moment, I was hoisted on to his shoulders, spun around and thrown to the ground flat on my back. The crowd fell upon us, and the most enthusiastic of them stomped on my chest. Someone bit me on my shoulder.

Later, I stood by the well, washing the dust off me, listening to the speeches. A man named Aplon Arouge was making the welcome speech. Edavanatt Padmanabha Menon and some others who had come on the boat at the lake sat on the stage, waiting for their turn. My opponent was on the other side of the well, drawing water and pouring it over his head. He peeped into the well, stuck out his lips and whistled to attract the attention of the fish, and then smiled at me. I smiled back.

'Who are you, buddhoos?'

Although I did not like the way he spoke to me, as though to a little child, I smiled at him.

'Have you eaten anything?'

'No.'

'Come on, then.'

He took me to a chai shop near the jetty and bought us tea and some fried snacks. I made up a story on the spot, telling him that my name was Bhasi, that my home was down south, and that I had left home wanting to be part of the freedom struggle.

'Ha, ha ... People like me went all the way to Kozhikode and Karachi to join the struggle whereas you've come to this backwater?' he said, laughing. 'See this hand? I've touched Gandhi with it.'

'Kandi? Really?' the chai shop owner, who was grinding the rice for the next day's snacks, asked, intruding into our conversation.

'Really. His hands are so soft, softer than women's breasts.'

He paid up and walked out without looking at me. I followed.

'What caste are you?' he asked.

'Oh, who cares ... One caste, one religion, you know...' I knew exactly what to say to get into the good books of such people.

'Ha, ha ... Now I know what caste you are.'

'It's not that,' I said. 'When I meet people, I just feel that whatever their caste is, that's mine too.'

'In that case, you can think of yourself as a Muslim when you're with me.' He stopped for a second, and with a playful expression on his face, he asked, 'Are you by any chance a see-eye-dee? They're the ones who behave differently with different people.'

The first thing I had learned in this job was the expression to assume if someone looked me in the eye and asked that question.

He took me by my shoulder and pulled me aside. 'Eda, I think in the last few days a see-eye-dee has been following me,' he said, lowering his voice.

Like everyone who is told something like this, I immediately turned and looked behind us.

That night, we slept in a shed that stored rope in a place named Mayithara. We shared the place with at least a dozen young men who were State Congress workers. Two of them were from a place named Panangad in the neighbouring country of Kochi, and one man, whose name, if I remember correctly, was Kunjiraman, was from Malabar. Listening to their chatter, I soon gathered that the gusthikkaaran was not someone important in the Congress hierarchy. He was energetic and brave, but he talked to everyone in a jovial tone as though he took it all to be a bit of fun. And yet, everyone behaved more respectfully than was usual towards him. Some people called him 'Ashaan' – guru – part jokingly and part seriously, and he seemed to enjoy that. He introduced me to everyone saying, 'He's our own boy, keep an eye on him,' and needless to say, I made full use of the opportunity.

He was adept at telling stories about his extensive travels. As we put the kerosene lamp out and lay down, mosquitoes buzzing enthusiastically around us, he told us about an experience he had at the Kabul border. It involved the acute embarrassment he suffered after he had eaten in a hotel and realized, when it was time to pay, that his purse had been stolen, and the mysterious man who had come to his rescue. The story underlined the weird behaviours that the strange creature known as human being was capable of and the inherent goodness that slumbered within even the cruellest of us all. By the time the story ended, I could hear two of the men lying next to us sobbing. Even I was close to losing control of myself. Such a powerful story!

Before we slept, a man sang a song which angered me.

Let go of king worship
It's time for country worship
Rulers of men, rulers of men
Monarchs of oppression...

Horrible lines written by a traitor to the country named Bodheswaran. I stared quietly into the darkness, aware that an emotional response would be detrimental to the responsibilities I had to fulfil. There was also a strange kind of happiness within me. So many of us did this job, but the developments today might help me complete my mission as no one else could. Adventure, intrigue, disguises ... these were the things that attracted people like me to this job. As a torrential rain started outside and droplets weightless as dust fell through the thatched roof of the shed, I dozed off and soon began to dream.

Heavy rain was falling on an expanse of sand, except in a large circle, like an arena, in the middle of it. I was standing in this circle beckoning people, challenging them to a fight. My mind was turning over illegal locks and cheating techniques. Finally, when no one took up my challenge, I looked up, and that was when I realized I was inside a cage made by the rain. A perfect trap, like the bamboo ottaal used to catch fish. I was the fish caught in it, about to take my last gasping breath as soon as I was landed.

A heavy raindrop fell on my chest like a bullet and I jerked awake. A pinprick of fire glowed in the dark. The gusthikkaaran was sitting up, smoking a beedi and talking to himself. Suddenly, he looked towards me, and I froze as though I had been caught. The raindrop had pierced through my body. I felt its warmth on my back as it transformed into blood, seeped through the mat and spread across the floor.

4

In the morning, we set out for Alappuzha on foot. By then, everyone was treating me like I was one of them. The gusthikkaaran was gone by the time it was light, but no one said anything about it.

Alappuzha – where, a month later, a meeting of the Thiruvithamkoor Labour Association was to take place. We were going to take part in the planning meeting. Around thirty of us squeezed into a room on top of a textile shop near Kalarkode, belonging to a Konkani man they called Rao. The first to speak was a man named V.N. Krishna Pillai. He described the problems that followed the banning of the Association after the agitation for Utharavada Bharanam last year. He criticized the leadership of the State Congress, especially Pattom Thanu Pillai and T.M. Varghese, which earned him an enthusiastic applause from the listeners. A welcome committee was formed, and someone suggested my name too to be on it. The person who made the suggestion was a man from Karunagappally I had been talking to on the long walk here, and he was honouring our newly formed friendship. The man who spoke last (I don't remember his name now) criticized Krishna Pillai's speech. Do not join Sir C.P. Ramaswami Iyer and his cohort in disrespecting the State Congress leadership, he said, and cautioned us to remember that the government was trying to belittle C. Keshavan, Kunju Pillah and others by refusing to engage with them politically and entrapping them in silly police cases like poultry theft.

That day, five of us stayed on in that building. I had decided to hang on with them – I told them I had nowhere else to be – and to establish a closer relationship. None of us had eaten anything yet.

By evening, someone brought some muthira, the small legumes they usually feed to horses, cooked into a watery soup. I realized that these people didn't have two coins to rub together and were hungry. Was that their problem? Was that why they wandered across the land ranting and raging against the government? As we were eating, the man who had suggested my name for the welcome committee told us about the time when the chenkodi – the red flag of the revolution – was hoisted in the country. I watched his animated face as he talked. The flag had come all the way from Palakkad in Malabar in British India to our neighbouring country Kochi, passed from hand to hand in great secrecy, and it was his responsibility to pick up the flag in Ernakulam and bring it over. He told us the adventures he had, avoiding capture at the border checkpost in Aroor.

'A couple of policemen were doing whole-body searches. You can imagine what would happen if they found the chenkodi on me. My companion was Mani, the son of Chidambara Iyer. I was sure I'd be caught, so Mani began creating a scene with the policemen, and I just sneaked quietly away as they dealt with him. Pretty soon, he too escaped, beating up the policemen. What a fellow!'

I would come to know later that this Mani was only a boy, seventeen or eighteen years of age. The talk turned to his adventures – how he had quarrelled with his father, who was a Pattar, a Tamil Brahmin, and left home to join the Congress, how he could eat five lengths of puttu and a whole pot of kanji in one sitting. Their leader went on hunger strike at the drop of a hat, but these men, his followers, thought of nothing but food, even in their sleep! Why else would they tell such stories?

Sometime later, when I tried to step outside, one of them stopped me.

'Where to, at this time?'

'Oh, just stretching my legs...'

'Be careful. We are always under observation.'

'I know. I just want to sit on the beach for a bit.'

'Don't worry,' he said, placing his hand on my shoulder. 'You must be missing home. All this is for the independence of our country. The next generation will remember our sacrifices.'

The beach was deserted, and thankfully it was not raining. In the dim moonlight, I leaned against a boat and wrote a report of everything that had happened in the last two days. By then, I had remembered where I had seen the gusthikkaaran before and included that in my report.

It was around four years ago. There were four of us young men, annoyed that our studies were being constantly interrupted by a section of students who called for strikes whenever they pleased. On most evenings, we went for walks around Thiruvananthapuram, marvelling at the beauty of the capital city of our country, its wide promenades, shade trees, graceful old buildings, mansions, palaces and fortifications, zoo, the Maharaja's College, railway station ... Was there any other country in the world as great as this, a country that was owned by the deity Bhagavan Sree Padmanabhaswamy himself. It was our good fortune that we were born in this place. We would take it all in and then head towards Kizhakkekotta fort in time to see His Majesty the Maharaja on his way to the temple. His gorgeous car progressed slowly along the road, and he sat in it smiling respectfully with his palms pressed together at the people gathered on either side. His resplendent figure would fill our eyes with joyful tears, and we would bow to him with our veshtis removed from our shoulders and tied around our waists over our mundus. Often, I would find it difficult to talk after that. When he descended from his car at the temple, a thaalappoli, young women holding little trays with flowers and lamps, would be lining the path.

(Let me recall an unsavoury event here. One of our fellow students, a man from Nedumangad, once told us that, in the old days, women, wearing no upper garments, would hold lamps and stand in a line to display their breasts to the kings. I only came to know later that the man who told us this was a disciple of the extremist leader of the State Congress, Ponnara Sreedhar. If the king liked one of the women, her family would be informed, he said, and they would hire a Tamil Brahmin to cook a feast of one hundred dishes, and wait for the king. The king would arrive and lay with the woman. And with that, the family would rise in social position. Let all ears that listen to this filth burn, we cursed, and beat him up thoroughly and pushed him into the drainage canal. We also lodged a complaint with the police which earned him a five-year jail sentence.)

Most days, as we friends walked along, we would pick a serious topic and discuss it. On the day I am talking about, our topic was an incident that had happened in Kozhikode in Malabar, which was part of British India. *Malayalarajyam* had published a news item about a meeting of the Kerala Pradesh Congress that took place there, in which they tabled and passed a resolution for the eradication of Thiruvithamkoor and Kochi in order to establish an Aikyakeralam, a united Kerala. The newspaper had also published an editorial opposing the plan. No matter how much we discussed it, we could not understand their motivation. Were they aiming to eradicate our great nation and make us lackeys of the white sahib like them? How strange!

By then, we had walked past Chalakkambolam, and further ahead, in an open space was a pandal. Banners in English and Malayalam said, 'Akhilendia Women's Conference'.

'A women's conference? Really? That's all we need now!'

We went in, wanting to know more. There were about fifty people in the audience, almost half of them men. Those sitting on the dais were all women. Someone asked us to sit, but we remained standing at the back. The first speaker was the foreigner, Aruna Asaf Ali. After her, a middle-aged madamma named Margaret Sanger began speaking. The person who introduced her said she was a social activist and a writer from America – a book of hers was banned in her own country apparently. She spoke disrespectfully, unmindful of the fact that she was a guest in our country. Nowhere else had she seen women as subjugated as they were in Thiruvithamkoor, she said, where a woman did not have the right to choose her own partner and was forced to live with one man as her husband even if they were not psychologically compatible. We could not believe our ears, and we stood there shocked as she continued insulting our women and publicly instigating them into prostitution. Even more shocking was the fact that the audience sat there listening to her patiently. Then she went on to say that women had the right to decide when and from whom they should get pregnant and to even control the number of children. When she began explaining how one could have sexual relations without the fear of pregnancy using a thing called 'condom', my friend lost control and began heckling. The four of us rushed forward, shouting that such indecent talk would not be permitted in our land. Some of the people got out of our way, and when we began throwing the chairs around, the madamma stopped her speech.

'Stop it, sons of bitches!' a man got up from the audience and shouted at us. I didn't remember until now that he was the same gusthikkaaran I had met the other day. There was also a short woman shouting at us angrily. Just as I ran into him recently, I had also run into her another time. Last year during the Maharaja's birthday, some people had come to the capital under the pretext of making a submission to the king and unleashed terror. She was their leader. Akkamma Cherian – that was her name, and she was currently in prison.

I included this incident in my report as a warning about the gusthikkaaran. After writing all this, I felt I should also include a line about the young man named Mani whom the State Congress men had talked about. Something in my gut told me that he could be dangerous. I would be proved right later.

The next day, I ran an ad in the weekly newspaper, *Dinaprabha*, published from Kottayam. It said:

Wanted: Male elephants with excellent reproductive ability.
A commercial breeding centre for female elephants is looking for strong, male elephants below the age of thirty. On long-term rent or for purchase.
Contact: Andrews, Kallupura, Kannamali, Kochi.

It was, of course, an address that did not exist, and as the newspaper was not circulated in the country of Kochi, people there would not see the ad. Some of the four or five hundred readers of *Dinaprabha* might read the ad and wonder what it was about. However, some important people – people who employed me – read newspapers not for the news but for coded messages and secret signs. The message was for them, and they would understand the precise information it contained. The reports I sent did not remain secret. The clerks saw them too. But this message would let the important people know that I had arrived at my destination and that I had some significant information to impart. They would send messengers to me.

Dinaprabha's office was in a stuffy little room near the taluk court in Thirunakkara. A man sat on the floor, stacking newspapers and tying them into bundles. He read the material I gave him over and over and stared at me.

'Are you sure this is what you mean?' he asked.

'Yes.'

'Sure you haven't made a mistake?'

Without responding, I gave him the money for the ad and walked away.

'Is this really possible?' he asked, following me out.

'Why not? If it happens in the wild, why not in captivity?'

'Still...'

5

It was after all these incidents that I spent some time working in Malabar, which was part of the Madras Province of British India. I think it would be good to talk briefly about it here.

At the time, I went by the name Avarachan, a Mar Thoma Christian from Niranam near Thiruvalla. To look the part, I shaved my head, dressed in a single mundu with no upper garment, and came to the railway station in Aluva which was a part of Kochi and at the border between our two countries. I was aware that the train north was not until the next day, but had arrived a day earlier on purpose.

A large crowd, literally hundreds of families who had no idea when the next train would arrive, sat or lay down on mats or on the bare ground all along the station road and in the compounds of the houses along its sides. One could tell they were all Christians just by looking at them. There were families with three members, and those with as many as fifteen or twenty members. Most were men around the age of forty with their wives and children, and in some cases, siblings. Old people were almost entirely absent. Women, dressed in the traditional chatta and mundu with its end pleated into a fan and tucked at the small of the back, sat before small cooking fires preparing the night's meal. Men mingled with their fellow travellers, chatted and smoked rolled-up tobacco leaves. I hung around, listening to their talk that was laced with the anxiety and uncertainty about their destination. Should they get off at Kozhikode or at Thalassery? Where would they go from there, and by what means? Where would they live? How much would the land cost, and would it be any good? Would they be taken advantage of?

There were a handful who had already found suitable land and settled in, and were travelling back up after coming home to take care of some matters. Others surrounded them, wanting to know what it was like, to learn more, and as they spoke, they looked anxiously at the sky. All of them had bundles containing essential clothes, a few utensils, dried tapioca and other foodstuff, and if it rained, everything would get wet and soggy.

As darkness fell, I got myself acquainted with a man named Devasia from Pravithanam in Pala. I was relieved when he told me that it was the first time he was meeting a Mar Thoma person. Almost all of the migrants to Malabar were Syrian Christians, and if I claimed to be one of them, more questions would follow because they had people of their acquaintance everywhere they went. Devasia seemed to be an interesting person, and his face reflected the anxiety and vulnerability of travelling outside Pala for the first time.

'Are your priests allowed to marry?'

That was the first thing he asked me. He then took me to his wife who was preparing the night's meal. She was a fair-skinned, slightly plump, beautiful woman, dressed in a new chatta and mundu as befitted the occasion of long-distance travel. The happiness that all women feel when starting a new life was writ large on her face.

'Where are you from, kochey?' she asked me as she struggled to get the firewood going on the damp soil.

She was around my age, but she called me 'young man' because as soon as they are married, all women feel they are older than their male contemporaries.

'A bit south – Niranam,' I said, squatting next to her to help her light the firewood.

If you arrange the firewood in a specific way, it will catch fire quickly. Place a large piece of wood at an angle at the very bottom without sticking it too much into the space between the three stones that form the fire. Pile some kindling on top with enough space for airflow. Light it and blow, and the fire will do its job perfectly. In those days, I was certain that this was how human beings needed to work as well – plan properly, allowing space for things to develop organically, and things would develop at the rate and time we envisaged. But if you ask me now, I will give you a different opinion. Fire is a dangerous thing that does not submit to our control. It is our ignorance that makes us think we have it under control within the confines of a box of matches.

Devasia and his wife – her name was Elikkutty – looked at me as though they had never seen a man tending to a cooking fire. So many things I will have to do in this job of mine, I thought to myself. There are no wrongs in this job, only rights, or, if one thought about it, the opposite can also be true. It required doing what is considered forbidden, making friends with people one didn't like, spending nights wherever there was space, changing one's name, pretending to be part of a group while keeping a distance deep in one's heart. Above all, making sure that everything one observed was safely noted in one's mind without allowing any of it to get jumbled up or confusing. People like me were at risk of falling into a trap: the tendency to think that the assumed identity we had been living under for a while was our real identity. So, it was important to always tell ourselves, 'This isn't me, isn't me, isn't me.'

A man named Luca sat near us on a mat with his family – wife and two brothers – getting ready to say the evening prayers.

'Don't you all have paddy fields where you come from?' he asked me as though wondering why I was going to Malabar.

'O ... but not much use that is. When it is harvest time, people come from all over and you'll be lucky to find one row to harvest.

My appan is a ploughman. Had two bulls but both died a couple of months ago.'

'Ah. Must have let them graze in the summer sun. Too much sunlight is bad for them.'

I told them that we, eight to ten Mar Thoma families, were planning to come to Malabar together, and that I was headed there now to look for a suitable piece of land. Good soil, not too expensive, and if it was somewhere with people we could trust, so much the better, I said.

'Buying enough land for you all together in one place ... that would be difficult,' Luca said. 'You could look in Govindapuram or Nilambur. Mind you, haven't seen your type of people there though.'

The next day, as the sun began to set, the train arrived. Most people were seeing such a thing for the first time in their lives. They were reluctant at first, but when a couple of people ran to it and boarded, everyone heaved forward. I helped Devasia carry his bundles on board. The monster vehicle rested on the platform for half an hour before crawling north, belching smoke and coal dust. Some of the passengers were crying while others sat anxiously listening to the unfamiliar rhythm of its heartbeat. The racket it made as it went over the bridges across rivers, as though something was collapsing underneath it, was reflected on the faces of the passengers. Carrying those who had abandoned what had broken by the wayside and those who had decided never to return, the train sped forward at times, and at other times lay still in unremarkable places as though it would never move again.

Almost all the women sat on the floor with their children even though there was space on the wooden benches. Spreading a cloth or a mat on the floor, they created imaginary boundaries, and sat watching their neighbours, anxious that they would try to expand their own territories. As though to establish their ownership, they pointlessly cleaned the space they occupied, placed random belongings on the borders, lay down stretching their bodies from one end to the other. Eventually, smiles were exchanged and some of them began chatting with those who sat on either side of them. Soon objects that established the boundaries between them were removed and spaces joined, and they began exchanging things and petting each other's children. Their men sat on the benches, watched them and smiled at one another, and began chatting until deciding to get off at the same station and to look for land together.

The train pulled into Kozhikode station in the morning. I had already decided to get off there with Devasia and Elikkutty. This land used to be ruled by kings as powerful as our own Maharaja, but now it was under British rule. The place had wide roads, many rickshaws and plenty of chai shops, and was crowded day and night. The people were mostly Muslims, and their dialect was difficult for us to understand. As we got off the train at the station, we saw some people standing around, middlemen waiting for the newly arrived migrants. Elikkutty was overwhelmed. Devasia and I calmed her down, sat her under a tree with their possessions, and ventured out to get the lay of the land. Devasia walked with one hand holding the waist-fold of his mundu securely, which contained the money from the sale of his land back home. He believed that the chances of being robbed increased as soon as one stepped outside of Pala, and the farther one went, the more the number of thieves.

'I'm glad we met someone trustworthy like you,' he said.

'Of course you can trust me,' I said, smiling inwardly and outwardly. 'I am dependable, always do what is asked of me.'

By the time we had some tea and returned to Elikkutty, we had decided on our destination – Thiruvambady. One could buy or lease land there, we had gathered, and since our countryfolk had not reached there yet, the prices were still affordable. Hoisting our bundles on to our heads, we began walking. In about an hour, we stopped by the side of a stream where we did our morning ablutions, and made some kanji and ate it. By then, Elikkutty had taken me on as her responsibility, and began questioning me about everything – property, relatives, marital status...

'There will be none of our people there...' Devasia worried about our destination.

'You'll be the first,' I said. 'Won't be long before others hear about it and come to join you.'

'Why don't you go back home and bring our people over?' said Elikkutty to me. 'We can all live there together.'

'That's up to them, isn't it?' I said, and to change the subject, I asked, 'How come you didn't bring your children with you?'

There was no response as Elikkutty and Devasia looked at each other. For the rest of the days I spent with them, I never again brought up the subject.

We spent the night on the veranda of a Muslim house in a place named Arambra. The next morning, we woke up early and set out, reaching Thiruvambady by the time the sun was up in the sky. Very few people lived in that place, and they came out of their houses to watch us staggering by with our bundles. They were most intrigued by Elikkutty whose clothes were different from theirs. Besides, there were no women in that place who exuded such enthusiasm and walked so confidently.

I spent around twenty days with Devasia and Elikkutty. Staying with that isolated family was not helpful to my objective – there was nothing I could learn from them – unless I endeavoured to recruit them to my mission. It would have been a clever thing to do, but every time I prepared myself to do so, something, some feeling contrary to the objectives of my job, stopped me. Let me briefly describe what happened in those days.

Devasia paid the asking price and leased five acres of land from a man named Mannidath Nair. A wooded area with very little undergrowth. With the help of two locals, he constructed an erumadam, a dwelling in the trees raised up from the ground, and began the work of clearing the land for cultivation. It was a sight to behold. Devasia was a strong worker, but his wife ... If ever they invented a forest clearing instrument, it would work like Elikkutty. After cooking the morning meal, she set out with a vaakkathi, a bill hook with a long handle, cutting and slashing away at the roots and stumps, setting fire to the debris as soon as the leaves wilted a bit in the sun. Small animals ran for cover as the greenery exploded in the fire. She glanced at me, struggling with even the twiggy growth, and laughed.

'What, Avaracha? No strength in your arms or what? Are all your countryfolk like you?'

That was when she became aware that I was watching her. She looked me straight in the eye and froze for a moment, then turned back to her work. For the rest of the day, she did not look in my direction at all, and continued to ignore me at the evening prayer before our meal.

By the time we cleared an acre of land and prepared the beds to plant tubers like yam and colocasia, Devasia caught a fever. Five days later, when he sat up and had some kanji, I got ready to leave, saying that if I set out now, I could reach the town by morning. At that moment, we heard someone hollering from near a tree. It had been days since we had seen anyone. Happily, I stepped out to see who it was, Elikkutty at my heels and Devasia following behind gingerly.

There were four of them. One of them looked around sixty and had a thoppippala, a hat made of the sheath of an areca nut palm leaf, on his head. The other three looked much younger. They said they were from Changanassery and had come north around six months ago, and now were cultivating some land in Nellippoyil, around eight miles from where we were.

'Only yesterday we heard there were newcomers here,' said the older man, 'so we thought we'll come around and see for ourselves.'

'Good,' said Devasia, happily. 'It's good to know there are our people nearby.'

Elikkutty lit a fire and began boiling coffee shells in water.

'What's that scar?' Devasia asked, looking at the faded mark high above the navel of one of the men. He had prominent cheekbones and a broad physique.

'O, nothing. Just an old wound when I fell over as a child,' he said.

'Some scars become clearer and clearer as they grow older,' said Devasia as though he was consoling him.

I sat with my eyes trained on the floor. I could recognize the scar of a knife wound when I saw one.

They told us that they had cleared the land they bought in Nellippoyil and were waiting for the rains so they could start planting tapioca. They had nothing to do until then, they said, and were happy to help out.

'We're one and all migrants here. We must help each other.'

'No one ventures out here with their women in tow, Devasiacha,' said one of them as Elikkutty began handing out the coffee sweetened with a bit of jaggery. 'There's all sorts of danger.'

He stepped into the darkness to urinate. On his way back, he slapped the trunk of a tree under which we had set down our spades and axes.

'Why haven't you cut this one down?' he asked.

'The landowner has told us not to cut down mature trees,' Devasia said. 'Wants to cut them down himself. To sell the timber, it seems.'

'Nothing will work out if you pay attention to all that,' the older man warned. 'He wouldn't even have stepped foot on this land in his life! Mark my words, if the soil is shaded, tubers won't grow properly.'

'Just light a tiny fire at the bottom,' said the man with the old scar as he gestured authoritatively to Elikkutty for more coffee. 'It will burn down slowly and steadily. Might even take a month.'

I took my leave and set out on my way. Elikkutty followed me in the dark up to the boundary of the land.

'Bring everyone back,' she said as she handed me a torch made of tightly bound coconut leaves. 'And quickly. We'll all get land next to each other. And even if no one comes, you come back, mind.'

As I walked on, darkness and the world of insects came rushing at me. I walked until I was sure that the torchlight would seem smaller than a firefly if Elikkutty was still watching, and then stubbed it out and threw it away. I changed direction and resumed walking. I had a different path from now on.

On and on I walked, until my legs began to ache. I began to consider that darkness was light, that it was darkness that showed us the true nature of things. Suddenly, a sight before me stopped me in my tracks, a sight that light hid from us during daytime. There on a hillside was a huge tree with its interior burning, just as the man with the scar had told us. There were no flames, but the darkness revealed its long, smouldering core as though it were a tree that glowed as it died, its insides folding into itself slowly like a funeral pyre of green firewood. Embers are hotter than actively burning wood. I walked away slowly, turning to look back at the red pillar reaching for the sky, listening for the sound of its exploding skull and ribcage. Darkness also showed me the magical sight of it melting slowly to the ground. In that moment, I thought about returning to the two-person family I had left behind and staying with them for a few more days.

For the next three months, I roamed all across the eastern parts of the Malabar district under the pretext of looking for land to purchase. My travels took me to places such as Peravoor, Iritty, Kodanchery, Nilambur, Vettilappara, Nileshwaram and Chemperi. The information I gathered on this journey was as follows:

There was a veritable influx of Syrian Christians from our country to this area, and their numbers were only going to increase in the days to come. An important reason for this influx was the plentiful availability of cultivable land to purchase as well as to lease. The custom here was to pay the lease in kind, in agricultural produce. Transactions were rarely conducted in cash, and so those who migrated from our country with cash resources were welcomed here.

The arrival of Syrian Christians was bound to change this place. The locals were, by nature, laid-back, and they watched the hard-working migrants with a sense of awe mixed with envy. It wouldn't be long before villages and small towns with a majority Christian population would be formed in the eastern parts of this area. The other thing of note was that they did not seem to be engaged, at least in any obvious way, in activities against our country. Although most of the migrants were followers of the State Congress, it did not seem to be active in this area, but there was no guarantee that it would not become active in the future. And it would be difficult to collaborate with their counterparts back home given the inadequate transport links. Still, there were two significant things to note:

1. These people had succeeded in spreading the falsehood that our country was under the rule of non-native Brahmins and Nairs. They had made the locals believe

that our Diwanji was anti-Christian, and that they were forced to leave their country because of religious persecution. As an example, they told them about a Christian by the name of Mamman Mappila and accused the government of destroying the Quillon Bank that he owned and seizing the newspaper he published. The anti-national uprisings that took place over the past year were presented here in a different light. All these stories being spread through word of mouth were causing damage to the glory of our country.

2. There were other stories being circulated that were simply unconscionable. That the supreme ruler of our land, Sultan Bahadur Sree Chithira Thirunal Balarama Varma, was mentally challenged, and that the diwan was the one who took all the decisions and ruled the land as he pleased; that our beloved Amma Maharani routinely thrashed her son, the Maharaja, with a golden cane because he failed to learn, even at this age, the Malayalam and English alphabets; that the 'Mylapore Set' – a Tamil Brahmin group which included many of Diwanji's friends – was cunningly moving the country's wealth across the border into Madras. Once, I even had to sit and listen to a bunch of migrants in Peravoor insinuating, as they got together for an evening of drinking, that there was an illicit relationship between Amma Maharani and Diwanji, and watch them jeering and laughing about it.

6

A whole year passed before I ran into the gusthikkaaran, Basheer, again. Up until that meeting, I lived in Thangassery. An area – less than a hundred acres that included Thangassery – within the city of Kollam was in the hands of the British, and so was part of the district of Tirunelveli in the state of Madras. Our police and magistrates were forbidden entry into this area. The population was made up almost entirely of fisherfolk of Catholic persuasion and the mongrel breed, the progeny of locals who had mixed with white-skinned foreigners, that jabbered on in English. The enmity these people entertained towards our Maharaja who was a devotee of Sree Padmanabhaswamy was, as everyone knew, no secret. Even when they travelled outside Thangassery, they behaved with the arrogance of being the subjects of the British emperor. Taking advantage of this situation, murderers, State Congress followers dodging arrest warrants, why, even dangerous traitors belonging to the Youth League, went about openly and disdainfully in this place. Our government had several discussions with the Resident Sahib about this issue, but nothing came of it given the opposition from Christian priests. All that was achieved was the construction of an archway at the point where the public road crossed the boundary between the two countries. And as though to laugh in the face of our country, people sauntered back and forth through it.

One evening, dressed from head to toe in khaddar, I went to Thangassery. Walking past a couple of palatial bungalows belonging to the mongrel breed and past the church, I came to the shameful sight. A building thatched with coconut palms, and hanging from its porch, a board with 'Thiruvithamkoor State Congress Committee Office' written on it. On its whitewashed wall was a picture, drawn with the sap of some ground-up leaf, of Gandhi. Couldn't they find anyone other than this foreigner to be their leader? And could we ever trust these white people, I wondered. They who pretended to be our friends could easily get rid of these troublemakers if only they set their minds to it. I hung around outside the building until I saw some people of my acquaintance before walking in. My presence and activities in those days in Muhamma had ensured that there were many in the State Congress who now recognized me.

Inside, three people sat chatting on the floor, and another man lay on a bench reading a newspaper. One of the men on the floor was someone I had seen at meetings in Alappuzha and Kayamkulam, and he scrambled up when he saw me.

'Ah, Bhasi!' he said, surprised.

At that moment, two people came out of the inside room, bending their heads to clear the top of the doorframe. I recognized one of them immediately – Ulloor Gopi, who was the Thiruvananthapuram taluk secretary of the State Congress. He and a man named Mannanthala Karunakaran had once scrambled up the Huzur Court building in the dead of night and planted the tricolour flag of the Congress on top. Karunakaran, who had returned to the scene of his valiant deed the next day, was swiftly arrested by the police. The *Malayalarajyam* newspaper reported that the police jeep had snatched him up like an eagle pouncing on a chick. Gopi had been in hiding since.

'Who are you?' asked the man with Gopi in an unnecessarily gruff voice.

This man, with a generous beard shot through with grey, looked to be over forty years old. He had calm eyes, but they looked piercingly at everything. Sensing danger, I told him that my name was Bhasi, a State Congress worker originally from Nedumangad, and that I had come to Thangassery to avoid the police as there was an arrest warrant in my name.

'But you speak differently for a person from Nedumangad,' he said.

'I left home when I was a boy,' I said.

'And where in Nedumangad is your house?'

He came close to me and looked me in the eyes as he asked this question. I realized that he was paying attention to the slightest of movements on my face, the twitch of my eyebrow, the change in my breathing.

'Bhasi is a friend of Basheer's,' said the man who had met me before. 'They had a gusthi at the meeting in Muhamma.'

My interrogator's face relaxed, an expression of mischief replaced the suspicion.

'What, with our Basheer?' he said, laughing. Everyone laughed with him. 'And where is he now? Haven't seen him in a while.'

He put his arm around my shoulder affectionately, sat me on the bench and began chatting with me. It was obvious that Basheer was widely respected by all of them. The mere mention of his name brought joyful smiles to their faces. I gathered that what they felt was not fawning reverence, but the indulgent affection people feel towards someone who is harmlessly mischievous.

'It's been a while since I've seen him,' I said.

'I need to see him soon,' the man said. 'Anyway, tell me, what have they charged you with?'

'When we took out a procession to Pulinkunnu during the Utharavada Bharanam agitation, the Rajabhakta Sangham threw stones at us. But the police say we are the ones who did the stone throwing.'

'Ah, well, at least it is a decent charge. See what they have done to great leaders like C. Keshavan ... Charged him with poultry theft! That no-good Pattar! He thinks he can make a joke out of our leaders, but the people know who the real thieves looting the country's wealth are.'

He tightened his arm around my shoulder even as he ground his teeth in anger. 'Don't worry, young man, be brave,' he said. 'No five-rupee police will dare come around here.'

Five-rupee police – the derogatory nickname given to the temporary workers hired to enforce the law, on a monthly salary of five rupees, because the actual police force could not keep up with the chaos unleashed by these people in the name of Utharavada Bharanam!

'Do one thing,' he continued. 'Don't stay here at the office. There are CIDs everywhere. No one can be trusted.' He beckoned the man who had been reading the newspaper when I came in. 'Eda, Naduva, come here.'

He asked Naduvan to take me to an alternative accommodation – an indication of his fondness for Basheer. As I walked out of the office with Naduvan, they were still discussing Basheer's doings and laughing appreciatively.

'That was Ponnara Sreedhar, didn't you know?' Naduvan asked as we walked to a building near the disintegrating fort of the British.

I tried desperately to hide the sudden surge of excitement I felt. That gusthi in Muhamma and the relationships that had ensued because of it ... it was taking me to places I had not envisaged! Ponnara Sreedhar was one of the most important leaders of these people – alongside Pattom Thanu Pillai, C. Keshavan and T.M. Varghese – the man who had formed the Youth League because he thought the State Congress was not revolutionary enough. Could anyone say that one person's timely interference would not end up changing the very fabric of a country? That day, when Basheer started the gusthi to energize the crowd in

Muhamma, I could have stayed back and not involved myself in it. After all, the only job expected of people like me was to prepare faithful reports of what we observed. I remembered the simple lesson I had learned at the beginning of my job – that trying to do anything beyond what was expected amounted to recklessness. Taking risks was all right as long as they were calculated, controlled, unemotional, and only when one was absolutely certain that one was ready to face the consequences if things went wrong. Any success was to be taken for what it was – momentary. No matter how clever the people making the plans were, there was always a chance that they would go awry. Even if plans fell into place, they could slip away further ahead. Imagine that we found ourselves unexpectedly on top of a peak with our enemy, and that the wind was pushing him towards the deep chasm below. We might help with a gentle nudge. Or he might fall in without any action from us. Either way, we would have to make absolutely certain that he fell in. Warning myself to be extra careful in my future steps, I walked along with Naduvan.

As arranged by Ponnara Sreedhar, Naduvan took me to the headman of a fishing port. For the next few days, I lived with him as his helper.

'Andrayose Mooppan is our man,' Naduvan told me. 'He can be trusted. Still, don't tell him your real name. Tell him it is Chakrapani.'

Mooppan had been a deep-sea fisherman for forty years. Not able to do it any more, he took on the work of repairing fishing boats, which brought almost no income. Still, when they had a good haul, the other fishermen gave him a share of the catch.

A couple of days later, Mooppan asked me, 'What caste are you?'

'Vaalan,' I said, 'from Vaikom.'

'Ah, so our kind only,' Mooppan said, getting up from his mat and coming closer. 'But when you go out, don't tell people your name. It's not a common name here in Thangassery. Tell them your name is Lasar. That won't raise suspicions.'

Lasar who is Chakrapani who is Bhasi ... An alias inside an alias inside another alias!

'No need,' I said. 'Why tell lies unnecessarily? They only come tumbling down one day or the other.'

'You're right!' Mooppan's face brightened. 'Like Gandhi says, if truth and courage are on our side, why tell untruths? Even if there is a storm and our boat capsizes and we end up swallowing salt water, we will swim to the shore.'

I spent my days with Mooppan and my evenings at the State Congress office, sleeping wherever I could in the nights. This was what I gathered during those days:

The State Congress was in a dire, volatile state compared to what it was two or three years ago. The cadre was frustrated and angry with the leaders. They were under the impression that there was some sort of secret understanding between the government and leaders such as Pattom Thanu Pillai and Nataraja Pillai. It was also evident that the socialists in Kollam and the communists in Alappuzha were gaining influence within the organization. That the moderates kept having to change their stances according to the whims of the Congress leadership in British India was increasing popular support for these factions. The socialists were led by N. Sreekantan Nair and T.K. Divakaran, while M.N. Govindan Nair, T.V. Thomas, Varghese Vaidyan, and so on were leading the communists. Kumbalath Shanku Pillai, Thazhava Keshavan and Ponnara Sreedhar were fond of these young men.

I reported the whereabouts of thirty people who were in hiding in Thangassery. Among them, Ulloor Gopi, who had gone into town to meet the student leader K. Balakrishnan who had just returned from Madurai, was caught by the police. I was sleeping under an upturned boat in the misty night when Naduvan woke me up. He seemed to be in a serious mood as I followed him. On the way, as though suspicious of something, he made me walk in front and followed carefully. We walked through lanes created by fenced-in compounds, and through the front and backyards of huts to a small alcove with a crucifix that sat with its back to the sea. Next to it was a shed for storing fishing nets. I stepped in, and immediately Naduvan locked the door from the outside. Inside, in the light of a dimly burning tin lamp, sat Ponnara Sreedhar, wiping the sand off his arms and legs with a cotton towel. His eyes scrutinized me as they had done the day we met.

'How long has it been since you came here?' he asked.

'Two months,' I said, taking time to pretend that I had to think.

He grunted, and picking up a blunt flick knife, he began to cut the thick, overgrown nails of his toes. It was a horrible job requiring time and patience. Like hard old wood that refused to submit to the chisel, his big toe resisted the iron blade of the knife. It was clear that he was deep in thought, and that he would not later remember this job he was doing unthinkingly to focus his mind.

I assessed my surroundings. If things went wrong, I could break through the feeble palm-leaf wall of the shed and run out. Naduvan, who waited outside, was not a strong and healthy man.

Ponnara stopped battling with his nails, got up, folded the knife and stuck it in his waistband.

'Do one thing,' he said after a few more minutes of silence. 'Don't worry about outsiders, but you keep an eye on our people. Don't tell anyone about it, not even Naduvan. Someone among us ... or it could be someone among the people who are helping us here ... If you suspect someone, let me know.'

As I walked back, lifting my feet off the sodden sand, I was thinking of something else. That there was something in the expression on my face or in my behaviour that others noticed, even if subconsciously. Otherwise, why was this job given to me? Or was it that this job had become part of the way I looked, behaved and spoke? Suddenly, a wave ran up my legs, and with it came a terrible smell. I looked towards the sea and saw pinpricks of light scattered over its surface. It was a time of abundant fish, a time to be careful with the sea.

The dusk that followed found me standing at the same spot. Boats loaded with big, fatty sardines had been coming in since afternoon, although the prices seemed low and transactions few and far between. Andrayose Mooppan stood beside a six-foot tall, dried plant with a vessel full of sardines. A clutch of naked, dark-skinned boys stood around him. He was hanging the sardines, their tails, heads and scales intact, from the branches of the plant, as though he was decorating a Christmas tree like the ones the Anglo-Indians had in their houses. When the branches were loaded with the sardines, he made the children stand back from it and set a fire at the bottom. Flames flared up the plant twice, and before the fire went out entirely, he picked up the sardines one by one, ran his fingers up from the tail end to remove the scales, and handed them to the children. They ate the flesh, holding them by the head and tail and slowly rotating them. Several of them burned their lips. As I stood watching them, I began to feel upon me the eyes of a man who was helping to drag the boats on to the shore. Refusing the sardine Mooppan offered me, I walked into the water and joined the people dragging in a boat filled with plump mackerels.

As we pulled the boat in, with the rope twisted securely around our waists and accompanied by rhythmic chanting, he asked me, 'Must the monkey paraded at the temple festival learn English?'

A nonsense question which was a signal meant only for me.

Immediately, without even waiting to say goodbye to Mooppan, I left Thangassery. After a long walk, I reached the jetty in Thevally. It was late in the night by then, but thankfully I found a boat to ferry me across the lake. It took almost an hour and a half to get across the water. From Kadavoor on the other side, I must have walked along non-existent paths for another two furlongs before I saw the building of Athangavidhwamsini Arya Vaidya Sala. In actual fact, it was only a small room connected to a house. It was closed, but I could see the light of the lamp inside through the gaps between the wooden planks that shuttered its entrance. Quietly, I removed one of the planks and entered. A woman, close to middle age, sat on the floor pounding dried areca nuts soaked in water. When she saw me enter, she covered her naked breasts with a cotton towel.

'What is it?' she asked.

'Heartburn,' I said. 'Can't eat a thing.'

'What about motions?'

'Difficult.'

She stepped outside and came back after a while with a small parcel wrapped in a piece of paper.

'Take this choornam dissolved in warm water for seven days. Avoid spicy, sour and salty things. You can have induppu, rock salt, if you wish. And drink lots of water.'

I paid her and stepped outside. As I pushed the plank back into place, the lamp inside went out.

Somehow or the other, I got back into town. I opened the paper parcel she had given me, shook the choornam out into the nearby drain, and stood under a street lamp to read the paper. It detailed further instructions for me, and ordered me to start immediately. As I tore the paper into tiny little bits, I looked towards the west. The glow from the Thangassery lighthouse was reflected in the sky and in the ocean. If I were to disappear suddenly without a trace, there was no doubt that Ponnara Sreedhar would know I was the spy. It would undo all the progress I had made so far.

7

In those days, receiving a postal letter at one's home address was a rare event. Only the very wealthy or the most respected were destined for it. The arrival of a letter by post could also transform an ordinary person into a respected one. The postbox was a most venerated object, and the postman its revered representative. Taller than an average man and stuck in one place permanently, the postbox was under watchful eyes at all times. Older folk, doddering along leaning on their walking sticks, dawdled in front of it, stared at it for minutes on end. Putting something into it in private was out of the question. The person doing so was expected to divulge the letter's purpose as well as its recipient to those gathered around, and it was best to provide an explanation without hesitation because failure to do so would give rise to a storm of stories, each one more inaccurate and salacious than the rest. The situation was much the same when one received a letter as well. All and sundry followed the postman to the recipient's house and did not leave until the letter was opened and its contents read out several times. And if by some miracle a person generally irrelevant to the local state of affairs were to receive a letter, the postman took it upon himself to open it and read it out to everyone before handing it over to the addressee.

The Raktarekha Case changed all that. It transformed the general sense of pride and pomp that surrounded the postal letter into anxiety and apprehension. The postal system in itself is one that underlines our faith in progress and development, and in the general goodness of human beings. Time was when people would set off somewhere, and the only way we would know they had reached their destination was when they came back. But now ... To be able to communicate with those far away, to exchange ideas, to share love ... So, it had not occurred to anyone that this system, this emblem of all that was great about humanity, would be abused, misused for criminal purposes.

The person who had the misfortune to experience this abuse was Sharngadharan, a permanent policeman at the toll office in Aroor. A letter arrived at his home address in Katakkarappalli, and it read:

> *Greetings, dear friend.*
>
> *You'll agree, surely, that our country used to be a little flower garden brimming with beauty. In the embrace of its peaceful air, every night its citizens slipped effortlessly into restful slumber filled with pleasant dreams. Even a small child would have felt a certain pride in being born in this land, this Vanchirajyam of scintillating prosperity. We are well aware that we are writing to one of the rude souls responsible for turning this glorious land into a cremation ground, and that any interaction with such a person bears the risk of poisoning the thoughts of even the most pristine of minds.*
>
> *The administrators of this land are blind to the atrocity you unleash towards the abject, starving citizens who are forced to leave our motherland and travel across its boundary. But we see it. We understand it. Be warned that if your own karma does not deliver just punishment for your cruel endeavours, we will ensure that you receive it.*

At the end of the letter, written in the clear, slanted letters of an educated hand, was a dark red line like a signature. A line drawn in blood, a raktarekha. The newspapers reported the incident and its aftermath by that name – the Raktarekha Case.

The letter wrought significant changes in the life of policeman Sharngadharan who had, up until then, amassed considerable money and other material benefits at the toll office in the form of bribes. He was not at home when the letter arrived, so the postman had opened it and read it aloud to his illiterate father and mother, his tongue stumbling over its complex wording and sentence structure. Not one of the fifteen or so people who had assembled to listen to the letter being read aloud could fully comprehend its message, and because of it, they were convinced that it was of great import, and that Sharngadharan was about to experience something, some calamity of major significance. Besides, words, when written down, acquire greater believability. No one thinks that someone would write something false and improbable down in a letter and post it. A collective wail rose from that house as though someone had died. Carrying the letter, a large group walked all the way to Aroor in search of Sharngadharan. He was not at the toll office, so the letter travelled from place to place as the crowd continued searching for him, and in all these places, literate people were forced to read the letter aloud to everyone assembled.

Finally, the threatening letter reached Sharngadharan. He took it to his superiors, but they reacted as though something terrible had already happened to him. He had, every month, dutifully handed over to them a share of the bribes he received, and yet they wrinkled their foreheads as though faced with evidence of dealings he had concealed from them. At the toll office, those who usually ran for cover at the sight of the pointy police cap now arrived to catch a glimpse of him, to secretly rejoice in his misfortune while publicly commiserating with him. Sharngadharan had only six more months to retire, but his entire service now came under the dark shadow of the letter. On the day of his retirement, the day he would go back to being the ordinary son of an ordinary fisherman, a large crowd gathered at the market junction in Katakkarappalli expecting something dramatic to happen to him. And when nothing happened, some of them beat up the former policeman and then took him to his home.

What happened to Sharngadharan was only the beginning. Letters arrived at different times, addressed to different people: Gopala Panicker, the sub-inspector of police in Cherthala (the State Congress called him 'Master of Torture'), two tehsildars, prominent landlords Parayil Ittichan and Kattiyatt Shivarama Panicker, and several others. The varied yet liberally embellished language of the letters – and the fact that they were vague about what would be done to them and when – created an atmosphere of great anxiety. The appearance of the postman at the homes of people famous for one reason or the other began to be considered a bad omen. Then it was the turn of the postboxes themselves. When postboxes were opened in Alappuzha jetty, Changanassery and Harippad, all prominent locations with good footfall, the post inside had been destroyed, eaten by some sort of liquid poured over them. In the following week, *Malayalarajyam* reported that a terrorist group was active in Ernakulam in the country of Kochi too, pouring acid into postboxes, sending letters to prominent citizens, and writing anti-British slogans on public walls. The newspaper published two editorials on the Raktarekha Case. A man named T.K. Varghese Vaidyan was eventually arrested and sent to jail, but the letters kept coming for over a year afterwards.

All this happened quite some time ago. I have studied, as part of my job, some of these letters. While working among the State Congress activists in Ernakulam, I have noticed the free circulation of pamphlets and books banned in our country. Ernakulam was the playground of State Congress people who had left our country, scared of the cases filed against them. And they sneaked back in whenever they had an opportunity, organized strikes, created mischief, and ran back across the border to Kochi. The fact that our Diwanji and the Kochi diwan Shanmukham Chetty did not get along only seemed to facilitate the situation. Meanwhile, I had made myself familiar to them and was able to infiltrate their meetings and visit their lodgings as I pleased, without having to invoke Basheer's name. And because of this, I did not go to the place where he lived, not even once, even though it was not all that far from where I was. Then, one day, after attending a condolence meeting in Thoppumpadi for Prakkulam Padmanabha Pillah who had passed away, I was sitting in the last boat to Ernakulam. One of my companions – I can't recall his name now – handed me a four- or five-page pamphlet.

'Have a look at this,' he said. 'The Pattar has banned it. The language! He must have been mortified!'

I read it. And the very next day, my mind going over the similarities between the words and constructions that appeared again and again in the pamphlet and in the Raktarekha Case letters, I set out for Basheer's abode.

8

It was called Seethi Buildings, but it was in fact an old house with a large number of rooms. It must have been the home of a family – wealthy, no doubt – at some point, because such a large house, with so many rooms spread over two storeys, was a rarity then as it is now. It was a lodge now, each of its narrow rooms rented out to three or four people, and they slept in there on mats or on the bare floor. A singular smell, of woodwork rotted in the rain mixed with palm civet urine, enveloped the place. Thick cobwebs hung heavy in the corners of walls and from the ceiling. No one brushed away the old cobwebs, and with no interest in weaving new ones, lazy spiders sat around motionless until they died of boredom. There were two halls in the building, one on each floor, and several people, unaccounted for in the owner's rent book, lived there communally with no regard for privacy. They were acquaintances, or acquaintances of acquaintances, of the formal tenants obliged to pay rent. Basheer lived in the kitchen.

To be fair, it wasn't much of a kitchen. There were two cooking fires, the type with three support stones planted well into the earth that required one to squat on the floor to tend to the fire. There were also two or three mud pots (empty), a couple of ladles made of coconut shell (broken), and a pot for cooking fish. A salt pot seemed to dangle from the sky, suspended as it was in an uri – a hanging potholder made of rope – whose other end disappeared into the congealed darkness above. A couple of cockroaches travelled up and down the uri. The room itself was of a fair size, and although Basheer occupied the far end opposite the cooking fires, everyone assumed that the entire space was his domain, under his control. It was also the heart, the focal point, of the whole building. It had things that were not to be found in any of the other rooms: a woven-rope bed, a clean table and a chair, and on the table, piles of books arranged neatly. Still, the space under the bed on which Basheer slept was chaotic, filled with secrets and mystery. A wooden chest could be glimpsed there, but beyond that was treacly darkness that concealed vague shapes of other objects. The cooking fire was rarely lit but the starving occupants of the other rooms imagined that a veritable bounty of food items was stored there. And given that, other than politics, food was the only subject that occupied their daydreams, they loitered outside the kitchen. Depending on his mood, Basheer chatted with them or shooed them away, and those he chatted with expected, hoped, that, like a magician, he would conjure up something from the darkness under the bed and give it to them. This never really happened, and yet stories about people who had experienced such generosity circulated among the occupants of the building. Whenever he went out, Basheer bolted the door that connected the kitchen to the rest of the building from the inside, and padlocked the outside door. It was assumed that, in order to find out whether some enterprising person was overcoming these precautions, Basheer placed a strand of hair where the two panes of the door came together. 'You didn't think I was going bald for no reason, did you?' he would remark threateningly, unsmiling, whenever he could.

When I arrived in front of Seethi Buildings, Basheer, dressed only in a cotton towel around his waist and his body slick with oil, was getting ready to exercise.

'Ashaaney...' I raised my hand and called out from the lane.

'Aha, you're right on time,' he said, his face bright. 'Come, let's try a hand.'

'No, my guru. Not wrestling with you until I learn how to do it properly.'

'Come, then, I'll teach you right now.'

I hesitated for a second; then, leaving my clothes on the veranda, I stepped in.

Basheer did a squat, and said, pointing at my mundu, 'Remove that too.'

I glanced around.

'To stand your ground, the first thing you need is to have the right clothes,' he said. 'No point in feeling shy. If not, all our attention will be on our clothes. Something around our waist that can withstand any move, that's all we need. Why do you think Kalari masters go on about tightening the kaccha? I clocked your ignorance that day right when I saw how you tied your mundu!'

'Yeah, well, still I stood my ground for a bit, didn't I?'

'Only because I let you. There's no fun if the game ends too quickly.'

Dressed only in my underwear, my body smeared with oil, I stepped into the godha. We had only begun grappling with one another when some of the other occupants of the building, who had stepped outside to pick mango leaves to clean their teeth, gathered around us. They began to cheer me on, only to annoy Basheer, and he took the bait, got angry, and effortlessly slamming me to the floor on my back, began pontificating about gusthi.

'Eda, listen, when it comes to gusthi, there are four ashaans, four exceptional maestros – Hanuman, Jarasandhan, Jambawan and Bheeman. Me, I'm Hanuman's disciple, part of the Vanarasena,' he declared.

We washed ourselves at the well, drawing water with a pail made of an areca nut sheath. Back in his room, Basheer began making tea. The fragrance of the black tea infused with cardamom and cinnamon brought four or five hangers-on scurrying in with clean teeth and freshly washed faces. Mercilessly, Basheer ignored them.

'Ashaaney,' I began, blowing into my tea to cool it. 'I have to confess something and also ask your forgiveness.'

Basheer gave me a grave look. 'What, are you the see-eye-dee who's always following me? Does your lot confess?'

'What? No! You're still being followed by a CID?'

'Still? Look over there ... If you sit on a branch of that tree, you'll have a clear view into this room. For all of last week, an owl has been sitting on that branch, staring this way non-stop!'

I laughed. Basheer did not like that. I was also confused. How much of what he said or did was serious and how much in jest?

'What I meant to say is that I had no clue then that I was wrestling with the man who wrote the banned book, *Dharmarajyam.*'

This seemed to please him. Just then, a young man with an ingratiating smile on his face came in, picked up a broom and began cleaning the room.

'It's not a book, it's a pamphlet,' Basheer said. 'I've written hundreds of them for the Congress and for the communists. Without putting my name on them, mind you.'

'Some writing this is...' I said. Pulling out a sheaf of papers, folded and creased by the many hands that they had passed through, I began to read aloud: 'There! An elephant in musth! Running amok, free of its chains ... roaring, trampling through the flower garden that is the abode of God himself, toppling plants, trees, bowers ... Hark! There! Its death knell echoes!'

The young man sweeping the room had his head raised and was listening carefully.

'Eda, Swami, do you know, the elephant in musth ... it's the diwan Sir C.P. himself,' Basheer said, looking at him. 'All these gormless folk who hang around here mouthing revolutionary ideas ... As if any of them have the balls to call him such names!' He turned his gaze back on me and said, 'The useless Pattar didn't just ban it, he also sent the police to my home! A whole boatload of police! They made my umma, bappa, brothers and sisters stand out in the yard, in the blazing sun. Told them that when they found me, they'd break my arms and legs and throw me in the river. Then they went inside the house and stole my books and my empty trunk. Showered abuse on my umma!'

He stopped, pointed at Swami, and continued, 'Know what I did? See this guy here? He's an Ezhavan. Back home we call them Chovan also. I appointed him as my servant. I call him "Swami" like they all call Sir C.P. Ramaswami. His real name is something else, can't remember. Eda, Swami, come here.'

Swami walked up to Basheer with a reverential expression on his face.

'Go, get me a bundle of beedis,' Basheer said, handing him a small coin.

Swami took the coin and left. He really didn't have much to do around the place. Basheer did the cooking himself. Swami kept the tiny space more or less clean, and was available when any of the tenants suddenly felt the need to rage against Diwanji. They could take it out on him, shower him with as much abuse as they desired, and he would stand there, wretchedly receiving it all as though the abuse was directed at him personally. Thankfully, there was no physical abuse, given that these were ahimsapremis after all. There was no salary attached to the job. If he was around when food was cooked, he would be given a share. Things had come to such a pass that he now had the constant expression of a guilt-ridden person yearning to own up to his crimes. Even overhearing a snippet of conversation among strangers about Thiruvithamkoor made him slip away with a deep sense of personal wrongdoing.

That night, Basheer told me a story. A romantic story titled 'Premalekhanam' – Love Letter. The way he narrated it, I felt he had a version of it written down on paper in his head and he was reading it aloud. The story was about the love affair between Keshavan Nair, a bank employee of the Nair caste, and Saramma, a young Christian woman at the house where he rented a room. I listened carefully. A handful of words that were in *Dharmarajyam* were in this story too, but by and large, the language employed was conversational. If it were to be published, the government would most certainly have to ban it because it was the kind of story that fuelled communal disharmony. Especially given that, following the failure of the agitations for Utharavada Bharanam, Nairs and Christians were at loggerheads. The Christians were quite upset that the Nair Service Society, under the leadership of Mannath Padmanabhan, had erected a marble statue of Sir C.P. Ramaswami Iyer in front of the legislative assembly building. And would the Nairs keep calm after reading a story about one of their own running away with a Christian woman? Still, I told Basheer that it was a wonderful story.

'The ending is great,' I said, 'although initially I kind of expected one of them to kill themselves.'

Basheer opened the door and stepped outside to urinate, and to clear his throat, loudly hawking up phlegm and spitting.

'There's one problem though...' I said when he came back in. 'The language the people in this story use ... They sound illiterate, uneducated. I suppose you'll change all that when you write it down?'

'Eda, buddhoos! You want me who is a Mussalman to write a story in Sanskrit?'

'But the characters are not Muslims...'

'So what? All the Nairs around here speak in Sanskrit?'

'Anyway, how come there are only two characters in such a long story? A chittamma and appachan are mentioned but they don't really come into the story...'

'There's that place near Ponkunnam in Kanjirappally – Kothazham it is called, land of idiots. Plenty of stories about the people there and their stupidity. Ever heard of it? When two people are in love, their world is the only one that exists. What? You want all and sundry to wander through their world?'

I held my tongue and lay there silently, staring into the dark. From above the ceiling came certain noises. Perhaps one of the young men, living a half-starved life in that building, scared as they were of the laws of our country, was trying to pleasure himself in a world of his imagination, assuming that everyone else was asleep. They all looked the same, these young men, each with two hollows on either side of their necks, each with bloodless, drawn cheeks. Dark, knobbly marks were visible on their backs and sides in the light of day, bitemarks from bedbugs. They stank of dirty, unwashed clothes, their bodies desiccated by the mad thoughts and ideas that churned their minds.

'All I was wondering...' I ventured, eventually. 'I mean, what will happen if a story like this comes out? Nairs and Christians in our country are not all that friendly with each other, so...'

'Poda! Catholic bishops have presented the diwan with a mangalapathram, felicitations scrolled in gold leaf and put inside a gold casket. The Chovans have, too. Meaning, the wealthy – Chovan, Nair and Christian alike – are with the Pattar, while we have with us the hapless and the hopeless! They can't tolerate people loving one another even in a story? That so?'

The next day, in the afternoon, Basheer took me along and boarded a boat to Mattancherry. He did not tell me where we were going or why. Mattancherry is an important trade post in the country of Kochi. To its east is the Vembanad Kayal, the vast lake fed by the waters of the rivers of our country. Beyond that is Willingdon Island, an artificial island built by the British. To the west, beyond Kochi, is the Arabian Sea. And to the south, the seaport. It adjoined the border of our country, its natural position conducive to loading and unloading ships, and because of this,

Diwanji had promised all support to the development of the port. But nothing came of it because of the conniving interference of Shanmukham Chetty, the diwan of Kochi.

Mattancherry was chock-a-block with Muslims, Jews and other communities. By comparison, Malayali Hindus who belonged to the three varnas were fewer in number. The town had many warehouses and storage facilities with high security. The managers and bookkeepers in these places were mostly Konkanis and Pattars, Brahmins both, but they often overlooked observing customs of purity and pollution in favour of the conveniences of their jobs. We got off the boat and set out towards the marketplace, proceeding at a crawling pace through the thronging crowds. The air was thick with the combined fragrance of spices – nutmeg, cinnamon, cardamom – piled inside shops or spread on mats to dry. These were spices brought from areas around Peerumedu and Devikulam, underlining the importance of this port town to the interests of our country. Basheer seemed to know a lot of people around here. A Parsi, doing busywork in a shop, ran out to greet him. Finally, as we reached the most crowded part of the town, Basheer led me into a shop. It had a stove packed with sawdust; a pot of water, constantly on the boil, sat atop it. He ordered two glasses of tea.

'For today, I've appointed you as my see-eye-dee,' Basheer told me in full hearing of the man who made the tea. 'Something is about to happen. I want you to sit here and sip your tea. Listen to everything that's being said and watch the expression on people's faces.'

The words were hardly out of his mouth when he got up and stood right in the middle of the road. The flow of activities – bullock carts trundling past, one behind the other, coolies passing bundles of merchandise from head to head – stuttered for a moment, and in that moment, Basheer flexed his knees, lifted his arms as though pulling them out from deep under the earth, and in the loudness of voice that is possible only once in a while, shouted:

'Inquilab zindabad!'

The market of Mattancherry came to a standstill. Conversations and bargaining, hollers and murmurings, all quietened.

'Inquilaaab zindabaaad!' Basheer shouted again.

No way a human being could raise their voice any louder than that! I feared that blood would flow from his torn throat. Then, from various corners, came answering calls.

'Zindabaaad! Zindabaaad!'

Young men – around thirty of them, at least – with moustaches matching Basheer's, their ends twirled upwards, walked towards us. Basheer continued calling out slogans and they responded, and when his voice began to crack, another man took up:

'Shaheed Bhagat Singh zindabad!'

'Sukhdev, Rajguru zindabad!'

'Mahatma Gandhi zindabad!'

'Vanarasena zindabad!'

The demonstration made a circuit of the market and set out down the road we had arrived by. A large crowd followed fearfully, careful to keep a distance from it. People squeezed to the sides of the road, clearing a space for the men to proceed. As they left the market and its shops behind, women and children, their eyes wide open, came running out of their homes to watch them go by. When a significant event unfolds, the rest of the world goes still. Nothing else happens, or even if it does, it would be pointless. Basheer was the protagonist of the single, significant event that was taking place in that port city of different languages and diverse human beings. It seemed as though every single person there was looking only at him. And those thirty-odd men who formed the demonstration, they did not seem to be a group of individuals. In their shared passion, as they raised their arms in rhythm and moved forward in unison, they seemed to be a single person with the face of Bhagat Singh, the young revolutionary from the Punjab who was hanged. I followed, taking care not to be part of the procession, keeping to the crowd in its wake, paying attention to things. I looked at the arms of those who were watching the procession go by. They were covered in goosebumps! Even I felt strange sensations as the unique rhythm of the event carried me forward. All creatures have the instinct to join in when the rest of their kind moves as a collective. No one knew how much time had passed or how far they had walked. By the time dusk settled, we had walked all the way to the harbour. Anglers and cast-net fishermen stopped what they were doing and stared at us. As the westering sun imbued everything with a red hue, the strong eastward currents of the high tide were clearly visible. Basheer's voice was powerful as he took in the blood-red sea and the backwaters and continued calling out the slogans. He would never stop, I felt. Every single person there had the same expression on their faces, of the expectation that something monumental was about to happen, and of the conviction that they were the driving force that would make it happen. At that moment, an enormous merchant ship, flying the colours of many different nations, passed through the shipping channel in front of the crowd, and it tooted its horn as though it was the vehicle of change and it was greeting them.

'Red salute! Red salute!'

Basheer, the young men, and all of Mattancherry called out as one, as though they were returning the greetings from human revolutions the world over. The backwash created by the ship came right up to their feet. I looked at Basheer. In his eyes and on his face was madness, dancing like the waves.

9

About a month later, the latest two-page edition of the newspaper *Ujjeevanam* was being prepared with reports of the Vanarasena's demonstration in Mattancherry. Basheer was the chief editor of *Ujjeevanam*, and these reports were all written by him but under different bylines. All made-up names such as Kulathoopuzha Ayyappan Nair, Sukumaran Chavara and Janakiyamma Perumbalam.

'Let the Pattar's see-eye-dees read these and run around looking for them until their feet fall off!' he declared.

'If that's what you're trying to do, better get rid of the name Janakiyamma Perumbalam,' I said. 'Women in this line of work are well known. Besides, Perumbalam is a tiny islet. Everyone knows everyone there. The police will see right through it in no time.'

'Not bad, you!' said Basheer, striking 'Perumbalam' from the byline.

'Why do you writers attach place names to your names anyway?' I asked.

'To tell one apart from the other, what else? There are plenty Sivasankara Pillais in our country. Adding "Thakazhi" helps identify which one we are talking about. Same with "Ponkunnam" Varkey.'

'Then how come we don't say "Neyyattinkara" C.V. Ramanpillah or Kalidasan "Ujjain"?'

'There you go again, being clever and all!' Basheer looked carefully at me. 'You're right, though. No one says Moscow Tolstoy or Shakespeare London. Them big-shot writers don't need to add place names to their names. But us piddling ones do.'

'Meaning none of you have the ambition to become big writers,' I said.

The first step in bringing out a newspaper was, of course, writing up the content. Day and night, Basheer sat in his room wrestling with pencil and paper like a man possessed. Sometimes, he spoke what he was writing out loud. Edited and re-edited three- or four-page matter down to a paragraph, and then tore it up into pieces. Replaced one unsatisfactory word with another, experimented with ten more, only to come back to the original word. The other occupants of Seethi Buildings stayed well clear of the kitchen during these days. Swami came into the yard a couple of times, but quickly made himself scarce as though he had picked up a whiff of something bad. A week later, when I arrived and opened the doors hesitantly, Basheer was done.

'But these are like stories,' I said after reading what he had written. 'Even I find it hard to believe, and I was right there!'

Reading what he had written, anyone would imagine a major uprising involving ten thousand people, not the procession with thirty-odd members. The writer had, in no uncertain terms, concluded that the world had changed irrevocably because of it, that Mattancherry was the centre of a worldwide revolution, and the Vanarasena its advancing guard. At one point, I began to think that even Subhas Chandra Bose and Captain Lakshmi were present at the event. Was it, I couldn't help wondering, the sea-conquering warship of the Indian National Army that had passed before us on that day at the Kochi harbour?

'Well, most people live inside stories, don't they?' Basheer asked. 'What else do we have besides stories? Take your name for instance. Bhasi ... Isn't that a story?'

I felt a jolt of shock.

'I mean, what have you got to do with that name?' he continued. 'If my bappa had named me Usman instead of Basheer, I would be Usman now.'

In those days, however, I had little faith in stories. My job had taught me to go after fact, not fiction.

'Eda, how do animals die?' asked Basheer.

'Other animals eat them ... Or they die of disease or old age.'

'And humans?'

'Also of old age and illness. And, of course, by being shot at or stabbed...'

'Nonsense! They begin to die from the moment they are born, listening to story after story. And even after death, they become story. And as if that's not enough, they've written a novel called "God" and fight over it thinking it's fact.'

'So, are you saying there's no God?'

'I'll kill you if you say there's no God.'

'Let me ask you this,' I said, changing the subject. 'Why do you revolutionaries shout the slogan "Gandhiji ki jai" when all you do is make fun of his non-violence, calling it foolishness?'

'All sons are against their fathers, but that doesn't mean they go around shouting slogans for their downfall,' said Basheer.

Carefully concealing the written matter in a cloth bag, we went to get the newspaper printed, but the owner of the printing press drove us away. This was the third edition of *Ujjeevanam*, but he was yet to be paid for printing the first. Basheer delivered a short speech on the importance of this edition and the changes it would bring around the world. Instead of being moved by the speech, the man reminded Basheer of all the lofty ideals he had espoused the last time he was there to get the newspaper printed.

'You don't want independence and Utharavada Bharanam, then? Is that what you're saying?' Basheer was enraged.

'You have to ask? No! I don't want any of it,' countered the press owner. 'What do you think will happen if you let the cattle in the barn roam free? If the sahibs go, our fate will be like that of the cattle. At least now we have hay and kaadivellam to eat. You'll see ... We'll starve to death otherwise!'

'At least we'll die free!'

'Well, I don't want to die. If they are to govern themselves, people have to be reasonable. Whereas here ... Each caste is after the other, like the god of death, Kaalan! Anyway, leave this here. Let's see if you all will come back for it.'

He took the cloth bag from us and threw it in a corner of the room – surety against money owed.

That night, Basheer locked up the kitchen and disappeared. He came back after a week with some money he had organized from somewhere.

'Did you go back home?' I asked.

'Ei! A see-eye-dee is on the prowl there waiting for me to come back. Every single day.'

'A CID?'

'Yes! I ran into a neighbour of ours on the boat the other day. Palunkan Kochukunju. He told me that this see-eye-dee goes to my house every day, sits outside by the gate in the scorching sun until evening, and then goes back. My poor umma feels sorry for him and gives him a glass of kanjivellam. Now it's difficult to say whether he goes there looking for me or for the free drink!'

We went to the printing press with the money owed. The press owner took out a bundle – two hundred copies of the new edition – and handed it to us.

'Cruel, you are! You were having us on, weren't you?' Basheer grabbed hold of him and planted a kiss on his head. 'Let the revolution come. We'll make you the manager of the press printing the people's newspaper!'

But his joy was short-lived. It turned into rage as soon as he read the printed matter. The press owner, a Christian Mappila, had taken it upon himself to make some changes to the copy. 'Althirakku' – crowd – had become 'jananibidam'; 'vaakkutharkkam' – argument – changed to 'vagsamaram'; 'kaayalkkara' – shore of the lake – morphed into 'thatakatheeram', and so on and so forth.

'Who asked you to change all this into Sanskrit?' Basheer shouted at him.

'Well, it's being printed in my press, so it should have some standards.' The man refused to be intimidated.

'Actually, "ujjeevanam", the name of the newspaper ... that's Sanskrit, too, isn't it?' I ventured.

Basheer lost all control and grabbed me by the throat. 'Ask me another question like that and I'll cut you to pieces,' he said, even as the printer and two of his employees got involved and released me from his grip.

That night, Basheer told me another story. We were on our way back to Seethi Buildings via Thoppumpadi after distributing almost half of the printed copies of the newspaper. I had noticed that people regarded Basheer with an obvious respect, but as soon as they got their copies, they forgot everything and were immersed in reading. They seemed to display a greed for letters more acute than their greed for food, their hands shaking and their faces reddening. Some were even on the verge of tears. Seems to me it is people with a heightened emotional sensibility that venture into such things as revolutions without thinking through or even considering the dangers involved.

'Will these many copies do?' I asked doubtfully.

'Even one copy will do,' Basheer said confidently. 'It will go from hand to hand, and everyone will get to read it.'

He then told me how, when the first edition of the newspaper had come out, several people had brought him copies without realizing who he was.

'Like *Ramanan*,' I said, laughing. 'Maybe people will write the whole thing down to read and to keep a copy for themselves.'

The story Basheer told me this time, about the love between a comparatively well-off Muslim man and a poor woman from the same community, was also like *Ramanan*. Except in *Ramanan*, the celebrated poem by the romantic poet Changampuzha Krishna Pillai, the woman is well-off and the man poor, and they are Hindus. Their love is doomed from the start. Each time it seems like it will survive, something disastrous happens. In Basheer's story, it is the woman who dies in the end, and instead of the betrayal by the rich woman in *Ramanan*, it is fate that deals the final blow.

'I don't understand,' I said. 'You all are always talking about the good times to come when everyone will be equal. Then how come all your stories and poems end in disaster? How come they all end with no hope at all? Don't you believe in your own vision?'

Basheer did not respond until we were back home and in our beds.

'It's not that,' he said then. 'We're talking about the world as it is now and the disasters that happen here. And when people read them, they will obviously imagine that a better world is yet to come.'

He sounded as though he was unconvinced by his own words.

'But all you do is tell stories. How come you don't write any more? What, one story was banned and you're scared now?'

Basheer was silent for a while. Then, getting me out of my bed, he took me outside. We sat on the bare earth at the spot where we had wrestled. It had not rained for days and the ground was dry. The moon was bright and a gentle breeze blew. It was then that I realized Basheer never slept. His mind was aflame with thoughts, he said. People like that barely slept, barely felt the chill even on foggy nights.

'Truth be told, I'm scared,' he said finally. 'But it's not like you think. I'm not scared for my life. If that was the case, why would I take the risk of publishing a newspaper? Why would I organize young men to terrorize the country?'

'What then? Are you scared it won't come out right if you write your stories down?'

'Poda! This Mussalman writes better than anyone else around here. What? You doubt that? Does anyone else have the kind of stories I tell?'

'Of course not!' I said, recalling the story he had told me the other day about a policeman's daughter who helps a prison escapee.

He remained quiet for a long time. Early birds chittered, signalling daybreak. Other birds took up the chorus, went far away with it, and came back after some time.

Eventually, Basheer broke his silence with a question. 'Eda, tell me, what is the most dangerous weapon invented by human beings?'

'Gun,' I said.

Basheer said nothing. His silence told me that I was wrong, so I tried again.

'Cannon? Chemical weapons? No, I know ... That terrible bomb they say the Americans are making.'

'No. It's none of these. The most dangerous weapon invented by human beings is the story.'

'The story! Really!' I laughed. 'How is a story dangerous to anyone?'

'What's the difference between a human being and an animal? Animals live for a while and die. Human beings make up stories, tell them to others and listen to the stories they tell.'

'So? That's a good thing, isn't it?'

'Yes, it is. That's how the likes of Jesus got people to congregate around him. No better way to control people and make them do your bidding than a story.'

'Well, good. What's the problem then?'

'Then there are only problems! Just think ... How many people have been killed because people believe his stories and the stories about him? Meanwhile, the Muslims also killed a whole bunch of people saying *their* stories are the truth. All because of stories! Imagine that ... Imagine killing one another arguing about the truth or falsehood of a story! Ha ha...'

'Well, yes, but, Ashaaney, why should any of this stop you from writing your stories? No one is going to fight over them. It's like I said earlier. Write stories that will make people happy.'

'All stories must be feared! A story has the capacity to make people love, hate, go mad ... kill!'

'Again, like I said, it should be used for good.'

'Using something for good does not stop its misuse. If something can be used as a weapon, it is dangerous. A machete is used to cut open a young coconut, but that doesn't mean it won't be used to cut someone's head off!'

Basheer scooted closer to me, lowered his voice and continued, 'I'll tell you a terrible secret. My fear is that an intelligent but horrible person will find out about this particular use of a story. Someone like Sir C.P. ... Think about it, imagine what he could do with it. He'll be able to control the whole world. Feed people one type of story and they will sit obediently in a corner. Feed them another type of story and they will fight with one another. Go to war over yet another. A timely story for all times ... Like putting grass and water in front of cattle. An animal living and dying within a story, and returning to it as a ghost, can be controlled.'

'If that's the case, these sahibs who are supposed to be so clever ... won't they have figured this out already?'

'To be honest with you, watching this war that's been going on, I think they already have. It's been going on for how many years now? Ho! It seems endless. It might actually never end, I'm beginning to think...'

The next day, in the end-of-month report that I sent to my superiors, I wrote clearly that the man named Basheer – the author of the banned pamphlet *Dharmarajyam* who had fled to Kochi and continued to mastermind subversive action – was in the grip of madness.

10

The sesame is a unique plant that sprouts in highland fields and grows rapidly without the aid of fertilizers. When the plant is as tall as a person and the stems start to yellow, it is harvested by pulling it out, roots and all. Gather up a few plants together and beat them against a stone set on a mat, and black seeds the size of mustard will scatter everywhere. Sweep them up and dry them in the sun, then put them through a mill, and they give up a first-class, dark-hued oil. Those who apply this oil to their head before a bath will have an intense sheen to their faces and bodies, and their hair will be imbued with its everlasting fragrance. There is, however, another, even better, use for sesame seeds. Toast them and put them in a syrup of melted jaggery. Before the mixture cools and hardens, pick up bits of it and roll them between the palms into neat little balls. These sesame balls – ellunda – will last as long as desired without spoiling. The combined taste of the bitterness of the sesame, the sweetness of the jaggery, and the moistness of the oil it produces as it is chewed is beyond description. Hunger will be sated with just two or three of these balls.

It was widely believed that, in the dark, secret world under his bed, Basheer had a bharani, its mouth secured tightly with a piece of cloth, filled with ellundas. The half-starved occupants of Seethi Buildings believed that this was why he was so obviously, indefatigably energetic, despite being broke, despite the kitchen fire rarely being lit. The only person who occasionally got to sample one or two ellundas was K.C. George, a forty-year-old dedicated socialist ideologist who was also said to work secretly for the Communist Party. He walked with a limp. His room on the upper floor of the building had many similarities to Basheer's kitchen empire below. Half the room was taken up with books and notices, and a wooden trunk filled with more papers, printed and unprinted, which was also used as a table to write on while sitting on the floor. But it was not as clean and tidy as Basheer's room, and it had other occupants. K.C. George was the only person other than Basheer who had free rein in the kitchen. And he had, for no apparent reason, taken upon himself the role of Basheer's guardian. Some days, as part of this role, he would deliver long sermons full of advice, and Basheer brought out the ellundas at strategic moments to silence him.

However, the ellundas became the cause of a serious, unexpected argument between the two of them.

'After the revolution, when a people's democracy is in place, private property like this that individuals keep hidden will all be confiscated, and the owners punished,' George said, swallowing the juice of the masticated ellunda in his mouth.

'Like hell they will!' Basheer said. 'Let there be no illusion that they can confiscate my ellundas. It is the surplus value of my hard work.'

'Under socialism, it is not possible to own private property. Accumulating surplus value to make oneself a capitalist simply will not be allowed. The state will provide for everyone. In fact, secreting resources is a crime even under capitalism.'

'But why should private property be confiscated? If the people are convinced that socialism is a better way of life, they'll willingly give up private property.'

'Ah, you're just repeating Gandhi's philosophy there. That human beings can be persuaded into changing their behaviour. Humanism. Similar to what people like Trotsky have said.'

'What does it matter who said it?' Basheer lost his patience. 'What are you hoping to achieve that doesn't involve people changing for the better?'

By then, the argument had attracted the attention of the other occupants of the building. The kitchen filled rapidly, and those who could not find space inside stood on the veranda and in the yard, joining in the argument. Two people were even hanging off the shutterless window through which Basheer aimed long streams of spittle at the yard. Basheer pulled out the bharani from under the bed and distributed the ellundas to everyone.

'Now see, this is typical Gandhian strategy ... undergoing a sudden change of heart and giving away what is in hand,' George remarked, finding a chink in Basheer's action. 'One can easily see that it is the pressure of the circumstance that brought this about. But the question is, what should be done if a person does not do the right thing even under the right circumstance?'

Use of force, opined more than half of the assembled people. Only Basheer and a small minority disagreed.

'How is that any different from the current government's behaviour? Are people to be beaten shitless to make them do things? Is that what socialism is about? What of values like freedom and self-respect?'

'Self-respect is a feudalist ideal.'

Soon, the discussion moved on to wages for labour under socialism. Basheer argued that those who laboured more should be rewarded with more wages. Others disagreed, arguing that they would then accumulate surplus value and turn into neo-capitalists. In this matter, George was in partial agreement with Basheer. If those who worked hard and those who sat around being lazy were paid the same wages, it would affect productivity. The economic disparities and contradictions it would engender, and how to handle them, needed further debate.

By the time it was midnight and the meeting dispersed without matters being resolved, Basheer had come to a decision – he would urgently prepare a blueprint for the state of affairs that would emerge after the imminent revolution. This plan was also met with disagreement, some saying that this was a task for the people's council that would be formed after the working-class revolution. George said there was no need to oppose this plan, even though it was being instigated by a person who was neither a party member nor a member of the working class. Whether or not the blueprint should be accepted could be considered after the revolution, based on the overall situation that would emerge. Even after he retired to his room and Basheer bolted the kitchen door, two people stood in the yard discussing the class behaviour of writers well into the wee hours of the morning.

The task of preparing the post-revolution blueprint for the nation seemed boundless and everlasting. Basheer spent his days locked inside the kitchen, thinking and scribbling, emerging in the evenings to sit on a bench in the hall, holding a bunch of papers. Then followed discussions and analyses of what had been written that day. The vast majority disagreed outright with everything, while a few hung on to a single word, endlessly debating its appropriateness – it took two nights to pick between 'government' and 'governance' and come to a decision. But the first serious debate was about *where* the revolution would actually take place. It was obviously a matter of the common good, affecting all of humanity, but it was important to the planning that a specific location was identified. A whole month went by as the pros and cons of various locales were discussed – Thiruvithamkoor; the area where Thiruvithamkoor and Kochi met; the entire land of the Malayali; all of the Indian subcontinent – without reaching an agreement.

By then, the news that Basheer was involved in this very important task had spread far and wide, and a veritable river of interested parties flowed towards Ernakulam. A large number of these were from the Malabar district, and each and every one of them dreamed of a vast and free country that included, along with the Indian subcontinent, the North-West Frontier Province, Afghanistan, Burma, Ceylon, Tibet and Malaya. A post-revolution India where linguistic nationalities would have the same place the Soviets did in the Soviet Union. Of course, there were quite a few who were opposed to this idea.

As the debate went on and on, one day, a man named P. Krishnapillah, who was active in Malabar, arrived as though he was in a great hurry. That night, he took Basheer out – they were countrymen and old acquaintances – and when he came back, Basheer had decided to move on from this topic.

And so the discussion turned to other matters: the distribution of land after nationalization; the handling of feudal lords who refused to join the working class; whether or not to impose a complete ban on religion; the role the Party – the advance guard of the working class – would play in the government; how to respond to counter-revolutionaries; how to educate the masses on socialist ideology; the direction post-revolution literature could take; whether or not to rehabilitate current government officials and the police through ideological re-education; whether the surplus from collective agriculture should be made a public asset. Someone proposed the topic of how to deal with Gandhi, but Basheer did not encourage this discussion.

'Gandhi will have to change...'

'Stubborn, he is. Won't change his ways even if he has to die!'

Seethi Buildings had transformed. It was difficult to say who was an occupant and who was a visitor, with the rooms, halls and the veranda overflowing with people. Reedy young men with no apparent need for food or sleep sat around day and night, talking with great enthusiasm and intensity. An almost foolish energy pulsated in their eyes and their faces, as though a great explosion was waiting to happen. Often, they shouted loudly, fell out with one another, and walked away. Some of them came right back as quickly as they left, caught in the thrill of a new idea that had popped into their heads. An argument between Gopalakkuruppu and Raghavakkuruppu from Chengannur about the role of women, their familial relationships, sexuality and chastity, in post-revolution society ended in actual fisticuffs. Raghavakkuruppu was the brother of Gopalakkuruppu's wife.

All night, Basheer scurried around, listening to people and making notes, taking part in debates that seemed important. Since he could not be in several places at once, he would go into a room and ask for a summary of what they had discussed. However, often matters unfolded in such a way that no one could remember anything substantial, and they would give Basheer irritated looks for interrupting their discussions. A lot of them did not know who he was.

'Where's that Basheer? Call him. It is he I want to talk to,' one young man, a student leader who had left his studies in Madurai, shouted at Basheer without even bothering to show the respect due to his age.

What truly confounded Basheer was the fact that the same people spouted different opinions on the same subject on different days. And if he pointed this out, referring to his notes, they denied it, except for the small minority who might concede and rationalize their change of heart.

'Just think of the people in this house as one person,' said K.C. George one day. 'A single person, an individual who has many ideas and many dilemmas. The cacophony around is the thoughts and soliloquies he voices as he strives for clarity and purpose. A process that needs time, nothing to worry about. The final answer to all of human beings' problems will soon be found.'

I was afraid that Basheer's head was about to explode, filled as it was with complex ideas and contradictory thoughts. He had no time to rest, often seemed to be sleeping with his eyes wide open, and he walked around like a somnambulist. One time, during an argument, everyone had stopped talking and fallen silent, but Basheer continued a one-sided conversation until someone tapped him on his shoulder.

'Oh, I just closed my eyes for a bit,' he said. 'What day is it?'

One night, when Basheer set out for a walk with some others, I tagged along. Going for a walk after midnight was a peculiarity shared by everyone who resided at Seethi Buildings. They seemed to imagine that they were experiencing absolute freedom while strolling along the deserted lanes, talking at the top of their voices. And when summer came, they seemed to be more energetic than usual. That night, we were headed towards the railway station. Basheer believed that watching people waiting for trains that would take them to faraway destinations made one happy, that it gave relief from the troubling thoughts one held inside. He said it reminded him that even if things went bad here, there were so many other places to go to.

A man with a mighty physique walked with us. 'Guru, this is Bhasi, my disciple,' Basheer introduced me to him.

He was T.V. Thomas, the man who had taught Basheer gusthi.

'He's all right, except for one thing,' Basheer continued. 'He's always full of doubts, asks endless questions.'

'Is that right, Doubting Thoma?' Thomachan asked, beckoning me closer. 'We should always have people who ask questions of us.'

He put his arm around my shoulder and began asking me questions. When I said I had given up my studies, he began giving me advice. As he talked, his gaze fell on a man who was walking along with us, a familiar face I had seen many times in the halls of Seethi Buildings over the last few days. Thomachan's gaze seemed to disconcert him, and when his expression changed, Thomachan took his arm off my shoulder. The man took a couple of steps back, but Thomachan stopped him and began interrogating him. There was nothing extraordinary about the man, just a face that looked harmless and a presence too insubstantial even to leave a shadow. As he hemmed and hawed trying to answer Thomachan's questions, he took a fearful glance behind him. The next moment, Thomachan had kicked him into the drainage ditch by the side of the road.

'Go on, go to Thiruvananthapuram and tell your Swami about this too!' he shouted.

The man scrambled up and ran away without even pausing to pick up his mundu that had come undone. Thomachan turned to Basheer and scolded him for allowing complete strangers free range at the house.

'Always remember that we have eyes watching us,' he cautioned.

An immediate decision was made to purge Seethi Buildings, to ensure that everyone who came and went would be questioned in detail. I was entrusted with the responsibility of doing this. I was to take down the names and addresses of everyone and verify them with State Congress workers who lived in various parts of Ernakulam.

'No one will dare infiltrate us if they think we are being careful and thorough,' said Thomachan.

But none of it came to pass. The next evening, K.C. George was apprehended by the police near the boat jetty and placed under arrest. This might have seemed like a good thing at first, but the way the arrest was made was symptomatic of the soft approach the Kochi government took towards these people. The only reason at least one of their ilk – people who lived in hiding in Kochi and continued to work against its neighbouring country – was arrested was because of the pressure our government put through the

British government. But they did it in such a way as to alert all the others and give them ample time to be prepared. If they had arrested someone like K.C. George not in broad daylight in public, and had questioned him in secret, they could have easily put an end to State Congress and communist activities centred around Ernakulam. But neither the Kochi government nor the police had any real interest in that. I had personally witnessed the police being friendly and tolerant with these people any number of times. Anyway, things happened exactly as they wanted. As soon as he heard of the arrest, Basheer and his servant Swami bundled up all the communist literature, books and papers in George's room and carried them on their heads to another house. A substantial number of people in Seethi Buildings disappeared overnight. A couple of days later, the police raided the place as though they were conducting a ritual.

II

It was in Kottayam that Basheer was finally arrested for his role in the Raktarekha Case and for writing seditious pamphlets. We were visiting a man named M.P. Paul who was the proprietor of tutorial colleges in Kottayam and Ernakulam. A meeting of an organization called Sahitheesakhyam was taking place there, and sitting in Paul's college which had no walls between rooms, we heard all that was being discussed, none of which is worth reporting. After the meeting, Basheer began telling Paul all that stuff he had told me about stories, and Paul, who seemed like an intelligent person, told Basheer off lovingly. We spent quite a while in the man's company. When we finally left, we climbed the steep rise behind the college and came up to the Kottayam–Kumali road. *Manorama*, the banned newspaper, used to have its offices on this road; the government had locked and sealed the building. Basheer stopped in front of this building and began chatting to a man named Puthencavu Mathan Tharakan. I glanced around me. They were there – Assistant Police Commissioner K.V. Raja and three policemen, all in mufti. They didn't know me by sight, so I gave them the signal – tapping my left ankle a couple of times with my right foot – and then quietly walked away a little, as though I was going to take a piss. Two of the policemen stepped forward, accosted Basheer and forced his arms behind him, and as a stunned Mathan Tharakan began to sound the alarm, they bundled him into a jeep that arrived and drove away.

Two other men were arrested that day in connection with the Raktarekha Case – Dr Thayyil in Cherthala and P. Keshavadev in North Paravoor.

I had some time to spend before the next stage, so I walked east towards Ettaam Mile until darkness fell. Then I walked back to Paul's tutorial college and went in, pretending to be out of breath from having run a long way. Paul was still there along with a bunch of people who had heard about the arrest.

Paul scrambled up when he saw me. 'Where were you?' he asked.

'I ran away,' I said. 'Down the slope and hid by the lake.'

'Well, good, you're safe,' said Paul. 'No one goes there even in daytime.'

They told me that Basheer was being held at a police station in Kottayam. Paul was acquainted with the sub-inspector and was confident that they would not hurt him physically. Arrangements were made for me to have a bath and something to eat, after which they got ready to go to the police station with a pillow, a mat and a mundu for Basheer. I began insisting that I wanted to go with them.

'Don't be daft,' Paul said, patting my head to calm me down. 'There's no point in presenting your head to them on a platter. We know these policemen, yes, but to trust them? They're slaves puffed up with the little power they've been given. They'll betray us.'

In the morning, Paul gave me some money, for transport he said, and saw me off. But I set out by foot to Pallam, which was not too far, to meet with a retired police inspector named Kunjukrishnan. A man who had spent more than half his years in service in suspension for taking bribes, he had acquired a considerable amount of land, a couple of shop premises in the city, and had a moneylending business, all of which made him more prosperous than most middle-class people could dream of. And yet, despite all this wealth, he engaged in a truly weird occupation – begging! Dressed in his good clothes, he would take a train from Kottayam and travel somewhere where he had no acquaintances. He would then change into some dirty, torn clothes, stuff his good clothes in an old tote, wander into rural areas, and go begging from house to house. To look the part, he also knew how to dislocate his right shoulder at appropriate times. A handful of rice, a coin, a meal – he was satisfied with whatever he was given, and if nothing was forthcoming, he would humbly take his leave. People said that he acquired more wealth in this manner. These days, he lived in an ashramam, just a hut with a palm-leaf thatch at a little distance from his home, all very spiritual.

Without getting into a long conversation, I told Kunjukrishnan why I had come to see him. A witness had to be found to give evidence against Basheer at the court. The police would find their own witness, but there had to be another, more believable, witness, and I asked him to be that person. I told him what he must say in court: That, around three years ago, as he was leaving after the evening prayer at the Cherthala temple, he had run into Basheer and three other men and had overheard their conversation. That Basheer had said horrible things about the Maharaja, Amma Maharani and Diwanji, and had threatened to topple the government. That he, Kunjukrishnan, had been distressed by what he heard and had to shut his ears with his hands. And that he had then watched the four of them walking towards the nearby postbox. All this and nothing more, in detail and without mistakes.

Kunjukrishnan balked at first, and I had to threaten him. I told him about the two files slumbering in the Huzur Court, containing information about his wrongdoings while in service, that would be enough to have his pension cancelled. The threat made him pliable, more receptive, especially when he considered that a favour garnered another in return and that the files could disappear forever.

The very next day, I had to deal with a matter relating to another Kunjukrishnan – the leader of the Thiruvithamkoor National Congress, Kottur Kunjukrishna Pillai. Although they had made noises about favouring Utharavada Bharanam, the TNC was patriotic and had, over time, functioned in support of the government. Kunjukrishna Pillai had even told Gandhi to his face that the seditious State Congress was trying to build a Christian nation within Thiruvithamkoor.

One day, I had been given an order to pick up two Chitpavan Brahmins at the island where the holy place of Rameswaram was located, which was part of the Madras Presidency of British India, and bring them to Kunjukrishna Pillai's house in Kottayam. The task had to be done in utmost secrecy. Their clothing and general appearance could give them away, so they were to travel like ordinary people, without their usual splendour. I had also received strict instructions on how to interact with them – I was to maintain physical distance and cleanliness, and speak, preferably in Hindustani, only when necessary and only about things that were urgent.

The journey to Rameswaram took three days. As had been prearranged, I met with the Brahmins in a house right behind the main temple belonging to a man named Pakshi Narayana Sastri. It was an auspicious day in the calendar, and the place was crowded with people from all over who had come to offer rites to the souls of the departed, a few among them speaking our language. In the midst of all this activity, we left in a hurry. The two men wore long coats over their clothes and had clean-shaven faces. One had round eyeglasses and a bald head like Gandhi. We took the train across the sea to Mandapam, and then to Madurai where we spent the night in a matam, a Brahmin household, as had been arranged. I took our host's advice not to travel by train and rented a horse carriage. We travelled through the next day and night until we got to Chenkotta. All this time, the two men barely spoke to me but conversed with each other in a low voice in Marathi strewn liberally with Sanskrit words. I suspected that they also discussed whether or not I was a Brahmin. On the second day in the early morning, when we finally reached the border of our country, the carriage driver insisted that he wanted to return. Having deviated from the plan and travelled by a different route from the train, I was anxious about how to complete the rest of the journey. But the two men seemed calm and showed no signs of being in a hurry. We got off at the toll post and walked for about a kilometre, and there was a car waiting for us. A clear sign that our journey had been under surveillance. The driver handed me the keys and scampered away.

Kottur Kunjukrishna Pillai's house was in the middle of a large property in Mayyanad in Kollam. It was left unoccupied most of the time, so no one paid it much attention. As I drove in, I noticed several people around the property pretending to be yard workers and gardeners watering the plants. As soon as I stopped the car, the guests got out, and Kunjukrishna Pillai got in without looking straight at them and sat in the front seat. It was clear from his expression that a momentous meeting was about to take place. The whole event had been carefully and meticulously planned, suggesting that the person the guests were here to meet, if it weren't the Maharaja, could only be one other – Sir C.P. Something monumental was about to happen, I too was certain. I drove back to Kollam and handed the car and the keys to another person, thus completing the job I had been assigned.

12

One night in August, Subrahmanya Pillah, the superintendent of the Central Jail in Poojappura in Thiruvananthapuram, welcomed me with the utmost respect and attention into his quarters. Pillah was the type of person who would genuflect in front of anyone he thought had some power or a bit of influence in high places while being utterly contemptuous of those who did not. Bend your back to those above your station so that they can step conveniently on you, and step mercilessly on those below even if they did not offer up their backs to be stepped on – this was the principle he lived by. It was late in the night, and I had already had my dinner, and yet he made black tea for me, generously adding sugar as a sign of his care and consideration. Was this the same man that the State Congress and the media portrayed as the cruel, heartless jail super, I wondered, as he sat there watching for the slightest twitch on my face so that he could spring into service. A person is not really the image of them in other people's minds, nor the image in their own minds. The real Subrahmanya Pillah, in that moment in time, was the man sitting in front of me, drenched in propriety and humility. The quarters were more well-appointed than most assigned to senior civil servants. I could see a couple of beds, a table and four chairs, all made of good wood, a cooking stove, and several copper and bell metal kitchen utensils. The cement floor was polished to the sheen of butter and the whitewashed walls had not a blemish on them. His family did not live with him there, but a woman's care was evident in the tidiness and cleanliness of the place.

'Well, best not show this much attention and care at the jail,' I said, blowing into my tea and taking a sip. 'There, I'm a prisoner, and you, my keeper. No one should suspect otherwise. In fact, show some extra irritation towards me.'

The unexpected handing back of power made his eyes glitter. The servitude he had felt obliged to show had made him sit tentatively at the edge of his chair, but now he sat back firmly, his breath easing and one leg rising to rest proudly on the other.

I suppressed a smile, and consciously changing focus, asked, 'Tell me, what has happened with Pandian's case?'

At once, his body language changed again. The leg came off to meet the other on the floor, back hunched, and the expression of servile mournfulness returned.

Before the agitations for Utharavada Bharanam, leaders of the State Congress had spread great falsehoods about our country in British India, especially in the Madras Presidency. In their meetings and demonstrations there, they claimed that freedom of press was non-existent and political torture was rampant. Lies repeated with the particular aim of embarrassing the diwan Sir C.P. Ramaswami Iyer in his own birthplace. The main instigators, it was well known, were P.T. Punnoose, Annie Mascarene and P.N. Krishnapillah. Their troublemaking incited the local Congress, and a demonstration led by a man named Shivaraja Pandian set out from Madurai and illegally entered our country at Chenkotta. An action that, as it turned out, defeated their own purpose as it went against the usual claim Gandhi made that the Indian National Congress would never interfere in the matters of other countries. It also turned out to be a moral victory for our government. Still, as any government responsible for the safety of their nation would do, the police arrested Pandian and locked him up at Kollam Kasaba station. Matters should have ended there. Pandian would either have been let go with a warning, or charged, found guilty and sentenced to a year in prison. But the unfortunate event that followed poured fuel over an agitation that had no great popular support until then.

Given the volatile situation out on the streets, the police had increased raids and patrols, working constantly with almost no rest. The night they arrested Pandian, only two policemen were on sentry duty at the station, and one of them, having worked continuously for three days, was sleeping, with the silent consent of his superiors, in a shed behind the building. The other policeman was Narayana Kurukkal, who had been showing signs of mental distress and instability for two or three years. He was almost near retirement, so was tolerated and relieved of any major duties. Two different narratives existed about the events that unfolded on the night six prisoners including Pandian were locked up there, Narayana Kurukkal standing guard on his own. One narrative went like this:

Late that night, a CID named Subrahmanya Pillah who worked at the station arrived in an inebriated state. He unlocked the cell and let himself in. Alcohol nurtures different emotions in different people. In Pillah, it brought forth patriotism and Swamibhakthi, intense devotion to Sir C.P. Ramaswami Iyer, our Diwanji. He began beating up the prisoners, Tamilians who had deigned to threaten the country of his Ponnuthampuran, the king as beloved as gold itself. Pandian, who said something in protest, was laid into mercilessly for almost half an hour. Then, as though nothing special had happened, Pillah locked up the cell, left the keys back where he had found them hanging from a nail on the wall, and went away. Pandian was taken to the hospital in the morning, and by evening he was dead. The post-mortem report showed heart failure as the cause of death.

This event made the agitations for Utharavada Bharanam, that only a few of our citizens were aware of until then, famous, and gave credence to the arguments put forth by its supporters. Jawaharlal Nehru and K. Kamaraj sent telegrams to the Maharaja making their displeasure known. A 'Pandian Day' was announced, and meetings and demonstrations took place across the country to commemorate it. Editorials in Madras newspapers claimed that the post-mortem report was falsified. Up until this event, Gandhi had remained unconvinced about the intentions of the agitators – C. Rajagopalachari, a friend of our Diwanji, had kept him informed of the developments. Pandian's death changed this, and Gandhi wrote a long essay in *Harijan* criticizing the government.

A departmental inquiry was set up to probe into Pandian's death, which pushed this other Subrahmanya Pillah, the jail superintendent who sat before me, into troubled waters. The prisoners who had been assaulted that day had identified the perpetrator as CID Subrahmanya Pillah. But Narayana Kurukkal, the sentry who was on duty that night and who had since been suspended, disagreed and insisted that the culprit was the jail superintendent Subrahmanya Pillah who had arrived unexpectedly at the station. No amount of questioning and persuasion by his superiors made him change his statement. There, of course, was no rationale to this. Why would a jail superintendent be at the police station? Still, the inquiry could not completely disregard the statement given by the only official who had witnessed the incident. So, both Subrahmanya Pillahs were suspended until the inquiry was over. The superintendent was back at his job not long after, but all his efforts to personally attest his innocence to Diwanji came to nothing. Diwanji refused to see him, his old faithful, and Pillah spent the rest of his service trying to prove his continued loyalty and dedication to his master.

Not soon after, CID Subrahmanya Pillah was embroiled in more trouble. Drunk as usual, he sprang up in front of a demonstration led by Akkamma Cherian and thrashed her car with a bamboo stick. When the volunteers tried to intervene, they too were beaten silly. This Subrahmanya Pillah was also doing these things to get into Diwanji's good books. In the next edition of *Deenabandhu*, the blame for this incident was once again squarely placed on the other Subrahmanya Pillah, the jail superintendent.

Sitting in front of me now, Subrahmanya Pillah described in great detail the troubles caused by his namesake.

'We're not even the same caste,' he said. 'He is a Vellalan. I'm a Nair.'

He could not comprehend how, given this fact, people could confuse the two of them. He was convinced that there were people in his department who were jealous of him. His eyes watered when he recalled how Diwanji had refused to see him, and looked at me with the hope that something could be done about it.

He then moved on to tell me the happenings at the prison. A woman named Ranganayaki Ammal was soon coming to the women's prison to look at their welfare and to raise consciousness about their rights.

'She's our person,' he told me. 'Now we'll know everything the women prisoners get up to the moment they plan it.'

I knew that Ranganayaki was the woman who managed a refuge named Vanchi Poor Home on behalf of Diwanji's mother, Seethalakshmi Ammal. When Pillah said her name, his lips and eyes acted as though they were hiding a secret that was known to all. It was also a ruse to let me know that he was hoping for some sort of connection with me. The Congress spread the malicious rumour that the poor home employed only good-looking women.

'Why have you told me this?' I asked, pretending to be angry. Pillah was the type of man one could play with, like a cat does with a mouse. 'Is this how you keep secrets? How do I know you won't go around telling someone else all about me?'

Realizing his foolish mistake, the superintendent hunched further into his seat.

In the morning, two policemen arrived, handcuffed me and took me to the jail. Having one's hands cuffed is a strange experience even if it is an act, as it was in my case. The key that locks the cuffs also fastens a lock inside. This was an unavoidable moment in the dangerous job I was engaged in, and yet, in that moment, as I looked out at the world, I felt a deep sense of shame. Living under assumed names, donning different guises, was not just playacting; it was real life, my life. In that moment, I was Bhasi the State Congress activist, and those cuffs tightening on my wrists were real. As the policemen escorted me to the jail, I looked up at the sky spread above me, a normal sky full of the invitation to take flight. No creature other than the human being locks up its fellow creatures. It is the rest of the world saying, we don't want you, you are a danger to us.

After the formalities of entering my name in the register and getting me into prison clothes, two wardens took me to the yard, and as was directed by Subrahmanya Pillah, beat me up. I cried out loudly and shouted 'Bharat Mata ki jai' at the top of my voice, and from one of the cells came the answering shouts of 'Vande Mataram' and 'Inquilab zindabad'. I spent my first night in prison in a cell with three men convicted of murder. I heard that P.T. Punnoose had begun a hunger strike demanding that I be treated as a political prisoner. In a couple of days, I was moved into their midst.

The Central Jail in Poojappura, as everyone knows, is a conglomeration of different types of prisons, a collection of buildings each with its own gate and different sets of rules and regulations. Behind the building that housed male political prisoners was a huge wall separating it from the women's prison known as 'ezhamkettu', or the seventh block. Among the twenty-five or so political prisoners were leaders such as C. Keshavan, P.T. Chacko, P.T. Punnoose and, of course, Basheer. It had always been obvious that these men, and not Pattom Thanu Pillai and T.M. Varghese who were still at large, were the real leaders and instigators of the strikes and agitations. It was in here that new plans were hatched. I was acutely aware that the successful completion of my mission inside the prison was crucial to my country's continued safety.

As I was brought in, everyone welcomed me, some shouting slogans, and Basheer introduced me to those who did not know me by sight. It was immediately clear that Basheer commanded respect inside the prison too, and was on friendly terms even with some of the prison staff. There was something innate in him – the way he spoke, or his mannerisms that exuded a kind of humanity absent in others – that attracted people. C. Keshavan also turned out to be a more interesting and jovial man than I had anticipated, but I think he thought I was just another gormless youngster.

'Is this boy old enough to be here? Give him a good thrashing and send him back home,' he said, making everyone laugh.

The political prisoners' ward was known as the solitary ward, and because the media and the public constantly watched what was going on at the Central Jail, it had many more facilities than other prisons across the country. Each of us had our own cells. The cells were small and built to certain specifications, with no windows, a door with iron bars at the front, and a small opening at the top of the back wall for ventilation. During the day, we were allowed to walk around the prison, but the high black-and-white walls, the buildings with dark interiors and the shadowy corridors created an atmosphere in which time became non-existent. Often, a minute felt longer than four or five weeks, and yet looking back at a certain point, it would seem that days had flown past with amazing speed. I was put to work as a kitchen assistant alongside V.V. Varkey and P.T. Chacko, and one day, as I stepped into the yard to gather up the firewood drying in the blazing sun, a month and a half marched right past me. I felt I had forgotten a fundamental principle of my job that required me to get close to people while maintaining emotional distance, and was becoming part of them, melting into them.

After several complaints about food, the political prisoners had been allowed to run their own kitchen. Chacko was a good cook, but the rations we were allocated were the same every week – white rice and pottukadala, desiccated beans partially hollowed out by weevils – and the only utensils to cook for all twenty-four prisoners were two large earthenware pots. So, the food, every single day, was payarukanji, the rice and beans cooked into a gruel. Some days, Basheer took on the cooking duties, which caused a palpable change in the atmosphere, an anticipation of something momentous. Basheer would start by telling everyone, at considerable length, some dish he had cooked and the enthusiastic appreciation of those who had eaten it. The poor souls whose afternoon naps were filled with dreams of good, tasty food would feel that they had themselves partaken of this feast, and soon everyone would be talking about what a fantastic cook Basheer was and the special creations of his they had once tasted. Come mealtime, it would be payarukanji in our plates, but the prisoners, their tummies already filled with tasty, imagined food, would finish their meal fulfilled and satisfied.

'See, this is what writers do,' P.T. Punnoose told me as we sat together eating our kanji. 'Watch and learn.'

Punnoose was a Mar Thoma Christian, a handsome man with an energetic way of speaking and a careful, piercing gaze.

'Nothing these people say is factual,' he continued. 'They just make up shit about places been and sights seen.'

'Utter lies, right?'

'Not quite, because they themselves believe everything they say. We're sitting here, right, having our kanji, and that, as far as we're concerned, is a fact. They've convinced themselves that they've been to other places and eaten other stuff.'

'Well, Basheer is all talk,' I said. 'He doesn't write anything.'

'True, but you know that everyone thinks of him as a writer. People can recognize those who are born writers. If he decides to write seriously, I bet he'll receive the Nobel Prize. Like Tagore.'

'Why doesn't he get on with it then?'

'Because he can't decide what to pursue – his writing or his politics. I'm just guessing here. In times like this, in important times, people tend to let go of everything else and jump into politics.'

'Can't he do both?'

'No.' Punnoose laughed. 'People like him, talented people, they tend to be single-minded. They can do one thing extremely well, but if they try to do two things at the same time, they make a mess of both.'

'But what if Basheer gives up writing and becomes a proper politician? What do you reckon will happen?'

'He'll be a legend, like Gandhi,' Punnoose said with conviction. 'You watch. This type of person, they'll pour all the madness of their writing into politics. Up the game to a level no one could even dream of. Just look at what Gandhi has done. Did anyone imagine that a man would step into the game of politics, dressed only in a piece of cloth around his waist and pontificating on ahimsa and satyagraha? Confounded the whites, didn't he? Just think about this – when everyone else wants to be like the sahibs, there is this half-naked fellow who goes all the way to a meeting in London in a ship, with a goat in tow! Even hearing his name makes the sahibs anxious!'

'So, you think Gandhi would have been a writer if he hadn't entered politics.'

'That's not what I said. Just that these people have minds that function alike. And, well, a lot of prominent politicians are good writers too, I'm sure you've noticed. Lenin, Nehru, Gandhi...'

As we spoke, Punnoose watched Basheer who was watering the little garden he had made near the prison wall, attending to each plant individually, carefully. He spent almost all his time with those plants. As though the welfare of those rose bushes was the most crucial element in deciding the destiny of the world.

There were predominantly four types of people among the political prisoners. The first were those who followed comparative moderates such as Pattom Thanu Pillai, T.M. Varghese and C. Keshavan. The second supported the extremists within the State Congress, younger men like Kumbalath Shanku Pillai and Ponnara Sreedhar. The third, mainly from around Kollam, followed the socialist ideals of N. Sreekantan Nair. And the fourth were the communists. All except the first group were extremely annoyed that a memorandum submitted to the viceroy, which contained personal allegations against Diwanji, had been withdrawn based on Gandhi's advice. C. Keshavan said somewhat apologetically that although they too were against its withdrawal, they had no other option than to follow the directive. Gandhi's moral stance had inconsiderable value, he explained, and without its guidance, the agitations taking place in our little country could not progress. The fact that Gandhi, despite his busy schedule, found time to write about Utharavada Bharanam in *Harijan*, and to exchange ideas with G. Ramachandran and others, was proof that he cared deeply about us. The other groups believed that a coterie of Brahmins within the Indian National Congress, including C. Rajagopalachari, spread falsehoods in favour of Diwanji and influenced Gandhi. What I found interesting is that, despite these differences of opinion, none of the groups said anything at all against Gandhi himself. To them, he was like a family elder, a karanavar who objected to a lot of things only because he was good, clear-intentioned, and had an unwavering moral conscience.

Interesting, too, that Basheer did not belong to any of these groups, and yet all of them held him in high regard.

Cohabitation usually makes differences of opinion more pronounced. But here in the jail, I witnessed signs of these differences getting resolved even when there were dislikes and displeasure. It was clear that the moment they were released, they would band together against their common enemy – Diwanji. Besides, there were problems within the prison that troubled them equally which served to increase unity.

The biggest of these problems was not in the political prisoners' ward but in the seventh block, the women's ward next door. Behind its heavy doors were incarcerated three political prisoners – Annie Mascarene, Akkamma Cherian and her sister Rosamma Cherian. The events that unfolded in the women's ward affected three people in the men's prison this side of the wall. One of these men was Varkichan, Akkamma's and Rosamma's brother. The other two were the communist T.Y. Punnoose and V.V. Varkey who was a State Congress man. There was quite a story behind this.

In all the work I did for king and country, there was a question that had always vexed me: Why was there so much unrest in our country when it was under the care of a benevolent king and a competent diwan? The journey to find an answer had taken me to a two-storey building in Pulimood Junction in Thiruvananthapuram. On its ground floor was a restaurant named Rashtriya Hotel run by a Nair from Mavelikkara. The name – 'Hotel Political' – attested to its character. The traitorous ideas of Utharavada Bharanam and an organization to spearhead the movement were first formed in the intellects of some lawyers who were frequent tea-drinkers at this hotel. The very first meeting to discuss these ideas took place in a lawyer's office, with C.V. Kunjiraman presiding, and it was rife with disagreements. Kottur Kunjukrishna Pillai made known his displeasure about working against the Maharaja, meaning that he was able, right at the beginning, to see through the conspiracy for what it was – an effort to bring our country, a complete Hindu rajyam, under a Christian government. Still, not long after, in a meeting held at the offices of a lawyer named Ilanjikkal John, the State Congress was formed with Pattom Thanu Pillai as the president and K.T. Thomas as the secretary. The committee was predominantly Christian, but they were careful to include some Nairs and Ezhavas. Their first task was to publicly agitate for Utharavada Bharanam, and in this they were supported by newspapers like *Manorama* and leaders of other countries like Gandhi. The Nair Service Society, under the leadership of Mannath Padmanabhan, was against them, while leaders of the SNDP, the Sree Narayana Dharma Paripalana Yogam that represented the Ezhavas, wavered this way and that.

The agitators sent our Maharaja a memorandum by registered post. With the express purpose of humiliating our country, they printed an English translation of it with the title 'Travancore Today' and sent copies to newspapers in neighbouring countries including India, to the viceroy, and to members of the British parliament. Several demands were made in the memorandum – the right to vote, freedom of worship, freedom to organize, freedom of the press, an independent judiciary – the likes of which could never be realized. Accusing our diwan, Sir C.P. Ramaswami Iyer, an administrator as great as Ramayyan Dalawa and Raja Kesavadas, of corruption, they further demanded that he be dismissed. They spread the falsehood that he was a womanizer, and that he, who had been a highly paid lawyer at the Madras court, had come to Thiruvithamkoor because of his clandestine relationship with Amma Maharani and his interest in the beautiful women of our land.

The protests they organized were as detailed and well planned as a battle, determined as they were not to give in without a resolution either way. Each stage of the agitation was overseen by a 'dictator', a person in full charge of the operations, and if that person was arrested, another dictator was appointed in their place. They were successful in generating enough public support that demonstrations and pickets all across the country were well attended. The first of these dictators was Pattom Thanu Pillai, but the person who was really in charge was M.M. Varkey, a man from Kochi. Just as the protest was about to begin, he dodged the police and sneaked away from Vanross House, the old Dutch bungalow where the State Congress had its headquarters, back to his own country. And sitting safely there, he began a campaign of propaganda about the protest through bulletins, pamphlets and newspaper reports, and saw to it that they were sneaked into our country. He brought people over from Malabar to Kottayam and Kollam and trained them to become part of a volunteer army. Under his influence, a man named A.K. Gopalan, from Perali in Kannur, led a large group of protesters from Malabar and arrived at Aluva railway station. He was arrested while trying to cross the border into our country.

Despite all this, our police and army faced up to the protesters effectively. Following Pattom Thanu Pillai's arrest, N.K. Padmanabha Pillai, younger brother of the exiled traitor Ramakrishna Pillai (he had the gall to call the newspaper he edited *Swadeshabhimani* – The Patriot!), became the dictator. When he too was arrested, riots broke out in Neyyattinkara and Thiruvananthapuram. The dictators who followed him – Neyyattinkara Vasudeva Pillai, A.K. John, Elizabeth Kuruvila, P.K. Kumaran, N.V. Chacko – were also arrested one by one, making the real perpetrator, M.M. Varkey, very anxious. It only intensified when an armed uprising at a place called Kadakkal was quickly and efficiently suppressed by the government. Varkey's plan was to prolong the agitations somehow or the other at least until the

Maharaja's Thirunal, the royal birthday, which was an auspicious day for our country, and to create havoc in the capital on the day. For this to be successful, they needed a new dictator, someone unknown, not on the police's watchlist, and highly intelligent. A woman would fit the bill perfectly, they thought, and racked their collective brain for just such a person. My fellow prisoner V.V. Varkey was also part of M.M. Varkey's gang, and his thoughts went to someone who had already occupied his mind, a beautiful, brave, twenty-eight-year-old woman – Akkamma Cherian.

According to tradition, Syrian Christian families married off their daughters before the age of sixteen. With a bit of money and a few pots and pans as dowry, she was sent off to her husband's family. The expense for the birth of the first child was also taken care of, but after that the family did not consider her to be their responsibility. If, for whatever reason, the daughter returned home, even her mother would ask what she was doing there. Educated girls rarely found husbands, and either stayed at home old and unwanted or shaved off their hair and joined a convent. But not Akkamma, the daughter of Kanjirappally Karippaparambil Cherian. She went to the newly opened women's college, St Theresa's in Ernakulam, and got herself a BA degree in history. She had already acquired a reputation for being arrogant while she was at the boarding school in Changanassery – she had successfully waged a hunger strike against the nuns who had refused to provide good, clean food for the boarders. And now, her studies completed, she was working as the headmistress of St Mary's School in Kanjirappally. V.V. Varkey had met her when he, along with P.T. Chacko and K.J. Thomas, had been house-to-house canvassing. As the protest intensified and most of the men were in jail, Akkamma and her friends organized a march by school students and began a fund-collection effort for the agitation.

Akkamma agreed as soon as V.V. Varkey proposed the idea. Accompanied by her sister Rosamma and brother Varkichan, she set out for Ernakulam, sending a resignation letter to the school where she worked along the way. It could be said that it is at this point that our government's intelligence service began to fail. In Ernakulam, Akkamma took over from Kuttanad Ramakrishna Pillai as the twelfth dictator of the agitation for Utharavada Bharanam. In order to avoid arrest, she went to Madurai. The plan was to take a train from there to Thampanoor, leading a procession into the capital on the Maharaja's Thirunal and hand an updated submission to him in person. The railway line and the station were under British administration; our police could not arrest anyone while travelling. As he had desired, the responsibility of furthering Akkamma's political instruction while on the journey was given to V.V. Varkey. P.T. Punnoose, meanwhile, was responsible for receiving them at Madurai station and making the arrangements for their stay. At the railway station, Punnoose gazed at Rosamma with the same wonderment that Varkey had when he had first laid eyes on Akkamma.

And now, a huge wall stood between them. On one side, the two women, and on the other, the two love-smitten men. The events unfolding in the women's prison were more worrying for them than they were for Akkamma's and Rosamma's brother Varkichan.

'No need to worry about her,' Varkichan said, referring to Akkamma. 'That job at the school. When she applied for it, the priest who was the manager wouldn't give it to her. Gave it to another woman. Only tenth-standard pass she was. Akkamma was so pissed off and was determined to find another job. So, she sat at home in Kanjirappally and bombarded the world with applications until she finally heard back from a school in Burma. I tried my best to stop her from accepting the offer, but she went to Madras all on her own. All packed and ready to board a ship to Burma!'

It turned out that, by this time, the woman who had been given the job had left. Akkamma was adamant that she would not reapply. Finally, unable to find anyone else, the priest had to come and beg her to take the job. More trouble followed. Discarding the traditional attire of Christian women – chatta and mundu – she went to her job clad in a sari and blouse, walked noisily around wearing sandals, took part in the All India Women's Conference when she went to Thiruvananthapuram for a teacher training course. And at the conference, when some people tried to disrupt the proceedings as a madamma talked about birth control, she confronted them angrily.

Regardless, the prison was not the school and Sir C.P.'s trustworthy wardens were not like parish priests. The world would never know what happened within these walls, and that worried V.V. Varkey and Punnoose. Every evening, at 5 p.m., before they were locked back in their cells, Akkamma, Rosamma and Annie Mascarene would sing 'Jana Gana Mana', the Bangla song Congress supporters were fond of singing. And the moment they heard it, the men, the prisoners on this side of the wall, would start shouting political slogans. It worried the superintendent, Subrahmanya Pillah, no end. It could deepen the displeasure Diwanji felt towards him for no fault of his. As a solution, he deployed a woman prisoner, a Kunjilakshmi from Muvattupuzha who was serving a life sentence for drowning a child in a pond. Pleasing the super might get her name on the list of prisoners to be pardoned on the Maharaja's Thirunal. So, as soon as Akkamma and her friends began their song, Kunjilakshmi would unleash a volley of obscenities at the top of her voice. It would fuel the energy of sloganeering on this side of the wall. Punnoose and Varkey were gravely concerned that the superintendent would instigate the criminal prisoners to cause bodily harm to Akkamma, Rosamma and the other political prisoners. They were convinced that Subrahmanya Pillah was under direct orders from Diwanji.

The men huddled together discussing the events.

'It's all right during the day,' Punnoose said. 'I've told them that, at the first sign of trouble, they should tie three or four khaddar saris together into a rope and throw it over the wall. We'll jump over somehow or the other. But at night ... The trouble is that the keys are always with the super.'

The memory of what had happened to Pandian gave Punnoose and Varkey sleepless nights.

'We'll find a way,' said C. Keshavan, consoling them. 'Next time they are taken to court, ask them to make a statement on the record. We'll see then. The whole country will be up in arms.' He was convinced that no one would dare touch them.

The seventh day of the month of Thulam in Kollavarsham 1114. A day that changed the country itself. That was the day Akkamma Cherian stepped off the train in Thampanoor, just as Gandhi had disembarked from a ship on to the damp soil that was the Indian struggle for independence. And just as he had led the Salt March, Akkamma led a people's march to the palace of our Maharaja. Thiruvananthapuram, our capital city, had never witnessed a crowd so large, nor would it in the future. There are some rare people who are made up not just of their body and mind. They are, it is believed, made up of all of us.

'How many people have the British massacred in Punjab and other places?' C. Keshavan continued. 'And yet, they don't hurt Gandhi. How come? Don't they still have their guns? They don't want anything to happen to him, that's why. Something happens to him, they're done for too. Some folks have that kind of power. They're untouchable.'

Akkamma, obviously, was one such person. Why else would General Watkins, a British man who was in command of the army, who had shot dead Neyyattinkara Raghavan without a moment's hesitation, give up in front of her? This is what had happened:

In Neyyattinkara, the superintendent of the CID, Raman Pillah, had arrested N.K. Padmanabha Pillai, the successor of Pattom Thanu Pillai, as the dictator of the agitation for Utharavada Bharanam. That led to a riot, with the police and the crowd throwing stones at each other. The army was deployed, and Raghavan, a young man, stood broad-chested and brave-hearted in front of Watkins Sahib's gun, daring him to shoot – and he did, without a moment of hesitation. Watkins Sahib was present when Akkamma led the protesters to the palace too, his gun aimed at the crowd, ready to shoot. But when the twenty-two-year-old woman stood in front of the barrel and challenged him to fire at her first, he doffed his hat, bade her goodnight and left. His Highness, the birthday boy, and his diwan had to admit defeat. Ordering the immediate release of all political prisoners, they sneaked away through the back door.

'There's nothing to worry about,' said C. Keshavan again. 'The Pattar is scared, that's why all this.'

He winked and smiled at his cellmate Natarajan, a man from Pothankodu, a meaningful smile indicating that they who were well past their youth understood why Varkey and Punnoose were more worried than was strictly necessary.

On the day of Akkamma Cherian's rally, a policeman had put mustard seeds inside a bull's ears and released it into the crowd. When the crazed animal charged at the people, it was Natarajan who had caught it and brought it under control with just the cotton towel on his shoulder as a weapon. A courageous act instigated by the bravery that had brought Watkins Sahib to his knees.

As Basheer had done on our side of the wall, the women prisoners had planted a garden on their side too. I joined Basheer sometimes, helping with the watering and the hoeing. There were several rose bushes – six deep red and two white – and a large gandharajan that belonged to no one in particular and was looked after by many of the prisoners who passed through the jail. It was assumed that there was a similar plant on the other side of the wall too. No other flower had the heady fragrance of the large white blossoms of the gandharajan. Even a withered, dropped bloom sent its scent deep into whoever sniffed it. But our gandharajan never flowered, while the one on the other side, it was said, flowered all the time.

'This one here is watered by gormless men, that's the problem,' Basheer said. 'Over there, it doesn't even need looking after. The beauty of the women who walk by, that is all the nourishment it needs.'

Clouds of fragrance wafted over the wall.

But when I flared my nostrils and inhaled, all I could smell was fresh air.

'I doubt there's such a plant there,' I said.

'It must be the scent of beautiful women, then,' Basheer said. 'Gandharanis! If I ever become the diwan, I'll make it unlawful for women to plant gardens. Women and flowers together? It's just too much!'

That was when we saw it. By the mango tree that stood at one end of the wall, a stick was being raised and lowered repeatedly. A signal from the other side. Varkey and Punnoose were waiting for it, and as soon as they saw it, they picked a few mangoes and threw them over the wall. After a while, a ball – two half-shells of a coconut tied securely together – came flying over the wall to our side. It contained a chammanthi made of coconut and the mangoes that had been thrown over.

'Ha ... what fantastic creations women are ... selfish and cruel,' Basheer said, his voice wistful. 'Lock them up in prison, or in hell itself, and they'll still make mango chammanthi, but only for their sweethearts.'

That night, Basheer told me a story titled 'Mathilukal' – The Walls. It took place on either side of a high wall in a prison. The hero was an imprisoned writer who looked after the prison garden. He had with him a copy of a story he had written, titled 'Premalekhanam'– Love Letter. The heroine was only a voice. The voice of a woman named Narayani, a prisoner on the other side of the wall.

'So, this is how you folk make up your stories,' I said. 'This story is only a quarter true!'

'No. This is the whole truth,' Basheer said.

'Not at all. I was there. Watched the whole thing with you, didn't I? Mangoes go over, mango chammanthi comes back. Two girlfriends there, two boyfriends here.'

'Poda, buddhoos. The story is the truth. What you think you saw is all in your mind. Jaganmithya, they say, don't they? The world is a mirage.'

'They also say brahmasatyam, the supreme and only truth.'

'And right they are too. The story is the supreme, and the truth. All else is illusion.'

There was also the night in prison when, unable to tell truth from illusion, fear stepped quietly into my mind – the night we realized that one of the guilty men in the Kadakkal revolt case was to be executed in the morning. The prisoners were not told about it, but all creatures are able to recognize the odour of death, just as they are able to recognize the scent of their mate. No one slept that night. Some spread their mats in the darkness and lay twisting and turning, not even complaining as usual about the mosquitoes. The thought of having been born as one among the billions of creatures on this earth which was a mere grain of sand in this universe made mosquitoes and bedbugs entirely immaterial. Some stood in their cells holding on to the bars, gazing into the darkness, thinking about the man about to be executed who must surely be awake, alone, in his cell, just like us. I was gripped by doubts akin to what I had felt when I was handcuffed before I was brought here. Was I, in fact, a criminal? Had I become Bhasi for real? Basheer and I chain-smoked, passing beedis back and forth. He, too, was quiet. I began to think that the trees outside had stopped moving, the wind stilled. These were just stories that our minds created at such times, attributing our thoughts and emotions to nature. Thousands of creatures died every single day, and the universe was unconcerned. Despite what Basheer said, stories are not the truth. They are just what human beings make up to escape from the truth, from reality. Even in that moment, we were only imagining that we were staying awake for the sake of the man who was about to die. What we were actually thinking about was our own deaths.

Hours later, we heard the hangman's horse carriage. Ah, what power he wielded! The ultimate power to extinguish the life of a human being, that other human beings had bestowed upon him. Why did he arrive in silence, in the cover of darkness, accompanied only by the hoofbeats of animals? Was it so that every person who heard those hoofbeats would imagine his own execution?

I turned to Basheer. 'Ashaaney, the question in the story you told me – why should I be free, who wants freedom?' I said. 'I want freedom. I'm going to break out of this prison.'

When I was sure that I had accomplished my mission, Superintendent Subrahmanya Pillah would secretly open the doors for me and let me out. Pretending to have broken out, I would go straight to his quarters, change out of my prison clothes, and write an urgent report for my superiors. It would contain the information that the State Congress, the socialists and the communists who had always been at loggerheads had started coming together, that protests larger and stronger than the agitation for Utharavada Bharanam were imminent, and that something urgent had to be put into action to create rifts among them. In the newspapers of the morning after, I would read that Bhasi, a prisoner awaiting trial, had escaped.

I heard the sound of the hangman's carriage going back. For now, the only truth was this silent and sleepless night. I looked at Basheer. It was in the early mornings that his eyes reflected the real intensity of his madness.

13

There is a theory that the consequences of the flap of an insect's wing could alter history. In my humble opinion, this is not true. No one can claim that their influence is what caused a specific event in history. It is the course of history that makes us. Whether we are involved or not, things that are to happen will happen, a bit differently perhaps, or a little earlier or later than expected. And suppose something that was to happen doesn't happen, upsetting the course of events? No matter, a new course of events will appear.

Perhaps because of the warnings in my report, the government found a way to create a rift between the various political factions that were forging common ground. A proposal for educational reform was announced, the most important factor of which was that the government would assume control and management of primary education as recommended in the report of the Education Reorganization Committee chaired by H.C. Papworth. It dealt a body blow to the Christians who were constantly trying to undermine the government. A large number of primary schools in the country were owned by them. The bishop of Changanassery, James Kalacherry, sounded a call exhorting his folk: 'Those who have swords, wield them; those who do not, sell the clothes on your backs and buy one.' Mannath Padmanabhan and Agamananda Swami welcomed the reforms. The Hindus and Christians within the State Congress formed factions and quarrelled with one another. R. Sankar stood by the government while P.T. Chacko joined the opposition. Within British India, support for our government increased with Pandit Madan Mohan Malaviya and

V.S. Srinivasa Sastri turning advocates for the reforms, and *The Hindu*, *Free Press* and *Bombay Sentinel* writing editorials in favour.

There was, during that time, a prevalent practice whereby newspapers that had their licences revoked would reappear, having paid the fees and registered under a different name. As a result, I kept a keen eye on the smaller newspapers. One day, in the newspaper *Bharathi*, printed in a press in Kumarapuram, I saw a news item with this title: 'Support for the Government Increases'. It reported that Mr V.D. Savarkar, the president of the Hindu Mahasabha, had sent a congratulatory telegram to Diwan Sir C.P. Ramaswami Iyer. He had also accused Christian missionaries of engaging in religious conversion in the schools they managed while receiving grants from the government. He demanded that the protests spearheaded by bishops who opposed the restructuring be suppressed mercilessly.

I looked carefully at the photograph of Savarkar accompanying the news item. The face, with its Gandhi-style eyeglasses, looked familiar. Was it on the journey from Rameswaram to Kollam that I had seen this man?

14

'Such fun listening to you, guru,' I told Basheer, pulling my legs up and sitting properly on the bed. 'Marrying her would be good, I think. She's beautiful, from what I've heard, and intelligent, educated. Has a job and is from a wealthy family. Yes, she's a Nair, and you're a Mussalman, but that doesn't matter really. Just go away to Madras or some place. I'm sure she can find a job there too.'

Basheer was listening to me carefully, which was unusual because normally he thought of me as a youngster without any worldly wisdom. But love transforms everything. Like an accomplished gusthikkaaran, it picks us up, twirls us around, and slams us on the ground on our backs.

'And if you marry her, you'll be the best husband ever,' I continued. 'Sure, you won't be a writer or a politician or even a gusthikkaaran because, well ... because once we achieve what we want, we won't have the enthusiasm for anything else, would we? You know how banana farmers stamp out new sprouts on seed stock so that a stronger one can sprout? I think your time to be stamped upon has come.'

To my own amazement, I was speaking with unusual sincerity. A positive conclusion to Basheer's love affair meant a positive outcome in my job. I could stop following the man around if he went off somewhere with his beloved and lived out his life without interfering in the world's affairs.

We were in his room on the top floor of a building near the magistrate's court in Punkunnam in Thrissur. The only room next door was a lawyer's office. On the ground floor of the building was a small hotel. By evening, both premises were deserted, meaning that Basheer's life here was the diametrical opposite of what it used to be in Seethi Buildings in Ernakulam. Still, I had my reasons for turning up here.

Between the time I had spent in prison and now, the world had changed a lot. The two atom bombs and the defeat of Hitler, Mussolini and Emperor Hirohito had ended the World War. It turned out that our government was right in supporting the British. Despite what they said outwardly, the freedom fighters, except for some diehard communists, were with Germany and Japan – one of their leaders, Subhas Chandra Bose, overtly so. Still, many things giving them hope had begun to consolidate, and there was even talk about the British granting independence to its colonies, including India. In the north, the Indian National Congress and the Muslim League could almost smell power, whereas here, in our country, the State Congress was mired in internal disarray and disharmony thanks to some clever moves by our diwan. The Nairs and Christians hated each other. The rank and file were highly suspicious of the leadership, especially of people like Pattom Thanu Pillai and T.M. Varghese. People had become aware of Pillai's secret discussions with the government, and when the political prisoners were released, they were questioned by the general public.

So, there were rifts and suspicions, and yet, an idea had begun to spread widely and take hold. That, when the British finally left India, our country would become part of India. An Aikyakerala Prasthanam, a movement to create a united Kerala made up of all Malayalam-speaking areas, had been started in Malabar, and the State Congress began working closely with it. It also had the support of the king of Kochi, Parikshit Thampuran. His jealousy of our country and its governance had driven him to seek out the support of the so-called progressives. The idea of Aikyakeralam was only a ruse that the State Congress used to distract its disgruntled rank and file.

Thrissur had become the place where all these sorts with all these ideas congregated. As it was far enough away from our borders, our government did not pay much attention, and it was near enough to Malabar for people to come and go easily. A meeting of the Aikyakerala Prasthanam was planned for April, with the support of the king of Kochi, and my objective was to follow the developments closely. I had gathered that leaders from Malabar such as K. Kelappan and E. Moidu Moulavi were already in Thrissur. Basheer was my best bet to get in close proximity to them.

But on my very first day in Thrissur, I realized that Basheer living there in a rented room all alone had nothing to do with what was going on; it was just that the politics was unfolding all around him. As P.T. Punnoose had predicted, he had not made a choice between his two passions, politics and writing. Other than a handful of political pamphlets, the last thing he had written was a one-act play titled *Pattothinte Pekkinaavu* (Pattom's Nightmare). It ridiculed Pattom Thanu Pillai who had betrayed the Nivarthana Samaram, the abstention movement which demanded equal representation in the legislature for all castes and religions. Basheer was bored with politics and had again swung towards his writing. He was working on something titled *Kamukante Diary* (Diary of a Lover). The room was littered with papers and notebooks scribbled all over, not to mention the debris of torn and discarded drafts.

'Is any of this true or is it all your imagination?'

Flicking through a few pages, I asked Basheer the most ridiculous of all questions, then dove anxiously into his story world where place and time intermingled into a bloody mess. The story took place here somewhere and also in some other place;

the events had already happened and yet could never happen; the characters included real people, people who could never be real, and those who were half real. They spoke exactly as ordinary people would, but also said things that no one would ever say. There were diary entries, letters between the two lovers, descriptions. Some letters from the girlfriend were in the boyfriend's handwriting; some diary entries were dated in the future. There was delicate, ethereal love and mad scribblings oozing carnal desire.

'"I sniffed it, and it had the smell of Devi's sweat,"' I read aloud. '"As I sat there sniffing at the letter and the envelope, I was overcome with desire. Penninte manam! The scent of a woman!" This sounds like the diary of a madman,' I said.

'Yes, there is a book with that title,' Basheer said. 'Written by Gogol.'

I raised my head and looked at him. And suddenly, to my utter surprise, I found that I had not broken out of prison, and he had not been released. In the night that had never ended echoed the sound of the hangman's horse carriage, returning after executing an unfortunate. A little ahead was the big wall of the prison, and beyond that the fragrance of gandharajan blossoms. Remembering what Punnoose had said, I looked carefully into Basheer's eyes. He had me trapped in unwritten stories.

The next day, we stood in a lane in Punkunnam, waiting for Devi.

'If you continue to write, you might receive the Nobel Prize,' I said. 'If you marry, you'll merely be a husband.'

'What's the difference?' Basheer asked. 'Being able to find a mate is the best prize. Everything else only leads towards it.'

Basheer's lover, Devi, was born out of a melding of his imagination and his writing. As they stood there talking, I observed her carefully. She was an amalgamation of an ordinary young woman, thin and fair-skinned, and a soundaryadhamam, the epitome of beauty in Basheer's specific language. What he saw, really, was a woman glorified by his own writing. Her sister, Vanaja, had come with her. She was darker, less attractive, and like me, she stood a little away from them. Just as it was written in *Diary of a Lover*, Devi had removed her glasses and was holding them in her hand – a clear indication that, even as she refused, she wanted her eyes kissed. Would they kiss in public? I looked around fearfully. I saw that Vanaja, too, was scared. I don't know what she was scared of.

According to *Diary of a Lover*, Devi was the middle child among several children. Vanaja and a brother were the youngest. Devi was twenty-two and taught at B.T. College, which was nowhere near Thrissur. In one of her letters to Basheer, she said that her parents were separated, but in the story, Basheer talked about having met both her parents when he went to their home. There were also mentions of stories he had not yet written. Devi asked him questions about Saramma, the character in his story 'The Love Letter'. It was Basheer the writer she was in love with. He edited the silly stories she wrote wanting to emulate him.

'There are a lot of incongruent things in here,' I said, reading passages of weird, crazed descriptions.

In some places, Devi was helpless, meek. In other places, she was described as hiding other love affairs, as having led men on with her charms. There was even a man who had gone mad because of her, and another, a married man, with whom she was said to be inappropriately familiar.

'Who told you that a story should be congruent?' Basheer asked.

'Well, shouldn't it at least have some continuity? Meaning? Otherwise readers will go crazy!'

'Writing is not about making meaning. It is about collecting together words and events from which readers can make their own meaning.'

In the lane, after chatting with Devi for a while, Basheer introduced me.

'This is Bhasi. A State Congress man. A brave man who broke out of the Central Jail.'

Vanaja looked at me with worshipful eyes.

Basheer's mental and emotional states were messily mingled with his writing and in the letters written by Devi or by him pretending to be Devi. Love, suspicion, hate, fear, anger, disgust, sorrow and love, again, but the most prominent of all was lust. Love was a conspiracy between lovers to hide this singular, strongest of all, feeling. In order to prove that what he felt towards Devi was simple, pure love, he had invented, in his life at the lodge as well as in his writing, others in whom he had only sexual interest. A curd-seller named Rasham; a young Brahmin woman who delivered the milk; a nurse who, after taking one look at him, agreed to sleep with him; another young woman who pursued him because she wanted to join the Communist Party; and another named Savithri who competed with Devi for his affections.

One morning, having woken up before Basheer, I stepped out of the room and saw the woman who brought the milk. Basheer had written that she had big breasts, and that she might feel bad if he didn't look appreciatively at them. I stood there watching her, her poor, emaciated body, as she placed the milk pail by the door and walked away without a backward glance. I stood there until I finished smoking my beedi. People like him, what all they think up and write down. O God above (if there is a god, that is), why did you give these people a thing called common sense? Isn't that just another name for madness? Because of it, we, each and every one of us, imagine that we are doing something special and specific for this world, that we think about past and future, cause and effect, collecting it all in our memories. Life is only about living it out. It does not require anything more than the intelligence of a spider.

I went back in, and overcome with a sense of sorrow, began reading *Diary of a Lover* again. It had changed from what I had read a month ago – the characters had become different people, events had become mixed up, dates had changed. Much later, from one of its crossed-out and edited pages, Basheer rose. His cheeks were puffed up, and he had bags under his eyes from having gone to bed late.

As he pumped up the kerosene stove, lit it and made tea, he said, 'Whatever you read, just think of it as the truth. Then there is no problem. Don't try to connect any of it to what happens in the outside world. If you do, you'll feel that all this is madness.'

'Actually, I do it the other way round,' I said. 'I think about the outside world and all that human beings do as madness. Someone gave me a name, and now I go around thinking that's who I am. We give names to creatures and convince ourselves that's what they are. The crow ... ha, ha ... the crow doesn't know that its name is "crow"! To expect that, at some point in time and place, all humans will think and do as one, to imagine that we will have some sort of value even after our death ... If all this madness is allowed, anything can be done within the confines of our writing.'

Even as I spoke, I wondered, was it me who was saying all this? The constant association with people like him might be rubbing off on me.

'Still, like Gandhi said, if I became the ruler of this country, I would release an emergency order to make you writers behave properly,' I said.

'What? You'll banish us from the republic?'

'No. Just that you write whatever you like as long as you don't mix up imagination and reality. Either immerse yourself in the world of your imagination and write pretend stories, or write factually about what is real.'

'Ha, ha, you idiot, is there a thing called reality?' Basheer asked, letting the tea fall in a long stream from the pot into the glass. 'Why do you drink this bitter water of boiled dry leaves? Because you add your imagination to it.'

I accompanied Basheer to his next rendezvous with Devi. As described in *Diary of a Lover*, he used to live in the house behind a wall on the other side of the lane from hers. No one lived there now, and she had given him a key to it. The arrangement was that he would let himself in and wait for her, and she would join him eventually. As soon as he went in, I ignored what I had agreed with him and positioned myself in the lane. Flanked as it was by high walls on either side, I was not directly visible from any of the houses, while I had a clear view of the surroundings. And if anyone came along, I could pretend that I was taking a piss by the wayside or picking fodder for goats from the verges. Devi's house was of a good size, with a seated veranda. No one was outside. A plant growing close under the eaves had wet leaves indicating that someone had watered it recently. In a while, Devi emerged dressed in a pretty khaddar sari, stepped out into the yard and walked casually across it into the lane. She came up to the wall on the other side and climbed over it using a wooden ladder that was already leaning against it. Unlike what was described in the story, I did not find the sight appealing.

When the doors to their secret meeting place closed, I walked into Devi's house. In the lowering sun, the clean front yard was shaded. I cleared my throat, and the sound brought Vanaja to the veranda. Having met several times within the story and out in the lanes of real life, we were now well acquainted. She glanced at the house beyond the wall, and so did I. We now had a shared secret. She smiled, and so did I. 'Come on in and sit,' she said, and when I hesitated, 'Don't just stand there.'

I sat on one of the chairs, cushioned like those in rich people's houses. 'In stories, when someone arrives like this, there usually is no one else at home,' I said.

Vanaja burst out laughing, and pressed her hand to her mouth as though she thought it was too loud.

Forgetting to offer me even a glass of water, she talked to me, asked me a lot of questions about the prison – What was life in there like? Did they harm you? Make you do hard labour? What was the food like?

'Prison is not like all this,' I said. 'It is filled with the scent of women.'

'The scent of women?' Vanaja's eyes widened.

So, I told her the story, 'The Walls'.

'Sshọ! What a story!' Vanaja said when I finished.

'No, not a story,' I said. 'It's what happened really. Saw it happening with my own eyes.'

When I got up to leave, our eyes turned inadvertently towards the secret house. Vanaja's face flushed like fire.

'I know what they'd be telling each other now,' I said. 'I've read *Diary of a Lover* several times.'

'What?' Vanaja asked, eager.

'Never mind. I can't tell you. I don't think it's appropriate.'

'Tell me.'

'No, it's inappropriate.'

'Go on, tell me.'

'Leave it, no?'

'You can't leave until you tell me.'

'Okay, I'll tell you. But don't tell me off after.'

'I'll be the judge of that. Tell me first.'

'"Devi, won't you show me your fair-fragrant flower, your secret blossom?" There!'

'Ayye!'

'What do you think her reply should be?'

'What?'

'"I'm yours, always and forever." They'll be talking to each other in literary terms, obviously.'

I laughed, but Vanaja did not melt into embarrassment as I had expected.

'Don't make fun of them,' she said, instead. 'How would you say it then?'

'Shall I say it?'

'Go on. Let's hear how the man who likes to poke fun says it.'

'I'd say, "Show it to me, penney!"'

Vanaja laughed again with her hand to her mouth. 'Ayye! You *are* shameless!'

'Don't you poke fun now. How would you have replied?'

'I'd say, "Look all you want, cherukka!"' she said, and ran into the house.

Basheer experienced a lot of distress with his writing. Common, I felt, in people who refused to compromise. He spent days agonizing over each event, each word. Writers are creatures who labour for weeks, only to mercilessly shred to pieces the fruits of their labour. He was gripped by a fearful anxiety about Devi, suspicious of her past, her friends, her future.

'She didn't tell me about her old love affair. Why?' he asked, staying up night after night, smoking one beedi after another, not letting me sleep either. 'What is her relationship with KS? He has a wife and daughter. Why does she have his handkerchief? And Karunan – first she said he was her muracherukkan, a cousin she was allowed to marry by custom, and now she says he's a friend.'

'Ashaaney, listen,' I said. 'The plants you looked after in the prison – didn't you plant them wherever there was a bit of space? If you had insisted you'd grow things only in perfect spots, you'd never have had a garden. Don't go looking for the most perfect words and events. Just use whatever is adequate.'

'But this is not the prison. This is the free, wide world, with perfect soil.'

'Well, the man who stubbornly waits for the perfect woman will have neither woman nor peace of mind.'

'I don't want that kind of peace of mind.'

At some point, when I finally managed to lie down to rest, I thought about leaving. My job was out there in the world, among real people, pursuing their secrets and conspiracies and immersing myself in them. The beings and becomings in Basheer's writing room were not of this world. I examined them side by side in my mind. What happened outside had some sort of rationale, didn't it, or was it also like it was in here? Were the people out there really characters living out their lives? If so, my job was brainless, and I was a fool to think it could be planned in advance.

Unusually loud voices woke me up and I opened my eyes to daylight. Basheer, the characters in the stories and everything else had disappeared from the room. Everything seemed as it should be, in order, as it is in the real world, each object exactly where it is supposed to be. Wind and sunlight entered the room through the window in exactly the quantities such a window would allow. Tentatively, I opened the door and then quickly descended the stairs. Outside, five or six people stood in a circle. In the middle of the circle was Basheer, lighting a bonfire of all his papers, discarded and otherwise. The voices I heard were of the villagers trying to stop him, concerned that he was destroying something important.

'Poison, these are, these stories. Cyanide,' Basheer said. 'Poison that you hate and love at the same time, that makes you want to eat it if you sit in front of it.'

In *Diary of a Lover*, Devi had also thought about taking cyanide.

Back in his room, Basheer sat down calmly and began speaking.

'I spent some time up north, trying to be a sanyasi,' he said. 'At one place, there was this clifftop. People would go there to jump off and kill themselves. Suicide Point, it was called. If you stood there and looked down ... Ho! It pulled you right in! I would have jumped into those stories and killed myself. I'm safe now.'

That night, Basheer was taken in a car to a psychiatric hospital in Vallappuzha run by Vaidyaratnam P.C. Govindan Nair, known to everyone as Vallappuzha Vaidyan. He has not written any stories since.

I stayed with him there, taking care of him as he went through the treatments of ennadhara and kashayadhara. Many were the times when I wondered why I stuck with him. Getting truly close to anyone was not good for people like me. Was I pretending that I was close to him, or was I convincing myself that I was acting?

'The earth and the sun have burned into cinder. A motionless wind blows. The world has shattered.'

Basheer muttered as he lay there after having a nasyam, a nasal flush with medicated oil that would have sent a dozen elephants into deep slumber.

15

It was while staying with Basheer at Vallappuzha Vaidyan's hospital that I became acquainted with the two socialists, N. Sreekantan Nair and Mathai Manjooran. Two men who had quite a few things in common. They visited Basheer often.

If Sreekantan Nair was a spitfire of a leader from our country, Manjooran was his counterpart from Kochi. Neither of them saw eye to eye with the ageing leaders of the State Congress who were scared of casteist and religious powers and their wishy-washy policies. They also disliked the communists who went on about 'the people's war'. Still, they had their share of disagreements with one another. Sreekantan Nair viewed the Aikyakerala Prasthanam as part of the Indian national movement, while Manjooran held that Malayalis had a national identity that was distinct from the rest of India. In their hatred for Diwanji, however, they were united.

Diwanji's smart and calculated moves had pretty much decimated the plans laid by the freedom fighters. The education restructuring created huge rifts along caste and religious lines. It was not as though our Maharaja could just hand over the governance of our country to anyone else because it belonged to the god, Sree Padmanabhaswamy. Neither was democracy, which could see non-Hindus coming into power, viable because governing our country included looking after the welfare of several Hindu temples. So, much to the displeasure of those waiting in the wings hoping to grab power as soon as the British left, a decree in the American model, specifying that the king and the diwan could not be removed from power was announced. With the State Congress pulled in different directions by the infighting between Nairs, Ezhavas and Christians, the socialists took over the leadership of the protests. Sreekantan Nair, in a dangerous manoeuvre, waylaid a delegation of British officials on their way to a meeting about the new governmental reform, and talked to them himself. When Diwanji went to speak at a school in Thevara in Kochi, run by the Anglo-Indian leader Stanley Lewis, the students, instigated by Manjooran, pelted stones at him.

With the British prime minister's comment that an interesting experiment was taking place in Thiruvithamkoor, it was clear that things were not going the way the freedom fighters wanted. Diwanji went to Delhi to meet with the Cabinet Mission to discuss, along with the administrators of Bhopal, Mysore and other princely states, the transfer of power. The country, under the leadership of the famous criminal lawyer Malloor Govinda Pillai, gave him a fantastic send-off. Diwanji would present our stance – that the princely states would cooperate with the government that was to be formed in Delhi on matters such as defence and foreign policy while retaining our full sovereignty in all other matters.

The foolish protests in Alappuzha – the revolt in Punnapra and Vayalar – spearheaded by the communists that took our government only three days to suppress made things so much easier for Diwanji. All the leaders were arrested, and the other accused, including socialists like Sreekantan Nair, had to abscond. This was the reason he was in Thrissur. Sreekantan Nair was a man who bowed to no one. But I thought, from the first glance, that he had an air of disappointment and dejection about him. Anti-nationals, it seemed to me, were not going to have a resurrection any time soon in Thiruvithamkoor.

Sreekantan Nair seemed quite fond of me. 'That's what real men do,' he said about my prison break. 'No point in going about like those gormless Congress men. Still, we should also be careful not to jump into things without thinking.'

The reference was to the events that took place in Cherthala and Ambalapuzha taluks. Sreekantan Nair had sent two men to K.V. Pathrose, the dictator of the protests there, with the warning that they should refrain from doing anything hasty. One was a young man he trusted, K.C.S. Mani, the man I had heard about in Muhamma from my Congress acquaintances and warned my superiors about, and the other was a student leader from Kollam named Janardhana Kuruppu.

'Doomed men take sensible men's words of warning as signs of weakness,' said Sreekantan Nair.

Basheer was well enough to leave the hospital and move into a room in a building near the Mangalodayam press in Thrissur. He had given up thinking deep thoughts and storytelling. Like broken and leaking pots and pans, his books were stuffed into gunnysacks and left on the veranda where they lay at the mercy of the sun and the rain. He did not tell jokes any more – in fact, he barely spoke – and remained uninterested even at the mention of Gandhi or Nehru or Bhagat Singh. Devoid of emotion, he sat sucking at his beedi. Visitors came expecting the old Basheer, sat around baffled for a while with nothing to talk about, and left.

'I was wondering ... whether to go home for a bit.'

Basheer was talking to himself, but Perunna Thomas, a writer who had come for a visit, thought he was talking to him. Thomas had been sitting there stumped, having exhausted possible topics of conversation – politics, cinema, religion, circus, story, drama – none of which had elicited a response from Basheer.

'To do what?' Thomas asked now.

'Start a grocery store in the market, maybe, or a booth selling karuppetti,' Basheer replied, assuming that he had asked himself the question.

Outside, as he was leaving, Thomas told me, as though I was responsible for everything that had happened, 'People who are not mad are useless. They do nothing new. Just go on living like cattle.'

'So, we don't need the hospitals that treat those who are mad? Is that what you're saying? I asked.

'I don't know about all that,' he said. 'All I know is that the God who burdened us with reason also gave a blessing with it – madness.'

'What about all the mad people who kill others in the grip of madness, then?'

'Well, most people who kill are those who claim to be sane. Madness is a unique thing that only human beings experience. You know any animal that goes mad?'

'You mean we received madness and reason side by side.'

'The two are one and the same,' he said.

He patted my shoulder and walked away, promising to pray for the return of Basheer's madness.

The room where Sreekantan Nair lived was also near the Mangalodayam press. Manjooran stayed overnight there a couple of times a week. Whenever I visited Basheer, I would also go there, and they treated me as though I was one of them. They didn't, in any case, seem to be involved in anything clandestine enough to keep a newcomer at arm's length. And they didn't often discuss the goings-on in Thiruvithamkoor, perhaps because things were not panning out as they had hoped. Besides, they might have concluded that these issues were short-lived, that once the British left India, the problems within the princely states would resolve themselves. Men like them were convinced that it was not the support of the people but the might of the British army that sustained the kings.

The newspapers had also moved on to other things. Barely anything was reported about prisoners who had been arrested in connection with the Punnapra–Vayalar revolt. Instead, the papers were now full of Jinnah, the Muslim League, Gandhi and Clement Atlee. In one newspaper, printed in an insignificant corner, was a statement by Diwanji, that getting all the princely states to be part of a unified India would be meaningful only if Pakistan was also part of it. Every nationalist I met talked furiously about Jinnah's demands and seemed convinced that Gandhi would pull off some miracle and defeat him. But Manjooran had other thoughts, different from all these people. Although inherently against the formation of a nation based on religion, he argued that there were hundreds of nationalities within British India and that each of them needed to be considered specifically and separately. The discussions in Sreekantan Nair's room in Thrissur, that went on inconclusively until the wee hours of the morning, reminded me of Seethi Buildings. On one of those mornings, before it was daylight, we went to the railway station to see Manjooran off. I took Basheer along as Sreekantan Nair had advised.

'Take him with you,' he would say to me often. 'If he's left alone here, he'll only think things up.'

It was still dark and deserted when we walked back from the railway station, signs of life, a couple of people here and there, evident only when we got to Swaraj Round. Old people on their morning walk, we said, laughing, sleepless because their time on earth was coming to an end. Suddenly, we saw two young-looking men who, with their dirty clothes and filthy bodies, seemed like beggars crossing the playground towards us, their faces becoming clearer as they came close. The stronger-looking of the two called Sreekantan Nair 'chetta' and hugged him and began sobbing. Nair's eyes, too, welled up. I had never seen this man before, but I knew that there was only person with whom Sreekantan Nair had such a deep bond – K.C.S. Mani, the son of Chidambara Iyer from Alappuzha. I guessed that the other man with him was Janardhana Kuruppu. These were the messengers sent to K.V. Pathrose with the warning to stop the communists in Alappuzha taking unnecessarily dangerous risks. We sat on the wet grass in a circle. As Sreekantan Nair and the State Congress had predicted, the uprising in Punnapra and Vayalar had turned out to be a human tragedy, the fallout of which, the two men said, could be witnessed even after months. No one knew the exact number of lives lost, and more were in prison with festering wounds. Women and children had left their homes and fled to the forest where they remained even now, starving.

'And yesterday near the Alappuzha court ... we saw...' Janardhana Kuruppu also began to cry.

A human train of dying men, bound to one another with heavy chains on their hands, legs and around their necks, being taken to the court from the prison.

'They couldn't have run away even if they were set free.'

Bodies covered in stinking sores; lice crawling down to their faces from their dirty hair; nails coming loose on their fingers and toes. The sorry lot included Janardhana Kuruppu's brother Gopala Kuruppu, V.S. Achuthanandan, T.K. Divakaran and T.V. Thomas, a tall, handsome man they could not even recognize at first. When the guards were distracted, Thomas beckoned to them. Thomas was ordinarily a man with a positive outlook on life, but he told them that they were beaten regularly and that they did not expect to leave the prison alive.

'We gave Thomas our word that we'll kill that man,' Janardhana Kuruppu told us.

Sreekantan Nair had tears in his eyes.

Mani had always been of the opinion that the diwan Sir C.P. had to be executed. He told us that he had visited Kumbalath Shanku Pillai in his ashramam in Panmana. Shanku Pillai agreed with him, but was not entirely certain that Mani was the man to do the job, that he had the strength and courage to do it. So, in order to convince him, Mani had vandalized the statue of Sir C.P. in front of the C.P. Sathram – a residence, named after Sir C.P., for travelling high-ranking officials to rest – near the Thampanoor railway station office. He was absconding to Kochi and had stopped off briefly in Alappuzha when he met the prisoners.

I sat there listening, stunned. The man who sat before me had destroyed the statue of the diwan who served my country. Plans to kill him, to commit a murder that would ruin the country, were afoot. An acute awareness of where I was gripped me in that moment. I was in the middle of a discovery that everyone in my profession dreamed of, and if I was careful, it would lead me to the most fulfilling task of my entire career. My throat was dry and my limbs shivered, but I controlled them and sat there listening intently to every word.

'This is not the right time,' Sreekantan Nair said. 'Rushing into things is always dangerous.'

In his view, as India's independence was imminent, there was much less to worry about. The native kings, who continued to rule only because the white man's guns protected them, would soon have to work for a living like everyone else, and so would the Pattar from Mylapore who ruled over us.

A belligerent man even under normal circumstances, Mani stomped off upon hearing his words. Janardhana Kuruppu went after him to placate him.

That night, I walked back to the railway station, bought some fried sweets and packaged them neatly. I gave this parcel to the loco pilot of the morning train to Thiruvananthapuram and asked him to deliver it to Varadan Pillah, a trackman in Thampanoor station. As a token of my gratitude, I gave him some small notes.

'What's so urgent with this?' he asked.

'It's my wife,' I said. 'She's pregnant – seven months – and she gets these urges for oily sweets. You know how it is. Pillah is my brother-in-law.'

'Why didn't you say so?' he said and stuffed the money back in my front pocket.

The parcel of sweets was a message to my superiors, code for urgent, serious news that needed to be acted on without delay.

Despite Sreekantan Nair's opinion, even leaders like Nehru and Gandhi had no clear idea whether Thiruvithamkoor would join the Indian Union after independence. At regular intervals, Nehru, N. Gopalaswami Ayyangar and others made statements about the new republic being one where the people, and not kings, held power. Use of force against states that stubbornly wanted to remain independent was not out of the question, Nehru had declared at the meeting of the citizens of princely states that took place in Gwalior. Diwanji had responded to it by reminding him of the history of our country. Thiruvithamkoor was the only country that had defeated a European power in a battle – the Battle of Kulachal that had seen the Dutch run away with their lives. Those who did not wish to see Thiruvithamkoor remain independent were welcome to leave the country, he said. There were some who saw Diwanji's statements as a kind of bargaining strategy. Meanwhile, the rifts among freedom fighters were clearly visible. At the meeting of the Aikyakerala Prasthanam in Thrissur, the socialist leader K.B. Menon tabled a motion arguing that what was needed was not an Indian Union or an independent Thiruvithamkoor but a United Keralam. Thamizhan or Malayali, Thiruvithamkoor had its own culture, a population of sixty million, and a tax revenue exceeding nine crore rupees, Diwanji countered, and that, come 15 August, no one could stop this country retaining its independence.

Everywhere I looked, I saw freedom fighters getting riled up by the increasing support for an independent Thiruvithamkoor. A.K. Pillah, who had been a Congress supporter, wrote and spoke publicly about the benefits. *Kerala Kaumudi* and *Malayalarajyam* supported independence. The SNDP passed a motion stating that the threats from the Congress affected the reputation of the country. Malloor Govinda Pillai declared that he would, despite his advanced age, fight for the king. Units of the Rajabhakta Sangham, dedicated supporters of the king and the royal family, sprang up spontaneously in each and every village.

I was present when the discussion about annexing Thiruvithamkoor to India through an armed struggle took place in Sreekantan Nair's room. P.T. Chacko was the most vociferous.

'What do we have to fear when we have people like them,' he said, looking at me and Mani. 'We have around two thousand people and local-made guns ready and waiting in Kottayam.'

'No,' Sreekantan Nair said. 'The diwan will play the hand Jinnah has been playing. Communalism.'

The next day, Sreekantan Nair left for Bombay on some secret mission.

16

You are all aware that 18 July is the second most important day in the history of our country, the first, of course, being the day the person who built our country, Maharaja Marthanda Varma, laid this land he had conquered at the feet of his beloved deity, Sree Padmanabhaswamy. I cannot leave this day undescribed. I was following a rally organized by Pattom Thanu Pillai, who had come out of hiding to take on the challenge thrown down by Diwanji. It would be August by the time the rally reached Thiruvananthapuram. They fantasized about raising the tricolour flag on top of the Huzur Court. The meeting at Vaikom when the rally got there was well attended but was dampened by the incessant rain. Thanu Pillai, too, seemed somewhat disheartened, perhaps because he was aware that the country's attention was elsewhere – Major General His Highness Sree Padmanabhadasa Vanchipala Sir Balarama Varma Kulashekhara Kireetapathi Manney Sultan Maharaja Rajaraja Sree Chithira Thirunal was going to address the country. No other maharaja before him had ever done this. The news made some people fall down in a swoon. Every State Congress person, every revolutionary I spoke to that day was in deep sorrow. It was unthinkable that the king, who had until then led the life of an ascetic, thinking only about his subjects and the holy feet of Sree Padmanabhaswamy, would, like a commoner, go into a radio station to broadcast a speech. The fear that he would announce his decision to abdicate was widespread. The State Congress also feared this because his subjects would never forgive them if the king was perceived to be shedding tears. Pattom Thanu Pillai, intelligent as he was, spent three-quarters of his speech praising the Maharaja, and concluded his words with barely any criticism of Diwanji. He then took himself to the home of Chakkayil Krishnan Nair, the only house in the vicinity which had a radio.

When we arrived, the radio had been brought out of the house and placed on the veranda in the front yard where several dignitaries had gathered. Spirits were up as the rain had passed and the sky had cleared. There were only two chairs, and these were reserved for Thanu Pillai and Nataraja Pillai. Several people sat on the steps and on the floor. Even the darkness beyond the yard had the shape of a group of people huddled and whispering together. I squeezed myself to the front and found a position that would allow me to watch the expressions on people's faces. The static emanating from the radio died and it went silent. As everyone looked at its owner Krishnan Nair wondering whether it had broken, that voice, soft like an ashareeri, a disembodied voice all the way from heaven, began to flow out of the radio. A sweet, loving, kind as well as magnificent voice, the likes of which I had never heard before. I watched the skin of an elderly gentleman standing next to me prickle even as two surreptitious streams of tears began to flow down my cheeks. Everyone, including Thanu Pillai, rose from their seats.

'On and from the 17th of August 1947, Travancore will reassume in full measure its independence and sovereignty.'

Thanu Pillai's face blanched right before my eyes. The Maharaja's message, delivered in English, was crystal clear, and his voice seemed to address the whole world. I did not see or hear anything after that. I walked, as though in a dream, towards the western entrance of the temple, drenched in the rain that had resumed. My country was going to be an independent nation. It would never again be a slave to anyone, a mere annex to another country. When, centuries ago, it made a pact with the British, my country had not sought permission from any of the other princely states, nor from the Congress which had only sprouted long after. And now, it did not need anyone's permission to declare its independence. This country, my country, had been in existence for hundreds of years, long before even the idea of India existed. It would exist again.

Coming up to the western side of the temple, I walked towards the lake. Basheer had once claimed that, twenty-three years ago, exactly on this spot, he had met Gandhi and touched his hand. All the State Congress folk who had been in prison with me would be sitting stunned before radios. I laughed, imagining the looks on their faces. At the jetty, a small boat, the type used by the police, was waiting for me. As soon as I stepped in, without a word, the driver sped away southwards. The surge of emotions I had been feeling quietened, and fear began to take hold. In the rain, the lake was dark and cold, and up above, light flashed in the sky as though there was a battle going on some place far away. The coming days would be crucial. The Congress had already promised unrest, starting with blocking the distribution of rice within the country. A cruel tactic, indeed. And it was almost certain that India would stage an army incursion as soon as the British left. Our country had not maintained a functioning army since the signing of an agreement after the uprising against the British led by Velu Thambi Dalawa, the diwan during the reign of Maharaja Avittom Thirunal Balarama Varma. The insurgents inside the country were to be feared even more. My thoughts went to K.C.S. Mani, the man who possessed a self-confidence bordering on madness. I had things to do now to conclude what was set in motion before I joined Thanu Pillai's march, and had to make a plan with clear objectives.

When Sreekantan Nair came back from Bombay, it was with the decision that the diwan Sir C.P. was to be assassinated after all. With him was a frail young man with barely sprouted facial hair who followed him everywhere like a shadow. His name was Varghese.

'You were right,' Sreekantan Nair told Mani when we all met. 'There's no other choice but to kill him. This man from Mylapore is asking us to leave the country! We're not scared of a confrontation but, don't forget, he is the master of underhand tactics. He has let loose a band of CIDs all across the land, spreading malicious rumours about patriots. Sent so many people to prison. And now he goes all around India, meeting with Jinnah on the one side, while, on the other side, soliciting support from the Brahmins within the Congress talking about caste. Even K.M. Munshi and Pattabhi Sitaramayya are swaying towards him. The Hindu Mahasabha and the RSS are already on his side.'

The RSS – the Rashtriya Swayamsevak Sangh. I was hearing about this Hindu nationalist volunteer organization for the first time.

'Well, I told you this already, didn't I?' Mani said, belligerent.

'It's up to you now,' said Sreekantan Nair. He pushed Varghese towards us and continued, 'But you also need a stand-in. If you get caught or something else happens to you, Varghese here will complete the task.'

Mani and Janardhana Kuruppu gazed at the feeble-looking man and were not impressed, but I understood that it was a clever, calculated move on Sreekantan Nair's part. To take on a man in combat, one needed strength, but it was not a necessary factor if the objective was to kill. If Mani failed, Varghese was most suited to take his place. No one, under ordinary circumstances, would even suspect him.

'What about me? I could be the stand-in,' I said, pretending to side with Mani.

'No, I have other jobs for you,' Sreekantan Nair said.

With the funds Sreekantan Nair had organized, Mani, Basheer and I set out immediately for Madras. Our task was to meet with a man named Ramunni Menon who was an acquaintance of Basheer's and a prominent leader at Madras Christian College. Janardhana Kuruppu and Varghese were tasked with travelling back and forth on trains without tickets, singing songs and collecting money until we came back. They were both good singers.

Ramunni Menon was trustworthy, but we decided not to tell him about our plans because Sir C.P.'s police and rowdies were always after us. Our primary objective was acquiring guns, but we told him that they were for our personal protection. Madras was a place where one could, with the right help, lay one's hands on guns. Menon enjoyed covert missions, and went off immediately to see a man named Bhayankarachari who could help, but we were told that it would be two weeks before we could take possession. We decided to wait, staying with an acquaintance of his in his room at the Christian College hostel for the time being.

But we had a problem – Mani. He was like a ferocious dog that obeyed only one master. All night, he paced around the room, restless, impatient, arguing that putting things off caused unforeseen problems. In the end, we decided to go and meet with Bhayankarachari ourselves, and without informing Menon, we set out as soon as it was morning.

Bhayankarachari ... The man personified the image his name conjured up – a bhayankaran, a terrible, terrifying fellow. We knew nothing about him, but everyone we asked knew something. Some looked at us, just for a moment, surprised, and walked away without saying anything. Some pretended not to hear us, and others, instead of responding to us, exclaimed loudly in local Tamil to passers-by. Eventually, a few people joined us and led us to an area where people of the lower castes lived.

As soon as we were in Bhayankarachari's presence, Mani, without hesitation or fear, said, 'Ramunni Menon was here yesterday to ask you about some guns, wasn't he? They are actually for us. The thing is, we need them immediately. We have to kill a man.'

Bhayankarachari paid attention to the Tamil Mani spoke. 'Brahmin, are you?' he asked.

'Yes.'

'Be careful then,' he said, addressing the rest of us. 'This man will betray you.'

I was certain that Mani, who did not appreciate his loyalty being questioned, would hit him. His fingers squeezed into a fist and his face stiffened as he ground his teeth, but he seemed to swallow the insult.

'The man to be killed is a Brahmin,' I said.

'There are those who hate their parents,' Bhayankarachari said, staring at Mani.

'Well, I've fallen out with my father,' Mani said. Anger had raised the pitch of his voice. 'And the man I'm going to kill is a Brahmin, the diwan of Thiruvithamkoor, Sir C.P. Ramaswami Iyer. It doesn't matter whether you give us the guns or not, I will kill this man.'

'That's all well and good. Do you even know how to fire a gun?'

We didn't, in actual fact, and we told him about our plan to find a deserted place and practise for a few days as soon as we had the guns. A meaningless plan, according to Bhayankarachari, as meaningless as a gun in the hands of those who did not know how to use it properly.

'If you're committed to killing this man, there are other ways,' he said. 'But it will be difficult to get away safely afterwards.'

'I'm not looking to get away,' Mani said. 'I'll do it alone, and I'm counting on being caught. What's the point in running away after the deed?'

Bhayankarachari told him that the best weapon for an up close and personal attack was a knife. It guaranteed death. He drew a picture of a knife on a piece of paper, a curved knife of a kind I had never seen before, that would, with one strike, slice through a person's neck. Show the picture to a blacksmith and have one made in iron, he said, paying attention to the width and weight of the handle and blade. If the height of the person to be killed could be estimated beforehand, so much the better. The neck was the part of the body most difficult to aim for, but also the most vulnerable, a small area that stood closest to death and nothingness.

'And if, before he dies, he has the opportunity to see the knife slicing through the air towards him, he will most definitely know who is behind it.'

Bhayankarachari said this with a secretive smile. Every minute I spent with the man, I felt his enthusiasm increasing.

17

When I got to Kollam in a boat, a car was waiting for me. At Varkala, another car began to follow us. After about six miles, I got off and got into the second car which took me all the way to Bhaktivilasam, one of the official residences of the diwan of Thiruvithamkoor. It was not yet 2 a.m. and most of the lights outside the beautiful palace were switched off. As soon as the car stopped, a man peeled away from the shadows by the gate and began walking silently towards the building. I followed him.

Inside, the high walls were decorated with framed paintings. A house, like the clothes a person wore, reflected the personality of its owner. The floors of Bhaktivilasam were paved with cool stones, its interior arranged with a grace, nobility and a mature simplicity rarely seen elsewhere. Past two grand halls with majestically carved cornices and a room lined with bookshelves, as we reached a door left ajar, the servant withdrew. I became a shadow and slipped quietly in.

Physically, Diwanji was not as big or tall as the reputation he had built for himself. Still, at first glance, his body revealed that it was used to daily exercise. Shapely, patrician nose, flushed cheeks, medium skin tone. Without the hat that was customary in the photographs I had seen, his curly hair was on display. His eyes were narrow, as though they were used to looking carefully at things. The expression of inchoate sadness that was constant on his face was undoubtedly attractive, and yet it radiated an amazing sense of command. He was dressed in a light-coloured dhothi, an upper garment and a shawl around his neck, and was standing by a table that came up to the top his stomach. An Englishman, seemingly over seventy years of age, with a strong body and a face with an expression of suspicion, stood opposite, his body language incongruent with the formal clothes he wore.

Without pausing in his talk, Diwanji came towards me, touched me lovingly on my shoulder and led me to the table as though I were a child. Picking up another glass, he poured whatever was in their crystal glasses for me too, and indicated with a gesture that I should wait until they finished their important discussion. The Englishman, too, looked at me, mouthed 'sorry' and continued with the conversation. The subject of their discussion was a sanyasi in Tiruvannamalai in Madras, a man who dressed only in a loincloth and had eschewed speech, and about the thought processes of the Hindus. With his exquisite pronunciation of English words and delightful table manners, he seemed more cultured than the real Englishman before me.

'I read "Saint",' Diwanji said, referring to the article the Englishman had written about his meeting with the sanyasi. 'One can look at it in two ways, but if you read it carefully, it is quite funny. A testament to your skills as a writer.'

'Ah, but not something that the disciples of Ramaṇa Maharshi would understand,' said the Englishman. 'I fainted because of the heat, but they think I lost consciousness faced with his spiritual brilliance!'

The Englishman laughed and then continued, 'The Hindus amaze me. I feel, compared to the European, they have less fear of death.'

'People think that's because of the belief in reincarnation. I disagree. It is possible that one is reincarnated as an insect, or a handler of corpses, a chandalan.'

'But this is it – it surprises me that even the highly educated believe in reincarnation!'

'And that's just as natural as Europeans – Christians – believing in the Resurrection of Christ and in Judgement Day. We assume these are rational thoughts because they are European, and because of it, one thought surprises us while the other doesn't. I'll be honest with you, I believe in reincarnation myself.'

It was the first time I was witnessing someone talk to a white sahib as his equal, or as his superior even. He showed no reluctance at all in disagreeing with the opinion of his friend while also remaining respectful.

'A friend of mine is of the opinion that the Hindu's beliefs originate in a profound sense of disappointment with life,' the Englishman said. 'Like poison, the proposal has a certain attraction. Like the bottom of a cliff calling to us.'

I was reminded of the day Basheer's madness played out. He had said the same thing this sahib was saying now, except that Basheer had been talking about stories while this man was referring to the thoughts of our people.

'I'm afraid I disagree with that too,' he said to the sahib. 'There is no such thing as Hindu philosophy, only a collection of thoughts, ideas. As for the sense of disappointment, well, it's most visible when you look into the eyes of Westerners. Here we call it nirmamathwam, dispassion. Can there be a more positive idea than the philosophy of karma? It inspires me!'

He stopped and turned to me.

'This is Somerset Maugham,' he said. 'The greatest living writer in the world, in my opinion. Very interested in Indian affairs. I'm proud to call him my friend. Let me also tell you this. There's a great novel of his – *Then and Now*. I am a character in it, by the name of Fra Timoteo!'

He laughed, a little loudly, and continued, 'Mr Maugham, I must say though that I'd have preferred it if you had used my real name – C.P. Ramaswami Iyer. That way, I would have been immortalized.'

Maugham, too, laughed and said, 'You'll be immortalized as the administrator of this country.'

'Ah, but who knows whether I'll be the villain or the hero in its history? I'm as proficient in making enemies as I am in making friends. Well. Now, this man here, he is our smartest, most capable employee. Most capable, I must repeat, because at this young age, he's achieved some very significant things. We are, in actual fact, meeting in person for the first time. Our work together has reached a crucial point.'

He heaped praises on me, I who was at the lowest rung of the ladder of my profession.

The great writer shook hands with me. 'I can guess some things,' he said.

The conversation then moved on to the political climate that would develop in India after the departure of the British. He was of the opinion that, within a year, most of the prominent leaders of the Congress, including Gandhi, Nehru and Patel, would be assassinated, and that there would be a civil war and great bloodshed in the country. The writer agreed with him. It was conceivable that British India could break into at least six pieces. Army incursions into Kashmir, Punjab and Assam would be never-ending. If, instead, the country split only into two, India and Pakistan, parts of Pakistan could end up within the borders of India and vice versa, creating endless conflict. Communist revolts and the Soviet Union's interference could be expected.

'If there is a third world war and a new Hitler, its origins would be here,' declared Maugham.

After a further fifteen minutes or so, Maugham retired to his room to sleep. Diwanji led me into another room.

It was a small room with little ventilation. Our voices would not escape it. The room was furnished only with two wooden chairs. He sat in one, and when I hesitated, he compelled me to sit in the other.

'Power is a state of mind, which is why it needs outward symbols like the crown, the jewellery and the throne,' he said. 'Even Gandhi dresses the way he does to show that he has power. This room, however, is to be entered with the self-awareness that we have no power. So, let's sit together.'

He then asked me what I thought of Maugham.

'I don't really read books,' I said. 'I've never heard of him before.'

'Somerset Maugham is not merely a writer,' he said. 'He used to be one of the best spies in the world.'

He told me that, as part of the British Intelligence Agency, Maugham had worked in Switzerland, Russia and Germany. During the First World War, when Virendranath Chattopadhyaya and others created the Berlin Committee to fight for India's independence, it was Maugham who helped break it up.

'Just think! What would have happened if the British had left India then,' he said. 'More bloodshed than would happen now. Delhi would have come under the rule of the Japanese or the Germans.'

Maugham had said that he had been late getting into Russia. Had he reached there six months earlier, the October Revolution, which took place only because of German and French sponsorship, would never have happened.

'If Maugham had succeeded in his mission, the world we know today would have been very different. We would never have heard the names Lenin, Stalin and Trotsky. Even in our Alappuzha, so many people would not have died.'

'True,' I said, agreeing.

'It will take at least another fifty years to recover from it.'

'But they have so many supporters now. Mostly younger people.'

'I've read their books too,' he said with an expression of scorn on his face. 'Things, ideas that will never come to fruition. Interesting to read, mind you, like science fiction, that's all. People like to pursue the madness that quickens their minds, and then there's no use trying to stand in their way, to reason with them. They'll only run over us. But not for long, only until another madness grips their minds.'

He went silent and sat there watching me.

'I think...' he began after a while. 'Well, I think that intelligent people need to get involved, not just sit back and let things evolve organically. Certain actions, taken at the right time and at the right place, can redirect the course of events, and what will follow will follow. I had felt, until quite recently, that our country was being dragged along by a current and would float away into the middle of the ocean no matter what we did. I don't think that any more. Now I'm confident that there is a way to stop it floating away. Because of you.'

As he said this, the expression on his face was not quite congratulatory, but that of a player who had found a crucial move just as he was about to concede defeat. His eyes shone with the affection as well as the sympathy inherent in carefully persuading someone to do one's bidding. Those who are persuaded by such people would do anything for a mere glance from them. I was overcome with a feeling of embarrassment that all I had done for him so far was inconsequential. Praise from great people makes us indebted to them.

'Perhaps it is because I've spent the evening with a great writer, I feel we are characters in a novel,' he said, this time in English. 'Characters who will redirect the course of the narrative. The story, thus far, had one ending, but now, right here, we are about to change it. There are speculative novels that imagine what would have happened if a certain historical event had ended differently. Like the one by Louis Geoffroy, the title of which escapes me now. It imagines what would have happened if Napolean had defeated the English.'

When I left Bhaktivilasam, the sky had not lightened. Yet some smart birds, perceptive of possibilities, had risen early and started rushing around in search of worms.

18

From the next day on, as was expected, trouble erupted in British India and in Thiruvithamkoor. The brave statement that the Maharaja made on the radio perplexed the British and the Congress leadership alike. What he said was indeed lawful; the agreement was that, when the British empire abdicated the governance of India, the princely states that had accepted imperial power could choose to join India or Pakistan, or to remain independent. The British, by and large, refrained from commenting, although Lord Mountbatten issued a statement calling on the princely states to be realistic in their decisions, meaning, essentially, that the British did not back our choice.

Gandhi, meanwhile, declared that the people's decision was more important than that of kings. To which Diwanji gave an appropriately strong response. We welcomed the will of the people, he said, and that the Maharaja and the people of Thiruvithamkoor were always of the same mind. Nehru's response, despite appeals from Sardar K.M. Panicker, V.T. Krishnamachari and N. Gopalaswamy Ayyangar to join the national mainstream, was provocative. He said that India would not recognize the sovereignty of princely states, and that if any foreign country recognized it, it would be treated as an act of enmity towards India. In effect, he was repeating what he had said in a meeting of the All India Congress Committee, where he had threatened to forcefully annex to the Indian Union those princely states that tried to retain sovereignty. Diwanji ridiculed him, saying that Nehru's own country – Kashmir – had not even considered the choice of joining the Indian Union.

The newspaper *The Hindu*, which had always supported Diwanji, published an editorial by A.K. Pillah which provided a strong foundation for the idea of an independent Thiruvithamkoor. At no time in history had Thiruvithamkoor, or its previous incarnation, Venad, been part of any of the empires of India, Pillah argued. No empire – the Maurya, the Mughal, the Maratha, the Vijayanagara – had ever reached close to one of its borders. Neither Hyder Ali nor Tipu Sultan, those belligerent sultans of Mysore, had succeeded in their efforts to conquer us. Even with the British, what we had was an agreement, not complete surrender. Pillah dismissed the idea that language formed the basis of nationality; people of Thiruvithamkoor had always spoken Tamil and Malayalam. Pillah, however, did not fully support royal rule. What he imagined, he said, was an independent Thiruvithamkoor that would eventually become a democracy.

Muhammad Ali Jinnah, the leader of the Muslim League, and V.D. Savarkar, president of the Hindu Mahasabha, sent messages of solidarity to Diwanji and to the Maharaja. Jinnah supported, in no uncertain terms, the argument that the princely states should make their own decisions about their future. Savarkar's concern, based on the large-scale religious conversions that had taken place, was that the Congress and the communists were using Christians to destroy what was essentially a Hindu country.

Diwanji allowed the newspapers to publish a letter he had written to G.D. Birla. 'I believe wholeheartedly that a Hindu country like Thiruvithamkoor is not only capable of standing on its own two feet,' he said in the letter, 'but deserving of the full support of people such as yourselves who are loyal to the ideals of Hinduism and the Hindu way of life and thought.'

Diwanji appointed the former inspector general of police, Karim Sahib, as Thiruvithamkoor's ambassador to Pakistan. Jinnah reciprocated by sending Mirgebul Muhammed as his representative to Thiruvithamkoor. A hearty welcome, organized by League members and merchants, was waiting for him when he arrived.

The State Congress was still conspiring to instigate civil war in the country. They spread exaggerated reports of the shooting in Petta in the beginning of July. Pattom Thanu Pillai exhorted the masses to disobey all of the government's prohibitions. At first glance, our country's prospects did not look hopeful. It seemed certain that India would send an army to attack our country, defenceless because we had not, as stipulated in the agreement with the British, maintained a strong enough army of our own. The Congress had already started blocking, at the borders with India, the train wagons carrying rice into our country. Declaring that he would not stand aside and watch as the people of Thiruvithamkoor starved, Jinnah offered to send supplies, but ships from Pakistan would take at least a month to reach us. Of all these developments, the most hurtful was the response of the British whom we had loyally served for centuries. Lord Listowel, the secretary of state of India, made the declaration in parliament that Thiruvithamkoor and Hyderabad would join the Constituent Assembly of India. Diwanji's response was to ask him to reread the portion in the India Bill that set out the rights of the princely states. The British, in effect, were proving their own untrustworthiness. The people of Thiruvithamkoor wanted independence.

25th July, judgement day. For almost a month now, I had been living in a room adjacent to a buffalo shed run by some Tamils in Kumarapuram. My name, currently, was John, and I helped out with the chores at the shed. That morning, standing in the straw and muck by the well and pouring a bucket of water over my head, I thought about my tiny country. Around me, the world was cloaked in silence except for the rhythmic sound of streams of liquid hitting metal pails as the buffaloes were milked. Each person was rendered lonely on judgement days. My country, too, was lonely now. People and countries engaged in the process of preparing agreements and contracts with such care and formality, and yet, to one's utter amazement, the other began to act as though they had no recall of any of it. If one were to believe the Congress propaganda, a thousand fortified vehicles were waiting in Delhi, battle ready, and if, on 16 August, they came revving towards us, the lakes, mountains and forests at our borders would be rendered insufficient barricades. The enemy had more soldiers than the entire population of our country.

I changed my clothes, made sure nothing of mine was left behind, and set out from my temporary abode. In the town, I went into a small hotel and had a meal as if preparing for a full day ahead immersed in my tasks. After the meal, as I walked to the overbridge, I watched the people passing by, people who expected their mornings would always be as calm and beautiful as today. Perhaps it was good to be like them, to choose not to remember that our circumstances were such that unexpected things could happen at any time. Their lives would be different tomorrow. The man who is going to change your lives forever is walking by you, I wanted to shout. You will never know it; there will be no record. Don't you know, people, that what gets recorded are all lies anyway, humongous lies that we want everyone to believe are the truth? Why else do we take great care to record these things? Truth should be widely known, shouldn't it, without it having to be written down? Have a rummage through everything human beings have written down – scribblings in notebooks, carvings on rocks, deeds, dictionaries, declarations, grammar texts, agreements, contracts, life histories, everything that he and she and they have written. All lies. Made-up stories. In fact, writing was invented for the express purpose of turning lies into truths and preserving them for posterity. Ha, ha! Only athmakatha – the story of the self, life story – is the truth, and only because of the fact that it is a story is already acknowledged. Doesn't matter what India's leader Gandhi says, it is not truth that is God, but lies.

When I got to the room at G.B.R. Boarding, K.C.S. Mani was still sleeping. Either he was stressed and had not fallen asleep until late, or his innate carefree nature made him indifferent to the importance of the day. Varghese and Basheer were in the next room, already awake.

I tapped Mani's foot.

'Did you come in a horse carriage?' he asked, waking up.

'No,' I said.

'I thought I heard a horse carriage in my sleep.'

I remembered the sound of the horse carriage at the Central Jail, the hangman's carriage.

I spent that day with Mani. Unusually for him, he talked a lot about himself, about his dead father Chidambara Iyer, and about his falling out with him. Still, his favourite memory was from his childhood, of walking to the paddy fields with his father. 'There are types of paddy that do not surrender to human will,' Mani said. 'We call them weeds and varinellu, try to pull them out of the walkways and verges, but they self-seed and secret themselves in our fields and grain stores, preserving their posterity, their continued existence.' He had made the decision to live as a free man, he said, and had left the fields behind. His amma, unlike his father, was a poor soul, clueless about all this.

'Don't worry about your amma,' I said. 'She'll be fine.'

Sreekantan Nair and Kumbalath Shanku Pillai had promised to look after her, provide for her. Sreekantan Nair was like a brother to Mani. He had spent more time in Nair's house than in his own. Nair's amma, knowing how fond of food he was, would serve more in his plate than in her own son's. He was the best person to kill C.P., he said several times that morning, and that it was good that the assassin was also a Tamil Brahmin. In a country like ours, where everything was based on caste and religion, it would be more dangerous for someone else to do the job.

In the afternoon, Mani bathed and got ready as though he was going to a wedding. He stuck a pretty moustache on his usually clean-shaven face. He wrapped a mundu over khaki shorts and pulled on a jubbah. The knife, made by a blacksmith in Karunagappally to the specifications drawn by Bhayankarachari, was at the waistband of the shorts. By four o'clock, we settled the bill for the four or five days he had stayed at the boarding house and were on our way. Varghese would continue hanging around there until six and then move elsewhere. His next task would depend on how Mani's mission turned out. Our destination was the Swathi Thirunal Sangeetha Academy, where the centenary celebrations of the demise of the musician-king, after whom the academy was named, was taking place. We took two different routes – Basheer and I together, and Mani on his own.

Although he had begun to take an interest in things, Basheer was still not quite the man he used to be.

'They say if the Indian army comes, the government will bring in the American army to confront them,' Basheer said, as though trying to diminish the significance of the imminent event he was going to be part of. Some of his old jovial tone was back.

'American army! As if!' I said. 'Ashaaney, they're just making up more stories.'

Perhaps it was the mention of 'stories', but Basheer did not say anything else. We had been walking for about fifteen minutes. By now, they would have arrested Varghese at the lodge, and police, in mufti, would be ready and waiting inside and outside the Sangeetha Academy.

The area around the Academy was fairly crowded. The event inside would be attended by members of the royal family, important officials and dignitaries, and music aficionados who had already purchased passes. We watched as Mani showed his pass to the security at the gate and entered, and as was desired, found a seat in the back rows close to where the guests entered. I left Basheer to hang around near the gate and walked away. According to our plans, my next job was to safely leave the country and meet up with Sreekantan Nair in Palakkad. After his mission, Mani would, like the valiant Veera Bhagat Singh, surrender himself to the authorities. He had sworn that he would shout slogans loud enough to echo through the Central Jail, all the way to the gallows. Basheer's task was to let the outside world know the outcome of our mission.

I kept walking until darkness fell. By then, the Maharaja and Diwanji would be in the music hall. Ignoring our plans, I veered off the main path, and cutting through backyards and breaking through some fences, made my way back to the Academy, and waited in the darkness in the compound of the Model School next door. I could hear the proceedings. The Maharaja spoke a few words inaugurating the function, which was followed by a speech, in beautiful English, by Diwanji. Each time he said the words 'the independence of Thiruvithamkoor', goosebumps broke out on my skin. There was a secret between us, one that only the two of us knew, and thinking about it, I felt that he was speaking only to me. How did a person speak with such self-confidence even in such a crucial, decisive moment?

Usually, the Maharaja would leave soon after inaugurating a function, but today he would stay on. His love of music was well known, so it would not seem untoward.

Soon, the concert by Semmangudi Srinivasa Iyer, who was also the principal of the Academy, began. He was Diwanji's countryman. Deviating from his usual routine, Semmangudi began with a rendition of '*Smarahari paadaaravindam*', and the applause that followed when he finished made my heart race and I began to sweat. When Semmangudi began his second song, '*Janani maamava*' in Raga Bhairavi, I climbed to the top of the school's wall. Perching there, I could see the movements on the stage and the audience which was behaving itself because of the presence of the Maharaja. No one moved unless he moved. The king was Padmanabhadasan, the humble servant of Lord Sree Padmanabhaswamy, and his attendance at the concert was akin to the god himself attending.

After the third keerthanam, the Maharaja stood up, and bidding adieu to the audience with his palms pressed together, he prepared to leave. Mani would not expect this. Events where both the Maharaja and his most important minister were in attendance were rare. Protocol decreed that at such events, the diwan must arrive first and wait for the king and could leave only after His Royal Highness left. How Mani would react to this unexpected turn of events was unclear. But plans were in place even if he did nothing.

As the Maharaja got ready to leave, the audience, Semmangudi and his orchestra rose from their seats and bowed low. The Maharaja made his way slowly down the aisle with two security guards on either side. Diwanji followed a few steps behind with his own four security guards. From my high perch, I watched carefully. The Maharaja passed the row at the very back, where Mani stood. And as Diwanji neared the row, I saw Mani lunge at him even as three or four people standing right behind grabbed him. Two other men were closing in on Basheer who was by the gate. Precisely at that moment, I took the stick I had brought with me – a long bamboo stick with a piece of copper wire attached at one end – and used it to pull together the electric cables running overhead along the wall. The wires shorted and the surrounding area, as far as the eye could see, was plunged into darkness.

Perhaps because I had created it, the darkness felt thicker than any I had experienced. Even the sky was devoid of light. I heard screams and unclear voices, and then ... chaos. Sounds of chairs falling over, people running ... In an effort to calm my mind, I began counting slowly, and when I was sure enough time had passed, I withdrew the bamboo stick and released the cables. Then, moving faster than light, I jumped off the wall, hurried across the school compound to the wall on the other side, and clambered over it on to the road. And as though I was a harmless family man returning home after a day's work, I walked calmly along, melting into the shadows on the verge whenever I thought I heard footsteps approaching behind me. Before I could collect my thoughts, Basheer passed me by in a great hurry. I could have stopped him, used the weapon at my waist on him. If I had, the remaining story would have unfolded differently. There was another man behind him, running along shouting, trying to attract people's attention. I veered off into a lane and walked away, wanting to put as much distance between me and them.

Eventually, I got to Thampanoor and walked along the railway tracks until I found an empty wagon and rested in it. After about half an hour, I continued to Kizhakkekotta as agreed and waited. It was past nine o'clock by then and barely anyone was around. A few police vehicles passed by, driving faster than usual. Soon, a car approached slowly from the south and pulled up to the side of the road, and as soon as I got in it took off westwards. My destination was an old house right by the sea, to the south of Vettukad church. It had belonged to a Tharakan, holder of a writ of social privilege from the king. But it had been foreclosed and seized by the government a few years ago. Boatmen used its veranda during the day to take a nap or to smoke a beedi, but by evening, with no other houses in the vicinity, it was deserted. Instructing the driver to park the car a kilometre ahead and wait for me there, I walked to the house. A kerosene lamp burned inside the house, protected from the sea breeze by a wall. The man waiting by the door came forward and greeted me. Without responding, I looked inside through the window. K.C.S. Mani was inside, being beaten by two strong-looking men. I heard the sound of finger bones snapping and Mani's half-conscious screams.

'Who's he?' I asked the man.

'Don't know, sir,' he said. 'They said they'll wait for you before deciding what to do next.'

Was there any point in looking Mani in the face again, I wondered. It would only cause him more hurt.

'Why beat up a man unnecessarily? Especially when he's going to be killed? What's the point in torturing him?'

'Right, sir,' said the man.

He went inside, and in a few minutes, I heard Mani's death struggles and the ugly sound that emanated from his throat as it was cut. Giving the men some practical advice on how to dispose of the body so that it would never be found, I walked away.

By the time I got back, the town was full of people who had abandoned their sleep and were milling around. A couple of processions passed by, angry people marching with hasty steps, shouting things other than the usual call-and-response slogans. A large crowd gathered in Kizhakkekotta as though expecting some kind of official announcement. As I walked ahead, watching people, taking it all in, I saw that Vanross House, the seat of the State Congress, was on fire. People were hurling stones and pieces of wood at it as though setting it ablaze had not been satisfying enough.

'What happened? I asked a man.

He gave me a look as though I was stupid. 'They tried to assassinate His Highness, our Maharaja,' he said.

'Ayyo! Who?'

'The State Congress,' the man said. 'Christians!'

19

That night, violence erupted all across the country, and continued into the following day, the people responding to the news of the attempted assassination as though they wanted to prove how much they loved their Maharaja. Protest demonstrations and meetings took place even in small villages, and people took part in them without being prompted, shed copious tears. Around fifteen State Congress members were killed. Churches and Christian institutions were attacked, including the Bishop House in Changanassery, which forced the bishop to go into hiding.

In the morning, the government issued a press release:

> *Around 7 p.m. yesterday, there was a cowardly effort to harm the Maharaja. It took place at the concert that was part of the auspicious centenary celebrations of Sree Swathi Thirunal, just as the Maharaja and the diwan were leaving the venue. As the Maharaja reached the exit where his car waited for him, the assailant pounced on him armed with a swordstick. His Highness faced the attack with a calm presence of mind even as our Diwanji Sir C.P. Ramaswami Iyer, who was by his side, tried to intervene with nary a concern for his own safety, and in the process, sustained minor injuries to his face and fingers. He is recovering at the hospital.*
>
> *The assailant has been arrested and has been identified as Varghese from Thrissur in the country of Kochi. His accomplice escaped capture. This man has been identified as Muhammad Basheer, a State Congress operative and a communist, who had been previously jailed for writing and*

publishing treasonous materials, and for his part in the infamous Raktarekha Case.

It is clear that the attack is part of a large-scale conspiracy. An inquiry is under way to expose this.

For failing to stop the attack and allowing one of the assailants to escape, the deputy superintendent of police Sankaranarayana Iyer has been suspended from service.

Deviating from routine, the day's *Jayakeralam* newspaper came out in the afternoon and was circulated only in a few places as there were no vehicles or boat service. The government had already cancelled the train service the night before in order to reduce the chances of those involved in the attack escaping the country. *Jayakeralam* carried detailed reports of the assassination attempt – where it took place, when and how it happened, how Diwanji and the bodyguards stopped it. A special report analysed how the attack might have been planned and who might be responsible, arguing that the communists disgruntled by the failure of the revolts in Alappuzha, the State Congress instigated by outside powers, groups who would be adversely affected by the Education Bill could all be involved, and that they could all have conspired together. Two conclusions were made about the sudden power failure at the time of the attack: if it was planned, it pointed to the presence of a third assailant; if it was coincidence, it was the miraculous intervention of Sree Padmanabhaswamy to protect His most favourite servant and His country.

The day's editorial was praised widely. When transportation services were restored, it was read aloud in school assemblies all across the country, and cut out and pasted on the walls of government offices without any instructions to do so. It began with an exposition of the singular fortunes of our country, this Vanchirajyam: the blessing of Sree Padmanabhaswamy; the sea that formed the borders to the south and to the west; the mountains of the Western Ghats; the boundless natural resources; the royal family that cared only for the welfare of the people. Added to all this was the priceless blessing in the form of the services rendered by Brahmins from lands outside our country. Occupying high seats in our government, they had been selflessly serving our country for a very long time. It was because their minds were filled with the knowledge of the Vedas that they were able to love so wholeheartedly the people of another country who, it would seem, were their intellectual inferiors. And had we rewarded them adequately for their service? All we had done was make fun of them, calling them gluttons, freeloaders at our bhakshanasalas who ate us out of home and hearth; went on strikes accusing them of taking our jobs; referred to them pejoratively as 'Pattar' instead of clearly as 'Brahmins'; accused them directly and indirectly of being devious chancers. The editorial described the services rendered by Tamil Brahmins, from Ramayyan Dalawa who was the diwan during the rule of Maharaja Marthanda Varma to V.S. Subrahmanya Iyer during the regency of Maharani Sethu Lakshmi Bayi. It then went on to discuss our great minister, the extraordinarily talented Sir C.P. Ramaswami Iyer. His excellence in governance had been leading Thiruvithamkoor to progress and prosperity that was unachievable for other countries. Because of his efforts, we were, at this moment in time, at the entrance to independence and sovereignty. And how had we repaid him? By accusing him of corruption, calling him an autocrat, making up falsehoods that were too shameful to repeat. Now he had shed his blood in service to this country, confronted, unarmed, the despicable criminal who tried to assassinate our Beloved Golden Majesty the Maharaja. Brahmins from other lands were foreigners no more; they were citizens of this country, fully capable of defending it with their blood. Our country was eternally grateful to them.

All that day, the radio broadcast updates on Diwanji's health. The news at 7 p.m. reported that all activities of the Thiruvithamkoor State Congress, the Communist Party, the socialist wing of the Congress and the Youth League were banned. It was also ordered that, with the exception of Sunday worship, Christian communities had to obtain prior permission from the government for religious gatherings.

The attack on the Maharaja made waves in British India and around the world. People were blown away by the realization that Nehru, Gandhi and Patel, who had consistently ridiculed our country's desire for independence, nevertheless entertained a deep affection of our Annadatha, the Provider, Maharaja. Each of these Indian leaders released statements condemning the attack. Gandhi sent the Maharaja a letter wishing him a long and prosperous life, and stated that he would assume personal responsibility for any Congress associate who had deviated from the path of ahimsa. Muhammad Ali Jinnah declared that the ahimsa of the Congress was a mere mask, and that they should respect the right to self-determination that all nations have. He vowed Pakistan's military assistance should Thiruvithamkoor need it. Savarkar, meanwhile, said that Muslims, Christians and communists were conspiring to destroy a Hindu nation, and warned that any move to send the Indian army into Thiruvithamkoor would be met with robust resistance from the Hindu Samajam in India.

On 26 and 27 July, there were attacks on Christian institutions in Bengal and the Central Provinces. In Gorakhpur, which was part of the United Provinces, mobs beat two Malayali missionaries to death. Huge rallies, led by sanyasis and the Hindu Mahasabha, took place in many different parts of British India and in the princely states, chanting slogans demanding a separate nation for the Hindus if the Muslims were given one. The Congress could demand that Thiruvithamkoor join the Indian Union only if they guaranteed that Hindustan would be for Hindus. The Nizam of Hyderabad was also refusing to join the Indian Union, so how come the Congress did not send someone to assassinate him, they demanded to know.

Even the British response to the princely states' desire for sovereignty changed because of this incident. Around thirty British MPs signed a statement insisting that the clauses in the India Bill be adhered to. Britain was duty-bound to protect the rulers of these states who had abided by their contracts with the empire and helped it in times of need including raising resources for Britain's efforts during the World War. It might, if the need arose, even consider supporting an army in Thiruvithamkoor for the protection of the country. Rulers of many world nations wrote to the Maharaja asking after his welfare.

The message, in short, was clear. No force could now stop our country's march towards independence. Only Nehru's voice remained unchanged. No one would be made to join the Indian Union by force, but no ruler had the right to stand in the way of the people if they desired to join the new India. The Indian government would not stand aside and watch this happen, he repeated.

On 28 July, Diwanji left the hospital. That same night, the government released a document with Varghese's admission of guilt. He claimed that it was the statements made by Gandhi and Nehru against Thiruvithamkoor's independence and the anxiety that it would not be possible to spread the religion of Christianity in a free Thiruvithamkoor that drove him to taking such an action. In committing this crime, he was assisted by the State Congress and the communists, he declared. The document contained details: That it was N. Sreekantan Nair who had, with help from some others in Tamil Nadu, organized the funds and the weapon; that his accomplice, Basheer, seemed, in the few days Varghese had known him, to be a Muslim who harboured a deep resentment against the idea that Thiruvithamkoor would continue to be a Hindurashtram; that the man who helped them in Thiruvananthapuram and brought them to the venue of the assassination attempt was a State Congress man named Bhasi, and that this man, whom he knew only by sight, was a close associate of Kumbalath Shanku Pillai, a leader of the State Congress.

Several arrests were made that night, including State Congress and Catholic Congress leaders T.M. Varghese, Pattom Thanu Pillai, C. Keshavan, Akkamma Cherian and P.T. Chacko, and the leader of the Nair Service Society, Mannath Padmanabhan. Kumbalath Shanku Pillai and Ponnara Sreedhar went underground. The newspapers on 29 July printed photographs of N. Sreekantan Nair, Janardhana Kuruppu and Muhammad Basheer. These were wanted criminals, it was reported, and even ordinary citizens had the right, and indeed the duty, to apprehend them, dead or alive. Since no photograph or permanent address of the remaining criminal Bhasi was available, all known details were printed: age, around thirty; skin colour, dark; hair, curly; physique, stout; height, around six feet.

I was preparing a list of second-tier leaders of the State Congress when I came across this news item. 'Havoo, good! That doesn't sound anything like me,' I said to myself, getting up to look at my face in the mirror.

On 28 July, with his face still patched up, Diwanji had called a press conference. The attempt on the Maharaja's life was done with the full knowledge of the Indian National Congress, he'd said, although he did not think Gandhi was party to it. British India and Kochi allowed enemies of Thiruvithamkoor to come and go as they pleased, and our country was paying the price. He had blamed the king of Kochi by name, accused him of relinquishing his country to the Congress in the name of Aikyakeralam, a united Kerala, and giving the dissidents of Thiruvithamkoor a safe haven.

In the following days, widespread raids took place in many parts of Kochi and in Malabar which was part of the Madras Province. Kochi banned all activities of the Thiruvithamkoor State Congress. Several activists of the State Congress and the Communist Party were arrested.

In between all these hectic happenings, two people were murdered. One death went unnoticed by most people, and the other gifted the renegades of our country a martyr.

The first was the death of Bhayankarachari. The police surrounded his house, and he fired at them with a local-made handgun and was killed within minutes. *The Indian Express,* a newspaper published from Madras, printed a short news item about the incident. It described him as a member of the Kallar community, a lower-caste people who had made banditry their traditional work. The kingly dynasty, Thondaiman, that had, a very long time ago, ruled Pudukkottai, was of this caste. Having lost its kingdom to the British, it had turned to thieving. The man who ended its reign of terror in Thanjavur was the deputy collector Ramaswami Iyer – our Diwanji's grandfather. The newspaper reported that Bhayankarachari's grandfather, Anakkudi Arunachalam, had tried to murder the deputy collector.

The other death was that of Sreekantan Nair. He was arrested in Thrissur along with Mathai Manjooran. Kochi police held on to Manjooran who was a citizen of their country, and took Sreekantan Nair to Aroor at the border and handed him over into the custody of the Thiruvithamkoor police. He was being transported to Thiruvananthapuram under the strictest security when, as they reached Thankikkavala near Vayalar, Nair declared that it was the perfect place for him to die and attacked the police. He was, of course, killed. Cremating his body right there instead of releasing it to his family turned into a huge controversy. How could a man in handcuffs launch an attack on armed police, asked the Congress. They accused the police of mercilessly torturing him until he died. Nehru declared that Thiruvithamkoor was turning into a field of death for political activists. Insinuating that there was something mysterious about the effort to assassinate the Maharaja, he demanded an independent inquiry into the matter. Unrest erupted in Kollam and in parts of Karunagappally and Alappuzha. The people of Thangassery came out on to the streets declaring that they did not want to be part of Thiruvithamkoor and wanted to join the Indian Union. The police fired at them, killing two.

The Hindu Mahasabha declared 5th August as 'Thiruvithamkoor Day' and called for it to be celebrated all across India. In Calcutta, large numbers of Hindu refugees from East Bengal took part in a demonstration led by Shyama Prasad Mukherjee. Under government directive, meetings took place everywhere in our country, and there were large processions organized by the Rajabhakta Sangham in Alappuzha, Kollam, Thiruvananthapuram, Kottayam, Thakkalai and Nagercoil. Still, in India the news was that Thiruvithamkoor was slipping into civil war. V.P. Menon, a confidant of Sardar Patel, tried to organize a meeting with Diwanji, who flatly refused saying that it would be considered if and when the Congress stopped their malicious attacks. In a letter to the Maharaja, Gandhi wrote that he considered Thiruvithamkoor to be his country too, and that he hoped the diwan and the Maharaja would base any decisions about its future on the welfare of its people.

Then, on 6 August, Lord Mountbatten, the last viceroy of British India, invited Jawaharlal Nehru, the interim prime minister of India, and the diwan of Thiruvithamkoor, Sir C.P. Ramaswami Iyer to a meeting.

The crowd that assembled at the airport to see Diwanji off was unlike any the capital city had ever seen. Even Amma Maharani was present, breaking all protocol. A group of Catholic bishops and priests arrived, garlands in hand, but the crowd ran them off booing and throwing stones. Before he set out for Delhi, Diwanji released a statement addressing the country. 'I'm sixty-seven years old, an age at which freedom is immaterial to me personally,' he said in the statement. 'But my people, the people of Thiruvithamkoor, need their independence. This country belongs to Sree Padmanabhaswamy. Neither I nor the Maharaja have the right to give it away. This will be my last trip to Delhi. I will either spend the rest of my days there in a jail cell, or come back holding the sovereign flag of Thiruvithamkoor aloft.'

On the twelfth, I went to Madras via Chenkotta and on to Dindigul and then, in a roundabout way, reached Palakkad, tired and dishevelled. I needed to find out the current state of play, so I went to the Congress office in town and introduced myself as Bhaskaran, a State Congress activist from Thiruvithamkoor. Four or five people were in the office, getting ready to celebrate the imminent independence of India, but they seemed disheartened. An agreement had been reached in Delhi and signed by Mountbatten, Nehru and Diwanji, which meant that the Congress would finally have to accept the sovereignty of Thiruvithamkoor, at least for the time being. By mid-August, along with India, Pakistan and Hyderabad, Thiruvithamkoor would become a free, independent nation. The railway and the postal services would continue to be India's responsibility. Nehru tried to insist that Thiruvithamkoor should not have the right to make decisions on foreign affairs and defence, but he was thwarted. Thiruvithamkoor was to have its own flag and national anthem. It would not send representatives to the committee that would prepare the Indian constitution. However, when the constitution was prepared, there would be a public consultation, supervised by the United Nations or another mutually agreed entity, to determine people's views. Only then would a final verdict be passed on whether or not Thiruvithamkoor would join the Indian Union. In return, our government would allow free and unencumbered political activity until then and release all political prisoners who were not directly involved in violence. India was forbidden from stopping the free flow of goods and materials to Thiruvithamkoor from other countries, and Thiruvithamkoor would have the right to use the seaport at Kochi which was part of India.

The men at the office invited me to spend the night there, but I refused saying that I had to try and find my friends who had all scattered. They gave me some money and sent me on my way.

Our agreement was that, after Mani completed his mission, we would regroup at the home of the old king of Kollankode which was in Palakkad town. Its current occupant was a man named Ravi Menon who held a deep and long-standing enmity with Sir C.P. He was somewhat distant with me, suspecting, perhaps, that I was a secret agent. I told him I had nowhere to go, so he opened up one of the rooms and allowed me to stay there. That night, he went away somewhere, returning just before the sun rose. He then took me to a place called Ilappulli. I arrived there to find Basheer waiting for me. Menon, ever loyal, had walked all this way and back the previous night to ensure that I was trustworthy before bringing me to Basheer.

As soon as he saw me, Basheer ran to me and embraced me, planted kisses on my eyes and my forehead. He was deeply sad that things had not gone according to plan and, in fact, had the opposite effect. But when he heard that the police had taken over his house and evicted his umma and his brothers, his sorrow turned into anger.

'What happened to Mani?' I asked.

'They must have killed him, what else?' Basheer said. 'Cut him to pieces.'

Mani would not have told them anything, this much Basheer was certain. Otherwise, they would have been at Menon's house by now.

'And now they'll be playing with that little snippet of a man,' Basheer said, referring to Varghese. 'All of us warned Sreekantan chettan that he was not up to the task.'

Basheer had his own suspicions about Varghese's arrest. C.P.'s CIDs were everywhere, after all.

'He must have been caught immediately after we left the lodge. In one of those routine raids,' I said. 'And no doubt beaten to make him talk.'

Basheer did not buy my explanation. No one could have planned such an elaborate incident as what took place at the concert in such a short period of time. Then he turned his suspicion on me. I had already served a prison sentence, so how come the police were not able to find any information on me – no photo, no address?

'Maybe they didn't connect that Bhasi to this Bhasi?' I said. 'Besides, Varghese didn't know me all that well, did he?'

'That's good then, right?'

All that day we talked. Mostly about Sreekantan Nair who, we agreed, was one of a kind as a leader. Basheer declared that he would avenge the death of Sreekantan chettan, just as Bhagat Singh had vowed to avenge the death of Lala Lajpat Rai. I recalled what P.T. Punnoose had said to me when we were in prison. Basheer was, like Gandhi and Subhas Chandra Bose and other men like them, single-minded. It was impossible to predict what would happen if he set his mind to something.

'I'm going back to my country,' I said. 'I'll continue our work there. Let them kill me if they want.'

That night, we lay on our backs in the field outside the house, staring at the stars in the night sky above us. I remarked that if we considered what happened up there, everything down here would seem insignificant. Basheer did not seem to hear me. 'Tell me another story,' I said, 'like "The Love Letter" or "The Walls".' He suggested we try a round of gusthi instead. Who knew when we would meet again ... Surrounded by bundles of threshed paddy straw arranged like the crowns of so many kings, we stood facing each other, our arms locked. The dark of the night and the light of the moon jostled us like the spectators in Muhamma all that time ago, moths and other creatures of the night flapping, screeching, egging us on. I saw him smile for the first time since we had met.

Later, as I got ready to leave, thinking that it would help me complete my mission, I asked him, 'Ashaaney, why don't we go back home together?'

'If I ever go back there, it will be under one of two circumstances,' Basheer said, stroking his head that seemed to have become balder. 'Either I'll be witnessing the people chasing the Maharaja and the diwan out of the country. Or I'll be leading a very large army.'

As he spoke, I saw all the madness that Vallappuzha Vaidyan had leached out of him with oils and kashayams and tonics and nasyams sneak back into him. I fingered the weapon I had kept hidden on my person. Why didn't I use it against him? Fearfully, I looked around me at the darkness, the sky that made me confused about time and place, the haystacks and shadows closing in surreptitiously. Was madness contagious? With increasing anxiety, I looked at the man lying next to me on the ground.

The day after I left – two days before our great nation of Thiruvithamkoor attained full independence – the police discovered the old raja's house in Kollankode and the house in Ilappulli. But, by then, Basheer had disappeared. Still, for a long time after, the Congress folk in Palakkad maintained that Basheer and Ravi Menon had been caught by the police.

PART II

I

Many were the opinions among astrologers, Vedic pandits and esteemed officials about what the first course of action of Thiruvithamkoor should be when it gained full independence on 17 August 1947. The final decision, arrived at after much debate, was this: The members of the royal family, together with their entourage, would visit the important temples in the country, including Suchindram, Ambalapuzha, Ettumanoor and Vaikom. They would set out without delay. But there was another matter to be taken care of before this, about which Diwanji had no doubts. The Maharaja must sign the death warrant of Varghese. The decision and its implementation had to be under the utmost secrecy. The political prisoners who had been released had submitted that Varghese must be given a fair trial. There was also news that his family members had petitioned the governor general of independent India, Lord Mountbatten, that they be allowed to visit him. Mountbatten was already upset and angry that Thiruvithamkoor had, against his expectations, decided to remain independent. So, the Congress hoped he would decree that Varghese be released to the custody of his country to stand trial according to their laws. A sovereign Thiruvithamkoor was not obliged to obey him, but it would be foolish to annoy the British at this time. So, the execution had to be kept under wraps. It would have the benefit of appeasing the patriots who were most aggrieved by the assassination attempt.

Because of this need for secrecy, Varghese was not informed of his punishment by death, nor given the opportunity of receiving the last sacrament from a priest. The usual preparations – testing the rope for the hanging, trialling the procedure – were also done away with. Not all prison staff was trustworthy. If the prisoners got wind, it would soon be out of hand.

Soon after midnight, I arrived at the hangman's house in a car. Leaving a lamp burning on the veranda, he and his wife were waiting inside the house in the dark. A thousand insects fluttered around the flame of the lamp. I was irritated. He, too, had been told not to give any indication to anyone about what was happening. What else would people think if they saw a light in the hangman's house at an odd time of night? Sticking a large piece of tobacco in his mouth, the hangman came out carrying his sack bundle. Inside it was the rope that would form the noose. His family took great care of it, as though it was the holy jewellery of gods. The occasion demanded nothing other than gravity, but he gave me a friendly look. A starched white mundu, like one worn on special occasions, stood stiffly around his waist. His small face was clean-shaven. He was unremarkable in his physique, and yet, when he passed me, the shadow his small body left behind, oh, was terrible, becoming more and more monstrous as he walked further away.

He did not seem to like being in the car instead of his horse carriage, and sat in it with the discomfort of having deviated from his routine. The rituals surrounding his job were more important than the job itself. And they had started going awry since yesterday. Perhaps he was worried that, without these rituals, what he was about to do would amount to murder. I told him he could put his bundle in the back seat, but he sat rigidly next to me holding it tight in his lap. With the buzz of modernity instead of the hoofbeats of tradition, the country's official death carriage sped forward, eager to reach a living being whose time had come. As darkness controlled our movement through the tunnel it created, I felt I could play a game by increasing and decreasing the speed.

Stopping the car a little away from the jail, I told the hangman we would walk the rest of the way in order not to wake up the prisoners. This seemed to increase his discomfort. He did not want to be responsible for deaths that came surreptitiously. Subrahmanya Pillah was waiting for us at the wide elephant gate of the jail. Opening the wicket gate set into it, we entered, bowing our heads to the walls. Seeing us enter, two guards snapped to attention, but only Pillah accompanied us, leading us towards the gallows across the well-lit yard. As I followed him, I glanced at the block where the political prisoners had lived. I imagined that, from the dark shadows, they could see us illuminated. They might bide their time and pounce on us. The wall that separated the women's prison could not be seen. Would the rose garden Basheer had created still be there?

The hangman perked up as soon as we reached the building that housed the gallows. Inside it, he was the supreme power. His journeys to and from this place, as the rest of the world slept, were akin to the meanderings of the gods. Taking more time than was strictly needed, the hangman set about his task. He took the rope out of his sack, laid it on the floor and examined it over and over. Walked around the hanging post, looking at it as though he were seeing it for the first time. It had been built aeons ago, planted so deep into the floor that not even an elephant could move it, and yet he slapped it with his palm as though testing its strength. It seemed that he wanted to worry us, his helpers, a bit, make us consider the lateness of the hour. Or was he trying to make up for the time he should have spent here the previous day? At one point, for no reason whatsoever, he gestured to us with his eyes, asking us to step back a little. Subrahmanya Pillah was more than a little anxious. My worry was that, outside, time might be racing to bring light in quicker than usual. Finally, the rope was in place on the pole, its knots checked and rechecked. The hangman indicated that he was ready. Pillah opened the door and stuck his head out, giving an instruction without speaking, and came back. And now, it was the hangman who displayed signs of impatience. He twisted his mouth and yawned as though wondering why things were not proceeding as planned. Stroked his arms. I remembered the large gandharajan bush that had stood by the wall. I could smell its intense fragrance. The smell of some flowers is more detectable at a distance, not in close proximity. Flowers like champakam, screw pine, ilanji, pala and, of course, gandharajan.

The door opened and four people, their faces masked with cloth below the eyes, came in leading Varghese. He looked like he had been yanked out of bed and brought here. Frizzy hair lay on his forehead as though he were a child. Sleep puddled between his eyes and cheeks. Having been denied baths, two lines of dirt ringed his neck. He was frailer than he had been when I had seen him in Thrissur with Sreekantan Nair that first time, and at the GBR Boarding House. His already thin body had emaciated further and caved in at the middle. Arms elongated with the loss of weight were held on either side by the men. Entering the bright room from the darkness outside, he stood blinking for a moment. All of us inhaled the fragrance of the last flower that was meant only for him. When his eyes settled on me, the expression on his face changed to one of hope, of seeing someone who might be able to save him. He must have thought that he was still sleeping and caught in a dream. He kept glancing at me. I thought he even tried to smile, even after seeing, quite clearly, the hangman's rope with the noose at its end. His expression now was one of puzzlement. Why was he here? Who was going to be hanged? Pillah muttered something and then began to read out the Maharaja's order in a low voice. Even he himself could not hear it.

The hangman stepped forward and began to pull the black hood over Varghese's head.

Suddenly, one of the big men holding Varghese grabbed the hangman by his neck and pushed him away. Another man hit Varghese's stomach with his fist. As Varghese crumpled to the floor, the four men kicked him, breaking his limbs and his ribcage. Rained blows on his head. Twisted his neck. Broke his kneecaps. Crushed his feet. All this, enough to make a feeble creature entirely motionless.

Three of the men picked Varghese up and hung his body from the noose. Blood flowed from his eyes, mouth, ears. As soon as he was in the noose, the three men stepped back, and the fourth pulled the lever. It was clear that they would not have been able to do all this so well without having choreographed it and practised it earlier. The rope stiffened but did not move. Varghese was already dead. In the three or four moments when the sound of the dropped plank echoed through the jail, my attention was on the hangman. In the darkness of the shadow of a small pillar, he stood like a man who was not there. Suddenly, noises began to rise from the cells, the whole jail waking up. Prisoners could hear and identify the sound of the dropped plank of the gallows even in their deepest sleep. The hum of their disquiet would have travelled across the wall into the women's prison too.

Finishing up the rest of our task, as we stepped out, we could hear the isolated slogans rising from the cells. The prisoners had guessed what had happened.

'Martyrs zindabad...'

'Comrade Varghese zindabad...'

I heard someone with the voice of Basheer who had been imprisoned in a treason case shouting.

'Zindabad, zindabad...'

The voice of Bhasi, his cellmate, returning the call.

On our return journey, the hangman was exhausted, his vainglory knocked out of him. He would have felt that he had been suddenly rendered insignificant. Utterly servile now, he kept glancing at me, began to speak and then stopped himself.

'Didn't take as long as we thought it would,' I said, driving the car through the night that seemed endless.

'Yes, only about an hour and a half, in all,' said the hangman.

After dropping the hangman at his house, I drove to the western part of Puthankotta, to the place where the city's garbage dump was located. By then, the men in the masks had brought Varghese's dead body there. They burned it, using petrol, sugar and other combustibles collected from the dump. I stood beside them and watched until the flames died down.

One of the men said, 'This was where the old Kalippankulam used to be.' He flicked debris off his body.

Uncomprehending, I looked at him.

Around two hundred and fifty years ago, there was a pond here, he explained. People would come to sit on its sandy beach and enjoy the breeze. Umayamma Rani, who became the regent queen after king Aditya Varma was fatally poisoned by his enemies, had lived around here for a while. Her five sons were heirs to the throne. And it was in this pond that they were drowned one night by those who did not want them to become kings. People became scared even to look at Kalippankulam – 'the pond where the children used to play' – and soon, they began to kill it by throwing their garbage into it.

'If you hurt innocents, you'll pay for it,' the man said as our wait for the flames to die down continued. 'There is, after all, someone called God. Those who did those terrible things. Their entire clan is gone now. Where their household used to be, there's a pond instead. Even their women and children were sold off at the port.'

'Can't say for sure that God will avenge such things,' I said. 'Sometimes things are avenged and so we remember them. There are plenty that are not.'

'No, no. God will demand answers. That's a fact.'

'Right, as if he has nothing else to do. Busy as he is looking after the whole universe, you think he has time to meddle in our piddly affairs? Plus, if you think about it another way, who is to say he is not making us do all these things?'

It was 6 a.m. by the time I was back in my room. At 9 a.m., the press release about Varghese's execution was read out over the radio. It went like this:

> *The man who was found guilty of the attempted assassination of the Maharaja, the crazed Christian fundamentalist Varghese, was executed this morning. The body was buried according to Christian customs. Even in the moments before his death, Varghese declared that he did not regret his actions. His dream, he said, was to turn Thiruvithamkoor into a Christian nation after it joined the Indian Union. As he was brought to the gallows, however, he acted like a coward.*

In the afternoon, hearing a commotion outside, I cracked my window open. A procession of the Rajabhakta Sangham was passing by, celebrating the execution. They had captured an old Christian fisherman and were making him walk at the head of the procession, carrying a wooden crucifix.

2

If Independence Day and the days that followed were marked by revolts and fleeing in India and Pakistan, in our country they were days of joy and expectation. Saffron flags imprinted with the sinistral conch fluttered in the breeze everywhere. Schools took out processions singing the anthem 'Vancheeshamangalam' and distributed packets of sweetened aval to the students. Temples had poojas and special offerings in the names of the Maharaja and Diwanji. A rally organized by the Rajabhakta Sangham started at the northernmost border of our country in Paravoor and walked to the southernmost tip at the Cape of Kanyakumari, singing patriotic songs all along the way. Members of the royal family, after worshipping at the temples of Suchindram and Thiruvattar, stayed on to watch the magnificent fireworks display at the place where the three oceans met.

Gaining independence brought changes even in those who were, until then, involved in anti-national activities. Mannath Padmanabhan, the leader of the Nair Service Society, suddenly declared that the Christians had hoped to unleash terrible violence in the country, had they been successful in their attempt to assassinate the Maharaja. The NSS, he said, had always argued for independence, but under royal rule. If Christians and Muslims were to ascend to power through a general election, it would be detrimental to the smooth running of Thiruvithamkoor's ancient and important temples. The Nair community had, for centuries, served this Vanchirajyam, our Thiruvithamkoor, as faithful citizens and as its soldiers. This community, protectors of Hindu customs and its temples, had stood with the government throughout the struggles around the Nivarthana Samaram, the Utharavada Bharanam and the Education Bill. The day after he was released from prison, Mannath led a procession to C.P. Sathram in Thampanoor, the members swearing to replace the statue of Diwanji that anti-nationals had destroyed in the exact same place it had stood.

Traitors and communists will have no place in the SNDP, declared the Ezhava community organization's leader R. Shankar. It would be best if the likes of C. Keshavan and K. Balakrishnan left of their own accord, he said. The country was ruled by His Golden Majesty, the benevolent Maharaja who assured the social upliftment of the Ezhavas through temple entry and establishing educational institutions. In return, members of the community were ready to lay down their lives in service of the country. Meanwhile, messages from Catholic bishops were read out at Sunday service in churches, proclaiming that Christians were never against the great country of Thiruvithamkoor or the royal family. The maharajas of the country were known to have shown kindness to Christ's faithful, right from the time of Thomasleeha, St Thomas the Apostle. It was on land donated by them that the country's churches and schools were built. We protest, in the strongest possible terms, the crime against the Maharaja perpetrated by the foreigner bearing a Christian name, they declared. Those who were not faithful to the king and to God could not call themselves Christians. The school that had been named in honour of Diwanji's sixtieth birthday had been renamed Thiruvananthapuram Bishop St Mary's School only because it was believed that the country would join India. In one night, it changed back into Sachivothama Shashtipoorthy Memorial School.

Of the political prisoners, the first to get out of prison was Pattom Thanu Pillai, the president of the State Congress. As soon as he was released, he went straight to Bhaktivilasam in a car and had an hour-long meeting with Diwanji. A press conference followed, in which he declared that he was using his prerogative as the president to dissolve the Thiruvithamkoor State Congress. He was never against royal rule or an independent Thiruvithamkoor, he claimed; all he had always demanded, still believed in, was Utharavada Bharanam – a responsible government under the rule of the Maharaja. But Nehru, Patel and the communists were hell-bent on destroying this country, and even Gandhi was under their influence. The revolts that took place recently in Punnapra and Cherthala were communist plots aimed at creating unrest in our country, and it was only Diwanji's clever, timely leadership that had saved it. There was a faction within the State Congress leadership that supported the communists, and they, he accused, had suppressed an inquiry report that detailed what had really happened in the Alappuzha revolts.

The following day, in the mega assembly that took place in Shankumukham, Pattom Thanu Pillai and his followers joined the Thiruvithamkoor National Congress. Kondoor Krishna Pillai stood down to allow Thanu Pillai to take over as its new president.

3

Events surge like floodwater at every historical juncture, making it difficult to account for them in a systematic manner later. Also, looking back after so much time has passed, it becomes clear that most people won't even remember much of what would have seemed highly significant at the time. So, it is perhaps better to provide a chronological description of all the things that happened, and their consequences, in the days after Thiruvithamkoor took back its sovereignty.

20 August 1947

Political prisoners were released, including prominent figures such as T.M. Varghese, C. Keshavan, Paravoor T.K. Narayanapillah, A.J. John, A.P. Udayabhanu and Annie Mascarene. As there was concern that their release might instigate unrest, and that patriots, still upset by their actions, would threaten their safety, the government arranged vehicles to take them directly to their homes at different times. Still, there were some minor skirmishes in the north of the country following the news of Narayanapillah's release.

The electric fence at the border between our country and India was not yet in place. All that marked the border were some stones placed at important points, with 'ko' for Kochi written on one side and 'thi' for Thiruvithamkoor on the other. And so they became 'kothikkallu', or kothi stones, in common parlance. Only a few roads and the main crossings had police toll posts. Like birds and four-legged beasts, humans went back and forth across the border as they pleased, had relationships with people on the other side, got married. Lands belonging to those who lived close to the border traversed the boundary line. Some had houses sitting on top of this invisible line. They cooked their kanji in kitchens in India and ate it sitting on verandas in our great Vanchirajyam, and when they finished, they crossed back into India, into their bedrooms to have sex with their partners. The vayattattis who delivered their babies went back and forth across the border, lighting their way with palm-leaf torches, and the babies came into this world belonging to both countries. For a long while after independence, people around these areas were unsure of their citizenship. When the Mysore rulers Hyder Ali and Tipu Sultan had advanced on our country, we had put up a great resistance, and as a result, we had territory that spread into the north of Old Kochi. So, if someone from, say, Thrippunithura or Ernakulam wanted to go to parts of Kochi beyond Angamaly, they would have to cross over to our country and back again. This meant that, after independence, a not inconsiderable chunk of India, including Munambam, Nayarambalam, Kochi and Ernakulam, protruded into our country. Products and merchandise from the Kochi seaport, and essential goods into Kochi from other parts of India, could only be transported through what was essentially Thiruvithamkoor. A straightforward border between two sovereign countries was difficult to establish, so imagine what it was like between Thiruvithamkoor and India. It was in 1729–1798, during the reigns of the maharajas Marthanda Varma and Karthika Thirunal, that the current borders of modern Thiruvithamkoor were shaped. I have heard that the diwans at the time, Ramayyan Dalawa and Raja Kesavadas, had ambitions of subjugating the kingdom of Kochi and redefining the borders. Had they been successful, the history of our country would have taken a different course. Well, anyway, I mention this only to describe the confusing political situation that followed independence.

That evening, a prison services vehicle took T.K. Narayanapillah to Paravoor, but he refused to take a single step and sat firmly on the road, accusing the police of trying to exile him to India. The police tried to explain to him that, in order to take him to his house, they would have to walk through some properties that were within Indian borders and back out into Thiruvithamkoor. He did not believe them. So, what ensued was a tug-of-war between Narayanapillah and the police, right there in front of the kothikkallu that marked the border at that usually deserted place. Pillah tried with all his might not to step over the border of his country while the police tried their best to pull him across. Soon, there were spectators, locals who had no idea what the altercation was about. Looking for better spots to watch the ensuing drama, they walked back and forth over the imaginary line at the border, some even treating it like a game of kilithattu where the player had to advance across rows without stepping on the lines or getting caught by the players of the opposing team guarding the rows. They were familiar with Narayanapillah – he was from a respected family – so it was not long before they took his side. Besides, as this was one of the last areas to be annexed to our country, and as they were quite used to interacting with citizens of another country, these locals, northerners, were, compared to the people in the south, somewhat slack in patriotic fervour. The police, in the end, had to leave Narayanapillah be and return. Meanwhile, events were brewing and led to violence that evening and the following morning all across Paravoor.

Similar problems unfolded in Kanjirappally on the following Sunday. The police had, in great secrecy, under the cover of darkness and isolation at midnight, taken Akkamma Cherian and her sister Rosamma to their house, and had tasked four plainclothes policemen to watch them. But the very next day, Akkamma gave them the slip, climbed up on a chumaduthangi – a shoulder-high platform built by the roadside for people who carry heavy weights to rest their loads – and addressed her countryfolk as they returned home after the morning Qurbana at the church. She told them, in the loudest voice she could manage, that the diwan Sir C.P. had lied to Nehru and Mountbatten about releasing political prisoners, and that they, including herself, were in fact under house arrest.

'Good people of the State Congress, communists, God-fearing folks, people of all castes and religions, please know that what we have here is a government that says one thing and does another,' Akkamma Cherian said, addressing the passers-by. 'It's been many days since India achieved freedom, but our country is still in chains. We are being taught lessons in patriotism by a Tamizhan who is not our countryman. If we disobey this foreigner, we are charged with anti-nationalism. Have you ever heard such foolishness? Sir C.P. is exactly like that man over there in Pakistan, Muhammad Ali Jinnah; they are both men instrumental in partitioning our country. He has Jinnah at his left hand and Savarkar at his right. Make no mistake, if we don't act now, it will be too late, and it is our children who will suffer the consequences, much more than what we've suffered so far.'

According to police reports, even as Akkamma Cherian spoke, over a thousand people, including women, assembled at the spot. Roused into violence by her words, and led by a man named Kochuthomman, they beat up and chased away the mufti policemen guarding her house. She was immediately charged with treason and instigating violence. The police who came to arrest her the next day did not face much opposition, but things got out of hand soon enough because of a statement made, while she was being escorted into the police vehicle, by the police inspector Achyuthan Pillah.

'We all know, don't we, why people gather below when a woman hitches up her sari and climbs on to a stone.'

Pillah said this almost like a victory statement, just as Akkamma had come out of the house voluntarily and was pacifying her followers who were restless about her re-arrest. He would have, in all honesty, regretted the words even as they came out of his mouth. But uttered words are like chucked stones, impossible to retract, and even before the wheels of the police jeep began to roll, the words were carried away in all directions. Crowds of protesters arrived from Kanjirappally, Changanassery and Kottayam, and clashed with the police. The story, by the time it reached Meenachil, had changed, and it was now said that Akkamma had been forcefully undressed and paraded naked down the streets. Huge protests with crowds of people, including women dressed in the traditional Christian attire of chatta and mundu, took place in Pala, Bharananganam and Ettumanoor. Two village offices were destroyed. Police rule was declared the very next day, but it had little impact. The unrest grew when the police action at a meeting in Pavithranam ended in the death of a thirteen-year-old child. Churches across the area were raided by the police, and two priests were arrested, accused of speaking in a threatening manner. Things started cooling down only after the bishop of Changanassery called for peace and visited the area with the tehsildar. The government closed the churches in the Pala area for a period of one month.

22 August

Barrister A.K. Pillah was appointed as Thiruvithamkoor's representative to the United Nations General Assembly, and the former inspector general Kareem as our ambassador to Pakistan. Gandhi kept his cool and remained silent, but Nehru responded angrily to these developments. Thiruvithamkoor, as was made clear in the agreement between the countries, was not fully sovereign, he declared, and it was duty-bound to join the Indian Union when the writing of the constitution was completed. Diwanji scoffed and replied that he had no intention of engaging with someone who had not bothered to read and understand the terms of the agreement to which he was a signatory. Thiruvithamkoor and its people owed nothing to anyone. He could understand, Diwanji added, the psychological issues an inexperienced person would have to endure when ruling a country dealing with civil strife and besieged by refugees.

The appointment of A.K. Pillah, a former Congress man and the author of the movement's history, was helpful in establishing the image of our country internationally. He was the first of the representatives of the countries that had attained independence from the British to speak at the United Nations General Assembly. In his first speech, he sought to focus on the remarkable specificities of Thiruvithamkoor, a tiny nation in South Asia, while discussing the problems common to all countries that had become free of colonial rule following the World War. The biggest challenges these countries faced were civil strife and an atmosphere of mutual distrust. The idea of a nation state didn't take root easily in communities not used to the idea of democracy. Power was going into the hands of those who did not welcome the changing world order. Thiruvithamkoor had played a small but crucial role in bringing down fascist forces in the World War. It had unequivocally supported the Allies while those who currently ruled the country next door were busy calling 'Quit India' and attacking Britain. Remember, he appealed, referring to Subhas Chandra Bose, that a former president of the Congress had even led an armed group that had sided with Japan and the Axis powers and fought against the Allied forces. The United Nations was born out of the success of the Allies, and so too, as an organization, it had the responsibility to protect Thiruvithamkoor from its neighbour's desire to expand its territory.

Meanwhile, in Pakistan, Kareem Saab received a magnificent welcome. Representatives of the Malayalis from Malabar, a part of India, who lived in large numbers in Karachi, called on him. Speaking at the industrial fair, where he visited the Thiruvithamkoor pavilion, Kareem Saab reiterated that Pakistan and India would be on an equal footing in his country's dealings with them, and that he would not, in that moment, comment on the situation in Kashmir. The next day, two ships carrying a cargo of rice set out from the port of Karachi to our country. I think that it is the events that followed that should be set down in writing as the first decisive episode in our relationship with India, our neighbour.

The ships arrived in Kochi in less than two weeks, but then they were denied permission to enter the Kochi seaport and were made to linger in the open water for almost a month and a half. And in that period, in complete disregard for the agreement between the countries, the government of India delayed releasing the quota of rice promised to Thiruvithamkoor. Even the few wagonloads that were sent were blocked by Congress activists. Their aim was to create a situation of food scarcity that would upset the people and provoke their ire against their government. And in this, they were partially successful. But our government did not simply sit back and watch the crisis unfold. Diwanji wrote a strongly worded letter to India's governor general emphasizing our rights to the seaport at Kochi. When Kochi was attacked by the kingdom of Mysore, it was our armed forces and our financial resources that came to its aid. The great lake on which it was positioned, the Vembanad Kayal, was geographically three-quarters in Thiruvithamkoor, he stated, and in all this time, 80 per cent of exports that went through the port belonged to our country. India responded to his letter claiming that it had not blocked anyone's food import intentionally, that the delay was natural given how busy the port was and because the ships required additional security checks as they were from Pakistan.

A.K. Pillah wrote to the secretary general of the United Nations. Blocking food imports was unheard of even in times of war, he noted, and it was a blatant act of disregard for international agreements and cooperation. British newspapers and *The Hindu* published reports about the incident. Then came a proclamation from Gandhi that the people of Thiruvithamkoor were part of India and that he would also go hungry as long as they were deprived of food. The next day, the ships were given permission to dock, and two trainloads of rice reached Aluva. In what could only be described as bizarre behaviour, the State Congress (the ban on the party had recently been revoked) used the occasion to heap praise on Gandhi and to argue that their bias towards India was justified. They marched all across the country, shouting 'Gandhiji ki jai'. People began to refer to the rice that became available in shops at a reduced price as 'Gandhi rice'. All in all, a weird state of affairs, like the lion caged in the zoo proclaiming its love for the man who fed it meat.

Still, this unfortunate turn of events paved the way for something good. Realizing the importance of agriculture, the government began making plans to develop Kuttanad and Nanjinad, our most important paddy-growing areas. We began modernizing agriculture way before India had even thought about their acclaimed Green Revolution. New seed stocks were brought in from Southeast Asia, and the first tractor arrived by the end of 1948. More cultivable fields were built, dredging up land from the marshes of Kuttanad. The government also took decisive steps to develop the ports at Alappuzha and Poonthura. It would come to be that the single most important factor that led to Poonthura becoming the busiest port in all of Asia was India's misguided attempt to starve our country.

30 August

Elections to the Sree Moolam Popular Assembly were declared. A third of the members would be nominated by the Maharaja. The others would be elected by the only people with voting rights – those who paid land taxes. Questions were asked about universal adult suffrage, but the government fielded these by saying that Thiruvithamkoor had not yet reached the required readiness. The government depended on taxes for revenue and the right to choose representatives who would be involved in making governmental decisions lay with those who paid the taxes. This did not mean that the government was against democracy. Indeed, our aim was to bring everyone in the country to a level of prosperity that would see them all contribute to the running of the country as taxpaying citizens.

As expected, the State Congress did not participate in the election. It was their contention that the election at this time was unnecessary and malicious, when in a few years there would be a people's vote to ascertain the country's wishes in relation to joining the Indian Union. Besides, the entire state machinery was being used to ensure that those who supported the government would be elected. Just look at how universal suffrage was sidelined, they argued. The Nair Service Society welcomed the government's decision. The SNDP complained that restricting voting rights only to those who paid taxes would affect their representation in the assembly, and yet it hoped to deal with the shortcoming in the nomination of its candidates.

The elections took place two months later, and the majority of the seats, including in areas where voting took place, went to members of the Thiruvithamkoor National Congress and the Rajabhakta Sangham. A handful of seats in Kanyakumari went to members of the Tamil Nadu Congress. The government hailed the victory as a sign that the people of Thiruvithamkoor supported its sovereign status.

5 September

The national emblems of Thiruvithamkoor were declared. Mahakavi Ulloor S. Parameswara Iyer's poem 'Vancheeshamangalam' that hailed the lord of the great land of Vanchi would continue to be the national anthem. The saffron flag emblazoned with the sinistral conch would remain the national flag. The remaining emblems were to be as follows:

Bird: the krishnapparunthu, the favourite bird of Lord Vishnu, the brahminy kite with a collar of white around its neck
Animal: the holy cow
Tree: the arayaal, the sacred peepul
Flower: the kanikkonna, the tree that covers itself with showers of golden flowers at the beginning of summer
River: the Pamba, the longest river in our country

The day after these were officially advertised in the gazette, K. Balakrishnan came out with a parody statement that ridiculed the government. In it, he named more emblems:

National foreigner: Diwan Sir C.P. Ramaswami Iyer

National caste: Pattar (the local pejorative name for the Tamil Brahmin)
National slaves: the people of Thiruvithamkoor
National dress: the unwashed konakam, the long strip of cloth that Brahmins used to cover their privates
National opportunist: Pattom Thanu Pillai

K. Balakrishnan was immediately arrested and charged with treason. *Mathrubhumi*, a newspaper published in Malabar, was prohibited from being sold or brought into the country. All natural responses from the government of an independent nation, but the Congress, of course, saw it as yet another attempt to establish a Thiruvithamkoor nationalism even before there could be a people's vote to ascertain what they wanted. A protest march by the Aikyakerala Prasthanam, led by E.M. Sankaran Namboothiripad and Moidu Moulavi set out from Malabar, but the police stopped them at our borders and sent them right back.

The next edition of the Gazette published instructions for citizens on how to respect the national emblems. As it had been since time immemorial, the right to keep cows would continue to be restricted to the four savarna castes, from Brahmins to Sudras. Others outside these upper-caste groups – the avarnas – could keep cows with the permission of the savarna castes, but they would not be allowed to milk the cows. Also to continue was the ban on cow slaughter. Cows that died of natural causes were to be buried with dignity and respect. It has been noted that certain heinous castes were skinning these dead cows, using the hide for leatherwork and consuming the flesh. This practice was now banned. There were murmurs about the caste-based restrictions on keeping cows, but the government addressed them with great maturity. Rights accorded to special groups were signifiers of the diversity of our nation. Not everyone can have equal access to everything. Could Hindus claim to have equal rights to the appam and the veenju, the Holy Sacrament that the Christians have at the Qurbana in their churches? For Hindus, the cow was a holy animal. Claiming equal rights to it would be sacrilegious.

These decisions had repercussions in our neighbouring countries too. In India, sanyasis took to city streets demanding a ban on cow slaughter. Many of them openly praised the Maharaja. A group of them set up a camp in Delhi and lived in it for years. Witnessing the incident first hand, the English newspaper *The Guardian* reported it thus:

New Delhi, 30 September

The old Mughal city that we vacated only a month and a half ago after granting independence to India is now wholly unrecognizable. Walking around the city for a day and night, this reporter cannot help thinking that Churchill was right after all when he said that this country was not ready for democracy. All around are large groups of sanyasis, some clothed and others naked. 'Stop killing cows; kill Muslims,' shout some in loud voices. With the help of an interpreter, I spoke to several of them. Most of them had no idea why they had decided to set up camp here in the city. They had not even heard that we had been ruling their country for nearly two hundred years. Only one person told me about a southern Maharaja who had banned cow slaughter, and was living a healthy life at the age of a hundred and thirty because he drank cow urine every day. And yet, the sultans who ruled Delhi were busy eating the flesh of the holy cow, he told me. When I told him that there were no more sultans and that India was currently ruled by a Brahmin named Nehru and his group, he looked at me utterly surprised. He had not even heard the name 'India'. I walked on. All around me was human faeces as though someone had purposely strewn it around. These people have no aversion to their own waste, or the shit and urine of their animals, and will eat and sleep in the middle of it, and smoke ganja like there is no tomorrow. Winter had arrived early, and the fumes they exhaled hung in the city's atmosphere like low-flying clouds. I walked through it, witnessing magical sights whose veracity was difficult to judge. Perhaps because the ganja had affected their ability to tell time, the people I met generally claimed to be two hundred or even five hundred years old. And there were those who claimed not to have been born yet, and those who said this world was not the real world. I saw men walking around with heavy stones tied to their penises, and those who put their yoga skills to use and tried to drink milk with those organs. Having inadvertently inhaled those fumes for a while, I came to a realization. There was, in this country, no such thing called reality. Those who think there is such a thing are not equipped to live in this country. In fact, I suspect that, in the two hundred years we spent here, we were trapped. We might think we had ruled this place, but that, really, is only an illusion. We were here, that's all, and it is good that we have now escaped.

6 September

The Civil Protection Group has been formally instituted with the deputy superintendent of police Vaidyanatha Iyer, who had suppressed the communist revolt in Punnapra and Vayalar in Alappuzha, at its helm. In a press meeting held the next day, Vaidyanatha Iyer reiterated that the CPG, as the name indicated, was tasked with the protection of the country's civil society. To this end, it was necessary to gather intelligence from within and outside the country. People wrongly call this process 'the secret service'. But the only job of this department is to bring to the government's attention matters that are not immediately apparent that impact the security of this country. It is not, as some political troublemakers have insinuated yesterday, the reconstituting of the old five-rupee police. And it most definitely is not for meddling in political affairs. Governments come and go, but what is important is the indivisibility of the country. He did not address the question about the relevance of Thiruvithamkoor's indivisibility when a people's referendum to decide whether or not to join the Indian Union was imminent. Thiruvithamkoor was, and continues to be, the Cherasamrajyam, the empire of the great Cheras, that existed before the birth of Keralam. This is why the Maharaja is called Perumal, The Great One. It was, he said, only recently that other nations had been carved out of the subcontinent. The reporter who asked the question was arrested the next day for possession of indecent reading material.

10 September

The government announced that the traditional observance of Murajapam would be revived and conducted between the end of November and early January. Murajapam, a period of ritual chanting of the Vedas for the continued blessing of the country's deity, Sree Padmanabhaswamy, has been conducted once every six years ever since Maharaja Marthanda Varma began it at the time of the formation of modern Thiruvithamkoor. The last time this ceremony was conducted was in 1936. During British colonization, the viceroys who came and went tried to obstruct the practice, often citing financial difficulties, but the maharajas and the diwans always found ways to go ahead. Except in 1942 when all resources had to be set aside for the World War. And the country and the people suffered the consequences. Unrest and disarray like never before, that resulted in so many deaths. Atheism and heretic thoughts on the rise in society. Even an attempt on the Maharaja's life. The country itself was on the brink of being lost. The government's press release made it clear that as our land was just about recovering from these adversities and the people settling into a peaceful life, it would now turn its attention to the timely observance of Murajapam.

The next day, a circular was released detailing, in numbered sections, the roles and responsibilities of each government department in the proper organization of Murajapam. Usually, preparations for the next ceremony would begin as soon as the present one concluded. On this occasion, however, time was tight, so all involved were ordered to work on a war footing in the coming months. The finance department was tasked with releasing an annexure with details of the funds allocated for the ceremony. The most important task was gathering all the material resources necessary. Various departments, organizations and the citizenry were ordered to get to it immediately. Diwanji would see to the overall coordination while the tehsildars in each taluk would be responsible for local preparations.

Having deemed the situation an emergency, a halt was called to all work at the village office level so that the collection of food resources for Murajapam could begin. Special attention was needed to collect the mango, bitter gourd and long beans to be pickled in brine. Entire crops of paddy about to be harvested were to be bought with a fixed, average price. Individuals storing more grain and other food items than was absolutely necessary for personal use was deemed a criminal offence. The order also contained a list of almost two hundred and fifty items needed for the ceremony, including banana, ghee, sugar, areca nut, tobacco, lemon, mundus of high quality, cotton towels, straw mats, reed mats, earthenware pots, and so on. Targets to be met by village offices and higher offices would be released soon.

It was estimated that around five thousand Malayala Brahmins would attend the fifty-five-day-long event. One and a half lakh rupees was set aside for their travel expenses alone. A special envoy had been dispatched with a personal invitation from the Maharaja to the Azhvanchery Thamprakkal, the elder of the Brahmin family of Azhvanchery Mana, the recognized authority over all Namboothiri Brahmins. Invitations had also been dispatched to other dignitaries – Tharananellur Namboothiripad, Akavoor Namboothiripad, Thekkedathu Bhattathiri, the priests of Cherumukku, Panthal, Kaplingadu, Perumpadappu, Kaimukku and Thaikkad, and the scholars in Thirunavaya and Thrissur.

On the same day as the circular was released, a man named Sahodaran Ayyappan, a member of the Kochi legislative assembly, told the newspapers that what had been feared was already happening in Thiruvithamkoor. The centuries-old custom in princely states, of using the hard-earned resources of the oppressed castes to feed the Brahmins, was being institutionalized in the country which had always been at the forefront of these backward practices. This was a land where any idiot with a piece of thread worn over his left shoulder and under his right arm could live a happy, well-fed life without ever having to do a day's work. The king of Thiruvithamkoor was so enslaved to the idea of Brahminism that he was willing to squander the land's resources to feed not only Malayala Brahmins but the Namboothiris and Pattars of other lands too. He demanded to know why Nehru was not already sending his army to defend the ordinary people of this land.

11 September

The Thiruvithamkoor State Congress declared that the country was entering a dangerous phase. The government had, for aeons, wasted the financial resources it raised from its hard-working ordinary citizens. It would seem that it was set to continue on this path even after British rule had ended. The same government that accused India of not sending the quota of rice that was contractually agreed upon was confiscating the food produced by its toiling citizenry. A huge famine was on its way, they warned. Once Murajapam was over, the streets would be strewn with dead bodies. The State Congress appealed to the governor general and to the Indian government to intervene and stop an impending disaster.

A.K. Gopalan and P. Krishnapillah vowed that volunteers would be deployed at the borders to stop Brahmins from Kochi and Malabar from crossing over to Thiruvananthapuram to take part in Murajapam.

12 September

The Indian government was carefully watching the food scarcity in Thiruvithamkoor and the administration's responses to it, Nehru declared. The people of Thiruvithamkoor were citizens of India, he said, and India would do everything in its power to save them from starvation. But it also had a responsibility to ensure that any supplies sent across were used appropriately to stave off the hunger of the people. An armed incursion was not currently in consideration, Nehru said. After all, as was detailed in the existing agreement between the two countries, Thiruvithamkoor would soon be part of the Indian Union.

25 September

An order was passed prohibiting people of the lower castes from entering temples until Murajapam was over. A measure aimed only at the convenience of those who were taking part in the ceremony, the order clarified, and in no way a retraction of the world-famous 1936 Temple Entry Declaration. The government was, as ever, duty-bound to uplift the lower castes and to ensure that they had the right to enter and worship at temples.

1 October

The latest edition of the Hindi magazine *Kalyan*, published from Gorakhpur, came out with a picture of the Maharaja on its cover. Usually, the magazine had gods on its front covers. Its editor, the eminent Prakash Poddar, had also written a detailed essay about our country. Hindus were being slaughtered all across Bharat, he said in the essay, while Gandhi and Nehru were busy protecting Muslims. Sanatana Dharma, the very foundation of the Hindu way of life, was being abandoned. Its only hope was the great nation of Thiruvithamkoor, a nation that, by rights, belonged to Lord Mahavishnu in His avatar as Sree Padmanabhaswamy, and was being served by His faithful servant. The Congress and the Christians were doing their absolute best to destroy Thiruvithamkoor, Poddar insisted, and it was the sworn duty of every Hindu to protect it.

Kalyan was popular all across northern India. Its regular writers were those with a deep knowledge of the Vedas and the Upanishads. Even the illiterate bought the magazine for the beautiful pictures of gods it printed. It could, in fact, be argued that the images of their gods that Hindus had in their minds were created and nurtured by *Kalyan*. The support that the magazine and its editor Poddar extended to our country at this time was invaluable. Thiruvithamkoor became ensconced in the minds of Sanatanis all across Bharat as a holy land, their spiritual home. They accepted the photograph of the Maharaja on the magazine's front cover as another avatar of Bhagavan Mahavishnu the Protector. The walls of countless ashrams and houses across India were adorned with the cover, the Maharaja finding pride of place as one of the Dashavataram, the ten incarnations of Mahavishnu.

A month later, at the assembly of the Hindu Mahasabha in Shimoga, the organization's president Bhoopalam Chandrashekaraiah tabled a motion declaring that Thiruvithamkoor would henceforth be the sacred refuge of all Sanatani Hindus just as Palestine was for the Jews. Thiruvithamkoor was not to be made part of India until an undivided India, with the *Manusmriti* as its code of law, became a reality. In fact, it was not the governance of India that should spread to Thiruvithamkoor, but India that should accept Thiruvithamkoor governance.

2 October

Riots broke out in parts of our country that were within the borders of India, especially in Paravoor and Gothuruth. 2 October was Gandhi's birthday, and the police had stopped State Congress activists in Paravoor from organizing a celebration. Was there really any country in the world that allowed a public assembly for celebrating the birthday of the father of another nation? Still, the people got riled up, resorted to violence and attacked the checkposts. Unfortunately, there was not much of a police presence in the area on that day. Rioters set fire to our national flag, and by noon a large demonstration took place in Paravoor. They beat up some policemen and made them carry the Indian national flag and march at the head of the procession. Technically, the incident took place in our country, but it was instigated and supported by Congress workers from places around the area that were within Indian borders. And the Indian police, dressed as ordinary people, helped attack and subdue our police.

Then, in a meeting in a school ground, T.K. Narayanapillah and some other communists declared that Paravoor would henceforth be part of India and that no Thiruvithamkoor official would be allowed entry. Indian police, having blocked all our roads leading to Paravoor, began patrolling the area openly.

News about the developments in Paravoor led to riots in Gothuruth, an island with a dense population of Latin Christians. Both Thiruvithamkoor and the erstwhile kingdom of Kochi had claims to the land. But the locals assembled in the church and came out as one, pulled out the kothikkallu marking the borders and threw them in the river, and declared that they were now part of India. They barricaded the river with their boats, stopped the police boat that reached the area by nightfall and set it on fire. One policeman lost his life, while others swam away barely escaping with their lives. The Tamil Nadu State Congress organized meetings in Kanyakumari and Nagercoil which, thankfully, did not turn violent.

Diwanji was utterly outraged by these events in the north of the country. He shot off letters to Nehru and Mountbatten underlining Thiruvithamkoor's resolve to ensure its safety and security by any means necessary. G.P. Pillah, too, sent an urgent memo to Trygve Lie, the secretary general of the United Nations. Nehru's response was to insist that the Indian government had no involvement in the events that transpired in the places mentioned in the letter. He would not allow the Thiruvithamkoor police access to these places through Indian territory to suppress the people. These places, he insisted, were part of the old Kochi and so were now rightfully part of India. However, in reality, records dating back to the time of Raja Kesavadas, the diwan during the reign of Maharaja Karthika Thirunal Rama Varma, and Captain Eustachius de Lannoy prove that these lands belonged to Thiruvithamkoor as was agreed upon by both countries.

7 October

Akkamma Cherian, Annie Mascarene, T.M. Varghese and some others were rearrested. They were charged with treason because they had supported the violent events in the north of the country.

Writing in *Harijan*, Gandhi expressed his sorrow that the celebration of his birthday had led to violence in Thiruvithamkoor. He recalled the deep affection the people of Thiruvithamkoor had shown him every time he had visited, and said that he hoped to visit the land again soon.

10 October

The first group of refugees from the Madras Province – Tamil Brahmins including women and children – reached Thiruvithamkoor, travelling up the Aryankavu ghat roads.

In their submission to the Maharaja, the group said that, as Brahmins, they were no longer safe in their own country and were constantly subjected to attacks and indignities. Brahmin-haters had begun calling for Tamizhakam, the land of the Tamils, to become a separate, independent nation. If it were to happen, it would be a real threat to their lives and property. Already they were being told not to use Sanskrit mantras in temples and to use Tamil instead. Thiruvithamkoor had always welcomed Brahmins, and they, Tamil Brahmins, had been serving the country for generations. They appealed to the Maharaja that they be allowed to live here, embracing it as their mother country.

16 October

Great unrest unfolded in the city of Thiruvananthapuram and in coastal areas such as Poonthura. At the forefront of it, and instigating and taking part in violent altercations, were people of the Nadar, Ezhavar, Muslim and Christian fisherfolk communities. In Neyyattinkara and Kulathoor, large crowds faced off against the police. Ten people were killed in Beemapally and Valiathura when the police opened fire. An even larger crowd of demonstrators set out from Chala, setting ablaze shops and government offices along the way.

Subrahmanya Pillah, the old jail superintendent at the Poojappura Central Jail, had, by this time, retired from service, and was living in a big house near the fort in Virakupura. More recently, he had married two women, twins who were almost thirty years younger than him. The crowd pulled him and the twins out of the house and beat them to death.

It took four days to bring the situation under control. The State Congress said that the unrest was in response to the government's move to forcefully displace people of the lower castes from city precincts to make room for the Brahmins. Peaceable people have been forced to take to the streets in protest, they said. The government dismissed the accusation, swore that such an action had not even been contemplated. All they had done was to rehouse temporarily those living in the vicinity of the temple so that the guests arriving to participate in Murajapam would not be inconvenienced. The real problem, the government contended, was that organizations like the State Congress that had their loyalties aligned with the neighbouring country were engaged in misleading the people.

17 October

Twenty-five detainees, including K.C. George, T.V. Thomas, Niklaav, P.K. Padmanabhan and Kumaran Vakeel, broke out of prison. Having been jailed for their part in the Cherthala and Ambalapuzha riots, they were idling behind bars hoping that royal rule would soon end and that they would be freed. But recent events had disheartened them. They had even attempted to write to Nehru saying that they expected to be killed in prison. A man named Loovees Pramani, serving time for his part in the attack on the police station in Punnapra, had changed his allegiance while in jail and sided with the government. Some of the jailbreakers, already at odds with Loovees, got into a fight with him when they were out of their cells for their baths. Prison staff trying to break it up also got hurt in the process. The fight swiftly spread across the prison and became a riot, the guards, much fewer in number, unable to contain it or call the police for help. A large part of the police force was in any case unavailable, having already been deployed in Thiruvananthapuram to control the rioting there. By evening, the rioters had managed to break out of the prison. But, in the process, a young man named V.S. Achuthanandan was killed. He had fallen off while attempting to scale the high perimeter wall of the prison. However, the story that the rioters would tell, for years to come, was that he had been shot down by a guard.

18 October

In the night, a man named Chulli Chakrapani was killed in Punnapra. There was no doubt that the deed was done by the jailbreakers. It was known that during the Punnapra uprising Chakrapani had helped the police who had camped at the house of the State Congress leader Aplon Arouge.

Meanwhile, in Kodungallur, in a meeting that took place at the police station ground, a new organization called Aikyakeralam was formed. Kochi newspapers reported that over five thousand people attended this meeting. It was also here that Kumbalath Shanku Pillai and Ponnara Sridhar, two of the accused in the case of the attempted assassination of the Maharaja, were seen in public for the first time after that incident. The main organizers of the meeting were P.T. Chacko and K. Balakrishnan. Three of the jailbreakers – T.V. Thomas, Niklaav and P.K. Balakrishnan – were felicitated at the meeting. Its name would indicate that the objective of the organization was the formation of a united Kerala. In his speech, however, Chacko reiterated that Aikyakeralam had nothing to do with the Aikyakerala Prasthanam, the old movement for uniting Kerala, nor was it affiliated to the Thiruvithamkoor State Congress or to the Indian National Congress. This new Aikyakeralam had only one purpose, and that was to rescue Thiruvithamkoor from the tyranny of raja rule and diwan bureaucracy as soon as possible and make it part of the Indian Union. The entire Malayali community was behind it, he said, and despite differences of opinion, the Congress, the communists and the socialists would work together until this objective was fulfilled.

Kumbalath Shanku Pillai also made a speech that day and newspapers all over India printed it with great prominence. The attempt to assassinate the Maharaja was mere theatre, he said, a drama written and directed by the diwan. The country's government was killing innocents with no compunction. He contended that, like Varghese, Basheer had also been murdered. He implored the crowd, made them swear, that they would avenge, by whatever means at their disposal, including armed attacks, the killings of Sreekantan Nair, Varghese and V.S. Achuthanandan.

26 October

Aikyakeralam activists raised the Indian flag in Annamanada at the northern edge of Thiruvithamkoor. Surrounded as the place was by Indian territory, they did not face any opposition.

27 October

Aikyakeralam opened its first office – in the old Seethi Buildings in Ernakulam.

Azhvanchery Thamprakkal, who was on his way to Murajapam, was waylaid by a group of people and forced to go back.

28 October

Led by Mannanthala Karunakaran and Polycarp, Aikyakeralam opened another office in Thangassery in Kollam. Before independence, Thangassery was under direct British rule. But it was within Thiruvithamkoor territory. So, the opening of the office was taken to be an action intended to provoke. The very next day, some members of the Rajabhakta Sangham entered Thangassery and destroyed the office. They then proceeded to the Thangassery lighthouse, climbed to the top and hoisted the Thiruvithamkoor national flag. Violence broke out all along the seashore and a great many huts and boats were set on fire. The rioting then spread along the coast to Neendakara and Chavara.

30 October

Several organizations publicly expressed their support for the government. A united Keralam was not something that should be born out of a bloodbath, said Mannath Padmanabhan, the leader of the Nair Service Society. The same troublemakers behind the erstwhile Nivarthana Samaram, the abstention movement that had demanded governmental reform, were instigating the violence, he said. He warned that if anyone entertained the dream that the Maharaja could be shamed and made to run away, it would remain unfulfilled. The members of the Nair community would never allow it.

The bishop of Kollam announced that the Christians in Thiruvithamkoor were proud citizens of the country. It was despicable that poor fisherfolk were being attacked in retaliation for the deeds of others.

6 November

Kumbalath Shanku Pillai announced that Aikyakeralam was prepared to block Murajapam. Conducting Murajapam, which had to be postponed last time, at a time when the country was going through a crisis was not a sign of affirming faith and tradition. Instead, it was, he said, a strategic move to allow the Pattars – the Tamil Brahmins who had been coming into Thiruvithamkoor in large groups – to settle in the country.

7 November

Various Indian newspapers reported that Thiruvithamkoor was heading towards civil war. *The Times of India* reported that several armed groups had appeared within and around the country. Large groups of Brahmins from Tamil Nadu were going to Thiruvithamkoor, their arrival prompting an exodus of Christians across the border into Malabar. The policies that the government had formed after attaining independence gravely worried the minorities and the marginalized lower castes. The newspaper predicted an armed struggle, led by Aikyakeralam and mobilizing those who had become refugees in their own country, as well as revolts led by the communists. In southern Thiruvithamkoor, the Rajabhakta Sangham and a vigilante group, led by a goonda named Simson, who called themselves the Simson Pada – Simson's Army – was attacking the State Congress. The Indian government must study the situation carefully, concluded the newspaper, and get itself involved if necessary. There were indeed other concerns, such as Bhopal and Hyderabad, princely states yet to join the Indian Union, but the situation in Thiruvithamkoor was uniquely worrying.

8 November

Sardar Vallabhbhai Patel invited Diwanji for a discussion. The government declined.

9 November

Diwan Sir C.P. Ramaswami Iyer addressed the nation on the radio. These were the salient points in the hour-long speech he gave:

> *Thiruvithamkoor is standing firm on the terms agreed between India and itself, mediated by the British government before independence. This country is also willing to go ahead with the people's referendum as stipulated when the Constitution of India is charted. Until that happens, and until the will of the*

people indicates otherwise, Thiruvithamkoor will remain an independent, sovereign nation with a seat at the United Nations.

The behaviour of the Indian government, however, is in breach of the agreement. It is offering its support to those who are unleashing a campaign of armed revolt against the country. It is imperative that the culprits in the case of the attempted assassination of the Maharaja – Muhammad Basheer, Kumbalath Shanku Pillai, Ponnara Sridhar – are extradited into the custody of the Thiruvithamkoor police.

India is to cease its efforts to unlawfully grab parts of Thiruvithamkoor. The country's officials must be allowed into those parts it has already appropriated.

As it has become abundantly clear that those responsible for the violence within the country are in fact insurgents from the neighbouring country and their cronies, anyone wanting to travel into Thiruvithamkoor will now need to procure prior permission. Official procedures will be announced later.

Thiruvithamkoor is a country which keeps every one of its citizens safe. Do not listen to malicious rumours and feel pressured to leave the country.

The organization Aikyakeralam, which calls for an armed insurgency, is hitherto banned. The government is carefully observing whether the State Congress is collaborating with them in their activities.

A safe passage is to be prepared to transport goods and merchandise from the seaport in Kochi to various parts of the country. Smaller vessels will now dock in Alappuzha. Plans to develop the ports in Alappuzha and Poonthura are well under way with the support of America.

Murajapam, one of our important traditions, is something that the country cannot abandon. Still, deviating from previous plans, this year it will be conducted as a pared-back ritual without fanfare.

10 November

Heeding Aikyakeralam's call to protest against Diwanji's announcements, violence erupted across the country. A boatload of people, protesting specifically against the requirement for prior permission to enter the country, arrived in Aroor and destroyed the police checkpost. Large crowds ignored the law and broke through the borders at Aaruvamozhi, Chenkotta and Devikulam.

Karunanidhi, the leader of the Dravida Kazhagam, said that Thiruvithamkoor's status as an independent nation was indeed for the citizens of that country to decide. But, he insisted, the Tamil people of Peerumedu, Devikulam and southern Thiruvithamkoor must also have the right to self-determination.

11 November

A dead body, not too far gone, was found at the bottom of the Kaduvakkuzhi hill by the bank of the Muvattupuzhayaar. The police assumed that it was Basheer. His old friends, Muzhayan Nanu and Chathankari Manakkal Sankaran Namboothiripad, looked at the body and confirmed the identity. But his younger brother Aboobakker insisted that, although the bald pate and the thick lips looked similar, it was not Basheer.

I had to find out the truth. So, that evening, I got on a bus and went to Kaduvakkuzhi, Basheer's bhaavanadesham, the world he had created out of his imagination. He called it 'Sthalam' – the Place – in his stories.

A small crowd of people who lived in this bhaavanadesham, the Place, stood before the jaggery shop run by an owl-eyed man called Undakkannan Anthru. The dead body was respectfully laid out on the veranda of the shop. A few policemen, always found hanging around the Place, stood about smirking, chewing on roasted jackfruit seeds, pieces of dried coconut and jaggery. In the crowd were the two thieves named for their heists, Aanavaari 'Elephant Scoop' Raman Nair and Ponkurissu 'Gold Crucifix' Thoma; Mandan 'The Gormless' Mustapa; Veerapandya Pandaram, the only snake-charmer in the Place; the one-eyed gambler Ottakkannan Pokkar; Palunkan Kochukunju and his daughter Kochuthresya; the aforementioned Undakkannan Anthru; two other local mischiefs named Driver Pappunni and Thorappan 'Bandicoot' Avaraan; Kandamparayan, the chief divyan – divine being – of the Place; and Karumban 'The Darkie' Chennan. They argued with Muzhayan Nanu and Sankaran Namboothiripad, insisted that the corpse on the veranda was not Basheer, and got very cross with the policemen. Also at the scene were the snake-charmer Veerapandya Pandaram's cobra, three dead piglets that had belonged to Kariyil Pathrose Mappila, Ottakkannan Pokkar's daughter Sainaba's kitten, six black cats and six black roosters, and three owls. Two elephants, Kochuneelandan and Parukutty, who were at the riverbank, had stopped eating the palm leaves strewn in front of them and stood watching the goings-on.

'You seeing how he lies there? It's him, no doubt,' Muzhayan Nanu said, fondling the muzha, a large bulge, on his head. Everyone knew that Nanu was clever and that the extra brain that allowed him to be clever was housed in this bulge.

'Poda!' Raman Nair said, raising his hand as though he was about to strike Nanu. 'No way he's pissing off and dying like this. Isn't he the one to decide our fates? What are we to do if he's dead and all?'

Pushing through the throng of creatures and characters, I approached the corpse and looked at it carefully.

'And who's this now? Never seen him around here...' I could hear them whisper.

'Didn't he go on about a see-eye-dee that was after him? Must be him and all.'

I called forth from my memory Basheer's eyes, nose, ears, the hair of his moustache. Examined the body I had wrestled with many times. No, it wasn't him. And yet, some things made it seem like him. What if he had gone away leaving something of himself here? Hurriedly, I turned and walked away. I had to get away as quickly as possible from this place, the Place, populated only by the characters from his stories, where only they were allowed to enter.

14 November

After his routine evening prayer, Gandhi spoke about his stance on Thiruvithamkoor. He said that he had been experiencing great personal pain watching the events unfolding there. He called for both sides to cease the violence. He was not against the king or against royal rule. The people in Thiruvithamkoor were Indians. And they had the right to want to be part of India. To tell them that they had to wait longer was unfair. Why should people of the same country need prior permission to travel from one part to another? India was always made up of several local kingdoms. And people had always travelled freely between them without having to take anyone's permission. This must continue. There was, in his opinion, no need for passports and travel documents between India and Pakistan either.

Gandhi said that he intended to visit the people of Thiruvithamkoor soon. He said he didn't expect that he would be asked to show his travel permit. He would first stop in Malabar to visit people from Thiruvithamkoor who lived as refugees there. And if they so wished, they could then accompany him to Thiruvithamkoor. In Thiruvananthapuram, he intended to visit

Amma Maharani, the Maharaja and Diwanji, and impress upon them the people's desire to join India. He was prepared, if need be, to live permanently in this beautiful, southernmost part of the country. He also said that, unlike some, he did not think it necessary to stage military action against Thiruvithamkoor.

15 November

Diwanji responded to Gandhi's comments. Gandhi would always be welcome in the independent, sovereign nation of Thiruvithamkoor, he said. The decision about joining the Indian Union was not his to make, but the people's.

P.T. Chacko, the leader of Aikyakeralam, declared that all public protest activities would be halted until Gandhi's visit. No one could stop Gandhi from coming to Thiruvithamkoor. Even the British couldn't stop him from doing what he set his mind to, so what hope did a Pattar from Thanjavur have? He said that, with Gandhi's arrival, a great people's uprising would take place in Thiruvithamkoor, the currents of which would sweep away even the thrones.

16 November

I received a message ordering me to go to the Bombay Province at once.

4

It was quite cold in Baramati, near Pune. An old town with a few unattractive buildings. All evening and through the night, the train travelled across cotton fields, and when morning came, the same fields stretched all around. By then, it was time to get off. I walked out of the station and stood by the side of a road for a while. A quiet, sleepy town. Nothing much to see because of the morning mist. I continued standing there until, as sunlight slowly filled the place, a handful of people became visible around me as though they had always been there. Half-naked bodies, like those that worked in fields, walked along, carrying tools and rolled-up gunnysacks. As the day brightened, the number of people increased. Hand-pulled rickshaws and motor vehicles began to appear, and still I stood there. Hours passed and the sun became strong. But there was a cool, intermittent breeze. I was dressed in a shirt and a pair of trousers, the usual attire of the long-distance traveller. A couple of rickshaw pullers looked hopefully at me as they passed. Finally, by around noon, when I began to feel less unfamiliar with the place, I started walking. Like our city, Baramati had fortified walls, but unlike ours these were not well maintained. The tops had begun to crumble. Plants like the peepul had spread their roots into the gaps between stones. The white sahib's rule had sent the kings of yore and all that they had built into obscurity. The arched doorways remained, and people walked back and forth through them.

I had walked some distance when a young man, dressed in clothes that might be considered modern in these parts – a mundu with one end pleated and tucked at the back and an upper cloth draped down the neck – fell in step with me.

'You're from Thiruvithamkoor, yes?' he asked me in Hindustani.

I answered and followed him for quite a while. All around us were fields of ripe sugar cane, their leaves beginning to turn yellow. The harvest was under way. Women hefted large bundles of cane and loaded them into bullock carts that had been driven into the fields. Further up, a few houses huddled together. He stopped in front of one of them, the doorstep of which had something written in Marathi in some white powder, gave me a smile and went away. The Brahmin with the Gandhi-style spectacles, whom I had accompanied from Rameswaram to Kollam, came out of the house and welcomed me.

'I'd quite like a bath,' I said to him.

He took me around to the back of the house and showed me a stone trough. Fetched me a towel to dry myself. I finished my bath, had a bowl of ragi porridge and sat down next to him. Without any preamble, I gave him the unclear message I had been entrusted with.

'Right,' he said, and then asked, 'Do you know what this means?'

'No.'

'Good. But you do know that this is about killing somebody?'

'Yes.'

'And that this man, the one who is to be killed, is an important person?'

'I guessed as much.'

'That'll do. There's another plot under way to murder him. If that doesn't succeed, our group will step in. What we need now is your help in finding the weapon to do the deed.'

'I'm aware,' I said. 'I have to go to Gwalior for it. Arrangements have been made. And I have the money. All I need is someone to go with me.'

He still had an aura of austerity and mystery about him, and yet seemed friendlier than at our first encounter. He asked me about the recent developments in our country. As the sun set, another person arrived. A thin young man who, at the very first sight, gave the impression of being an introvert. In the presence of the bespectacled man, his face flushed with shyness and a sense of subservience. As they talked, they stood close together with not even the distance between couples between them. He introduced himself, told me his name, and said that he was, until recently, running a newspaper. It was called *Dainik Agrani*. It reminded me of Basheer. People with extreme ideas everywhere think that they can change the world by printing what is inside them for all to read.

'He'll come with you to Gwalior tomorrow,' said the bespectacled man. 'You can start early in the morning.'

He took his leave.

Before it was too late in the night, we lay down under our blankets.

'Your name sounds strange,' I said, making small talk as my ears began to feel uncomfortable with the utter lack of sound. Back home, no matter how dark, the night was full of sounds. Frogs, crickets, birds, foxes, wind in the trees, spirits of the nights such as yakshis and chathans, gods who left their temples to stroll through the lanes ... Here, though, as soon as the people went to sleep, the world itself slept.

'When I was young, I was brought up as a girl,' he said. 'I even had a nose stud. Ram with a nose stud – that's what my name means.'

I remembered Varghese. Was this man, too, a stand-in for the person who would actually carry out the task, like Varghese had been? They were of the same body type, and had similar quiet personalities, their faces and bearing unthreatening. No one would suspect them of any wrongdoing. But they would fulfil the tasks given to them without fail. Then continue behaving within this aura of innocence. Until we fell asleep, without me prompting him, he told me all about his ideas.

We don't need to be told what to do, he said referring to the people in his group, we know what to do. The organization needn't get involved because the members, the activists, will do what needs to be done. That, in essence, was their principle. And that helped with the survival of the organization. There were many like him, he said, who had dedicated themselves to the service of the country, eschewing even marriage.

We fell asleep, and at some point, his hand crept unknowingly to my waist. Slowly, I moved it away. Then slipped into a dream.

Coming out of Naduvan's house on Thangassery beach in Kollam, I take just a few steps and find myself in Basheer's rented house in Punkunnam. Every now and then, the place also looks like the kitchen in Seethi Buildings in Ernakulam. The man in there is an older Basheer, one who has written several books.

'And now you arrive?' he asks, looking at me.

'What news?' I say, smiling.

'You're in my story "Communist Den",' he says. 'The CID who came to us dressed like a labourer when K. Damodaran, K.C. George and I were going to a movie, took a rupee from us saying he would get us tickets – that was you.'

He then reads a section from his short story 'Ente Charamakkurippu' (My Obituary) to me.

'"The time I have been allocated on this beautiful planet has come to an end. There is no more time. The only time left is in Allahu's treasury. Time that will never, never end ... endless ... endless time."'

The dream repeated itself several times. Finally, I jolted out of my sleep, stepped outside and stood in the cold of the sugar cane field. Was Basheer dead? No one seemed to know. He had given the slip to the Thiruvithamkoor government, the State Congress and Aikyakeralam, and faded away. After we wake from a dream, there is a short while when the dream feels like reality. I was still in that phase. So, I was not astonished to find myself standing here, on a dark night in Baramati, now, in the November of 1947, immediately after listening to Basheer reading to me from a story he had written in 1986. They were, I realized, the one and the same moment. Endless time.

In the morning, I set out for Gwalior with Nathuram. A member of the local royal family had entrusted an Italian-made 9mm Beretta to an arms dealer so that any trace on the gun would show that it had been sold. I could go back home as soon as I paid the asking price and bought it, and handed it over.

5

It was the night of 30 January, and I was in Naikkanal in Thrissur, talking to a bunch of Aikyakeralam activists I had recently befriended. By this time, almost all political activity in Thrissur had to do with Aikyakeralam. The place had become an organizational hub for those who had escaped from our country, and the State Congress and communist activists from Malabar. Party offices and low-rent lodges and houses were full of these people. The locals took great pleasure in feeding and fattening them. A large proportion of Christian refugees from Thiruvithamkoor used Thrissur as a midway resting place on their way to the eastern parts of Kannur and Kozhikode in Malabar. They camped for a few days in the open grounds of Thekkinkadu Maidanam, sheltering from the sun and the rain behind screens of plaited palm leaves. Despite troubles and tribulations, all the political activists I met seemed to be in a great frame of mind. With a common enemy firmly established, the Congress and the communists from Kochi and Malabar had decided to set aside their differences and work together. Gandhi's visit to Thiruvithamkoor was confirmed, only the date needed to be set. Everyone was ready and excited to charge across the border with him. There was no doubt that, if it were to happen, it would be a massive deluge of people. A rumour, a great falsehood, was also in circulation that, before Gandhi arrived, the Maharaja would abdicate the throne and let Thiruvithamkoor join the Indian Union.

It was around eight o'clock. We hung around talking pretty much only about what I have described above. The town was still awake, people milled about. Suddenly, a group of people appeared in the distance, carrying tricolour flags and, visible above them, flags in black. A strange time for a rally, we thought as we stepped away from the little paan shop and on to the road. Almost all of the flagbearers were weeping openly. Some shouted out, 'Mahatma Gandhi will never die,' and others repeated the call. Like trickles of water merging to form streams and then rivers, the procession grew before our eyes as people joined it along the way. A strange sound emanated from the two people standing with me. Watching them scramble to join the procession, I melted quietly into the darkness behind me.

I walked unhurriedly down lanes made secondary by the town's major roads. On both sides were backyards of houses with fences left unmaintained. The sound of the demonstration faded away. All that could be heard now was the clanging of utensils in kitchens about to shut down for the night and the scurrying of vermin looking for food in the backyards.

These lanes were so much more important than the main roads. These were the paths frequented by paramours, thieves and keepers of secrets. The real entrances were the holes quietly made in the fences. Accepted entrances, walls, gates and gatehouses were only to fool people. The most important space in a household is its backyard, its back door its real door, and those who come through it the real guests. I marvelled, as I walked along, at the many turns and myriad connections of these lanes. One could go around the whole world using just these. Most of the blood that flows through human veins is the blood of secrecy. The earth is full of lanes of secrecy. I walked. On and on I walked. As I walked, I became convinced that this, right here, was the right path. The world is full of secrets and concealed paths that lead to secrets. All that is made known is only to hoodwink people. The real body is the one that is secreted within clothes. Life, real life, unfolds in the darkness of a closed room. The real lover is the secret one.

The life concealed is the actual life of a person. Scared by my journey and by my own thoughts, I stopped and stood still for a while. Secrets are the only truth. What we reveal are the stories we make up. The world is full of things that are difficult to see. Creatures that cannot be seen. Their hidden universe surrounds me. When I walk, it walks with me. They are the only true things. I am a lie.

Suddenly, the world around me and within me terrified me. I peered at it, this way and that. Aiyo! All lies. Would I, from now on, be able to perceive the world only in this way? What if, every time I spoke to someone, I could see the lie in their breath, word, glance ... The lie that was written into their positions, names, clothes, ancestors, offspring, partners ... I would never again leave this lane I was in and walk on to a big road. I sobbed. Someone was following me, inside and outside. I looked carefully inwards and out. If one felt that one was being followed, it was then the truth. Basheer was not saying crazy things. Someone was following him. That must be why he had disappeared without a trace. Did he go away scared of the thing that he had created inside his mind? I worried now that I was created by Basheer, that he had written me into being. I stopped crying as a great anxiety filled me. Now, as I walked, the path beneath my feet began to frighten me by churning and shaking. Shadows moved relentlessly. Branches of night-darkened trees bent downwards as though they were the sharpened teeth and claws of demons. Everything I could see had something else in addition to its length, width, height, weight and colour. Things that never moved began moving. Holes in the hedges enlarged. Creatures stuck their necks out through them. Reaching out in a multitude of colours, moonlight stung my head. Hearing the ear-splitting sound of the back door of a house opening, I looked towards it. A large, clothed insect stepped out to throw away the remains of a meal. Leftovers, discarded, were the real food. Flies and tiny creatures rushed towards it with their teeth and nails sharpened. Grains of rice animated and stood upright, sticking their tail ends in the soil. All things never to be feared began to fill me with terror. Leaves, the gentle breeze, small noises, dust, soil, moss, tiny blossoms of the arippoo, fireflies, moths, the drizzle, all of it. I saw trees disappear into the earth and a generation of dead children rise up to take their place. Finally, when I began to scare myself, I ran. I ran and ran without stopping. And yet I followed myself. As I ran, I realized that a group of people armed with weapons was following me. Each and every one of those people was me. All along the way, I was hiding, crouching in the bushes, in the dark, round the bends. I pounced on me, cut me into pieces and strewed me in the dust. They ran again. I ran after them. And I ran after me chasing after them. In my panic, I grabbed at things. Each of those things scorched me. I lay down and the surroundings boiled. Each step I took, the ground beneath my feet became as deep as hell. I swam and I flew, only to have birds snatch at me. The endless lanes I ran through became narrower and narrower. Then I crawled through a tunnel. And when that too became impassable, I saw an opening, barely large enough to pass a thread, in a fence made of dried palm leaves. I inserted myself into that needle's eye and tumbled over to the other side. Aha! Another world.

A hundred small plants. Trees. The back of a building. Its secret world. True world. There, in the light of a burning lamp, Vallappuzha Vaidyan was waiting for me. He took me to the same room where he had treated Basheer. There, on a shelf, was a radio. It awoke. Capturing my mind as sound waves, it broadcast it to the world. It would reach Basheer too. Terrified, I curled up and hid in the weave of the mat spread on the bed. Like the inconsequential being that I was. Vaidyan rolled up the mat and handed it to an assistant and asked him to take it away. Part of me detached itself and went away with the mat. What was left lay face down on the bed, almost dead from fright.

'The treatment can begin,' Vaidyan said. 'No one comes here alone. Neither did you.'

'No, I came alone.'

'No. Basheer brought you.'

'I was the one who brought Basheer here.'

'Basheer brought you to me. And your treatment started on that day.'

'That ... was a long time ago.'

'Yes.'

Vaidyan began to prepare the nasyam.

A long time passed. The time it takes for the medicine administered through the nose to travel up through the nasal passage to the crown of my head, purify and return.

Endless time.

6

Vallappuzha Vaidyan grew, filling the room and the outside of it, as though the universe had suddenly become a grand old man. With his broad shoulders, hirsute body, nostrils thickened from inhaling the aroma of medicinal herbs, plump hands, and a jumble of black and white hair on his head, he sat warming and mixing potions. Leaves and roots marched into the room. As he pounded them on stone, a few of the minds that had been clinging to his body lost their grip and fell into the mixture. They screamed, along with the herbs, as he squeezed the juice out of them. And when their screams became unbearable, I shut my ears and lay there looking upwards. Tiny ants clung to the wooden ceiling way up there. They splayed their hands and feet and fell on top of me. Slowly, very slowly. A rain of ants. The room was lit only by a small lamp. I looked at the blackened wood of the walls. They seemed to be pulsating. Someone was shuffling the wooden planks as though they were a deck of cards. Aiyo. Aiyo. I screwed my eyes shut. In the darkness in my eyes, everything I had seen thus far came in as light. The world inside began to move faster and more furiously than the one outside. My eyes burst and leaked from the corners. I felt as though I was going to shout out everything that was inside me. Everyone was going to read me like an open book, licking their fingers and sticking their saliva on the pages as they turned them. I focused on my body. It wasn't there.

'No, don't speak,' Vaidyan said.

Or perhaps he didn't. He was not the kind of man who would say such things.

'This thing flowing out – it is all that you've been wanting to say. No need for anything else. Just think of God,' Vaidyan said. He understood even what was in my mind.

Would anyone who is filled with doubt say that there is no God? Whether he exists or not, he is all there is to hold on to.

Vaidyan brought an undamaged jackfruit leaf and folded it into a scoop like the one used to drink kanji. He helped me move further up in bed. The back of my body was pressed against the planks of the kanjiram the bed was made of. My head hung off the top end, ready to receive the medicine. Beneath my head, the world somersaulted. Vaidyan inserted the pointy part of the jackfruit leaf scoop with the medicinal oil into my nostril. As he blew hard on the oil, I inhaled as forcefully as I could. Daivam thampuraney ... God almighty. What a hard moment that was. A vicious bitterness exploded inside my head. In a split second, even roots of hair became bitter. The bitterness of the kashayam began to leak out of eyes and ears. Urine, shit, nails and teeth blackened. Heart and oesophagus shrank. Brain was caught in the current of herbal potions cooked and proved over a long time. The medicinal water entered each of its folds and washed it clean. I called out to my mother. All around me was the bitter sky and the bitter air, and having taken it in, bitterness became my abiding taste forever. Microbes detached and left. I became hollowed out. Emptied. I lay in the darkness, unable to think even about not being able to think. There was nothing.

The morning after the nasyam, when I opened the door and stepped gingerly out, the plants in the yard and the compound had grown. Large trees had grown new branches. Vines sprouted from fallen seeds had borne fruits. The chirping birds were of the fifth generation. Many days ago, on a day with no visitors, I, who was Basheer's companion while he was being treated here, had sat on this veranda with him, arguing. Basheer was gazing intently at Vallappuzha Vaidyan who was rooting around among the medicinal herbs.

'He's not that good,' Basheer said.

He was under the impression that Vaidyan was not the same person we had met when we came here, but a son or even a grandson of that man. He insisted that it had been that long since he had entered the room for treatment. I disagreed.

'Onnu poda,' Basheer scoffed. He was angry. 'You think "Vallappuzha Vaidyan" is a single person? He is many. Like Vedavyasan and Sankaracharyar. They are several of them. We just think of all they do as the deeds of one person.'

'What, so you, Basheer, are also many people?'

'Are you making fun of me? Ordinary people do not come back into being again and again. When they are gone, they are done.'

'But you're not ordinary.'

There were people, Basheer said, who lived many lives in one lifespan. They would either be extremely cruel or completely mad. They even forgot, as they went on living, their own names and their real character.

'So which is good, do you think?' I asked.

'Ah, it's not about that. I once passed a sanyasi on the road and thought, ssheda, isn't that me!'

I stepped off the veranda and looked back at the building I had been living in. It looked older. The thatch of its roof had been changed several times. The oil stains on its pillars, where bodies and heads had rested, had become darker. Its floors had been repolished with several applications of cow dung mixed with powdered coal. I walked around the compound, looking at the soil that had changed with repeated tilling. The palm-leaf fence at the back was exactly as it had been. I peered into the needle-head hole in it. I saw the me who had crawled in here through it.

7

By the time I got out, our country had been in two battles with India. The first had begun on 5 October 1948. Hyderabad was a country just like ours, which, not wanting to join either India or Pakistan, had decided to remain independent. It had also sent its representative to the United Nations General Assembly. And yet, on 13 September 1948, India entered that country unlawfully. Hundreds of razakars, militant opposers of joining the Indian Union, were killed. India's action was in contradiction to existing agreements. The under-trained Hyderabadi army of barely twenty thousand soldiers surrendered within four days. That country was forcefully annexed by India.

The representative of our country, A.K. Pillah, was at Lake Success, the temporary headquarters of the United Nations. He protested against this event in the strongest possible terms and demanded that the Security Council get involved. He met with the secretary general and the representatives of several countries, and also organized an informal discussion about safeguarding the sovereignty of countries that had gained independence from colonial rule. Then he set out for London to request the British government to ensure that the agreements reached with its mediation were adhered to by the parties involved. In this, he had the firm support of the British Conservative Party. The British prime minister, Clement Atlee, addressed the issue in parliament. Ultimately, there was nothing A.K. Pillah could do for Hyderabad, but later events would prove that his actions were of great relevance to our country.

On 23 September, our government announced that it was stepping back from all agreements with India as a protest against the country's military action in Hyderabad. International agreements were not to be followed only by comparatively smaller countries. What justification did India have, a country claiming to be in the process of creating a democratic constitution, for using military force to subjugate its neighbouring countries?

Our country took this stance at the right time. India could not deploy its military against Thiruvithamkoor then because the entire international community was raising its collective eyebrows against the action in Hyderabad. Still, on 5 October, a group of armed men came by sea in around fifteen boats and landed in Thangassery. They claimed to be Aikyakeralam activists but were, in truth, Indians from Malabar and Kochi. They shot and killed the five policemen on duty in Thangassery harbour and then proceeded to Kollam city. Precisely at this time, Indian radios broadcast news stating that the people of Thiruvithamkoor had taken to the streets against royal rule, and that they were warmly welcoming the freedom fighters who had reached Kollam. From Kollam, the armed group tried to travel south quickly. Other than the blockades people put up using rocks and wood, they did not face much opposition. Meanwhile, another armed group, arriving by the Vembanad Kayal, declared that Alappuzha was now part of India. They imprisoned the police there and set free the prisoners, including dangerous communist criminals, in the sub-jail. Their next move was to get to Central Road, travelling east through Kuttanad. But neither of these groups were able to do so as quickly as they wanted because they had no vehicles. That night, in a press note, Diwanji said that what had happened in Hyderabad was happening in Thiruvithamkoor. He could not talk to his people via his usual radio broadcast because the employees at the radio station were subservient to the Indian government. Thiruvithamkoor appealed for help from the international community and the United Nations. The Maharaja sent a letter to Clement Atlee in which he noted that Thiruvithamkoor was left without an army because it was following the terms of the agreement with the British government. And now, another agreement, reached and signed with British mediation, was being broken.

The armed groups were trying to get to Thiruvananthapuram as soon as they could. But, on 7 October, our puny army, if it could be called that, set up a major resistance by destroying all the bridges across the Kollampuzhayaar. When the Indian army entered Hyderabad, they had the firm support of the Hindus there. But in Thiruvithamkoor, such expectations came to nothing. The people saw the groups, not in uniform and armed with dangerous weapons, as hooligans. On 8 October, Britain and France demanded that the military action against Thiruvithamkoor be stopped. India's position, however, was that there was no military action against Thiruvithamkoor. In any case, the armed groups disappeared the next day. The ban on the import of goods at Kochi port continued for months after.

At the end of the month of October, in Bali, an unofficial meeting took place between India and Thiruvithamkoor with the mediation of the British ambassador. Our country reiterated that both countries had to follow the terms of the agreement. India demanded that free political activity be allowed in Thiruvithamkoor. Our country acknowledged India's claim to Thangassery, which had been in British possession. But it set forth the condition that there would be no military presence in the area.

The second, and most horrific, battle that our country faced was in March 1950. On 26 November 1949, the Constituent Assembly of India adopted the Indian constitution. The very next day, Indian's home minister Vallabhbhai Patel sent a letter to Diwanji wanting to set the date for the people's referendum as stipulated in the agreement between the countries. Our country did not respond to the letter. At the beginning of December, the Maharaja received an official letter from the Indian prime minister. Our government refused the demand, and sent a detailed letter to the Indian government, the British government and the United Nations. There was a numbered list of the reasons why it had chosen not to honour the terms of the agreement, the most important of which are listed below:

1. The Indian government had never abided by the terms of the agreement.
2. India was still illegally holding the northernmost areas of Thiruvithamkoor.
3. Proper goods transport was not being allowed at Kochi port.
4. Aikyakeralam, an anti-national, armed organization, was being given all support, enabling them to enter the country and unleash violence.
5. The criminals involved in the attempted assassination of the Maharaja were still being protected.
6. The Indian army, dressed as civilians, entered the country and conducted unlawful criminal acts, including the murder of several innocents.

And yet, our country did not entirely dismiss the possibility of uniting with India. Thiruvithamkoor had a legislative assembly elected by the people. And it was that assembly that made decisions about the future of the nation.

Many were the reasons why our country took such a strong stance against our powerful neighbour. Significant among them was the fact that the port at Poonthura had been developed with the help of America and had become fully functional. This meant that we could move goods without having to depend on Kochi. We had also, within the last two years, formed a functional army. In addition to this, Thiruvithamkoor enjoyed a good profile among its international allies, all thanks to the diligence of A.K. Nair and the foreign visits Diwanji had undertaken on and off over the years.

India responded severely to our reply. It sent a letter demanding that Thiruvithamkoor's membership in the United Nations be revoked. On 1 January, it stopped all railway and postal services to our country. All goods transport was banned. The Indian navy constantly patrolled the Arabian Sea and blocked the shipping channels. On 26 January, India became an independent, sovereign, democratic republic. The map of India released on the day showed Kashmir and Thiruvithamkoor as part of the country. Most of our country was marked as part of the state of Kerala which was to be newly formed. Devikulam, Chenkotta and Nanjinad were marked as part of the Madras Province.

Criticisms of the new constitution emerged from within India itself. Different Hindu organizations questioned what right India, which had adopted a constitution filled with foreign ideas, had to order around a country like Thiruvithamkoor which was ruled according to the principles of the *Manusmriti*. But organizations like the Hindu Mahasabha could not mobilize wider protests because they had been banned following the assassination of Gandhi. On 10 February, India announced that it had confiscated Thiruvithamkoor's property in various parts of the country. Guest houses built in aid of pilgrims in places such as Kashi, Haridwar and Rameswaram were included in this. Ancestral properties belonging to Diwanji, in Madras and Mylapore, were also confiscated. In retaliation, our country shut down the radio station that constantly broadcast anti-national messages.

On 7 March, at midnight, India officially announced Operation Cape – military action against Thiruvithamkoor. The responsibility of Operation Cape, which involved fifty thousand soldiers, was with Major General Jayant Tripathi.

The Thiruvithamkoor army, led by General Roy Bucher, who had retired from the British army, gave more attention to protecting the border at Chenkotta. He had concluded, rightly, that our army would survive only a few days if it were to engage in an open battle. It had to be delayed as long as possible while waiting for international intervention. The Indian army would try to reach Thiruvananthapuram as soon as possible. As expected, it was the border at Chenkotta that the enemies breached first. It took them until the following afternoon to get across Puliyara and Kottavasal. Our army put up a brave resistance despite being inferior in numbers and weapons to the attackers. A brave soldier named Malaichami, a man from Suchindram who had fought with the British Indian army at Burma and Nagaland in the Second World War, courted a martyr's death in Thenmala. He would receive Thiruvithamkoor's highest military medal posthumously. Even after his companions, fifteen of them, were all dead, Malaichami put up a fight that delayed the Indian army's advance by a whole day and caused a loss of five covered vehicles and almost thirty-five soldiers.

The atrocities committed by its army during the military assault on Hyderabad had put India on a defensive footing. This was why they chose the sparsely populated area of Chenkotta, hoping to end the war quickly. But the unexpected resistance rendered all their calculations wrong. Meanwhile, A.K. Pillah began an indefinite hunger strike in front of the United Nations office. The news spread all across the country that the Maharaja had declared that he, too, would give up eating until the war ended. These were unexpected developments. Concluding that it would be dangerous to delay further, the Indian army breached the southern borders. Bridges across all rivers had been dismantled, which would have slowed down their advance, but they would have used other means and reached Thiruvananthapuram in two days.

Then, 12 March happened.

The government school at the southern entrance of the Vaikom temple was only walking distance from the place where the Congress had held a two-year-long satyagraha that started in 1924. The school, which began functioning during the time of Maharaja Sree Moolam Thirunal, was the only English-medium school all along the Vembanad Kayal which spread into the Kochi border. On the morning of 12 March, at 10.30 a.m., the headmaster P.A. Krishnaiyar conducted an open-air assembly in which he made a short speech about our great country and the dangers it faced currently. The assembly was over and the students, after singing 'Vancheeshamangalam' and shouting 'ki jai' to Amma Maharani and His Highness the Maharaja, were returning to their classes when an object, like a large ball of fire, fell into their midst.

The Indian army had, in the cover of night and in a range of boats, landed in Kadavu, Vaikom jetty and the place where the Kariyaar emptied, and nowhere in these places had it faced any resistance. A section of the army, in its haste to reach Thiruvananthapuram, had already crossed Kottayam by land. Given this, the army had no need to use such a strong bomb or cannonball. This horrific incident shook the whole world. India's defence that it had its suspicions about why a school was open and functioning in the middle of a war, and its call for an independent inquiry, were of no use. We'll hand you our country if you give us our children back, said Diwanji to that country. And with little regard for his own safety, he went to Vaikom. Not able to stomach the death of sixty-two schoolchildren and three teachers, Thiruvithamkoor roiled in anti-India sentiments. People took to the streets and waylaid military vehicles. The children's death struck a terrible blow to the international image of India and of Nehru. The defence minister Baldev Singh resigned. On 15 March, the Indian army withdrew from Thiruvithamkoor completely.

This war had a significant role in shaping the nationalistic fervour in Thiruvithamkoor in modern times. The miseries that arose from the sense of being besieged that went on for months had created anti-government feelings in the people. They had begun to believe that joining India would make their lives easier, more secure. But all of that changed suddenly. A common enemy who killed their children united the people. From then on, every year, 12 March would be observed as the Day of Sorrow and 15 March celebrated as the Day of Victory. The martyrdom of Malaichami became legendary in Thiruvithamkoor. He joined Ananthapadmanabhan, a great army leader from the time of Maharaja Marthanda Varma, on the list of heroic figures the Tamil people had contributed to Thiruvithamkoor. For a long time after, even the banned organizations Aikyakeralam and the State Congress did not dare voice the demand that Thiruvithamkoor join the Indian Union. They turned their attention to working on such issues as Malayali nationality and the challenges to democracy in Thiruvithamkoor.

The repercussions of the war of 1950 were significant. Our existence as an independent nation was clearly established. Ignoring India's objections, several countries including France, Israel, Portugal, the USA, South Africa and Sri Lanka pursued diplomatic relations with Thiruvithamkoor. By the time five more years passed, almost all world nations, except India and the Soviet Bloc, had accepted us as an independent nation. Learning from the lessons of the two wars, Thiruvithamkoor entered into a cooperative military relationship with the USA. A modern military, although not very big in numbers of soldiers, was formed. The Arabian Sea Union was formed with Sri Lanka and the Maldives as partners. Food security and sustainability was still a faraway dream, so rice was imported from Pakistan, Southeast Asian countries and China. Another major impact was the acceptance of Sir C.P. Ramaswami Iyer's infallibility in home affairs. As befitting a modern nation, he changed the name of his position from diwan to prime minister. From time to time, he appeared in military uniform, bringing good cheer and positive energy to the people.

8

Standing in front of the building in Punkunnam, I looked up at the room Basheer had been staying in when he went mad. Would he be in that room that had been locked from the outside, writing *Diary of a Lover*? Trying to recapture what had been set on fire? How long since there has been any news about him? Would newspapers in Thiruvithamkoor still be writing about him? Would anyone remember the stories he told? Where has he been hiding all this time? No one asks after some people, like Mani, Chidambara Iyer's son. They won't ever come back either. But was Basheer like that? Was anyone in this world, other than me, looking for him? No one remembers a writer who stops writing, a politician who miscalculates his politics, or an investigator who fails to find the subject of his investigation. Worthless are those who fail after trying to live life differently. As I stood there gazing up at the room, I began to feel that there was someone inside. That I had only stepped out to buy a bundle of beedis. That he was sitting inside writing a story in which all the characters were in a muddle. And that I, too, was muddled up in the muddle.

I talked to the owner of the shop on the ground floor of the building and located the landlord. He did not remember anyone named Basheer living there.

'My father used to take care of the building,' he said. 'Lots of people have stayed here. But Acchan never kept a record of anything. He just let out the room and collected the rent. That was all.'

He told me that the room needed some repairs and was unoccupied. When I insisted that I would like to rent it for a few days, he looked at me curiously.

'Why? Walk along a little and there are any number of lodges where you can find a room,' he said.

I told him that I had lived in this room with a friend once and wanted to relive my memories.

He was not impressed. 'You remember it, don't you? So, what's the big deal?'

I pressed him to let me have a look inside at least. He relented, finally, and sent a man with the keys.

Inside, the room was ordinary, unremarkable. There was no furniture, no table or bed. No windows opening to pleasing views. We open a room thinking in vain that the memories of a person will still be inside. But it was only in my memory that it acquired stature. Even if there was something of him left – a piece of cloth, a shred of paper – what significance would it have? Our minds latch on to something and make up stories. When we are gone, even the memory of our being gone will cease to exist. Tragic is the life of human beings. We live in the hope that we will be remembered. None of the other creatures on earth are made fools of by their own brains.

'You can lock it,' I said, stepping out quickly.

I walked along the lane in *Diary of a Lover* and reached the house in Punkunnam where Basheer's Devi lived. I don't have to describe all this. As it had been the last time, when I entered her compound after standing in the lane for a few minutes, I saw that the plants were wet. The ladder leaned against the wall that separated this house and the secret house that Basheer and Devi used for their rendezvous. The shadow of the person who had climbed up the ladder and gone over the wall lay at its bottom. I began speaking as though continuing the conversation I had when I was here previously. I had come to keep Basheer company.

As happens in stories, Vanaja was alone at home. She lied, said that she did not remember meeting me. Good thing she didn't say she did not know Basheer. But she showed no interest in talking about him. Why talk about a man like that now? Yes, there was a Basheer who lived in the house opposite many years ago, one who thought of himself, or whom others thought of, as a writer. He wrote, in his mad diary or a story by some such name, about one of the young women who lived in this house. According to this story, they were in love. And met in secret in the house on the other side of the wall. This woman, standing here, was witness to their meetings, their secret keeper. The man standing in the front yard might have come along with the writer once or twice. In the course of things, they might have talked to one another. She might have listened to his talk and laughed. What more was there to say? What else was there to discuss and deliberate? Vanaja looked at me with a face reflecting all these thoughts. She told me that Devi had left and that she knew nothing about her whereabouts. I thought about the timeline and concluded that Devi had gone away around the time Basheer had disappeared.

As she stood there wondering why I was still hanging around, Vanaja's gaze slipped towards the secret house. My gaze followed. And when we looked away again, our eyes made contact. I knew what was happening in that house where there was no one else. In the absence of the writer and his main character, the lover, without their knowledge, two insignificant characters – Vanaja and Bhasi – were cavorting with one another. Enjoying themselves in the great secret that they, the secret keepers, are in the process of creating.

'Tell me the truth,' Vanaja says with her head in my lap. 'Have you actually read it?'

'What?'

'What Basheer has been writing. *Diary of a Lover.*'

'Yes. We wouldn't be here together like this if I hadn't.'

'Does it talk about us?'

'A little. Just two minor characters. But now, we are, without Basheer and Devi's knowledge, where they were, doing what they were doing.'

'What does Basheer usually ask Devi in moments like this?'

'He says, "Devi, will you show me your sundara surabhila rahasya pushpam, your fair-fragrant flower, your secret blossom?" That's what he says.'

'Ayye!'

I looked at Vanaja standing on the veranda with no interest in talking to me. I felt that, even though she said she didn't know who I was, she was happy someone had come looking for her. We are glad when someone from some other time remembers us even vaguely. Her attention was on that secret house. She, too, knew what was happening inside. Whatever. It was enough that two of the characters he had created, from a story of his that had burned down, were still meeting one another even after he had disappeared. A testament to the strength of his mad imagination. I recalled what P.T. Punnoose said about him when we were in jail. Either he had disappeared forever, or something momentous was about to happen.

9

By this time, Ernakulam had turned into a hub of anti-Thiruvithamkoor activities that the neighbouring country was engaged in. Geographically, it intruded into Thiruvithamkoor territory, making it easier to smuggle people and weapons deep into our country through the waterways – the rivers, and the long lake, the Vembanad Kayal. Major attacks continued to take place in Kuttanad and in the northern parts of the country. Aikyakeralam activists working from within our country were being given all support from Ernakulam. The Thiruvithamkoor security forces regularly patrolled the lake, but it made little difference. The two countries were constantly squabbling about the ownership of the islands in the Kayal and the borders within its waters. The Indian navy chose Willingdon Island in the Kayal to set up its southern base. Its boats patrolled the waters and engaged our border forces in constant combat, thereby providing safe passage to insurgents. At this time, Thiruvithamkoor was trying to clearly delineate its northern borders and to secure vulnerable areas with additional guards. India's incursions by land, attacks and shootings were regular occurrences. Also by this time, the Thiruvithamkoor State Congress was almost dead; its members, along with the communists and the socialists, now worked as part of Aikyakeralam. Prominent leaders, including Akkamma Cherian, Kumbalath Shanku Pillai and P.T. Chacko, were all present in Ernakulam. Everything that went on in this town had to do with Thiruvithamkoor. Everywhere one looked were soldiers, exiles and refugees. There was also a large established ring that smuggled tobacco and alcohol into

Alappuzha and Kottayam. It was widely assumed that the Civil Protection Group, Thiruvithamkoor's secret service agency, was also active in Kochi. Aikyakeralam and the Indian government looked upon the CPG as something to be feared. Newspapers in Thrissur, Kochi and Malabar regularly printed stories about CPG spies. The unexpected death of Sankaran Namboothiripad, a man from Perinthalmanna who was the author of the book *Keralam Malayalikalude Mathrubhumi*, which argued that Kerala was the motherland of all Malayalis, was widely believed to be the handiwork of the CPG. The body of the prolific writer was found in a lodge in the Kodungallur area. Sankaran Namboothiripad was married to a Thiruvithamkoor woman. Following his death, his book became popular among the Aikyakeralam cadre and attained the position of a text fundamental to their cause.

Having been implicated in the case of the attempted assassination of the Maharaja, Kumbalath Shanku Pillai did not take part in public events. There was no doubt that the Indian government would use any public appearance by him as yet another tool for anti-Thiruvithamkoor propaganda internationally. Regardless, it was he who controlled all that happened in Ernakulam. So, it was Shanku Pillai I went to see first. I was under the impression that, although he had not met me in person, he would know that I was part of the event that shook the country along with Basheer, K.C.S. Mani and Varghese. But when I told him that my name was Bhasi and mentioned what had happened, he responded as though he had never heard of such things. Not only that, his face was suffused with suspicion. When I spoke in detail, he sat listening to me as though I was telling him a story.

'What is it that you want?' he asked when I stopped talking.

'Nothing really,' I said. 'I'd like to be active in our struggle.'

'Well, not yet. Let me think about it.'

Looking carefully at my face, he told me that there were some mysteries surrounding the assassination attempt. He said it was only now that he had become aware that there was one more link in the chain of events – me. No matter how much I tried to explain my long absence, I felt that he did not believe me. It was also clear, after talking to him for some time, that he had no idea where Basheer was. In fact, he seemed to believe that Mani and Basheer had both been killed. Everyone involved in that incident had either been killed or had disappeared. He considered all of them, including Sreekantan Nair, to be veeranayakans – heroes whose bravery would never be forgotten. Their task was well planned, precise, but somewhere along the way, it had been redirected. He gave me permission to hang around, sleep in Seethi Buildings or somewhere else nearby. I was certain that I would be under surveillance and might even be interrogated. But I had to find Basheer.

Seethi Buildings was now known as the headquarters of Aikyakeralam, an organization banned by the government of Thiruvithamkoor, and yet it looked exactly as it had in Basheer's days. Important leaders came to the place but rarely stayed overnight. Frontline workers came and went as they pleased, slept there on empty or full tummies, took active part in debates and arguments. Just as it had been in the old days, most of these were tired, unkempt young men. I did not find a single familiar face among them. In the intervening years, a lot of people had left and a lot more had arrived. What had happened to all those youngsters who had lived in these rooms, ideas their only sustenance, thinking that something magnificent, something that would change the world in a single day was about to happen? Or was such a life earmarked only for a few years in each person's lifespan? Some of them might surely have gone back to their ordinary lives. Others might still be engaged in work left over from those days. There were places like this in towns all around the world, I thought, where young people lived helpless, chaotic lives, believing that they were the catalyst for some major turning point in history. If you ever pass through some faraway town, look out for buildings that have been left unmaintained, their walls naked without whitewash, yards overgrown, threadbare clothes on clothes lines drying in the sun, lights still on even at dawn. These will be the Seethi Buildings in those towns. And the lean figures you might see through the windows might be going through the most decisive moments in their lives.

Some of the current occupants were aware that K.C. George and Basheer had lived in the building before. As I began asking around, a man, a self-proclaimed socialist ideologist, asked, 'Basheer? You mean the guy who was implicated in the assassination case? Do I know him? Ha, ha, it's people like him, brave people, that we need right now.'

I told him that Basheer used to write fiery pamphlets and produce the newspaper *Ujjeevanam*.

'Really! He was a writer too?' The man was amazed to hear it. 'So many talented young men sacrificing their lives for the cause...'

He too assumed that Basheer was dead. Or that the CPG had caught him and he was being kept a prisoner somewhere and tortured.

I met another man, from Manjeri, who was also acquainted with Basheer the writer. He had met him in person, he said, and had read a story that he had written, titled 'Paavangalude Veshya' (Poor People's Prostitute).

'No, he has never written such a story,' I said. 'He had, at one point, written a lot of essays. And he used to tell the stories he intended to write. But this one – no, he has never written it.'

'Ha, I'm telling you, I've read it. It's written like the narrator is telling the story to the nurse who is treating him.'

'And I'm telling you, you're wrong. He has not written anything. You probably heard the story somewhere.'

After an argument that went on like this for a while, he agreed that perhaps he was wrong. It was etched in his mind as though he had read it, he said. A real heartbreaker of a story. It bothered him that the brave actions of people like Basheer had not received the recognition they deserved. Like Bhagat Singh, Basheer and the others had stepped up with little regard for the consequences. If it had been successful, that assassination attempt would have changed the course of the history of Thiruvithamkoor and of India.

'I do, from time to time, think about a Kerala state that includes Thiruvithamkoor,' he said. 'It would be the most peaceful place in India.'

Only victors are remembered for their sacrifices, he said. Had Basheer and the others been successful, they would have been feted as heroes all across the land. But now, neither the Aikyakeralam leadership nor the Indian government wanted to be reminded of the incident. They were concerned that the shadow of suspicion would fall on them too.

'If what they did was wrong, then so is what Bhagat Singh and Subhas Chandra Bose did,' he said. 'They too tried to eliminate the enemies of the people. Basheer and the others were not successful, and now the people of Thiruvithamkoor are paying the price.'

All of the Aikyakeralam folk I met exuded an outward hopefulness but were disheartened inside. None of them believed, truly in their hearts, that Thiruvithamkoor would be rid of royal rule any time soon. They were deeply disappointed that the country could not be annexed by India in one fell sweep as had been done to Hyderabad.

'There are other games at play,' they said when we discussed these matters. They believed that there were many within the Indian government and in positions of power who secretly supported Sir

C.P. 'When things come to a head, the Pattar and Namboothiri here and the Tripathi and Chatterjee there join forces.'

Indian Brahmins looked upon Thiruvithamkoor as the only place where they, their people, were in power. It was true that they held power in all important areas in India too, but given that it was a democracy, their power and influence were waning, always under threat. The king of Thiruvithamkoor, meanwhile, put Brahmins – Bhoodevans, gods on this earth – and their wishes first and foremost. And while in India, they had employment reservations for the lower castes, in Thiruvithamkoor, they only appointed Brahmins to top-ranking positions. Aikyakeralam members were convinced that there were those in Delhi who saw to it that any action by the Indian government against Thiruvithamkoor was either softened or blocked entirely. The only exception to this state of affairs was Nehru. India still held on to its official policy of considering Thiruvithamkoor its territory and upheld people's right to travel between the countries without needing a passport or permit. This enabled Indian Brahmins to come to Thiruvithamkoor and take on jobs, go back home or settle here permanently as they pleased. Meanwhile, large numbers of people left Thiruvithamkoor as refugees for Kochi and Malabar. Put together, it was conceivable that Thiruvithamkoor would soon become a majority Brahmin country. But there were those who dismissed this idea outright. And I was, I must say, convinced by their reasoning. Brahmins would never build a country where they formed the majority of the population. Their lives depended on other people's labour and the fruits of that labour. They themselves did not know how to produce anything. So, their aim would be to build a country where they were in charge and controlled everything but still had other castes to do everything for them.

When I got to Seethi Buildings after all that time, the first place I went to was the kitchen – Basheer's old abode. In his absence, both doors to the kitchen lay open. No one lived in the room or lit the cooking fire. The short space between the two doors had been left uncluttered to allow people to pass through to the outside. On either side were piles of old notices and newspapers, broken beds and chairs, and other discarded items. There was nothing of Basheer there. Standing there taking it all in, I laughed at myself. What difference did it make if I found something of his, or something I assumed to be his, here? Old rooms and old things were just that. They were not markers of human lives preserved forever. Still, I looked at where Basheer's bed had been, with the mysterious world underneath it where the ellundas had lived. With the windows pulled shut, it was in total darkness.

I did not try to find out what had happened to Swami, Basheer's manservant. It was certain that one of the haters of the other all-powerful Swami would have taken out their hatred on his person.

I left Seethi Buildings soon. Waking up at 4 a.m., I walked a long way towards Mulanthuruthi and entered Thiruvithamkoor. By then, the day was bright, but to my amazement, no one stopped me. Birds in the sky and creatures on land went back and forth. And humans, too, without worrying about the fact that they had been relegated to this side or that, went back and forth to work in the fields, graze cattle, empty their bowels. Border patrol, war, incursions, these, I thought, were all performances. Games enacted with mutual consent of the parties involved, at mutually decided upon venues. Step and counter-step. That was all. With a gimmick or two thrown in every now and then to maintain the facade of seriousness.

10

Biding my time, I spent a few days in Kanjirappally, Alappuzha and Kuravilangad before making my way to Thiruvananthapuram. There were no messages waiting for me anywhere, so I rented a small room in a lodge near Thampanoor and decided to stay put. When people like me come out into the light of day, the information gets quickly and precisely to those who need to know. It was certain that, by now, those who employed me would know where I had been and what I had been up to. Yet no messages or directives arrived. And so, I picked the one place in the country that was under the most surveillance. For the next two months, I hung around doing nothing other than eating and sleeping. It began to feel that the situation would continue like this. Those in charge of getting things done in the lower rungs would not know of my significance in the overall scheme. After all, only one or two people were privy to the tasks I had been assigned.

One day, as I stepped out of my room, the owner of the lodge came up to me.

'Sir, are you staying here because you've fallen out with your folks and have left home?' he asked.

'Ey, no, nothing like that,' I said.

'Don't mind me asking, sir. It's just that, a while ago, someone else stayed here like you and then hanged himself to death.'

'Ha, ha, well, if I feel like killing myself, I'll be sure to do it elsewhere.'

'Ayyayyo! It's not what I meant, sir. So, what exactly do you do?'

'Nothing worth much. I'm writing a book.'

'Oho. Sorry for disturbing you, sir. What are you writing? A story? Like *Marthandavarma* or *Dharmaraja*?'

'Yes, something like that.'

'Then you should have looked for a more beautiful place, no, sir? With some peace and quiet?'

If a decision was made that someone like me was not needed any more, there would be no notice to the effect. I'd just have to accept that all I had done or was made to do had been erased. The reason things are done in secret is to be able to deny doing them. It might also be that I was being put under observation before I was given new responsibilities. If that was the case, it was best to go somewhere, take up an ordinary job, and wait it out. Still, I felt the need to warn them of the situation with Basheer. Everyone would have forgotten about him by now. But this job I do has given me certain insights and intuition. And they are usually right. Basheer's disappearance, with no trace and for so long, signalled danger. I knew that there were plenty of people who would recognize him at a glance. And he was not the type of person to live completely cut off from people. I was convinced that something big was coming, something entirely unexpected.

I began to make an appearance wherever there was bound to be a crowd in the city. Such a move was certain to elicit a response. I went everywhere – meetings, demonstrations, celebrations, concerts. Strolled aimlessly along the roads in the evenings, as was my habit during my student days. Made random acquaintances chatting with people in Kizhakkekotta and Chala. Went to places that sold bootlegged arrack, got drunk and came home late in the night. It was in the middle of all this that I understood something. In the period I had spent away, my country had changed quite substantially.

After many long centuries, Thiruvithamkoor was experiencing what it meant to have absolute power over itself. Ever since the time of the great Marthanda Varma, the founder king of the country, it had been more or less under the direct control of the East India Company and then the British government. Now, finally, there was no resident – the seat and symbol of British power – hanging over its head. Those who had operated against the country, safe under the might of the residency and of the Indian Congress and Gandhi, had all either left the country or been imprisoned. The rest, those who remained, had publicly sworn their complete allegiance to the king and the prime minister. Bouquets in hand, Christian priests and nuns lined the streets whenever Sir C.P. Ramaswami Iyer went out. Still, masses of Christians left as refugees and migrants for the neighbouring country. Newspapers that had consistently printed anti-national news became obedient. Now they regularly printed articles ridiculing India, Nehru and A.K. Gopalan, the communist leader and chief minister of Kerala, which was part of India. *Kerala Kaumudi* began an investigative series comparing Nehru and Sir C.P., their life, education, expertise in the English language, skill in governance, family background, and so on. It concluded the series with the finding that had Sir C.P. not dedicated his life to the service of Thiruvithamkoor, he would certainly have been the first prime minister of India. Articles criticizing Sardar Patel and V.P. Menon, his abettor in the Madras Province, were also plentiful. Newspapers from Kerala and the Madras Province were banned within Thiruvithamkoor but were available at the borders. The newspaper *Jayakeralam* changed its name to *Thiruvithamkoor Pathrika*.

Railway and postal services had been partially re-established, serving Thiruvithamkoor alone. A new radio broadcast, named Vanoli – 'heavenly voice' – had started. The emphasis was on Thiruvithamkoor nationalism. Not a nationalism founded on linguistic lines alone, and to underline this, Vanoli gave equal importance to Malayalam and Tamil. The most significant changes were in the transportation of goods. The infrequent trains were used only for travel. With the development of the seaport at Poonthura, shipping containers became a common sight in Thiruvananthapuram. Another interesting change was in Pangode. The area was set aside for the embassies of foreign countries. Construction was under way. In the meantime, the embassies of Pakistan and Portugal functioned from temporary quarters. A major development was the changes made to the Temple Entry Declaration, the historic policy that had, after a long struggle, allowed people of the lower castes the right to worship in temples to which they had been so far banned entry. The declaration was modified to exclude twenty-one important temples from its powers, including the Padmanabhaswamy temple, Thiruvalla Sree Vallabha Kshetram, and the temples in Suchindram, Ettumanoor, Vaikom and Aranmula. Free public movement around these temples was also banned. The government claimed that they were finally acting on the demands devotees had been making for the last two decades. Simultaneously, the government announced policies for the upliftment of the avarnas. These included yearly financial support for the kaavu – sacred groves – and other places of worship under their management. Indian newspapers reported that at least fifty people were shot dead in Ambalapuzha and Thiruvattar in the revolts that followed these announcements. In Thiruvananthapuram, however, things were different. Celebrations, under the aegis of the Nair Service Society took place in all major localities in the city. In Vaikom, there was a large demonstration by avarnas who supported the government's policies, which all the newspapers reported with great prominence.

In this short time, great changes had taken place in the country's internal politics too. Leaders like Pattom Thanu Pillai, who, after being released from prison following independence, had changed their allegiance and supported the government, were re-arrested and jailed for their old activities and anti-national speeches. Bhaktivilasam, the official residence of the prime minister, became an even greater seat of power. It was the prime minister who controlled the day-to-day running of the country. He used his weekly radio broadcast to remind the citizens of their duties. Twice a month, he went to the royal palace to visit Amma Maharani and the Maharaja and update them on matters. These journeys, and the Maharaja's daily visit to the Sree Padmanabhaswamy temple, became occasions of great pomp and glory, rituals that spoke loudly of the nation's splendour.

As the country gained full independence, several new faces appeared in the political and public spheres. Here I describe some of them.

Politics

K.K. Nair

Born in 1907 in Kainakari in Kuttanad, K.K. Nair was educated at the Sanatana Dharma School in Alappuzha. After coming back from England where he did his higher education, Nair passed the Indian Civil Service exam, which, in those days, was something most young people dreamed of. He then went on to work as a civil servant in the United Provinces in British India. In the course of his career, he created powerful supporters and sworn enemies in equal numbers. He had close relationships with the Maharaja of Balrampur and the leaders of the Hindu Mahasabha. He had developed a reputation as the bosom friend of corrupt politicians and cruel zamindars.

The temple of Ranopali Nanakshahi in Ayodhya had a large property running to over a thousand acres. Its mahant, a man named Keshavdas, was addicted to opium. By law, the distribution of opium was under the direct control of the district magistrate. Sitting in this position, Nair, who had a fair idea of the mahant's vulnerability, ensured that he was regularly supplied with opium. The story was that Nair succeeded in keeping Keshavdas in a constant state of intoxication until the temple properties ended up in his hands.

In Ayodhya, there was a long-standing feud between Hindus and Muslims about the ownership of a mosque. One night, K.K. Nair, a man named Digvijay Singh and a few members of the Hindu Mahasabha scared off the security guard and planted an idol of the god Ram in the mosque. The next morning, a large crowd gathered to celebrate the miraculous appearance of Ram Lalla, or Baby Ram, at the mosque. Nair's Hindi-speaking wife, Shakuntala, was also there to lead the bhajan singing. Ironically, it was Nair who held the responsibility of taking legal action against the unlawful planting of the idol. He refused, of course, and the Uttar Pradesh government, following direct advice from Nehru, fired him.

Upon the invitation of our prime minister, K.K. Nair and his wife returned to the mother country where they received a warm welcome. Representatives of the Hindu Mahasabha hailed him at the border as he arrived in Tirunelveli by train and proceeded to Thiruvananthapuram by road. After an audience with Amma Maharani and the Maharaja, Nair had a meeting with the prime minister. A citizens' welcome was arranged at VJT Hall. In his acceptance speech, Nair said that India had a curse on it in the shape of its prime minister who was an atheist, and that time would prove that his actions were right. And now he would put the wealth of his experience to good use in serving Thiruvithamkoor, his motherland. He called on other Thiruvithamkoor citizens who held high positions in India to stop serving an anti-Hindu government and return to their own country.

K.K. Nair's first appointment was to the important position of the prime minister's principal secretary. The appointment was viewed also as an attempt to appease the Nair community that had a long-held distrust of the administrative control that foreign Brahmins had. The chief minister of Kerala ridiculed the appointment as an attempt by Sir C.P. to improve his image. Having someone else with a worse image can only make him look better in the eyes of the people, he said. But later events would prove that Nair's appointment was critical. He was shrewd and soon became the second in command in the administration. Within a couple of years, the king and the prime minister became unreachable; the only access to them was through Nair.

A.J. Simson

It was in 1938–39 that a man from Kulachal named A.J. Simson came to public attention. Until then, he was a young man involved in minor goonda-like activities limited to the Vaniyakkudi, Panavila and Mandaikkad areas. Unlike in the Malayalam-speaking areas, the Congress and the communists were not so active in these Tamil-speaking areas in southern Thiruvithamkoor. Simson collected tithe for the church and for the owners of the fishing boats. When a few young people protested against the church and against the businessmen who trapped fisherfolk in debt and then worked them like slaves, Simson beat the protest out of them. He was also known to sexually assault the women in the households of the men he terrorized. It stopped people from speaking up or complaining to the authorities. But there was also talk that he was fundamentally a coward, scared to be alone or even go anywhere on his own. Following several complaints to the British resident, he was once arrested by the police and spent a night in jail. That night, scared out of his wits, he defecated all over the cell. The incident made him behave in an overly obedient manner even with the ordinary policemen who were on duty that night.

It was during the State Congress–led agitations for Utharavada Bharanam that Simson's activities expanded to areas north of Thakkala. With no prompting from anyone, he pled allegiance to the diwan and organized a gang of hooligans named Simson Pada. This gang worked hand in hand with the five-rupee police to suppress the activities of the State Congress and to disrupt their meetings in Kollam and Thiruvananthapuram. The gusthi performances that Kumbalath Shanku Pillai and Thazhava Keshavan had put on before these meetings began were aimed at scaring away people like Simson and his followers, and to give party workers the courage to stand up to them. Still, all through the period of the agitations, Simson collaborated with the government. It was the Simson Pada that began the practice of throwing faeces at the houses of prominent State Congress leaders. The Rajabhakta Sangham took it up and spread it all the way to the north of the country. Their particular practice was to put excrement into drinking water wells. As the country moved towards independence, Simson and his gang became busier. After the attempted assassination of the Maharaja, they drove away everyone who nurtured even the least sympathy towards the State Congress.

After independence, Simson grew to be an important centre of unchallenged power in southern Thiruvithamkoor. He was also the answer to the accusation that Christians in Thiruvithamkoor were being oppressed. With the arrival of K.K. Nair, he became even more powerful. He became Nair's most trusted assistant. Their relationship even gave rise to a saying – 'Nair thinks, Simson does.' Much later, the Catholic church would honour A.J. Simson with the title of 'Chevalier'.

Jayananda Rao

Jayananda Rao, born and brought up around the Thirumala temple in Ernakulam, belonged to the Konkani Brahmin community. He was the son of Ganesh Rao, one of the first volunteers of the RSS in southern India. Jayananda Rao became involved with the Hindu Mahasabha at a very young age. On the day after Gandhi's assassination, Rao, only seventeen at the time, celebrated the event by distributing laddus in Mattancherry and was quite badly beaten up. Life in Ernakulam, the centre of Aikyakeralam activities, had become uncomfortable. So, by the end of 1948, he left his homeland and moved to Thiruvithamkoor.

It was Jayananda Rao who began the Hindu Mahasabha's 'shakhas' in our country. Shakhas were local branches, and it was not the practice of the Hindu Mahasabha to set up such units. At that time, Rao had no real connections with the all-India leadership of this organization which was banned in India. Taking inspiration from the RSS, and with the support of some like-minded folk, Rao set up shakhas near temples in various neighbourhoods in and around Thiruvananthapuram, Cherthala, Kayamkulam and Alappuzha, which began to catch people's attention. In the initial days, the attendees were mainly Konkani Brahmins and a few people from the Namboothiri, Nair and Asari communities. These were people reluctant to get on with the wider communities in which they lived, and they came into temple yards as soon as it was dark to learn vadithallu – fighting with sticks. Because of their refusal to come out into the light, people called them 'oozhans' after the pesky little insects that lived under the soil by day and came out at night to cut through the stems of plants and suck their juices. No one ever saw these oozhans, but evidence of their troublemaking was everywhere. Rao was careful to collaborate with the Rajabhakta Sangham which had sunk its roots deep into the rich savarna sections of society. The Sangham was an organization in name only and was, in reality, a bunch of people come together. Over a period of time, Rao was able to take over its control and attract its members into the Hindu Mahasabha. Within the next two or three years, shakhas began functioning in almost all parts of the country. Operating in and around temples, they perfected a methodology by which, in a very brief time, they took over the administration of these temples and the minds of the faithful who came there to worship. Several were the privately managed companies that they took over in this way. As K.K. Nair gained more power in the administration, the Hindu Mahasabha became stronger. Soon, it began to operate as though it was an official organization of the state. Nair bestowed upon the young Jayananda Rao the responsibility of administering the temples under the Thiruvithamkoor Devaswam, the trust looking after them. In this role, Rao began the process of unifying the Hindu religious practices and rituals in Kerala. Indigenous gods like Bhagavati, Ayyappan, Vettakkorumakan and Kali were ousted from the kaavus, the traditional sacred groves, their worship now replaced with customs and rituals in the Vaishnava tradition. Schools for religious study were set up, and attempts made to force children to attend them. Rao's actions also brought displeasure from some quarters, especially from within the Namboothiri, Nair and Ambalavasi communities. Rao continued to be an important figure in our country until his accidental death in 1962 while engaged in overseeing Thiruvithamkoor's first Somayagam. He was burnt to death during the last ritual of the Somayagam when the yagashala – the place where the yagam took place – was set alight. There were calls for an inquiry into his death, but the government refused to heed them.

Many were the activities that the Hindu Mahasabha undertook under Rao's leadership. They dug out the names of those who involved themselves in anti-national activities in each area and gave them to the police. They called for the social ostracization of such people. As a step towards turning the entire country vegetarian, they banned the use of fish, meat and eggs within a kilometre of temples. Instead of letting the Parayar make use of dead cows for food and leather, as was the custom, they gave them ritual burials.

Except in its initial years, the Hindu Mahasabha in Thiruvithamkoor was organizationally and ideologically affiliated with its counterpart in India. Yet they insisted that they were separate movements. In actual fact, when their operations were disrupted in India, it was in Thiruvithamkoor that the Hindu Mahasabha found its base. Many of its leaders came here when they had to step away from India. Every year on 15 November, which was celebrated as Nathuram Godse Remembrance Day, they organized processions in all major cities, with speeches by leaders from Bombay and Uttar Pradesh.

Franco Raghavan Pillah

Puthiyaveettil Raghavan Pillah, a man from Kadakkal, received the name 'Franco' because of Sir C.P. In 1938, there was a revolt in Kadakkal, precipitated by the exorbitant taxes levied on the merchandise that came into the market. For two weeks, neither the army nor government officials could enter the place. Raghavan Pillah was the leader, and he declared that Kadakkal was now an independent nation and he its king. He also appointed a prime minister. Sir C.P. called him 'Franco' after General Franco of Spain to indicate that this too was an uprising like the Spanish Civil War and needed to be suppressed. But what the name did was to endow Raghavan Pillah with an extraordinary heroic persona.

Kadakkal Kalapam, as the revolt came to be known, was suppressed soon enough. But try as they might, the army and the police could not capture Franco. All the while, he was in Kadakkal, hiding among the people. No one gave him away to the authorities. Besides, households in Kadakkal began the practice of keeping a plate of food aside for him in the evenings. There was no telling where he might turn up, hungry and wanting something to eat.

I was pretty sure that this legend, of mothers waiting for Raghavan Pillah with a plate of food at the ready, was the inspiration behind the story 'Amma' that Basheer had told me. He had told me this story three times, in three different ways.

In the first version, Basheer himself was the hero. Enthused by seeing Gandhi in person while he was still at school, Basheer runs away from home to join the freedom fight. He ends up in Kozhikode. There, the Congress people think that he is a CID.

'Me! A CID!' Basheer said, interrupting the storytelling, and then looked at me with suspicion. 'What if, by chance, you are the CID?'

One of those Congress people tells Basheer that he looks like Bhagat Singh. In that excitement, he joins the Uppu Satyagraha, the Salt March that Gandhi organized as part of the civil disobedience movement. He is arrested along with his fellow agitators, and is tortured by the police. Time passes, and much later, one night, he returns home to find his umma waiting for him with a plate of food. She has been doing so every night since the day Basheer ran away.

The second time he told me this story, the protagonist was an imprisoned revolutionary. After serving ten years, the revolutionary is released from prison and arrives at his home one unexpected night to find his mother waiting for him with a plate of food.

When he told me the story a third time, we were in prison together and were having our evening meal. This time, the hero was Franco Raghavan Pillah himself. One night, while in hiding, he goes home and finds his amma and a plate of food waiting for him.

'Why do you always mix up fact and fiction when you tell a story?' I asked. I still could not understand this. 'Either tell the facts as they are or make up a whole story.'

'Why do you mix your rice with sambar? Why not eat the rice and the vegetables separately?' Basheer made fun of me.

In the one year he spent in hiding, the police never even came close to catching Raghavan Pillah. Fed up, finally, he surrendered and was given a custodial sentence. After coming out of prison six or seven years later, he was lying low, engaged in some small-time farming. But when Thiruvithamkoor became independent, he became active again unexpectedly. By this time, most of the Congress leaders had either been imprisoned or exiled. Armed with local-made guns and knives, Franco Raghavan Pillah and his gang organized public protests against the king and the diwan in Chitara, Nilamel, Trikkanapuram and Attingal. The next day, the gang had a direct altercation with the army in which five of the protesters and a police inspector named Assaria were killed. Once again, Raghavan Pillah went into hiding.

Later, in the absence of experienced leaders, it was Franco Raghavan Pillah who took up the helm of Aikyakeralam in Thiruvithamkoor. He and his gang organized stealth attacks in many parts of the country. Living in Kochi or in the Madras Province, P.T. Chacko, Kumbalath Shanku Pillai, Akkamma Cherian, K. Balakrishnan and others made sure that he had all the support he needed. Weapons passed across the border unhindered. Once again, the police were entirely unsuccessful in capturing Franco who lived among his people, sometimes in hiding and sometimes in disguise. Many were the times he came close to death, but each time he escaped miraculously. One time, operating on information that Franco was hiding there, the army attacked the village of Amburi. The attack resulted in the death of several people while Franco escaped unscathed. The incident was picked up and used by India to argue that Thiruvithamkoor was annihilating its own people. Newspapers in Kerala described Franco as a heroic leader, while in Thiruvithamkoor the papers published serialized articles describing his cruel and hideous deeds. Among the populace, too, there existed many and contradictory stories about Franco Raghavan Pillah.

DSP Vaidyanatha Iyer

The head of the secret service agency, the Civil Protection Group, was a man named Vaidyanatha Iyer who had been a close confidant of Sir C.P. Ramaswami Iyer from before the Punnapra–Vayalar struggle. Basheer had referred to him as 'Pattar's assistant pattar'. Vaidyanatha Iyer was born to a couple in Kumbakonam but had grown up in our country from the age of fourteen and then gone to Scotland for his training. There were those who believed that were it not for his decisive intervention, the Punnapra–Vayalar revolt would have been a success and the communists would have been in power in Alappuzha. With the establishment of the CPG, his influence multiplied; he was now answerable only to K.K. Nair and the prime minister. It was Vaidyanatha Iyer who oversaw the eviction of the inhabitants of Kizhakkekotta, Kannanmoola and other neighbourhoods to make space for Brahmin settlers.

Vaidyanatha Iyer grew the CPG into a true secret investigative agency that could compete with any such organization in the world. It was believed that CPG agents were involved in the murder of several Aikyakeralam activists inside and outside the country. In 1950, India declared Vaidyanatha Iyer a criminal. But the most serious allegation against him was about the death of A.K. Pillah, Thiruvithamkoor's representative at the United Nations.

After finishing his stint at the United Nations in 1955, A.K. Pillah lived in a rented house in Colombo, spending his time speaking at universities, writing and reading. He was widely respected for his mature and thoughtful analyses of international affairs. In December 1956, Pillah wrote an article in *The Statesman* titled 'The Future of Travancore'. In it, he explained that he had argued in favour of Thiruvithamkoor's independence because the country had an idea of nationalism that was different from and better than India's, and because it had a better culture and quality of life. And that had been the right decision at the time. But it was now time for Thiruvithamkoor to embrace democracy, he said, and appealed to the people that they should work proactively towards it without waiting for anyone's largesse. In 1957, at the beginning of January, A.K. Pillah was killed in a car accident close to his home.

Within the police department, Vaidyanatha Iyer had the reputation of being a hard drinker. But his family and friends, those who knew him well, had other stories to tell. At home, he was loving and caring. He had established a home for the destitute in Kollam in memory of his daughter who had died unexpectedly, a place where everyone, irrespective of caste and religion, was welcomed. He went there at least once a month and served food to the people there. It was also said that, at the beginning of his career, he was known to behave kindly towards even the worst of criminals and to be entirely incorruptible.

The Public Sphere

K.N. Ramanatha Kuruppu

K.N. Ramanatha Kuruppu – KNR as he was called – was known as a revolutionary poet. When communist and socialist ideas began to become popular in the Malayalam-speaking parts of British India, they were also seen reflected in the literature and art of the region. KNR's beginnings were also as a poet, and naturally for the time, his work showed influences of Changampuzha Krishna Pillah, known popularly as Changampuzha, the pastoral romantic Malayalam poet. Some of KNR's works were calls for societal change. Connecting stories and images from Hindu puranas and legends with socialist ideology, he tried to bring out their modern sensibility and potential. By this time, a chapter of IPTA – the Indian People's Theatre Association – was active in Thiruvithamkoor. Young people associated with IPTA wrote plays on socially relevant issues with popular and crowd-pleasing elements of performance stitched in. Earliest among them were *Pattabakki* by K. Damodaran and *Kudiyan*, a play by an Ezhuthachan from Palakkad. The plays that followed these – *Puthiya Bhoomi, Koythu, Communistukaran* – garnered public approval. Most enthusiastically received were the revolutionary and love songs in these plays written by KNR. These songs remained on the lips of many a Malayali for a long time to come. And KNR received the epithet 'revolutionary poet'.

All through the period when the country went through internal strife and when it was at war with India, KNR remained silent. Later he would say that he had forgotten poetry, concerned as he was with the fate of the country. When independence was a certainty, he made a comeback with two poems, titled 'Venadinte Punarjjani' (The Rebirth of Venad) and 'Nadinte Mahabhagyam' (The Great Fortune of the Country). In the second, he compared Diwan Sir C.P. Ramaswami Iyer to Hanuman Swami, the monkey god of the Ramayanam who loyally serves Sreeraman and saves the land. He went on to write several more khantakavyams, long narrative poems, that glorified the nation, with titles such as 'The Victory of Dharmaraja', 'The Greatness of Ananthapuri' and 'To My Country', all of which became prescribed reading in schools and colleges. He was appointed as a language teacher at Thiruvananthapuram Maharaja's College, and was soon given the important responsibility of leading the Bhasha Parishkara Commission set up to modernize the language. The objective of the commission was to ban Malayalam books that contained ideas detrimental to Thiruvithamkoor nationalism and to correct texts where necessary.

Some poems by Ulloor S. Parameswara Iyer who penned our national anthem, 'Vancheeshamangalam', were thus corrected or removed from circulation. For instance, the lines, 'Gandhi, Bose, Tagore ee moorthitrayangale naam / Santhwathil dhyanichu moksham nedam', where he compares Gandhi, Subhas Chandra Bose and Rabindranath Tagore to the Trinity of Gods, and suggests that quietly meditating on them would lead to salvation. The poem that began with these lines, 'Ente Matham' (My Religion), was removed from all books. So were other poems of his: 'Mahasamadhi', a poem about Tagore; 'Vijayaprartana' and 'Jayabheri' about Gandhi; and 'Prabhata Gatha' that called for every Bharatheeyan, anyone who considered themselves a citizen of Bharatham, to rise out of their stupor. Ulloor's poem 'Thammiladi' (Infighting) was until then understood to be about the failure of the Bharatheeyans of British India to achieve independence because they were busy fighting with one another. But KNR wrote an essay arguing that Ulloor had the people of Thiruvithamkoor in mind when he wrote it and directed that every child be taught the poem. Banned were also several of the works of Vallathol Narayana Menon: Poems that glorified the motherland including 'Mathrubhumiyodu', 'Ente Kritaghnatha', 'Vijayippoothaka'; poems that venerated Gandhi, including 'Ithile, Ithile', 'Om Shanti Shanti', 'Kaalam Maari' and 'Ente Gurunathan'; poems describing the significance of the charkha, the spinning wheel that personifies Gandhism, such as 'Chakragaatha', 'Khadivasanangal Kaikkolkinevarum' and 'Poraa, Poraa'; poems about Gandhi's life in prison, 'Somagrahanam' and 'Papamochanam'; poems written about the Congress assembly in Madras such as 'Thilakamandapam', 'Aa Potticchiri', 'Jayichupoyi', 'Mottusoochi', 'Sahavasiyude Sahasam' and 'Paadapaamsu'. In addition to the full ban on these specific works, all of Vallathol's poems were removed from textbooks. A ban was also imposed on the usage of the term 'Kavithrayam' – Trinity of Poets – that was widely used to describe Ulloor, Vallathol and Kumaranasan. Other banned works included poems by Sahodharan Ayyappan, G. Sankara Kuruppu, Bodheswaran, Vennikulam Gopala Kuruppu, Balamani Amma and Akkitham. KNR also went about revising some of his own poems from the early stages of his career.

KNR prepared a long-term plan to modernize the language and submitted it to the government. It contained ideas to formulate a Malayalam that would be different – he called it 'veritta Malayalam' – from the Malayalam used in Kerala, which was part of India. Many were the recommendations that he outlined in the plan, including the use of more Sanskrit words in prose and the gradual adoption of the Devanagari script. The plan highlighted Savarkar's work to modernize the Marathi language with the addition of vocabulary from Sanskrit. KNR introduced the use of Malayalam mixed with Sanskrit in government circulars and official papers. Some newspapers followed suit but soon abandoned the idea when the circulation plummeted.

Despite all these developments, the songs that KNR had written all those years ago for the theatre continued to be popular among the revolutionaries of Kerala. They were sung loudly and proudly in demonstrations demanding the swift annexation of Thiruvithamkoor by the Indian Union. No one found this weird or puzzling.

K.P. Sukumaran Nair

K.P. Sukumaran Nair, popularly known only by his initials KP, was part of a family from Palakkad that had settled in Kollam. He began writing poetry at a very young age. But it was a short story, published in a magazine from Kozhikode, that got him noticed. The story was widely read and appreciated, especially by those who were fed up with the new generation of writers, ever eager to insert unpleasant things into their writings and pepper them with obscenities. 'Here, finally, the Changampuzha of prose!' proclaimed one critic. Soon, KP turned his attention to writing novels and was hugely successful in this endeavour.

In their use of language, KP's works were the antithesis of works by other established prose writers of Thiruvithamkoor such as Thakazhi Sivasankara Pillai and P. Keshavadev. KP's writings gave the reader a sweet ache. Not that they did not engage with social anxieties. But the undercurrent was concern with issues such as the breakup of the family unit, the sorrows of the Ambalavasi and Nair communities who faced great challenges in these new times, nostalgia for an older time when different castes coexisted in camaraderie. The isolation of the individual was his major theme, and he used a language that was enticingly romantic and strewn with philosophical musings. The dialogue was not in the usual boring, ordinary speech. His characters had such exquisite names that his readers began to name their children after them. Love letters written in that time copied his language.

Still, the modernists within the literary world regarded KP with derision. It was the time when many of the stories Basheer told were being passed around orally. In *Panjajanyam*, a magazine published from Thrissur, there appeared a story about a man who went around making up stories based on experiences that were not his, who couldn't be bothered to write them down. The author's name was Somanath. The same author had also written a story about a clientless lawyer who went about trying to write stories, obviously aimed at ridiculing Thakazhi Sivasankara Pillai. The modernists were convinced that this 'Somanath' was none other than KP.

The most significant phase in KP's career began when Hamsakkoya Thangal, a businessman who was a great admirer of Sir C.P., began a literary magazine, *Udayam*, in Karunagappally. KP was appointed as the founding editor. It made him the authority who decided the literary sensibility not only in Thiruvithamkoor but in all Malayalam-speaking lands. He knew, quite clearly, that power was taken, not bestowed on a person. As the editor, he encouraged writers old and new, paid them well. But he also took the liberty of freely editing the stories and poems sent to him, changed their names, gave them pen names, had them rewrite their work over and over. No one took offence. Instead, they went about testifying that their works were elevated to a higher plane with a single stroke of KP's editorial pen. Others wished KP would give them the gift of a new name. Writers of the new generation discarded role models like Thakazhi and began copying KP's language and style in their stories. Being published in *Udayam* became the mark of literary success, and Karunagappally became a centre of literary pilgrimage. Silence was KP's hallmark. Writers sat in front of him wrapped in that silence, and when they came out, they gave it various interpretations.

Udayam and KP's stewardship of the magazine brought about several good results. Writers in Kerala too, which was part of India, began to be afraid of criticizing the Thiruvithamkoor government, stopped making even general adverse comments about autocracy and royal rule. Some began writing essays stating that India must respect other ideas about nationhood formed after independence, and that democracy was a European notion. Left-wingers wrote about the modernity, hidden but present, in KP's writings. Critics regularly tore to pieces works by writers KP disliked, including Thakazhi, Keshavadev and Muttathu Varkey. Fame-seeking writers interrogated them in public forums whenever they had a chance. KP himself rarely made public appearances, and when he did, he spoke softly into the mike, his speech punctuated by long intervals of silence.

K.P. Sukumaran Nair would later become the only writer to receive the highest literary accolades in both Thiruvithamkoor and India, two nations at loggerheads with one another. There were writers like Zacharia who called his writing 'painkili' – romantic drivel – while he was still alive. But even after his death, the fear KP inculcated followed generations of writers. Even in 2035, when a critic opined in a public forum that KP's works were the least accomplished in the last century, the audience booed until he sat down cowed.

Kunchacko

Malayalam cinema began with the artists in Thiruvithamkoor. Still, all production processes took place in Madras. Kunchacko, a native of Pulinkunnu, was a great patriot of our country. In the year we attained independence, he established a film studio, Udaya, in Pathirappally in Alappuzha and transplanted Malayalam cinema from Madras to our country.

After the first two, all the films he made were patriotic, devotional, or ones that glorified life in Thiruvithamkoor. Several of them – *Raja Kesavadasan, Veera de Lannoy, Sree Padmanabha Charitram, Ashokavani, Tipu Sultan, Vajramothiram, Paramabhakta Markhandeya* – were commercial successes. The songs in these films were written by KNR. A film that requires particular mention here is *Swami Vijayam.* Its subject was the attempted assassination of Maharaja Sree Chithira Thirunal Balarama Varma. In the film, it is the ruler of the neighbouring country, moved by jealousy towards Thiruvithamkoor's prosperity and a deep personal enmity towards the diwan, who sends the assassins. But the attempt is foiled because of the timely intervention of Diwanji. Sree Padmanabhaswamy Himself makes a divine intervention that causes the electricity to fail at the crucial moment. *Swami Vijayam* depicted Varghese and Basheer as heinous; Basheer is portrayed as raping two young Tamil Brahmin women. Students from schools and colleges all across the nation were taken to the theatres and made to watch the film. India banned the screening of the film in Kerala. A second part was made later, in which a new actor, a man named Prem Nazir from Chirayinkeezhu, enacted the role of a police inspector. The narrative follows him as he pursues Basheer and finally kills him.

It was through Kunchacko's films that Thikkurissy Sukumaran Nair, Prem Nazir and Sathyan attained their status as the greatest actors of Thiruvithamkoor. Their films influenced generations in the Malayalam-speaking parts of India. They helped reinforce the feeling that the people of Thiruvithamkoor lived happy, contented lives. In 1962, the government of India banned screenings of all films made in Thiruvithamkoor.

Murikkummoottil Outhachan

The prime minister had invited the American agronomist Norman Borlaug to Thiruvithamkoor for a visit. Borlaug travelled all around the country and made a few recommendations to the government. Self-sufficiency in food was an urgent and crucial objective. So, swiftly acting on Borlaug's recommendations, the government made changes to our agrarian laws and sanctioned subsidies to farmers. Murikkummoottil Outhachan was a man who quickly made use of the new policies. Creating a company on the American model, he began large-scale farming operations in Nanjinad, Onattukara and Kuttanad. He imported new paddy seed stock from Southeast Asia and from the Philippines. The sudden mechanization of agriculture had the adverse effect of starvation and death among the lower castes who lost their livelihoods as agrarian workers. Protests and violent events followed, but the government stood firmly by Outhachan.

Freeman-Thomas, Marquess of Willingdon

Lord Willingdon, governor general of India, had passed away in 1941, so how would he have become an important personage in post-independence Thiruvithamkoor? A legitimate puzzle, but it is true.

Even the Maharaja had seen Lord Willingdon in his bedroom once when he started awake from sleep at an ungodly hour. Dressed in his best coat, with his face clean-shaven and the edges of his trimmed moustache sharpened to points, his head beginning to go bald and eyes half-closed, the lord was staring at the Maharaja with great interest. The Maharaja had just had a dream in which he was a young boy. He sat up immediately and called to his sentry.

Thiruvithamkoor had been under regency rule when the Maharaja was a minor. His enemies propagated the falsehood that the British would never let him rule even after he reached maturity at age eighteen because he was mentally deficient. To prove them wrong, Diwan Sir C.P. Ramaswami Iyer took His Royal Highness to Lord Willingdon. Lord Willingdon studied the boy sitting alone in front of him and asked him a few questions. He then allowed His Royal Highness to ascend the throne. This was not because the lord was convinced of his mental capacity, said the naysayers then, but because, in order to pretend to rule a tiny native kingdom like Thiruvithamkoor, no one needed a full brain.

Following the Maharaja's sighting of Lord Willingdon in his bedchamber, people began to see him at odd hours all over the palace. Most of the high-ranking officials, with the exception of the prime minister, claimed to have seen him. People ran into him in the racks at the British Library, flicking through his friend Rudyard Kipling's book, pacing in the front yard of the old Residency Bungalow ... and so on and so forth. When this went on for a while, the Maharaja summoned the royal astrologers. There was nothing to worry about, they told him. Lord Willingdon was peaceful in his death, they said, and he had great fondness and sympathy for the people of this country.

I too was convinced of the whole Lord Willingdon situation after I stepped out of my room at the lodge and interacted with people. Many of them had also seen Lord Willingdon. One night, I was a little drunk and was walking along the railway tracks from Pattom to Thampanoor when I ran into two trackmen. One of them had seen Lord Willingdon.

'Where?' I asked him.

'Here, right here, just the other day,' he said.

I left them and went on my way. I had walked along a bit when I saw a man coming towards me. Railway workers were always walking along the tracks, so I did not pay much attention to his face or his figure. As we passed each other, suddenly he took out a knife and flashed it at me. Shocked, I fell, and he flashed it in the air once again and walked away. It was clear that he did not intend to kill me or harm me. Perhaps it was a message from someone, telling me that I was not needed here. Or I had become so unimportant that I had disappeared from everyone's memory. He had flashed that knife like he was shooing a fly away. Perhaps he had done it without thinking, or he was just having fun. He might not even remember the incident.

That same night, I left Thiruvithamkoor.

II

For the second time in my life, I was in Thiruvambady in Malabar, and by then, as I had predicted in the report I had written all those years ago, everything had changed. Except, that is, the exuberance of Elikkutty's youth.

Thiruvambady had ceased to be a forest and had turned into a place with all facilities. People had built dwellings all along the deserted forest paths down which we had walked when we came here first. Earth left undisturbed by human interference had been dug up, the soil turned by hoes with pointy blades brought from Thiruvithamkoor. Seeds from our country had sprouted, fruited and been harvested several times. Shops sprouted too, all over, trading in the harvests, and a church of the Sacred Heart and a school beside it. Oxen trundled up and down the wide roads pulling loaded carts. Landowners unused to working the land had sold off their properties, pocketed the cash and gone away. They left behind a generation of nephews and other descendants enraged at their action, and these young people joined the Communist Party. Wherever there was a village of migrants – Christian chettans from Thiruvithamkoor – there was, in close proximity, a communist stronghold. Completely different worlds, these two. In one, young men, with no particular occupation, sat around day and night, thinking and strategizing about equality for all on earth. In the other, in lands forsaken by their ancestors, people from another land, men and women with no particular ideological standpoint, toiled together, their thoughts only on survival. Were they to be told that there would come a time when everyone would be equal, they would smile.

By the time of my second visit, there was a bus service between Kozhikode and Thiruvambady. The bus arrived at its destination in the evening, and the driver spent the night there. By dusk, Thiruvambady was cloaked in the mild fragrance of charayam. If anyone unused to a day's hard work swallowed a mouthful of this potent arrack brewed from paddy by the chettans, their story would come to a swift end.

The night of my arrival, I sat drinking charayam with Devasia. He lay in his bed, and I sat beside him on a wooden chest that was used to store rice. Elikkutty stood a little away, watching us. Ever since I had left Vallappuzha Vaidyan's place, I had not met a single person who had known me. Everyone had forgotten me. Even the dead were remembered at least for a while after their passing. I had been forgotten while I was still alive. Perhaps I had not done anything in my life so far that was worth remembering. But these two people, Devasia and Elikkutty, whom I had met at the Aluva railway station many years ago and had spent twenty or so days with, had not forgotten me. They talked about me every day, they said, or at least thought about me. And I ... I guess I would have thought of them five or six times in all these years.

Unlike the last time I was here, there were no erumadams, the dwellings up in the trees that people, emulating their ancestors, had built. They had all climbed down the trees and built proper houses on solid earth. Devasia and Elikkutty had also built theirs. Only a single room at first, with twigs stacked between bamboo poles for walls. Then, two years later, a nice house with two rooms, with walls of red stone and a thatched roof. They cultivated the land around the house, planted yams, tapioca, kaachil, nanakizhangu, taro, banana. An acre was set aside to sow paddy, depending on the rains, and when it was ripe, husband and wife would harvest the whole crop in a week or two, thresh it and store it away. Devasia gave away seed stock to those who came looking for it. Now, with his health deteriorating, he had had to cut down on the work of ploughing, weeding, sowing. Elikkutty grew what they needed in the yards around the house, producing without fail just enough for both of them to survive.

In a spurt of energy, Devasia sat up in his bed and ate some kanji with a side of fried mullan fish.

'Avaracha, you won't believe the number of people who came up to Thiruvambady after you went back,' he said. 'Just upped sticks and came over. More and more came as problems there increased. Can't believe that the places we left behind are now in another country. Ho! To think Pravithanam is in another country!'

'Who's left back there, your relatives?' I asked, struggling to inhabit the name 'Avarachan' again. They didn't hear my question. I asked it again and still they didn't hear. I understood that there was no need to ask it again.

'Where's the chain that was around your neck?' Elikkutty asked me.

'Here, you too have some,' Devasia said, sliding the bottle of charayam towards Elikkutty. 'It's only Avarachan here. No need to be shy.'

'Ayyo, that. It broke,' I answered her question. 'It was old.'

'Put this on then,' Elikkutty said, picking up a string of beads lying next to the Bible. It had a small cross as a pendant. 'Men going around with nothing around their neck. It's unsightly.'

Sitting on top of the rice chest, I too had my kanji and fried mullan. Elikkutty had also made a little condiment, chillies and onions roasted over coal and crushed with her fingers together with salt, tamarind and a slug of coconut oil. It was spicy and sour. Devasia could not eat it any more.

'I used to love it,' he said, 'but no more. Whatever I eat, I get this heartburn, hear, and sour hiccups. And if I get the runs, it's more work for her.'

'I love it too,' I said, although I was eating it for the first time. 'My ammachi used to make it. She'd grind the chillies after roasting them, with onions and salt.'

'Where's Ammachi now? Still around?' Elikkutty asked.

'No, she's gone. By the time I got back from here, they had buried her. That's why I was late coming back. Some folks who said they would come up here went off to Kattappana. We didn't. And then, a couple of years later, Appachan also died.'

Recalling from memory the story I had told them all those years ago, I added a believable end to it. Long years lay stretched between us in the silence that followed. Insects, still around even after the forest outside had disappeared, called to the light inside from the darkness outside.

The meal was over and yet we did not feel sleepy. Taking a mouthful of charayam every now and then, we sat up chatting until the small hours of the morning. They had so much they wanted to talk about.

'Ennada, Avaracha, why are you so silent?' Elikkutty became the old, energetic young woman who had walked all the way from Kozhikode to Thiruvambady.

'O, what do I have to say. Lots of years just rolled on with nothing much to show for them. Go on, you tell me your news.'

'No need to get up early in the morning,' Devasia said. 'Nothing urgent to take care of.'

I asked them about the people, folks from Changanassery, who were already here when Devasia and Elikkutty arrived. My last night here, they had appeared at the bottom of the erumadam as I was saying my goodbyes and getting ready to leave.

'Ah, best not to talk about it,' Devasia said. 'It will only upset her.'

I looked at Elikkutty. She sat staring into the darkness outside. Devasia recalled the trouble they had caused, those who had come saying they wanted to help.

'Wouldn't let us have a peaceful night's sleep, that lot, hear,' he said. 'Who could we complain to? We didn't have the police and all that until much later.'

I helped Devasia up, and with small, slow steps, took him outside. He urinated into the darkness, a feeble trickle that dripped on his legs. It had been a long while since he had stepped outside like this, he said. Usually, he urinated into a mud pot which Elikkutty emptied.

'Because of them, I was this close to abandoning everything and going away,' Devasia said. 'But Elikkutty, she wouldn't let me. You'll be back soon, she said, with more of our people, and then we won't be alone. We believed you would too, hear, and that made us stand firm. Thinking about it now – I don't know how we stood up to those wild men. Every day, Elikkutty would tell me, don't worry, our folks will be here soon. In the end, it was good we had the courage to stay. After a while, they started fighting among themselves. The cruel don't last that long, as they say.'

'Stop harping on about all that. You'll only upset him,' Elikkutty said as we helped Devasia back on to his bed. 'Look, his eyes are wet. Potteda, let it go. When you didn't come back, we knew something serious must have happened.'

My lies had made them stay in this place, for such a long time. They had nothing to say to each other about the people they had left behind or about the children they did not have. As they eked out a living in this dismal, deserted place, all they had to talk about was the young man who had helped them get here and spent a few days with them. No one in the whole world remembered that man now. But these two people had only him to remember. The world that he had served all his life did not want him, but these two did. I felt that this place, right here, was the centre of my world.

'Ha! Avaracha, don't cry,' Devasia said. 'We didn't mean to upset you. Still exactly like you were when you were here last, getting upset over the silliest thing. Potteda.'

As I bent down to help him lie back, his hand touched the crown of my head.

Saying that I had to urinate, I stepped outside and stood looking at the sky. Would a man like me cry? Still, could the sorrow that I was feeling right now be just an act? What if we began to love the life we built on lies? These two people would have continued talking about me until I came back. If I hadn't come back, they would have talked about me until their death. Who else was there in this world, except these two human beings living in this remote corner, to talk about this useless creature?

12

I slept the sleep of the dead, all through the day, for the first time in my life. Elikkutty cooked their portion of a young bull that had been slaughtered in the neighbourhood. I woke up inhaling its aroma as it simmered in the pot in a paste of chillies and coriander. I helped Devasia up and sponged his body with lukewarm water, and then went out into the compound to have my own bath. Back inside, I sat on the rice chest, ready for my meal. Elikkutty handed me a large enamel plate with a mound of rice topped with the curry, and stood aside watching me eat.

'Go on, eat, fill your belly,' Devasia said.

'We can't eat like you easterners,' I said.

'You can too, if you work hard enough. Look at me now. Don't need much more than a couple of bits of tapioca and a glass of kanjivellam. I feel full up to my neck!'

They did not ask me what my plans were, or say that if I had the money, I could buy some land. Nor did they ask me why I had come back now, after all this time. Some people are able to recognize those who come to them with nothing to their name, no one to look for them. They will not worry the wanderer with questions. These two people, Devasia and Elikkutty, fed me as though I was an ancestral spirit come on his yearly visit.

I ate until it felt like I would never need to eat again, and then went to sleep again on a mat on the floor by Devasia's bed. This sleep was not like earlier. It was filled with trouble. Three people came into my sleep to disturb the peace. Varghese, Mani and an old man dressed in a single mundu whose face remained unclear.

He crawled into my head through my ear and played around in there. Scribbled things with a pencil stub. Vallappuzha Vaidyan came in and erased them by morning.

'The rest of your treatment will be here,' he told me. 'You don't have to ever leave this place.'

I woke up in the morning feeling calm. After a couple more days, I began helping Elikkutty with the work in the compound.

A large part of the five-acre plot that they had bought from Mannidath Nair had gone to weed, but the signs of Devasia's and Elikkutty's back-breaking work to rid the soil of rocks and stones and prepare it for cultivation were everywhere. Trees planted along the edge of the plot to mark the boundary had grown and blocked the view beyond. The sloping plot on the hillside had been terraced with stacked stones and mud walls. Basins, pits and channels had been built to let enough water seep into the earth and the rest flow away. They had worked the soil, compressed over a thousand years, and made it friable. There was a well they had dug themselves, and a cowshed built with strenuous effort. Elikkutty took me to the top terrace where, in their first year, they had planted bananas of the etha variety with a base crop of kuttypayar, short-podded cowpeas. Drunk on the water carried all the way up from the bottom of the hill and the dripping from leaves, the bananas had prospered until, just before the fruit bunches matured, a wind had come roaring in and floored them. The year after that, the crop was lost to a drought in which even the well dried. In the third and fourth years, Devasia harvested several bunches of bananas, but in the fifth year, another wind brought havoc again.

'It's just how it is,' Elikkutty said in response to my commiseration. 'It's how farming life is. Add up ten years of work and there'll be nothing to show for it either way. But we won't starve, that's there.'

We began hacking through the weeds and undergrowth that had taken over ever since Devasia's fall. When I stopped for a break, Elikkutty grabbed my hand and peered at my palm.

'What's this, Avaracha, your palm is like them akathammas who never do a jot of work,' she said. 'Barely gripped the koduvaal and the skin is already split and bleeding. And your face! Red and puffy from this little sunlight!'

She took off the towel flung across her chest and put it on my shoulder.

'Here, wipe the sweat.'

By the fifth day, we had cleared the upper terrace, and in the following week, hoed the soil. That night, precisely, it rained. In the morning, we climbed up carrying tapioca cuttings ready for planting. Sunlight slanted across the slope. Trees dripped the remainder of the rain. The soil lay wet and ready. I picked up the hoe and began preparing a bed.

'Ayye! Avaracha, is this how you plant tapioca?'

Elikkutty grabbed the hoe off me and demonstrated how to prepare the bed to plant tapioca. She drew the soil into a mound, like a big, firm breast. Only then would the tapioca take root and produce tubers. Laughing, she handed the hoe back to me. I gave it a try.

'Ah, yes, this is good,' she said. 'Make it a little larger though.'

By noon, we had planted half of the cuttings. Elikkutty went down to fetch our kanji. I stood up, stretched my back and looked around me. Not a single human being was in sight, not even their sound or smell. No one followed anyone suspiciously, distrusting. Gaze did not penetrate to the outside, nor came piercing inside. Countries cleaving into several or coming together into one was of no consequence here. It did not matter if they were ruled by the white man or by Gandhi. This, now, was my world. As Vallappuzha Vaidyan said, why should I ever leave this place? This was the second place I had come to, sad and desperate. And these people here were waiting for me like the mother in Basheer's story who had waited for her son all night, every night, with a plate of food. Like Vallappuzha Vaidyan in the light of the lamp in the first place, Elikkutty was waiting, peering into the dark. This plot of land, sloping downwards to the cover of trees at the boundary, populated only by these trees and plants, the two heads of cattle, and the three of us, was my world. Suddenly, a bird from another world flew in, picked up a worm from the soil I had hoed and flew away. I walked in the direction of its flight and reached the edge of the compound, the edge of our world. I looked at that other world outside, just to see the sights. It was in turmoil. Men tried to kill men. Earthquakes and hurricanes, floods. New songs, dance, films. Young people agitated in the streets. Smoked cigarettes and held discussions, convinced that their world would change in the next instant for the betterment of all. Kings became fewer in number. Others took their place and acted like kings. White men watched the world without stepping out of their homes. Humans built a machine that could travel around the earth like the moon, and sent it up into the skies. It traversed the sky above our world too. People fled, alone and in groups, some, only to return. Rowed boats in the oceans. Flew across the sky. Countries became one. Split apart. Secret discussions, public challenges, knife fights. Human beings wore too many clothes and then took them all off. Countries and houses built fences at their boundaries to stop people from moving freely across them. There were those who made holes in the fences. Thiruvithamkoor was also building a fence. And there, too, people tried to bore holes into it. Sir C.P. had taken to wearing a military uniform at all times to make known that the country was fighting. Courageously, he stood for elections and won 99 per cent of the votes. His opponents challenged his victory, claiming it was a lie. Thiruvananthapuram, now, was a city more peaceful than before, steeped in the mantras of regular yagams and Murajapam. In the raja's eyes, there were now only good citizens. Franco Raghavan Pillah continued to hide among the citizenry, like fish in water. Simson and K.K. Nair executed their jobs efficiently. Together, they suppressed the uprising of the Tamils in the southern end of the country. Blood flowed freely there. Vaidyanatha Iyer's CPG still had people killed. It was believed that K. Balakrishna Pillah and R. Sugathan were killed that way. KNR stepped back from his official duties to write an epic poem about the Venad Swaroopam, the mighty kingdom of Venad that preceded Thiruvithamkoor, in the model of *Raghuvamsam* by the celebrated Sanskrit poet Kalidasan. A film, *Marupadi*, produced by M.R. Vithal, was released. It portrayed Basheer as having escaped death and making a comeback to take another stab at assassinating the Maharaja. Before he was killed by the hero of the film, Krishnan Nair, played by the actor Sathyan, he apologized to the country.

'Why are you standing there staring that way?' I heard Elikkutty calling to me. 'Come and have your kanji.'

We ate the kanji, accompanied by a chammanthi of dried shark meat, and got back to work. We planted all the tapioca by the time the sun set and walked back to the house.

There were no years, no hours, in our house. Night and day came and went, rain and sunlight and, sometimes, fog. Hours of daylight passed, and afterwards it was difficult to say how many days had come and gone. Equally difficult was figuring out what lay ahead. Elikkutty and Devasia did not hold inside them the number of years they had lived in this place. They had an accurate estimate of the years cultivation went without a hitch. Once, I tried to recall when we had taken the train to Malabar together. Was it 1942 or 1943, I wondered aloud. Devasia was intrigued. Why – how – did you keep an account of time, he said.

Pandu, innaal, orikkal, annu, appol, aa samayathu, a long time ago, the other day, once, that day, then, that time. Any of this would do because we have the memory, don't we, he said. And whether we remember or not, what was the point in naming the year precisely? It might be useful if it was about something yet to happen, about the future, I said. We could then do what we needed to do at the right time. But what is the right time, asked Devasia as we sat together with a bottle of charayam between us. Isn't everything just a bloody mix inside us?

'Hear, now, when you went up to plant the tapioca, I was walking with both of you along the road from Kozhikode to Thiruvambady,' Devasia said. 'And when we got here, and you went back, and we cleared this place and started cultivation. I'm lying right here, and it all came to me, passed right in front of my eyes. We just think we have lived a long time. But lying here and thinking about it, it only took a minute. You go out to work in the compound and I think, how will I spend the time until evening? But then I close my eyes and open them, and it is already sunset.'

'Sometimes I feel I should have been born much later,' I said, 'or maybe long before.'

'That's an interesting thought, Avaracha,' Devasia agreed. 'I've thought that too, lying here alone. People should have been born several years earlier or later. Hear, Eeshomishiha, our Lord Jesus, he should be born now, after the rains in the month of Thulam.'

'Yes, and that means he'll die on the cross in 1991 or 1992.'

'He could be born in our cattle shed, why not.'

Elikkutty came in with the tapioca for our meal, her face shining in the light of the tin lamp.

'That Gandhi should have been born a hundred years earlier. Imagine what all he would have done.'

'Ha, ha, yes.'

'Sir C.P. should be born in 2001. And should slip on a banana skin and fall down and die, say in 2084.'

'That would be fun,' Elikkutty agreed. 'And Avaracha, you should have been born two Christmases ago. Then you would be a toddler waddling around here butt naked. And I'd be feeding you, mmumm-mmumm, ha, ha, ha!'

All three of us roared with laughter. As we laughed, Elikkutty picked up a piece of tapioca and put it in my mouth. 'Here, vavey,' she said, and we laughed again.

The next day, or the day after, or some other day, when Elikkutty brought our evening tapioca meal, Devasia and I were talking about something else.

'Avaracha, we should have come to Thiruvambady much later, no?' Devasia said.

'You're right,' I said. 'A hundred or a hundred and fifty years later.'

'Ha, ha, that's good.'

'Then we would have come here in an aeroplane.'

'Quite right. And the white sahibs should have left in 2035. Or just this morning!'

'Both of you have gone mad or what, filling your bellies with paddy water every night?' Elikkutty asked.

Unmindful of time, we sat up and talked crazy talk through the nights. And during the days, when Elikkutty and I toiled in the soil, Devasia lay on his back in his bed, staring at the ceiling. Sometimes, I felt that it was me in that bed. As I had been on the plank bed at Vallappuzha Vaidyan's place. This was the place where the bitterness that had been poured into my head would be cleansed. Elikkutty was the only one who had any connection with the world outside. She went there every now and then to buy salt, chillies and dried fish. She also attended church on rare occasions, and came back and told Devasia what was said in the sermon in great detail. He sat listening to her with his eyes closed. On those days, during evening prayers, he was unusually loud. His rhythmic voice travelled, slowly, sorrowfully, outside our house and into the compound, to the plants, to their leaves, buds, roots and new shoots. I found it in the mornings after when I stepped out, lingering still, until, as the sun warmed, it faded slowly away.

If you need to know about the people who live in a house, all you have to do is look at their compound. It was Basheer who said this. We were in prison, watering our plants.

'Take a look outside,' he said. 'The yards and surroundings of the men's prison are barren. But, here, nearer to the wall between us and the women's prison, it is greener. The men nurture, with great enthusiasm, flowering plants close to the wall. And women do the same, on the other side of this wall. People change, become different people, as they come closer and closer to this wall.'

The land around Devasia and Elikkutty's house had changed its behaviour after Devasia had his fall and became bedridden. But we, Elikkutty and I, changed it again. We cleared the beds of grass and weed, worked the soil, broke up the clods. Pruned the unruly branches of large trees and let light in. Fixed mud walls and stiles fallen to disrepair. Planted pineapple and fodder grass on top of them where they marked each terrace. To understand human beings, it is also enough to look at the plants and animals they take care of. In high summer, we dug pits and burned dry leaves in them. Topped the ash with soil and planted sections of yam dipped in cow dung and smoke-dried. Gave them a dusting of fertilizer made from mucking out the cattle shed. Covered them with green waste. They lay under there, hot and waiting for the rain. When it was almost time for the rains to begin, we made smaller beds and planted taro, kuzhikkachil and sweet potato seed stock just beginning to sprout. Alongside, in thin, long beds, we dug in fertilizer and planted ginger and turmeric that had begun to sprout, topped them with a protective layer of twigs and leaves. By then, in the bottom terrace, etha bananas that had been nurtured with plenty of water had put out dark, freckled hands and grown waist-high. We lay coconut leaves in the space between the saplings as they stood in orderly lines. Vegetable seedlings awoke and spread their roots as soon as the summer rains came. Bananas that threatened to lean over were given supportive poles. Yams and taro had the soil at their base hoed. Kachil vines were trained on to trees.

In between these oft-repeated tasks, one afternoon, in the languor of a bellyful of midday kanji, I lay napping on the top terrace in the shade. There was no breeze, not even enough to tickle the leaves. Like Devasia in his bed, I lay on top of the fallen leaves. It was not a comfortable sleep. Mani, Varghese and the old man dressed in the single mundu came again. The old man pricked my big toe with the sharpened point of his pencil stub, made it bleed. Then he climbed into my blood and began his mischief. I could see, in addition to myself, five or six others who were also me. They said what I said before I said it, did what I did before I did it, cried my tears before I shed them. They fell asleep before I did and saw my nightmares before I did. Then, in the end, came Elikkutty.

'Ennada Avaracha, why are you thrashing about in your sleep?' Elikkutty asked. She lay down next to me. 'Come here, vavey, there's nothing to be scared of.'

She stroked my head. Wiped sweat off my neck and shoulders. Pulled my face to her chest and held me close. It was fragrant there, like freshly sprouted seedlings. I splashed around in the water channels flowing there.

'Come, vavey, drink.'

She made me drink. Stroked my back and head in encouragement. Told me what to reach for and what to taste. Slowed me down when I got too fast and greedy. Pulled me up when I slipped behind her back and neck and made me lay face to face. Looked straight into my eyes. Was this the real me? That was her question to me. No lies. There were no lies in this game. We had cast away the lies with our clothes.

'I don't know, Elikkutty,' I said. 'I think, in this moment, I might be Avarachan.'

'No matter, vavey,' she said.

She pulled me closer and fondled me, all of me. Then, in a sudden moment, our play became faster. We attacked one another, experienced sweat and stench. Flung truths as curses in place of endearments. And then, finally, oh God, the world exploded as it did at the very beginning.

Coming out of Elikkutty felt exactly as it had when I came out of Vallappuzha Vaidyan's place, the same place Basheer had also lain in. By the time we caught our breath and our sweat dried, the plants had grown further. Pruned branches of trees had sprouted new leaves. The seeds we had sown had grown and set seed themselves. I got up from Elikkutty and walked naked to the edge of our world. Looked at the world outside through the screen of trees. Some things seemed the same there. But everything had changed.

New songs and new stories could be heard. Those who thought they would turn the world upside down were still around. Wars raged within and between countries. Autocrats were dethroned. And new ones took their place. New modes of dressing had come. Houses had better roofs and polished rooms.

The government of Thiruvithamkoor declared that the civil war that had been going on for over a decade was over. The official declaration came after Franco Raghavan Pillah was killed in Kadakkal, his own land. It was then that the government used the term 'civil war' for the first time. Until then, they had used terms like 'revolt' and 'interference of the neighbouring country'.

In the few years towards the end, Franco and Aikyakeralam were able to liberate some places. The largest of them was Devikulam, close to the Indian border. Other significant places were near the Vembanad Kayal and the borders of the old kingdom of Kochi. In addition, Raghavan Pillah had extraordinary support among the ordinary people in the area between Thiruvananthapuram and Kottarakkara. Aikyakeralam's practice was to declare areas in which they had support as part of India, introduce the use of the Indian rupee, and start exacting land tax. Goods and merchandise crossed borders at various places, and so the people used the currencies of both countries. Franco Raghavan Pillah and his folk had also connected the areas of their influence by water routes.

Thiruvithamkoor was able to take a strong stand because it used its diplomatic relations cleverly. India, by this time, was busy at its eastern and western borders. In international forums, Thiruvithamkoor raised the same accusations that India had raised against it – incursions across official borders, and instigation and support of insurgents. That country found it difficult to convince its allies of two contradictory arguments. It had to say, at least in public, that it did not support the armed rebellions in Thiruvithamkoor. Meanwhile, Sir C.P. made clever use of his personal relationships within the international arena. The Soviet Bloc had not recognized the sovereign existence of Thiruvithamkoor, and yet he ensured that the countries within the Bloc maintained impartiality. There was also the fact that in northern India the situation with Thiruvithamkoor was not an emotionally charged issue like Kashmir was. Those who still smarted from the wounds of Partition found it insufferable that a Muslim-majority region wanted to become a sovereign nation. Thiruvithamkoor for north Indians was like Nepal or Bhutan or Sikkim. Ordinary people were barely aware that these problems existed. The Hindu Mahasabha's strategy was to present the rebellion in Thiruvithamkoor as an attempt by insurgents to establish, in the style of Kashmir, an independent Christian nation in the south. They always took care to mention the Christian leaders of Aikyakeralam. And every time the question was asked why Thiruvithamkoor had still not become part of the Indian Union, they countered it by loudly citing the non-annexure of Goa and Pakistan-controlled Kashmir.

There were clear reasons for the early success and subsequent failure of Franco Raghavan Pillah and Aikyakeralam. Franco and his people had initially adopted a reasonable, not overtly violent way of working, positioning themselves among the people. Their protest involved attacking police stations and government offices. These did not cause loss of life, and the goods confiscated in the process were distributed to the community. They beat up officials who were corrupt or caused harm. Published their names and other details in newspapers. Made it so that being in government service began to feel shameful. Through all this, they had great support from the public. It became widely accepted that there was more dignity in choosing the risky life of an Aikyakeralam activist than living a safe life with a family and household. The government countered this situation with strategic attacks on Franco's followers. They were tortured in custody and killed. No area where Franco had support was spared. Property was confiscated and people jailed indefinitely. Naturally, in retaliation, Aikyakeralam had to resort to more violence. Soldiers and police officers were killed in stealth attacks. Government officials, like collectors who had magisterial duties, were abducted. Outside Thiruvithamkoor, these were hailed as inspiring actions, but within the country it had the opposite effect. In all of its long history, up until independence, the country had never been embroiled in a serious war. Even the rebellions and people's uprisings were resolved quickly, within a fortnight at the most.

The people of Thiruvithamkoor were not willing to put up with indefinite turmoil. As the unrest intensified, they began to view the government and Aikyakeralam as the same – violent and destabilizing. Another mistake Franco made was proclaiming the areas where he had support liberated and setting up parallel administration. This meant deploying traditional security and warfare to protect those areas. But it was not practical to engage an organized army in all-out, face-to-face battles. In the end, Franco Raghavan Pillah and his followers faced the fate that awaited all armed groups. They were pushed back and cornered in the one area where they had the most influence. And they were killed, massacred along with the ordinary people who had continued to protect them.

Franco Raghavan Pillah's death was a major setback for Aikyakeralam, both inside and outside the country. They had hoped that the rebellion in Thiruvithamkoor would continue to grow in strength, and that they would be able to take over governance with the timely assistance of the Indian army. Most hurtful was the silence of the international community. Thiruvithamkoor's sovereignty had been, in the long run, recognized widely. Only a few nations that were friendly with India held off official acceptance. In Kerala, too, Aikyakeralam's survival as an organization was under threat. Prominent leaders like Ponnara Sridhar, and many in the second rung of leadership, were dead, killed in numerous skirmishes. The Communist Party was in power, and it did not get on with the old Thiruvithamkoor State Congress leaders such as Akkamma Cherian and P.T. Chacko. They were, naturally, ideologically closer to the Congress Party that was in the opposition in Kerala. As the flow of goods and merchandise into Thiruvithamkoor slowed, Kochi's geographical and strategic importance was reduced to being an army base. Under the CPG's constant surveillance, it became increasingly difficult for the organization to operate. Seethi Buildings lay deserted most of the time.

Around this time, Nehru wrote an article titled 'State Within the State' in the *National Herald*. It reflected the disappointment of Aikyakeralam and the Indian government. It was one of the last essays he wrote. The title could be interpreted in two ways. In one sense, it was about the independence of Thiruvithamkoor, a state he believed to be part of India. In another sense, it alluded to the group within India that operated in support of Thiruvithamkoor. They, he argued, were persuaded by communalism and religious ideology. These were the same ideas that had, for thousands of years, relegated the people of India to a deprived and backward existence, that had resulted in the assassination of Mahatma Gandhi. And these were the same people who stood in the way of the popular desire that Thiruvithamkoor join the Indian Union. Nehru said that he had finally come to understand the extent of their influence within the bureaucracy, the judiciary and the military, and in the very veins of India. It was now up to the people of Thiruvithamkoor to decide their own future. He had full faith, even at this disappointing time, that the people's will could work miracles. A path would open up just as we were lost in the wilderness. It was in such a moment that Gandhiji had entered India's freedom movement. And it changed everything. Something similar might happen, something we might not be hopeful about.

The end of the civil war in Thiruvithamkoor was what prompted Nehru to write this essay. He used a large part of it to decry the atrocities the army was said to have committed. Particular mention was made of the incident where Franco Raghavan Pillah's dead body was brought to Attingal, tied to K.K. Nair's car – he had come there to celebrate the killing – and was dragged through the streets. A scene that would never fade from the collective memory of Thiruvithamkoor's people. He was saddened and pained, Nehru said, to think that such a man as K.K. Nair had ever worked in the Indian government, and that nations would end up paying a grave price for the deeds of men such as him.

Nehru said that the indignities meted out to Franco after his death had disgusted him, hurt him and made him feel helpless. No human being deserved to be subjected to such treatment in death. The act had dishonoured the people of Thiruvithamkoor and, indeed, all Malayalis who took great pride in their culture, wrote the newspaper *Express*, published from Thrissur, in its editorial. The perpetrator had learned such an act elsewhere and executed it here, sending Thiruvithamkoor tumbling into darkness and a deep silence.

13

In his childhood, his father Kunjuvareed had seen a man who had come back from death, said Devasia. This was before tapioca cultivation had started in Pravithanam. Only a few old families lived there then, and there were only a handful of houses.

'Appan was little then,' Devasia said. 'It was night-time, hear, and there was a scream from next door. Appan, his appan, his amma and his siblings ran across. A young man had died. Quite healthy he was too. It was like that in those days. Children are born and they start perishing right away. One or two might make it. Someone gets to fifty years of age, that's a huge deal. Make it to sixty and it is an occasion for celebration. But this man here, he had not even married.'

Elikkutty came in with the freshly cleaned pot that Devasia used to urinate in during the day. It lived under the bed. I wiped his body with warm water, cut his toenails with a small knife. Helped him sit leaning on a pillow against the wall. Poured the charayam into two coconut shells and handed one to him. Held his hand when it shook as he raised it to his lips.

'They lay the body on a bed, hear, and began reading the Pana, our Lord Jesus' story. That usually goes on until sunrise, yes. It was raining heavily, Appan said. It got to be sometime after midnight. Only five or six folks left around the bed. Then, hear, the dead man sat up rubbing his eyes. Scary it was at first, Appan said, but then everyone came to have a look.'

'What had happened to him?' I asked.

'What's to happen? It wasn't his time.'

'He must not have actually died.'

'Poda cherukka.' Devasia was irritated. 'He died, he said, and then was covered in this massive white light. Then someone tied him up with a thick rope and dragged him away. Then it was down a large cave. Like it would never end. He said he saw the shadows of all his ancestors as he was being dragged along. Then he heard someone say, quiet but angry like, "Who brought this fellow, it's not his time yet, you've got the wrong man." After that, all he remembered was sitting up in bed. Then, hear, another scream from the neighbourhood. My appan was not the kind to make crap up. Now hear this. In the morning, there were rope burns all over the man's body. Scary, it was. Appan even touched them.'

'There's talk like that here too,' Elikkutty said. 'A chedathi told me on the way back from church. There's this man, it seems, who was given a chance by God to start over. The first man to come up here from back home, but he was in quite a state. Worked really hard, he did, cleared away the forest and started cultivation. Was doing quite well too at first. But then, when everything was growing well, some folks came along and said it was their land and drove him away. He cleared up another piece of land and planted tapioca, but then got sent to jail for something or the other. When he came back, that land was gone too. So, he cleared up yet another piece of land and planted black pepper. The vines were just about setting wicks when he fell off a tree and ended up bedridden. That chedathi was telling me that God took pity on him and gave him another chance to start his life over.'

'Well, that's interesting. We were the first to come up here, no? So, who's this fellow then? One we don't know about? Ha, ha, or is it me actually?'

'I asked her that too. That chedathi said this man lives a bit further up north.'

'Start over from the beginning. From where exactly?' Devasia was puzzled. 'Like, it will be a right mess, won't it? Won't he have to go all the way back to the beginnings of his appan and amma and siblings?'

'I was thinking that too.'

'Well, possible or not, it's fun to think about,' I said. 'If it was possible to start over from scratch, what all would people do? Get rid of everything they had done so far, most likely.'

'I think we'll end up doing the same things,' Devasia said. 'I'll marry her only. Who else will have me? I only need this one chance, I'm not going to change anything. Even, hear, even getting stuck in this bed. What about you, Avaracha? Will you change anything?'

Pretending not to have heard the question, I dipped a piece of yam in the kandari chilli paste and put it in my mouth. I started looking back at my life, then, deciding against it, began thinking about other things. About what Varghese would have done if he was given this chance to start over. What Mani would have done. Would Gandhi have left South Africa and come back? Would Basheer destroy *Diary of a Lover* and stop writing?

Devasia fell asleep. I went into the room inside, spread a mat on the floor and lay down. Outside, the rain of many days fell ritually. The noise it made became the sound of the night and, sometimes, its silence. The ears, habituated to it, stopped hearing it. Basheer came into my sleep. He had died. We walked alongside swiftly flowing water. He was trying to convince me of the reason he had died. Listening to him, one would think he had taken his own life or something. Just before dawn, Elikkutty also came into my dream. Dawn is the time when greed is at its highest. Without bothering with foreplay, we fell enthusiastically into our game.

The rain that fell in our compound was a peculiar kind. It went on all night, making us believe that it would stop in the morning. But when morning came, it would only get stronger. The canopy of the trees around the house made it feel as though it was leaking water rather than raining. The earth lay darkened. Compounds that looked so forlorn in the rain existed only in our world. The trees, heavy with the dripping, bowed their heads obligingly, the vegetable plants leaned over. Dark green leaves turned black right in front of our eyes. The wind did not enter our world because of the tree screen at the boundary. Unlike in the outside world, the rain fell in straight downward lines, not slanted. Everything stood still, allowing itself to be drenched.

After sitting in the house for a few days, reluctant even to step into the yard, one afternoon I picked up the broad-bladed hoe and ventured out. Walked up to each of the terraces, hoeing channels to release the accumulated water. Scooped mud underneath plants caught in standing water. Cut off broken leaves. Only a few plants had perished. The rest would raise their heads again when the sky cleared. Still, through these days of rain, they would stop growing and stand frozen. Where the soil had washed away, the roots were white and visible. I reached the top terrace, the first one that Elikkutty and I had cleared together. From there, our world lay extended down the steep slope, the house at the very bottom. Right now, it was cloaked in mist. If I looked hard, I could see the faint figure of Elikkutty crouched over the yam stems she was chopping for our evening meal. Devasia liked the thoran made from the tender stems of yam cooked with beans. The rain took up again. Thick strings that made even what was right in front me invisible. Water falling by the potful, on the face and chest, pushing the body back. If it continued like this for some more days, all the worlds, not just ours, would be submerged. Or was this deluge only in our world? If so, an ark, as was described in the puranas of the Christians, would need to be made. A fun thought. Who would need to be given place in it? The three of us humans, Devasia, Elikkutty and I. What else? Hoes, pickaxes, vegetable seeds, rootstock of banana and tubers, the sack of dried tapioca ... I walked hurriedly back, happy that I had something interesting to discuss with Devasia. Darkness had followed the rain by then. Standing under the eaves of the house, I took off my mundu, wrung the water out of it, draped it back around my waist, and stepped inside enthusiastically. Devasia, sitting up in his bed leaning against the headboard, looked fondly at me. I looked back at him. As I watched, I became he and looked at the rain-drenched younger man coming in after work. Then I heard Devasia say something that sent a current through me. We were still in the world of impossibilities. Where gods gave human beings second chances. Where the dead came back because there had been a mistake. It was meaningless to think that what usually happened were things that were ordinary. Usual happenings were, in fact, things that happened in between unexpected, extraordinary things. Nothing to be amazed about. I had been expecting that something would happen about Basheer. Still.

When I heard what Devasia said following the question, 'Avaracha, have you heard?' I knew that the world had changed. As I blew into the black coffee Elikkutty brought me, I asked a pointless question for no particular reason.

'How did you know, lying here like this?'

'Why wouldn't I know? When a big thing happens, the world hears about it without anyone coming around to tell us. Did we need to be told to know about Gandhi's death? If the sky falls, do we need to be told? Even the calf in the cattle shed will know.'

After the evening meal, I got ready to leave. I had nothing to take with me. Elikkutty walked me to the edge of the compound as she had done the first time. The rain had stopped.

What else was there for me to do other than follow Basheer, I thought as I walked away in the darkness. No one had asked me to follow him. No one was left who would care if I found him and set him off in a different direction. No one remembered that a man like me existed. Even my name would not be in any record.

All that I had done was not done by me. The things I did became mine only if other people knew about them. I had been erased, as had my doings. Starting today, the history of my country would change. From now on, I would follow it. I would follow Basheer. From this day on, fact and fiction would intermingle just like in Basheer's stories. His reckless imagination had mixed with the history of my country beyond recognition. I recalled what P.T. Punnoose had said about Basheer all those years ago. That it was impossible to predict what single-minded people would do. But something like this was happening for the first time in this world. Had anyone heard anything like this anywhere, ever? Anxiety, fear, happiness, enthusiasm, I don't know what, but my heart began to pound faster, breath quickened, strides lengthened. I tried to slow myself down and failed. I was being swept along in the current that had taken me ever since I heard what Devasia told me. I knew something was coming, although I could not accurately guess what it would be. But I could foresee that, when it came, it would be most amazing, beyond anything anyone could imagine.

As it was with all nights after rains, there was no one around. The morning bus to Kozhikode lay quietly asleep at the junction. I was not the type to sit back waiting for it. I began to walk downhill along the path I had walked with Devasia and Elikkutty that first time. The cold enveloped me, entered me. A long time after, the path curved around a hill. On one side, blocking vision, the high rockface. On the other, the earth dropped away into the darkness. A low stone wall marked the verge. I sat on it with my legs dangling into emptiness. Eight or ten minutes later, when I got off it and resumed walking, I had begun to write this book of history in my head. What else could I do? Who else but me would do this? Now, to write about what happened after, I had to follow only one person. Basheer.

14

To begin with, I watched to see how people reacted. Eavesdropped on their conversations. Insinuated myself in discussions. Asked people direct questions. Went to see some of those who were of special interest. When some people, suspicious of my inquisitiveness, asked me questions, I told them that I planned to write about it. Most people found this explanation believable and opened up to me. Telling people that my objective was to write about this had its benefits, but it was also dangerous. People became more confident at the thought that what they had to say carried weight. And they began to talk freely and seriously about the matter. Some went one step further and poured out everything that was inside them. People liked the idea that their words would be recorded somewhere, even if anonymously. I recalled the special regard that the State Congress followers had for Basheer who told stories and wrote pamphlets. Except for a few dangerously practical people whose lives were lived entirely in the real world, everyone else had a special regard for writing. Ordinary people had respect even for those who were engaged in drab, mechanical jobs related to writing – writing notices on walls, preparing deeds and documents, proofreading. The danger was that they also wanted to know what kind of writing I was doing. If I told them I was writing an essay or a history book, they switched to a formal speech and started spouting stupid ideas authoritatively. If I told them I was writing a story or a novel – well, that was it. Their imagination took flight in all four directions. And the stories they told me would all have heroes none other than themselves.

The subject of conversations everywhere, and not just in Kozhikode, was, and had been for a while, Basheer and the recent developments. What had happened was utterly incredible. As unbelievable as the arrival of extraterrestrial beings on earth, or a water snake walking on two legs, or human beings suddenly forgetting the use of fire. At first, I was interested in knowing how people reacted to this unbelievable development, and the answer was unbelievable too. People were ready to believe whatever happened or the idea that things might happen. They viewed life and the world we lived in as though it were a novel in which unpredictable things could happen. If you told them that a bear, dressed in a pair of trousers and a shirt, went to a restaurant and asked to be served, their eyes would widen in amazement for a brief minute. True, but not because they found this unbelievable. They were amazed because they were happy – 'See, what I had imagined has come true,' they thought. The more details you gave about an incredible thing, the more they believed it. At the very least, they were happy that such a story existed. The most innate attribute of human beings is the readiness to imagine that anything can happen at any time. Children take everything we tell them seriously, don't they? It is only later, when foolish ideas that we mistake for knowledge enter their brains that people lose their sense of wonder and curiosity. And they resign themselves to the idea that life is about going on living until we die.

I purposely hung around for a few days on Beypore beach. It would be those who went to the sea who would be able to talk authoritatively about this incident. The rest of us could only stand on land and imagine the happenings in that vast space while they witnessed them. But by the time I got to Beypore, talk about it had died down. You easterners find all this incredible but for us it is ordinary, said the expressions on the faces of everyone – from the little kids picking up sardines on the beach to feeble old men mending fishing nets. I tried to talk to some people, but as soon as they heard my queries, they went silent as though thinking, what a fool this fellow is. Others looked at one another and exchanged meaningful smiles. Finally, I found a man named Pookunju who talked to me a little.

After roaming around the Chaliyam area, I was lying down on the sand in the shade. In front of me was the sea. Thinking about it, I was lying on the shore of an incredible wonder. All that was on land had climbed out of it. Lying here, the conflicting urges of running into it and disappearing and of running away from it before it came crawling up one day took hold at the same time. I saw one such who had come out of it, Pookunju, walking towards me. I had the thought that he wanted to talk to me, and he had the thought that I wanted to listen to him. I smiled, and he smiled back. Gave me a beedi when I asked for it. Decided to light one himself and stand beside me until he finished smoking it. An average-sized man who looked to be around thirty-five years old. He kept undoing and redoing the fold of his mundu as though it was an ingrained habit. Either he understood what it was that I wanted to ask, or this was how all conversations started these days.

'Ponnu changathi,' Pookunju began, addressing me as a friend, his gaze far away into the sea. 'What we see out there, we don't speak of it when we get back on land. What would be the point? We don't talk about it even to our own folks at home. We know we can't describe it in believable ways, and they know it is difficult to believe.'

He spoke, and I believed all that he told me. Creatures the size of fifty elephants, fish that fly, birds that are harbingers of oncoming storms, frogs that eat away entire nets. Considering what lived at sea, what was really there on land? Nothing. Humans, who would drown in water, walking about, some cattle that obey them, some plants. It wasn't like that out there. No one obeyed anyone else in the sea. We humans were inconsequential compared to turtles that lived for over five hundred years. When they looked at us, they seemed to be remembering something and laughing at us. No one listened to anyone. There were forests at the very bottom of the sea, larger than any on land.

'Have you seen them?' I asked.

'No! We won't survive down there. All we can do is play around at the top, floating on a piece of wood, catching what we can before getting the hell out of there. Those terrible creatures though, they go wherever they want, all around the world. There's no one to say, like we do, don't go there, don't come here. Making and obeying rules, that's something only we do. And, when we go to the sea, there are those there who watch to see what we do, whether we get up to any mischief.'

'Seriously?'

Pookunju told me that when he and his group, five of them, went to the sea, they saw someone follow them, swimming behind them as though unconcerned.

'A komban, a great white shark. We pretend not to notice him. He'll go away after a while, but don't for a minute think that it is because he trusts you. He will appear again.'

It was only a few days ago that they started hearing about Basheer, he said.

'There are a lot of Basheers right here,' he said. 'But this one, he's a southerner, isn't he, makes up stories and all.'

'Yes. From Thiruvithamkoor.'

'Wherever. Such a nuisance these people are. They make up things and keep talking about them until these things become true.'

'That's possible, is it? Talking about something and making it happen?'

'Possible!' Pookunju looked at me, amazed. 'Think about it, won't you. Them karinkannans, folks with evil eyes, they say things and jinx things, don't they? Oh, that's a lot of fish, they'll say, and there won't be even a karinathan to catch for days! Other people say things and they actually happen.'

'Still, what we've been hearing these days. Is it all really true?'

Pookunju dropped the butt of the beedi he was smoking and smiled at my scepticism.

'Have you actually seen it?' I asked, just to make doubly sure.

'No. It's a ways south,' he said. 'We don't usually go that way.'

Regardless, he insisted that what he had heard was true. No one really needed to tell them, he said, because they could gauge these things from the small changes in the wind, the waves, the currents. And if I must talk to someone who had seen it, I only had to travel a little this way or that, he said, to find people who would vouch for it. They saw a lot of such sights at sea, he said one more time, except that this time everyone was making such a hoo-ha about it. And with that, he walked away.

I rented a room near the railway station in town and lived there for a few days. It was a narrow room in an old two-storey lodge. Inside, there was a light with a naked red bulb and an insect with white wings. Every time I switched on the light, it flew around the bulb. There was also a bed with a straw mat spread on top, and a thick folded cloth to use as a pillow. The toilet was downstairs and to be shared by all occupants. In the night, I opened the window, stuck my head out through the bars like a goat that was trapped in the room, and looked out at the town. What had happened, I thought. What was happening?

Everything looked the same. Night buses drove past. Done with the last ride of the day, cycle rickshaws headed homewards. Hotels buzzed with activity. Trains lay as though dead for a long time, and then laboriously came back to life. People came out of the station and walked away until they disappeared in the distance. Nothing had changed. But something had happened. And the world was aware of it. Even though I was not hungry, I ate the fried pathiri I had bought at a hotel earlier. Watched the world full of people without them being aware of it. Were they acting as though nothing had happened? Or were human beings like this, going about their business no matter what? I imagined a group of savages riding into the city on horses and ransacking it. They set fire to buildings, killed people, raped women, looted money and jewellery. Then they left, and the very next day, people went back to their routine, acting as though nothing had happened.

As though nothing had happened, K.K. Nair had called a press conference in Kollam yesterday. Everyone assembled there knew, of course, that everything had changed. He knew it too. And to hide it, he arrived at the Residency Bungalow, in brisker steps than usual, dressed in a pair of grey trousers and a coat with large buttons. On his feet were Testoni shoes, made of high-quality Italian leather in its natural colour. Ever since he had come to Thiruvithamkoor and taken over his new position, Nair had been paying more attention to his clothes than the man who was his superior. He appeared in public dressed only in expensive, formal clothes. With each passing year, he became more meticulous about it. Pressed his subordinates to dress well. Told them, repeatedly, that they were the official representatives of the country and that their appearance, and the appearance of the main cities of the land, would raise the dignity of the country in international forums. This was also the rationale he gave when he ordered the eviction of the poor from Alappuzha and Kollam. The writer Thakazhi Sivasankara Pillai, who had left the country and moved to Ernakulam, had, after Franco Raghavan Pillah's death, written a story titled 'Coat'. It was about a caveman who comes to Thiruvananthapuram city wearing a coat. He makes friends and hobnobs with the people of the upper echelon. He uses the best perfumes to hide his natural stench. The caveman speaks in Oxford English and has better table manners than the sahibs.

Then, one night, he jerks awake from sleep and roars. Begins eating raw meat. This story was understood by everyone who read it as an allegory about K.K. Nair.

A beautiful dais made of rosewood was built in the lawn of the Residency Bungalow for the press conference. To its side, the national flag fluttered. Nair began by addressing by name a couple of reporters sitting in the front row. Something that he did on all such occasions. Once, when a reporter repeatedly asked uncomfortable questions, he responded by asking him about his family: Your wife still works at the Alappuzha Medical College, yes? And your children, in classes five and one now, I reckon? He also recalled precisely the reporter's accreditation number and the fact that he had begun the construction of his house. He made it a point to find out and commit to memory all information about the people he encountered. He usually called a press conference when something special or extraordinary happened. And usually, on these occasions he maintained a stern demeanour. But at this press conference, he had on a pleasant countenance and tried to appear jovial.

'I felt like seeing you all. That's all right, isn't it?' he said, laughing. Everyone laughed with him.

The first thing K.K. Nair addressed was foreign policy. He detailed the trade and defence agreements that the country had recently entered into with America. Nothing new in it because these had already been reported in the newspapers. Still, the journalists maintained an expression of wonder on their faces and took copious notes. He then moved on to the infighting between the countries that were part of NATO and the Treaty of Versailles, remarked that the brave picked sides when cowards remained wishy-washy. Everyone understood it to be a dig at Nehru and his policy of non-alliance. The attendees exploded in laughter while Nair maintained a straight face. He talked some more about the general situation in the country, and then it was time for questions.

The journalists' queries were about security, practical projects to nurture national pride, the secret behind the exponential growth in industry. Some stood up, and instead of asking a question, delivered a message congratulating the Maharaja, the prime minister and the principal secretary. Finally, Nair looked at a man sitting in the second row, a reporter from the *Thiruvithamkoor Patrika*, and said, 'You have a question, don't you, Narayanan?' This man, Narayanan, from Budhanur near Chengannur, was thought to enjoy a close relationship with the centre of power. One only had to read the *Thiruvithamkoor Patrika* to know what the government had to say about any matter of importance. In his column, Narayanan routinely predicted the actions of the government and the changes in policies. It was his questions that most often decided how a press conference turned out.

'The Indian newspapers...' Narayanan began. 'Well, there have been some insinuations about the prime minister's health...'

Suddenly, Nair's expression changed and his face was suffused with rage. His response was a long speech about Sir C.P. Ramaswami Iyer. He recounted every service Diwanji had rendered for the country, the personal losses he had to suffer. India had protected those who attempted to assassinate the Maharaja. The prime minister had risked his life to save the king. It would be a wonder if the newspapers of that country did not say horrid things about him. The prime minister was currently engaged in studies on how to accelerate the country's social, economic and technological development. He was, in addition, writing a book. And yet, he found time to be involved in the everyday administration of the country. Paid attention to even the smallest of matters.

'Our prime minister is not the type to wander around dreaming of things,' he concluded.

Once again, understanding exactly who the barb was aimed at, everyone laughed. They had already decided what the front-page news would be and what the headlines would proclaim. So, they knew there was something else Nair wanted to say when he called the press conference. He switched off the mike and turned to leave. Then, as though he had suddenly remembered something, he turned back to face the attendees and laughed. It was not an ordinary laughter.

'Ha, ha, ha, well. There is that other thing, ha, ha, ha,' he said, standing close to the podium without switching the mike back on.

The journalists, who had stood up and were getting ready to leave, laughed with him. Theirs was no ordinary laughter either.

'Well, what can I say about it. Ha, ha, ha. Has anyone ever heard of such a thing anywhere in the world?'

The listeners laughed louder.

'Complete madness. What else. Couldn't defeat us, so went raving mad. Ha, ha. It can be treated, yes. Application of nellikka thalam to the head. That should do it.'

'Some people are agitating around this and organizing demonstrations,' said Narayanan. 'Will there be any action on the part of the government?'

'What action? When temple festivals take place, some people get drunk and dance around all over the place. Do we take action? When the effect of the hooch wears off, they'll go home. Clowns!'

Nair's effort was to make light of the matter, convince everyone that the government did not take it seriously. But towards the end, it became obvious to everyone that he was grinding his teeth and his face had taken on a gruffer expression than before.

The night deepened, and I switched off the light and lay down to sleep. But sleep had not blessed me ever since I had left Thiruvambady. Inside, I was in turmoil. Body weakening. Eyes and mind refusing to rest. Lying there for a while, waiting, I got up, stepped out and shut the door. No lights anywhere on the veranda or outside the building. Lights were off in all the rooms too. Women of the night stood in a dark corner of the lane before the building. One stepped forward and beckoned me. I walked on and stopped at a shop that was still open, bought a glass of tea, and stood by the side of the road drinking it. It was warm. And there was a small breeze.

When I finished the tea and returned the glass, the man asked, 'Want another one?'

I took my time with the second glass of tea, paid for it, then crossed the road and walked into the railway station. The best place to spend time when one can't sleep. Not much of a crowd tonight. I sat on a bench, saw off a train that had pulled in, got up and walked back and forth on the platform a couple of times. Then I peeped into the room with the board saying 'Station Master' outside it. Seven or eight employees stood in front of a map of India on the wall. I understood what the subject of their conversation was. What else was there to talk about these days!

'Sir, can I have a look?' I asked, standing in the doorway, neither in nor out.

Without waiting for a reply, I entered and stood looking at the map with them. India still refused to mark Thiruvithamkoor as a separate nation on its map, showing it as a part of itself. I looked at the bottom of the map, to the south and into the blue sea to the west. It was true. There it was, a small dot, like a pottu on the forehead. An island that wasn't there even a few days ago. I looked at my arms. My hair was standing up.

'Where are you from?' asked one of the men.

'Thiruvithamkoor.'

Everyone turned their attention to me.

'Do you know Basheer?

'Yes.'

'Have you met him?'

'Have I met him? I've even touched him. Here, look, with this finger.'

15

Aikyakeralam, which had almost gone dormant since the death of Franco Raghavan Pillah, resumed its activities. The locked office in Kozhikode reopened. A huge rally took place in the city with no one really taking the lead to organize it. Thousands of people came singing songs of liberation and shouting slogans. In the midst of the chaotic crowd that flowed into Mananchira, a young man stood on a table making a speech with great enthusiasm. There simply was no limit to human beings' creativity and progress, he said. Science has already taken us to space, and if we soon found ourselves travelling to the moon and the stars, it would not be surprising. All of this was made possible by scientific socialism. Citing a section from Maxim Gorky's *Mother*, he said that behind all these advancements were great writers who were the driving force.

And now, here was this new development in Thiruvithamkoor. A writer showing us what could be achieved with his creative power. Had anyone heard of such a thing before? Would anyone now be able to stop the liberation of the people of Thiruvithamkoor? That great writer had made the most definitive declaration of independence. The scope of writing had grown beyond the ordinariness of words on paper. He announced, 'Sir C.P. and the anti-people king, listen, the countdown for your downfall has begun,' and then, as is done for the launching of a rocket, he actually began to count down. Ten ... nine ... eight ... With each number, the noise of the crowd increased in volume. Finally, hoisting the man on their shoulders, one group began shouting slogans.

As the crowd began to disperse, another man began to talk about Basheer. They had been friends for a long time, he said.

And they had been in prison together. C. Keshavan, T.M. Varghese and P.T. Chacko were also there at the time. He and Basheer had tended a garden near the prison wall, he said. On the other side of the wall was the women's prison. He spoke in a low voice. No one listened to him. It was a soliloquy, and he didn't seem concerned that no one paid attention. Some people speak only for themselves. Their minds are in turmoil. I thought hard but could not remember who this person was. But it also didn't seem like he was making up things. If we listen, we are able to distinguish between experience and imagination.

He walked away, finally, alone, and I followed him. A light-skinned man, past his youth, with hair that was beginning to grey. Looked like he had not eaten or slept properly in days. He walked briskly as though he was in a hurry. And yet, he stopped every now and then like he had forgotten his destination. Looked around anxiously and then started walking again. After a while, I came out of hiding and fell in step with him. We walked on either side of the darkness and looked each other in the eye.

'Who are you?' I asked. 'What's your name?'

'Bhasi,' he said.

We walked in silence for a while. When I lit a beedi, he looked at me surprised.

'When did you take this up?' he asked.

'Ah, been a while.'

A number of years passed us by as we stood there on the wayside, and a group of people shouting slogans, the last of the crowd that was in Mananchira.

'Fun to watch all this standing here, isn't it?' I asked.

When I left, it was to a house in Chalappuram that I went. My information was that a man named Appukkuttan, who worked at Akashvani and was a playwright, lived there. The house, shared by a group of unmarried men, was right by the roadside. Four or five of them were sitting on the stoop, playing cards. A couple of others stood watching them and eating their evening meal. Before I could finish asking if any of them was Appukkuttan, a man wearing a lungi came out of the house. He too had a plate of kanji in his hand.

'I'm Appukkuttan,' he said. 'What do you want?'

Seeing that I was reluctant to talk in front of the others, he invited me in. Took me to the back of the house to a small veranda. Finished eating his kanji and came and sat beside me. The glow of the hurricane lamp inside reached us, but we were mostly in darkness. Appukkuttan looked no more than forty years old. He peered at my face wanting to know why I was there.

'I want to write a book,' I said, somewhat embarrassed. 'But don't get me wrong, I don't have much of an idea how to go about it. I've not read many books. I don't quite know how to write either. For days now, writing has been going on in my mind, but I only realized it recently. So, I'm somewhat reluctant to speak to someone like you.'

His face showed that he had no clue what I was talking about. So, I quickly explained why I was there.

'The guy in the next room at the lodge where I live likes to listen to the radio. And he plays it loudly. It really annoys me. To be honest, I have no interest in the programmes, but I have to listen to them anyway. I was about to tell him to stop when I heard a fifteen-minute play. It was titled *Kaalaal*.'

'Yes, I wrote that one,' he said happily.

'Yes, and that's why I came.'

'And I gave voice to the character Prahladan.'

He seemed to think that I had come because I liked the play.

'Really?' I said, feigning surprise. 'Well, there is this bit of dialogue. Prahladan, who is a writer, says it to his lover. "Creative power can build an island of imagination in the middle of the sea." I was quite surprised by that.'

'Ah, it all comes from the inside,' he said proudly.

'No, I mean, they said at the end that it was a repeat, that it had been broadcast before.'

'That's right. I wrote the play a year or a year and a half ago.'

'I came because I wanted to know for certain that this was the second broadcast.'

'Yes, that's right.'

'Well, that's why I am surprised. When you think about what's happening now, it's like that dialogue was a prediction.'

'Ha, ha, that could be right.'

'Was there something in your mind when you wrote it? Or did you just simply come up with it?'

'Ey, couldn't say there was anything specific. A coincidence, maybe. Still, when you read things some people have written after a long time, they seem to have a prophetic quality. But this, now, it didn't occur to me until you pointed it out.'

He wasn't given much of a salary, Appukkuttan said, so it was a great reward when people commented on his writing. He went in and fetched some letters. They were from his listeners sent to his office address.

'One more thing,' I said. 'Do you believe that such a thing could happen? I mean the stuff that is happening now?'

He thought for a while. 'To tell you the truth I don't really understand what's been happening,' he said eventually. 'I knew Basheer. A long time ago, the two of us and some others had spent a couple of days together in Koyilandy. Sat up late telling stories and whatnot. What he tells as stories are really things that happen in ordinary lives. Like the writings of people like Keshavadev. But there is a kind of madness in everything he says. And after a point, it becomes unmanageable. For example...'

Appukkuttan took a while to come up with the example.

'For example, one story I heard in those days was about how he had a relationship with a female spirit, a yakshi who haunted the house next to the one he was living in at the time. Another was about how a man's nose kept on growing. When you consider all this, there's nothing so strange about what we are hearing now. It's just like one of his stories.'

'Those are all, well, stories. But what happened now, isn't it real?'

'That's where I am confused. If not completely, I do believe a little in rationality. It is not about whether it is real or not. The helpless people of Thiruvithamkoor were depressed, dejected. They had no one to turn to. So, they wished for the return of someone like Basheer. Imagined that there would be an island of freedom in the middle of the Arabian Sea to which they could escape. Think about it that way, and what is happening becomes real.'

Appukkuttan did not have even an iota of the ego writers usually have. I got up to leave and he walked me to the road.

'No one would believe any of this if you put it in a story or a novel,' he said. 'But in real life, people have no problem believing it.'

'Your play...' I said. 'Well, I have a few disagreements.'

'Like what?'

'For one, people talking in literary language. No one talks like that in real life, do they?'

'What we are doing is telling a story,' Appukkuttan said. 'A story! Remember. Those who listen are well aware of this. So, what does it matter how a character in that story speaks!'

He patted my shoulder and sent me on my way. He was right, I thought as I walked away. I had started writing inside my mind from the day I left Vallappuzha Vaidyan's place. What was the point in looking for rationality now?

16

The responses to the developments were several and varied. I think it would be pertinent to record here some of the information I have collected regarding this. One of the widely discussed responses at the time was that of the communist leader P. Krishnapillah. He was replying to a question from a reader, a Balan Nambiar from Kuttiyattoor, in his regular column in the newspaper *Deshabhimani*. The question was this: What did the Communist Party think of literature in a society where a people's revolution had failed and the viable circumstances for another revolution seemed impossible? Should literary writing that existed in such a context be rejected?

The Communist Party could only take a stand based on objective reality, Krishnapillah replied. He then quickly digressed and talked about Thiruvithamkoor and Basheer. Basheer had associated himself with the State Congress and the Communist Party, he said. Had operated outside of the Gandhian path. Gone to prison for taking part in the strikes against royal rule. The Thiruvithamkoor government had declared him an enemy of the state, a most wanted criminal. His writing was confined primarily to propagandist pamphlets. These were historical facts, Krishna Pillah wrote, and the developments in Thiruvithamkoor were to be analysed within this context.

Krishnapillah ridiculed those who took what happened in literature as fact. Art, of course, was a mirror held up to society. But it must be remembered that the reflection in the mirror is reversed. Writers do not faithfully record what happens in society. Moreover, writing that arises from a feudal society like

Thiruvithamkoor and from a socialist society must be seen as different. So, what Basheer has done here, what he is said to have done, can only be seen as a symbolic act. Remember that it happened on the same day that the newspapers reported that the old, anti-people diwan – the current prime minister – was sick and bedridden. In that sense, Krishnapillah wrote, it was a welcome development.

I was convinced that the questioner was an imaginary person. It was true that, in Kerala which was part of India, there were tensions between the Communist Party and the Aikyakeralam leadership which had a prominent presence of the old State Congress. Still, for the followers of both, Thiruvithamkoor continued to be an emotional issue. They welcomed the new developments enthusiastically without worrying whether they were fact or fiction. The leaders of Aikyakeralam did not feel the need to make their stance clear; they welcomed all good news. But for a political party that based their ideology on dialectical materialism, it was unthinkable that an island had mysteriously appeared in the Arabian Sea around fifty nautical miles from the coast of Thiruvithamkoor, that it was somehow connected to Basheer and to the struggles in Thiruvithamkoor, and that people believed this without questioning. Like everyone else, the Party too was confounded. This was quite clear from Krishnapillah's reply. What he spoke of was about the use of symbolism in literature. But could this be seen as a literary event? Was it writing that had happened here? If it was only an idea, would it have manifested as material reality? Krishnapillah could not argue, not openly at least, that people were making these things up, or falsely believing such things to be true because that was the argument of the government of Thiruvithamkoor.

The newspapers in Thrissur and Kozhikode were, naturally, in a state of great enthusiasm. They published with equal gusto news about the event and the rumours about Sir C.P. Ramaswami Iyer's ill health. If people from a different time were to read these papers, they would think that novels had shifted shape and form and were now published as news reports with narrative content that defied the laws of materiality. Plentiful old information about Basheer came out as news reports, and they were replete with the unbridled imagination of the journalists who wrote them. A main preoccupation was with the Raktarekha Case. Many had no real idea of what it was or when it had happened. During the Vayalar revolt, there was an incident where a man named Raman, a goonda of the landlord Kattiyatt Shivarama Panicker, was set upon and murdered. This had become known as the Raman Murder Case. Some reporters thought that these two cases were one and the same. And that the name 'Raktarekha' had come from the fact that, after killing Raman, Basheer and his friends had dipped their hands in his blood and marked the walls. Stories about the attempted assassination of the Maharaja also took on similarly imaginative flourishes.

At this time, I spent every single one of my nights in my room, sitting still or pacing, unable to sleep. There is a moment at night when all lights switch off and all sounds cease. A time when we think that the night, now, will never end, that time will never pass. Switching off the light, I sat in the darkness spending time minute by minute. Each minute stretched so long that I was exhausted by the time I walked to the end of it. Oh God, this doesn't end, I told myself. It was the world and the people around us that made time move. What was I to do when they had all gone to sleep? I switched the light back on. Spread the newspaper I had bought in the morning on the floor and looked through it. From it slowly emerged another image of Basheer. I began to examine whether the Basheer I knew had anything in common with this image that the reporters had drawn up with their words. According to them, this Basheer had travelled all around the world, had been a sanyasi, a beggar, a magician, a wrestler. He knew how to make bombs. He had touched Gandhi. And much, much more. The years he had lived so far would not have been enough to do all the things he was said to have done. As in Elikkutty's story, had God given him another chance to start over?

The image of Sir C.P. that emerged from the reports in the newspaper was also different from the man I had met, alongside another, a white man who had introduced himself as a writer, in Bhaktivilasam all those years ago. He had been a handsome, well-dressed, energetic man then, one who had controlled all the strings. Now, it had been more than a year since a photo of his had been published. Almost six months since he had attended a public function. Even high-ranking officials had not seen him in person for quite a while. There was a report that a medical team from America had arrived in Thiruvananthapuram. They had not returned yet. The newspaper tried to figure out what kind of illness the prime minister suffered from based on the names and details of the members of the American medical team. It also closely analysed a press note said to be from the prime minister that had been released a month ago. It dealt with the situation in Vietnam. It was not the prime minister's habit to respond to events like these through emergency press notes. This note felt like it was trying to convince the world of something. The newspaper also found two grammatical errors in the short note written in English. It was inconceivable that Sir C.P. Ramaswami Iyer, who was more proficient in English than the British themselves, whose thoughts even were, perhaps, in English, would make such errors. Equally inconceivable was the explanation that some civil servant had written the note and sent it out without Sir C.P. actually seeing it. He had always been adamant that nothing be done without his knowledge and approval. In the editorial page was an essay written under the pseudonym 'Soori', which wondered whether India and Thiruvithamkoor had started speculations about what would happen after Sir C.P.'s time. He had been instrumental in the fall of the Regent Queen Rani Sethu Lakshmi Bayi, and in shaping Thiruvithamkoor into what it was today. The country's decisions were his and his only. After independence, he formalized a model of government different from the old Thiruvithamkoor. It was because of the presence of a strategist administrator like him that the country escaped the fate of Hyderabad and Goa. If the reports coming out were to be believed, the Thiruvithamkoor royal family was about to face another crisis.

When time stopped moving again, I packed up my things. Took several night trains until I reached Kochi. By this time, Kochi had become a city in distress, its only significance its proximity to Thiruvithamkoor, being surrounded by Thiruvithamkoor territory its only remarkable feature. Only a thin corridor, made up of places like Paravoor, Munambam, Nayarambalam, and so on, connected it to the Indian mainland. Even this strip of land was constantly targeted by the CPG's destabilization efforts.

The first thing I noticed when I got off an early morning bus in Ernakulam was the reduced presence of the army. India now had more important borders to protect. Except for the navy boats on routine patrol around Willingdon Island and in the Vembanad Kayal around it, there were no other signs of security forces. The town seemed unchanged in other ways. A few boats sat motionless in the Kayal with men fishing with tackle nets. The streets were taking a long time to come to life. It felt like how it was when I had arrived here after leaving Vallappuzha Vaidyan's place all those years ago. As I walked southwards along the lakeside path, I wondered whether this place was on its way to becoming a dead city. There were still houses here that had palm-leaf-thatched roofs, something not common in other towns and cities these days. Signs of trade were few and far between in the market and Joothatheruvu, the main street in the Jewish part of the town. Instead of expanding out, the town seemed to have shrunk into a circle. There were no new constructions. Some streets were dirty and filled with stagnant water and others potholed and strewn with rubble. This was a place, until quite recently, abuzz with shops, clubs and movie theatres frequented by the families of the soldiers from northern India. These establishments were all shuttered now. Perhaps this was the fate of all places the army used as staging posts for its wars, its inherent power the destruction of civilizations. Their cities contracted until they imploded. As for me, had madness and freedom not captured me and given me a good shake, I would not have had these thoughts. I would have, instead, felt impressed, marvelled at their identical clothes, gestures and movements. Applauded their ability to turn a diverse group of human beings into a single, uniform entity.

What if things had unfolded differently, I thought. What if other things had happened in 1947 and 1948. If Thiruvithamkoor had, as shown in the maps verified by India, joined the Indian Union. This city would have been so different then. The island the sahibs built and its surroundings would have been one of the greatest seaports. Its position in the middle of the southern state would have turned it into its capital, the centre of its activities. The Vembanad Kayal, now the border between two countries, would have remained calm and placid. Some would have their mother's house on one of its banks and their father's house on the other. I had, by then, reached the law college established by Rama Varma Thampuran, the last ruler of Kochi. It too huddled back, its old buildings showing no signs of maintenance and its surroundings dirty. It did not look like a centre of excellent education. A vaka tree stood in the compound with a few of its branches hanging down broken. The beggars and elderly sex workers who spent the nights on its pitted verandas were only beginning to stir from sleep. As I stood looking at the two-storey building at the front of the property, I saw a picture on the upper back wall. Quickly, I walked towards it.

Standing in the grassy ground right below the wall, strewn with the waste of the itinerants who used the place as a public toilet, I looked up at the picture. It looked new, created perhaps only four or five days ago, because rain had not faded it. Someone, an unknown student perhaps, had painstakingly scratched away the moss on the wall to create the largish area where the picture was made. I looked at it more carefully and it dawned on me that it was the creation of not one person but several. The lines were of different thicknesses. But instead of clashing with one another, they had come together well. Only thick, deep red and black strokes had been used. They combined the slackness of art and the certainty of political conviction. Studying the picture, I got sucked into it. Blood seeped from its edges, from its outer lines. Eyes glittered in shiny black. Etched on that wall, the man I had been chasing all this time gazed fiercely at the lake across the street, at the sea beyond the lake, and at the island, born out of imagination, in the sea. Beneath that face, the student artists who had drawn it had written these energizing words: 'Continue as a creative. Continue as a fighter.'

It was possible to say at the same time that the picture was and was not of the Basheer I knew. One had to remember that it was the picture of a Malayali, somewhat dark-complexioned, short-statured, with a balding head and thickish, pouting lips. But something else was mixed in with it too. The face had been altered slightly in the drawing, enough to remind us of a revolutionary in South America or in Russia. Cheeks were sunken like those of a mineworker. The balding head was reminiscent of Lenin. The eyebrows were thin, and the eyes showed a romantic mixture of brightness and fatigue. The ears were not fleshy. The face, overall, was longer. Were they not able to draw the face of an ordinary Malayali as that of a fighter, I wondered. Or was it that our bodies and faces were unsuitable for such a representation? Did we, instead, have the figure of a coward, a slave, someone incapable of self-respect? It might be that when they drew this, those students were relying on the things jumbled up in their minds. Their hands might have moved in those ways. Still, the picture had a rare energy and intensity. It reminded one that several revolutions had taken place all around the world, were still taking place, and that there was something that unified all of them. Perhaps this was what they intended when they made slight alterations to Basheer's face. It was the Basheer inside them who stared at the sea beyond, the lawbreaker on the wall of the law college. There was an island in that sea, an island born of his mad imagination, that did not obey the laws of materiality. His characters, escaped from the ordinary confines of storytelling, might be there on that island. I too wanted to go to that island.

The followers of Aikyakeralam and the old State Congress, and the communists in Kochi were in a state of great enthusiasm. The news, still unconfirmed, streaming in from Thiruvithamkoor and the return of Basheer made them exuberant. They had been dejected because of the unchanging situation that went on for a long time. People are enthused only by things that are about to happen. Marvels must materialize in our own lifetime. Franco Raghavan Pillah's death had robbed them of hope. The fact that when India declared its independence, the native kingdom of Thiruvithamkoor also asserted its independence finally penetrated their minds. The land beyond the Kaithapuzha Kayal and the Periyar river was another country, as separate as Sri Lanka or Malaysia. It had its own currency, flag and army. But now, there was that old feeling again, that something was imminent. Every time I spoke to them, I remembered the picture the students had drawn on the wall of the law college. When they talked about Basheer, I felt they were talking about someone else. They had added other things to the Basheer I had known. The real Basheer must be this too, I felt, not just the man I remembered. Not just the man I had met at the Muhamma post office ground or spent time with at the Central Jail, but also made up of all that people said about him. Once more, I looked into myself. I was only this, this figure, this body. Without even a name. When I walked, not even a shadow walked with me.

Once again, I spent the night at Seethi Buildings. Like my memories, the building had also become old. The old owner's descendants had dismantled a portion at its back and sold the wood and stones. A dispute about ownership had broken out then and saved the rest of the building. Around ten people lived in it, a few of them with vague connections to Aikyakeralam. They had no idea how important this dilapidated building had been in its heyday. It was as good a place as any to live in when they came into the city to study or for work. And because of the dispute, they did not have to pay rent. I made their acquaintance, told them that I had once lived in the building.

'Yes, some people come around sometimes, saying that they had lived here once,' one of them said. 'They look around for a bit and go away.'

Perhaps those dreamy young men who used to hang around the place, I thought. The ones who had thrown themselves enthusiastically into the discussions and debates that went on when Basheer was preparing the blueprint for a post-revolution society. They must now be living a life of plenty or penury, alone or with a family, engaged in agriculture or trade or a government job or burglary or beggaring or fishing or small-time politics or card games or pimping. Why would such men come around here to have a look? And when they did, were they laughing or weeping inside? Or were they ridiculing themselves on finding how everything had, in the tide of time, turned into a big joke?

'Last time, when I came back from Vavubali, one chap was walking around the building,' another person told me. 'Hung around for quite some time. Looked like he hadn't eaten in a while too. I gave him some kanji and sent him on his way.'

Might have been one of the youngsters who had died before his time, I thought. It was the day of Vavubali, as the man said, the day of rituals and offerings of food to ancestral spirits. Perhaps this was where he came once a year when all spirits visited their families, this place that he had considered his home.

'Did he tell you his name?' I asked.

'Swami, I think it was.'

They balked at first, but in the end, they let me stay the night. I decided to sleep in the kitchen. In Basheer's old bed. The woven-rope bed was still there, not too damaged. No one paid attention to the kitchen any more. People still used it as a thoroughfare because of the two doors that were always left open. Two kerosene stoves sat where the cooking fire used to be. The pile of discarded furniture and other stuff on the opposite side had disappeared. I picked up the five or six sack bundles that were on the bed and put them on the floor. The others found it strange that I had chosen the kitchen to sleep in when there were other vacant rooms. One of them suspected me of being a thief, I felt. He locked the door that connected the kitchen to the rest of the house.

With no sheet or mat, I lay on the naked bed, my head leaning on the bar at the top and my eyes open. I lifted you up from such a posture, Basheer, and took you to Kottayam. You were caught by the police there. And I got caught in the trap of forever following you. I sat up, and as Basheer used to do, coughed up phlegm and spat it out through the window. A cold wind, the kind that made the lungs feel damp, came in. And when a rain took up a little later, I pulled the window shut. The darkness made no sound. Outside, the rain continued, one downpour after another. By the time I slept, finally, light had begun to spread outside.

Even as I fell asleep, I felt that this would be the deepest sleep of my life. The old ropes of the bed sagged in the middle, and I lay in it with my knees pulled up, my body curled, like a foetus in the womb. Floated gently in the warm, comfortable fluid that enveloped me. In the sounds of the unknown world outside that I would see when I left was the low, loving voice of someone calling me by my real name. I understood that I would forget that name as soon as I woke up. After a while, someone tried to shake me awake. His face was familiar from the first time I had come here to see Basheer. 'Here, get up,' he said, 'a lot of people are here.' I nudged him away. Other people began pulling things out from under the bed. I wanted to stop them. I couldn't. I wanted to sleep. I flipped myself over in the amniotic fluid.

It is sunny and windy, and I am at the boat jetty near the law college. But the lake in front of me is a different one. A boat stands ready to head out to the sea beyond. Other boats can be seen leaving the far shore. I beg the boatman unmooring his boat to take me too.

'You have any money to buy a ticket?' he asks.

'No.'

'Well, get in then.'

As I am about to step in, he asks, 'You have nothing to take with you?'

I look into the boat. Every one of the people on board has bundles or metal trunks. They are going to live there permanently.

By the time I woke up, it was noon. I boarded a boat from the same jetty as in my dream and went to Mattancherry. Went down the lane I had walked with Basheer and reached the place where he – he had a moustache like Bhagat Singh's then – and his followers had called out slogans. Not even a small percentage of the bustling trade and noise of those days remained in the area. The streets and the buildings were the same. I sat in the same old shop, sipping tea and staring out. There, right there was where he had stood calling out the slogans. And here, this was where I was sitting, watching how people responded. It was the events that happened here that he had filled the next issue of *Ujjeevanam* with.

I left the shop and walked the route the demonstration had taken. No one came running out to stand at the verges watching it go by. Noisy children played outside large old buildings where several families lived together. Nanny goats waddled along, their udders covered in cloth bags. I took my time and walked to the shipping channel. It was here that they had given the red salute to a fortified ship that had passed by blaring its siren. These days, barely any ships passed through the channel. Wharfs lay empty. Darkness fell in a single sweep as I stood watching. At the south-western corner of the sea, a light became visible. I stood looking in that direction for a long time.

A man came along smoking a beedi.

'What's that over there?' I asked him.

'Ayyo! You don't know what it is?' he asked, amazed.

'I guess I do,' I said.

17

Repercussions of the news about Sir C.P. Ramaswami Iyer's mysterious illness and of Basheer's return were evident all over, in all areas. Here, I will keep politics aside and talk about the arts. Despite the countries becoming separate entities following independence, Thiruvithamkoor and Kerala, the Malayalam-speaking parts of India, remained connected by that shared language. Movies made on either side were shown across the borders at least for a while. Writers published their works in literary magazines on both sides. Those writers who escaped from Thiruvithamkoor were welcomed and given public forums in Kerala. But Thiruvithamkoor had the upper hand in the literary field, with more opportunities for publishing and a proliferation of literary magazines supported by the government. Writers on both sides were scared of falling into the bad books of editors and writers of stature like K.N. Raghava Kuruppu and K.P. Sukumara Menon. So, in those days, Aikyakeralam did not enjoy the overt backing of most writers. In public forums, if they were asked questions about why speakers of Malayalam had ended up in two different countries or about autocratic governments, all they did was don a weird smile as though the questioner was a fool. With the new developments, things began to change a little. At least some of them made their stances public, consciously or because of their haste.

The first of such responses was an essay titled 'Why be Silent in the Face of Foolishness', published in the magazine *Arul* that came out from Kollam for over ten years before it was stopped. It was written by a professor of English at the Thiruvithamkoor

University, named Kumar Anandan. He had, to his name, such tomes as *Old Travancore Records in Marxist Perspective* and *A Comparative Study of Walter Scott and C.V. Raman Pillah*. Who was Basheer? What was the truth behind recent events? These were the questions Kumar Anandan engaged with in his essay. The first question he posed was whether or not Basheer was a writer. Clearly, he was not, he argued. Even Basheer would not claim to have written anything other than a few pamphlets. And even those were questionable because there was no proof that he had written them. Then there were the stories, folkloristic in nature, circulating in society that were claimed to have been told by him. Comparing a couple of these stories to the pamphlets attributed to Basheer, he argued that there were simply no similarities between them. What had happened in this case was a conscious attempt to reconstruct Basheer's image. The talk about the sudden appearance of an island in the Arabian Sea and its connection to Basheer was also part of this construction. It was beyond common sense. If, for argument's sake, say that a writer was capable of conjuring up reality from imagination. This argument fell apart when it was established that Basheer was not a writer. At least until it was proven otherwise.

Kumar Anandan was expecting a promotion in his career and the associated increase in salary. And the expectation would have come to fruition because he was known in his social milieu to be a harmless person, and he had a fairly commendable academic background. Perhaps he had written the essay thinking that a shove with the push might speed things up. But the essay that, on the face of it, seemed to support the government and ridicule Basheer, brought him nothing but misery. A cunning junior of his filed a complaint arguing that the essay was treasonous. The clerks at the university, tasked with putting the complaint on file, read the essay front to back and back to front but could not understand what it said. The professor wrote explanations upon explanations, some longer than the original essay, but to no avail. Finally, an order came from above asking him to answer one simple question: Why write about something that had never happened? Anandan had no answer except to apologize. It earned him a suspension, and he lost two salary increments and his promotion.

K.N.R. Kuruppu was the type of man who would have a fair idea of what was going to happen before it would happen. He wrote a poem at this time, one that seemed ordinary at first glance. 'Bird', it was titled. In a nutshell, it was about the poet standing on a seashore looking hopefully at a new type of brightly coloured bird that flies in from the west. He connects it to the migratory travels of birds. Where was its home? Would it be on an island in the middle of the vast ocean? At its sight, one's mind shed its worries and was filled with the joy of a hopeful tomorrow. The poem was read and interpreted in two ways. In Thiruvithamkoor, the bird was understood to symbolize the new defence agreement that the country had entered into with America. Its home, the island in the vast ocean, was taken to be Diego Garcia, off the coast of Africa in the Indian Ocean, where America was building a military base. Meanwhile, in Kerala, the poem was read aloud at Aikyakeralam meetings and demonstrations with great enthusiasm. In their interpretation, the bird was the people's revolution strengthening anew in Thiruvithamkoor. And the island. What else could it be other than the one that had taken birth out of Basheer's imagination?

The magazine *Udayam*, under the editorial leadership of K.P. Sukumaran Nair, did not engage with the new events despite them being discussed wherever there were Malayalis. There was nothing to fault in this stance. The magazine usually engaged only with issues of an old era. The stories and poems it published dealt with themes such as the Onam celebrations of yore, ponds, sacred groves where snake gods dwelled, romantic walkways through vast fields, murappennu – girl-cousins one could marry according to tradition – songs of the harvest, and so on. But KP dusted out the old pseudonym, Somanath, and wrote an allegorical story. A madman declares that he has seen a golden mango hanging from the topmost branch of a mango tree. People of the land believe him, and they gather around the tree waiting for the mango to fall. That was the story. The madman in the story was called Basheer. The message of the story was clear as day.

Somanath's story was published in a minor magazine. It coincided with an important event in the history of our country. Preparations were under way for Murajapam, the third since independence. In the old days, it was mainly Brahmins from Kochi and Malabar who came to attend Murajapam. But now, large groups of Brahmins arrived from all over northern India. Thiruvithamkoor was more volatile than usual lately, and the Indian government had tried to deny them permission to attend but failed. The conference of sanyasis that took place in Haridwar declared that Thiruvithamkoor was to the Hindus what Mecca was to the Muslims, and that Maharaja Sree Chithira Thirunal was akin to the Khalifa. Besides, it was the land where Adi Sankaran, the first of the Sankaracharyas, was born. If the communists in Kerala or the Dravida Kazhagam in Tamil Nadu tried to stop them from entering Thiruvithamkoor, there would be dire repercussions, they warned.

A fortnight before Murajapam, the towns of Kollam and Alappuzha and places such as Aranmula, Chengannur, Kumaranellore, Attingal and Punalur filled with people from north India. Large groups of naked sadhus arrived. When they saw churches in the country they had assumed to be the land of Brahmins, they turned violent and set fire to them. Ankamali and Kuravilangadu churches on M.C. Road were among the ones that perished. The government, under the stewardship of K.K. Nair, took more precautions than usual. Other religions were banned from communal worship until after Murajapam. People of castes below Sudras were removed from areas where accommodation for Brahmins was arranged. RSS volunteers from Vidarbha and Uttar Pradesh were called in. As with all occasions of Murajapam, the lower castes' right to enter temples was temporarily suspended. All food except vegetarian was banned. And to ensure that this was followed, fishing and butchery were stopped. Traditionally, Azhvanchery Thamprakkal, elders of the Namboothiri Brahmin family of Azhvanchery, had the most elevated position in Murajapam. But this time, the rituals themselves were recast so that the Sankaracharyas from Sringeri, Badrinath, Dwaraka and Puri had a more elevated position. North Indian food items were included alongside local delicacies. Travel allowances and dakshina, gift offerings for the Brahmins, were increased. More people than ever before were coming to attend the event, so collecting the necessary resources and food through village offices was insufficient. Besides, for the last two years, paddy harvest in the country had been less than ideal. K.K. Nair ordered that all food resources kept aside by the farmers of Nanjinad and Kuttanad be confiscated.

On 15 November 1966, without being prompted by anyone, thousands of people, including women and children, gathered on the beach in Alappuzha. Among them were fisherfolk, farmers, ploughmen, duck herders. Most were starved and emaciated. It was unclear what had driven them to assemble there at this time. There was also talk that the bodies of two children who had died of starvation were brought there. They spent some time wailing and cursing K.K. Nair and the prime minister, and then stood looking towards the light far away in the western sea. People who had never made a speech in their whole lives climbed up on whatever elevation they could find and began saying provocative things. Some old State Congress people arrived and tried to make them stop and to disperse the crowd. But with nowhere to go, they continued standing there. The news began to spread that some people had jumped into the sea with their children in tow. What happened next was without precedent. Pouncing on the handful of policemen around, they beat them up, and then the starving horde ran towards the city.

The looting in Alappuzha went on until the morning. After destroying the recently established Brahmin settlements near Mullakkal and the Sanatana Dharma College, the crowd set fire to two temples of the Gowda Saraswatha community and the courthouse. Temporary arrangements had been set up for those who had arrived from north India for Murajapam. These were attacked and the food stores taken away. The policemen guarding the old Aspinwall Building, where all the items for the ritual, to be sent to Thiruvananthapuram, had been stockpiled, ran away. By morning, more police arrived, but with people pouring in from all directions, the crowd had also grown. By the 16th, the riot had turned into a full-fledged anti-Brahmin revolt. Several people were injured, including many north Indians, but all those who were killed were the rioters. Police gunshots echoed from many parts of the city. By afternoon, the crowd, grown much larger than on the previous day, moved south along the main road. Their numbers increased steadily as they passed Paravoor, Ambalapuzha, Harippad and onwards. Grabbing whatever they could use as weapons, they destroyed the oottupuras and thanneerpanthals that had been set up all along the way to provide food and water to Murajapam attendees. By the time the crowd reached Kayamkulam, it had become an unbroken stream of bodies. Their sights set on the faraway seat of power, they ran madly towards it.

The revolt in Kollam was fuelled by the news about what was happening in Alappuzha. The people there were already fed up with the north Indian Brahmins who had been camping in all the main locations in the city under the protection of the government. The gosais, as north Indian Brahmins were known, had stunk up these places with their excrement and turned churches into kitchens. On the 16th, a crowd of Ezhavas and Latin Christians drove them out of Kollam. They then planted the flag of Aikyakeralam on top of the old diwan court.

As these events unfolded, another group, a calm and orderly procession, had set out north from Nagercoil. This was the Nanjinattu Koottam, a collective of the farmers of the area. They had set out with the clear objective of demanding payment for the paddy the government had bought from them in the last several years and for what was confiscated this year. They were determined to be present in the capital at the time of Murajapam.

The 1960s were a time when Malayalam saw the emergence of several writers who wrote in new and different ways. Ever since I decided to write a book like this, I had been, in preparation, reading everything I could lay my hands on, with the exception of poetry. Many were the short-lived literary magazines that came out at this time. Stories, written by younger writers with unfamiliar names, began to be published in them and also in the main, well-known magazines. They wrote in a way that made the imagined seem real and the real imaginary. Deciding to write like they did, I read what they wrote several times. And remembered the reports I used to send to my superiors. The things I had, like these writers, mixed in with the information in those reports. O.V. Vijayan's *Moonnu Yuddhangal* (Three Wars) had come out, and Zacharia's *Unni Enna Kutty* (The Boy Named Unni) and M. Mukundan's *Veedu* (House). If Basheer had been mad when he wrote *Diary of a Lover*, so were these people. It was not truth or lies that they wrote. Only the truth that was inside them.

In those days, I lived in Ernakulam doing odd jobs using neither of my names, Bhasi or Avarachan. Neither I nor the jobs I did were important enough for people to ask my name. One morning, I was lying awake in the narrow room I lived in, the floor strewn with literary magazines. In them were stories I had read and discarded, all of which dealt with Basheer's return. That was how contemporary these new writers were. They said nothing overtly about it. But the reality he had created with his imagination had changed the way they wrote. There was one story in a magazine named *Thudakkam*, published from Thrissur, that talked directly and only about it. It was published as a short story, but it read like an essay. The writer's name was left out. Purposely or not, I couldn't tell. I read it and immediately felt that I wanted to find the writer. First, because the language in some places resembled the Raktarekha letters, and second, I had never read anything like it.

The story was long and divided into parts, and started with the premise that the island in the sea was real. In the first part, right at the start, the location of the island was established with latitude and longitude. Then followed a detailed exploration: How far into the sea was it? Could we all get there? Was it always there and we discovered it only now? Were only a handful of people from Kaduvakkuzhi – the Place that was Basheer's bhaavanadesham – Undakkannan Andru, Muzhayan Nanu, Ponkurishu Thoma, etc. living there from the beginning? Then the story described the experiences of the people who tried, out of desperation or curiosity, to get there. What was interesting was that, as in K.P. Krishna Pillah's essay, facts about Sir C.P.'s ill health and details about the island were revealed simultaneously in this story too.

Reading the second part of the story, I felt that the writing was sarcastic and fantastical, purposely so. It began with the discussions at an international conference about the new island. One group argued that the island should be given the status of a nation. What was the delay? Did it not have borders? Inhabitants? Other experts argued against it. How could a land mass that did not exist until now, which had no history, become a nation? And its inhabitants, did they not exist only in stories? Were they made of flesh and blood, skin and bone? If it were to be recognized as a nation, it would mean admitting that novels were free countries. Were *Don Quixote*, *Madame Bovary* and *The Invisible Man* free countries? If so, how many republics could a writer create? Well, what was wrong with that, countered the first group. Go to the moon and look down, were any countries visible? They existed only in human imagination. Read the history of a country, any country, and it would become clear that it was a novel that had lost its central plot. God himself was a big novel. Made up of stitching together several novels, with dodgy protagonists. There was also, in this second part of the story, a summary of discussions that had been published in the English magazine *Granta*. In it, one commentator called the appearance of the island off the coast of our small country 'a momentous literary event'. This man – his name was Borges – asked the sceptics why they found it so hard to believe. Such islands and cities existed. That same issue of *Granta* had a review of a French film about just such an island.

The third part of the story began with a group of people standing on the beach at night looking out at the sea. It was not even clear which of the many lights visible there they were looking at. After a while, with a collective wail, the group moved towards the city. Looting the city was not their aim; they could then have run back home with whatever they could lay their hands on. What they did, instead, was desecrate the places of pomp and glory where their hard-earned resources had been confiscated and stockpiled. Their arrival, like rats out of the sewers where they had bred and multiplied, caused panic, and city dwellers fled in all directions. Buildings and storerooms burned. Their wails unending, the crowd then ran towards the centre of power. They were in a great hurry. Momentous events are not planned in advance. They just happen. The crowd, too, did not have a clear plan, but they, and those who joined them along the way, knew, clearly, their destination. Perhaps provoked by the news of their revolt, other revolts broke out in many parts of the country.

They were shot at, killed, and yet people reached the capital city, wave after wave. Watching the screaming arrival of walkers, women, children, the infirm, the destitute, the army scattered out of their way. Helter-skelter they ran, through the city that had, until then, denied them entry. They filled the streets. A few city dwellers stuck their heads out and watched them from the upper storeys of buildings. They realized that their days were numbered. Finally, the revolt reached the seat of power. Even the sentries guarding the place had grabbed whatever they could and run away. The crowd breached the wall and entered the garden in front of the building. Something gave them pause. A horrible stench. They wondered if, in places like this, even the flowers had a stink rather than a fragrance. Were these places occupied by people who liked the smell of decaying meat? Or was this stink their odour? The closer they got to the building, the more intense the stench. The braver among them entered the building. The grand halls and long corridors made them uneasy, scared them. Could they defeat those who lived in such large spaces, amidst such luxury? Would not such people be highly intelligent, able to foresee what was coming? What if they had cleverly enticed them here? They felt as if they were being watched from behind the pillars, sniggered at. That the shadows were of sharpened weapons. Finally, they stood before the door behind which was the man, the Almighty, the one who controlled everything with his fingertips. Their knees shaking, they waited, ready to apologize and surrender to their fates. Time passed and nothing happened. Then, a small breeze opened the door that had been left unlocked. They peeked inside. There was the Almighty, lying suspended in a tank of liquid, discoloured but undecayed. They couldn't believe their eyes. Was it this thing, this corpse, that had been ruling them all these days? Did he send out all those orders lying here in this bizarre coffin, this tank of formaldehyde?

I finished reading the story, put aside the magazine, and stepped out of my room thinking about the nameless person who had written it. The quiet streets were suddenly coming alive. Groups of people went along in processions. Vehicles blared their horns victoriously. In the time that it took me to read a story, the world had changed. All that had been certain and dependable had come tumbling down. Leaving behind what was in my room, I walked towards the lake. Boats and small vessels, with flags fluttering in the wind, rowed towards the far shore as though a dam had broken. They were filled with people shouting slogans and beating drums. I could also hear, loudest among all the noises, the name of the man I had been following. I looked at the faint green of the land across the water. It was time to go to my country, to Thiruvithamkoor.

PART III

I

As I stood listening to Akkamma Cherian speaking from the hastily assembled stage near the Huzur Court, I was thinking about the Maharaja hoisting the flag on the day our country became independent. I had stood aside from the crowd then, not wanting to attract attention to myself. Was Basheer here, now, doing the same? And just as the Maharaja had looked at me then, was Akkamma looking at him?

Akkamma was small-statured, but when she stood behind the mike, memories of her courageous acts and suffering seemed to make her much larger. Almost a quarter of a century ago, at a very young age, she had managed to bring this city to a halt. Forced the Maharaja and Diwanji into making compromises like no man in the entire country had been able to. Stood unafraid before the white sahib, challenging him to shoot her. Spent years in prison, and loved another prisoner on the other side of the wall. Gone to another country beyond the border and created a parallel government. And led a revolution from across the border back into her country. She had come back now when the palaces had crumbled in an earthquake created by the people. I remembered the twig that rose in the air as signals from the other side of the wall in the prison. Was this woman with a few grey strands of middle age showing in her hair the same young woman who had nurtured a garden of love in the prison yard? Did the somewhat rough voice that came out through the microphone belong to Narayani in Basheer's story about the walls? Was that the fragrance of gandharajan in the air?

As was familiar from the personal history that had been widely circulated, Akkamma Cherian was dressed in a white khaddar sari and blouse, with a white Gandhi cap on her head. Behind her, in a row of chairs sat P.T. Chacko, Kumbalath Shanku Pillai, Chandrananan, T.V. Thomas and other prominent leaders. Perhaps because of their tireless toil, living precariously in another country, they all seemed to have aged before their time. They had spent years battling hopelessly before being able to return to their own country. Some seemed to have difficulty believing that they were back here, in their own country. They aimed suspicious looks at the building nearby, the symbol of royal power. It would take some time for them to believe this victory, which had come at a time when all hope had been lost. But the crowd that was in front of them had no doubts remaining in their minds. Holding aloft the flags of the State Congress, the Communist Party and Aikyakeralam, and calling out slogans, they were in a jubilant mood. Walking long distances from all parts of the country, they coursed through the streets that were forbidden to them until then, taking in the sights.

Akkamma Cherian began her speech by stating that it was the people of Thiruvithamkoor who had stopped the last Murajapam in the land. The taxes that people paid would never again be used to feed and fatten one section of society. 'We have nothing against them,' she said, 'but they too must work like everyone else to earn a living.' The protests that had taken place in Thiruvithamkoor were without precedent. She then named several people who were instrumental in them. At the mention of Franco Raghavan Pillah's name, the crowd released a collective, mournful roar.

'I will not utter the name of the person who desecrated his body in death,' Akkamma said. 'I will not sully my own tongue saying that name. He has absconded to the neighbouring country where he has people to help him. But mark my words. They are yet to reap the suffering from the seeds he had already planted there all those years ago. Meanwhile, we have the job of pulling out by the roots what he planted here.'

Loud slogans erupted when she mentioned the names of N. Sreekantan Nair, Ponnara Sridhar, V.S. Achuthanandan and Varghese. She waited until the noise quieted down, and then said the name Basheer. Joyful screams rose from all corners and drowned out most of what she said next. In that moment, I thought of Mani.

Akkamma ridiculed the royal family that had fled the country.

'Allayo Raja! We might have shown you some respect if you had not been this cowardly. All these people assembled here might even have pardoned you, chosen to forget how you had ruled this country for months, hiding behind a rotting corpse. Because, unlike your acolytes, the ordinary people of Thiruvithamkoor are not utterly despicable.'

She then said that she had an important request which she wanted to present before the people and the leaders of the revolution who had suffered worse atrocities than she herself had.

'I want to be the prime minister of the independent, sovereign republic of Thiruvithamkoor,' she said.

Everything went silent. Each person sitting on the dais seemed to wonder whether they had heard these words or whether their ears were playing tricks on them. After all, for quite a while now, unbelievable things had become routine. The crowd stood still, unblinking, expectant of something momentous to follow. Every single one of the leaders who had spoken before Akkamma had declared that they had no interest in holding power. They had only indicated subtly that, were power to be bestowed upon them, they would humbly shoulder the burden.

'I ask you this not only for my sake,' Akkamma said, almost bellowing now. 'Men must stand aside now. Haven't you been the rulers all this while? Weren't the two world wars your doing? The atom bomb? The colonization of the whole world? Aren't you responsible for crucifying Eesho Mishiha, assassinating Mahatma Gandhi, and killing Sreekantan Nair in a staged encounter? Aren't you the ones who tied the dead body of the most heroic soldier of this land to the back of a car and dragged it through the streets? Aren't you the ones who ruled this land for all this time and made it what it is today?'

She then listed the names of all the queens, the maharanis who had been fair rulers of Thiruvithamkoor.

'Consider. Were they better, or are you?'

Almost all of the crowd assembled there, gleeful that they had finally been successful in the revolution, were men. They felt that they had suddenly been found guilty, the victors and the losers inseparable.

'Can you show me a single woman who had anything to do with the miseries that were unleashed since 1947? Aren't you responsible for all this?'

Some people began to feel that, in some bizarre turn of events, they had sided with Sir C.P. and K.K. Nair, and that they were now standing there defeated, their heads hanging in shame. Movements stopped, sounds died out.

'There is only one thing that women can learn from men,' Akkamma said. 'That no one hands power over; it has to be taken. If the humble and the empathetic stand aside, the evil and the demented will take their place. You – men – have taken your places in this way,' she said.

The rest of Akkamma Cherian's speech was in the voice of the ruler of Thiruvithamkoor. What she said next was addressed to the neighbouring country and its woman prime minister.

'We, the people of Thiruvithamkoor, respect you not because you are the prime minister of a country that is a hundred times the size of ours, or because you have a large army. Size does not beget significance. We respect you because, firstly, you are the daughter of a great, far-sighted man. Secondly, your name contains the name of the man whom we love the most. Both these men respected moral power over manpower. We can only hope that you have inherited at least some of their qualities. If not, we will have to agree with those in the opposition in your country that you are a mere puppet in the hands of a bunch of old men.'

She then went on to aim bitter criticism at India which had, when the people of Thiruvithamkoor had finally toppled an unjust government, tried to conquer the country by sending in the army.

'And what happened? Had to go back halfway, didn't you? The proud people of this country took to the streets unarmed and stopped you, didn't they? Didn't the whole world turn against you? The leaders sitting now on this dais, the people assembled here – these are folks who have worked so hard and for so long to create a unified Kerala, an Aikyakeralam. Just look at the name of our organization. We are people who fought to join the country ruled by Pandit Nehru. Thousands of people of Thiruvithamkoor gave their lives for the cause. Is there any province in your land which has rid itself of royal rule like this? We are indeed a proud people. We, the people of Thiruvithamkoor, will decide whether or not we want to join another country or remain independent. If you try to force the issue with your army, you will lose. Do not forget that the people across the Periyar are our blood relatives. Who knows, they might decide to join us.'

By this time, the crowd was worked up. Anti-Indian slogans rent the air. Akkamma understood that she was in the middle of a historic moment. Her words became sharper, shimmering with sarcasm.

'You say that you were, all this time, helping us. But the people who gave us asylum in your country were our relatives.

What were you doing meanwhile, when the people of this country were going through unconscionable suffering? Wasn't it your people who supported the horrible government here? Your sanyasis and communalists who held demonstrations supporting the king and the diwan? Ousted the oppressed communities here and planned to turn this into a Brahmin land? Weren't the king and the diwan starving our people in order to feed and fatten them? Let's keep this all aside for a moment and think about the man who disrespected our country for so long, who continued to rule this country even when he was a lifeless, rotting corpse. Wasn't he from your country? His trusted assistant, wasn't he your agent? We'll make the decisions from now on. The Hindu Mahasabha, which for so long clamoured for the protection of Thiruvithamkoor, why is it suddenly demanding military action against our country? It is clear that you are not concerned about the history of your country or its unity. All you really care about is that this country, our country, should be ruled by you.'

I stood there listening to this barrage, amazed, incredulous. How quickly things changed. Patriots became traitors and vice versa in the blink of an eye. What had I become? I walked amongst the multitude of people who had gathered around the Huzur Court building and spilled into the streets and by-lanes beyond. I did not come across anyone who knew me. No one looked at me. I insinuated myself into a conversation among three or four people. They did not even notice my presence. Not even as a shadow. I walked, and people passed me by. Finally, I came back to the dais and stood in front of it. P.T. Chacko sat directly above me. I remembered what he had said about Mani and me when we were with Sreekantan Nair. I was directly in his line of sight now. But his gaze passed me by and went beyond. My actions and I myself had been forgotten a long time ago. I felt an overwhelming sorrow. In my job, it was important that I remained anonymous, unnoticed, my actions unrecognized. But for this to be taken to an extreme where I was entirely erased? That there remained, in this world, not a single person who knew of my existence? Leaving the crowd behind, I walked aimlessly until darkness fell. Lay down in the veranda of a shop to spend the night and searched the whole world. Was there anyone other than Devasia and Elikkutty who remembered me? But as I lay there, I began to feel that Devasia, Elikkutty and their house were conjured up from the bitterness that Vallappuzha Vaidyan's nasyam had released inside me. I was afraid. What if I had never made that second trip to their place in Thiruvambady? I closed my eyes and dreamed of Basheer.

It was a dream that only had sound. His voice was that of a dead man.

'What you said then has come true,' I say. 'That you'll come back with a large army, or that you'll come when people run them off.'

He laughs softly.

'Everyone remembers you,' I say. 'The noise when they said your name ... But no one remembers me.'

'Why is that?' he asks.

I do not respond.

2

30 November

The new, interim government released some emergency policies. It was duty-bound, it said, to honour the terms of the agreement drafted at the time of independence between Thiruvithamkoor and India. The statement clarified: There would be a public election within a year, with voting rights according to the principles of adult suffrage. All sections of society would be ensured representation. An election commission would be formed and mandated with the tasks of deciding constituencies, preparing voters' lists and putting in place due processes. The election would be under the supervision of the United Nations. The newly elected people's representatives would have the task of deciding whether the country should join the Indian Union or remain independent.

No one should feel the need to leave the country because there is a new government, it reassured. For some time now, foreigners had been accommodated in the country in settlements specifically created for them. They had the choice to return to their countries or remain in Thiruvithamkoor. The election commission would decide whether or not those who chose to remain should be given voting rights. No special rights would be meted out to them. The process to repatriate those who had to leave the country seeking asylum in other places would begin imminently. Their properties, confiscated by the previous government, would be given back to them. Political prisoners would be released immediately. All cases filed against those who had fought against the royal government would be withdrawn. The ban imposed on some sections of people, on their free movement in main cities and on entering major temples, was revoked. So was the ban on the religious worship of Christian communities. Newspapers would not be censored. The mortal remains of Swadeshabhimani Balakrishna Pillah, who had died in exile, would be brought back and laid to rest in his birthplace. The United Nations would be informed of our protest against the neighbouring country which sent in its the army in an attempt to seize our country as soon we had rid ourselves of our oppressors through a people's revolution. In the process, they had breached the terms of the contract that they too had signed. The people of Thiruvithamkoor who stood up to them unarmed and sent them packing deserved our appreciation. The neighbouring country must be held to account for the lives lost in this process.

The government said that it was looking into reinvestigating several important events of the past years. These included the alleged attempt, just before independence, to assassinate the king, the death of Varghese, and the murder of innocent schoolchildren in Vaikom.

1 December

India made a submission to the United Nations asking that the new government of Thiruvithamkoor not be recognized. That country, it insisted, was still a part of India.

India's home minister Yashwantrao Chavan accused the State Congress, Aikyakeralam and the Communist Party of betraying the people of Thiruvithamkoor. They had fought, for so long, because they wanted to join the Indian Union. But now that they were in power, they were changing their tune. The Indian government was imposing a temporary ban on travel between the two countries, he said, because the new government of Thiruvithamkoor was trying to expel some of its permanent residents while trying to let others into the country. The promise of an election within the year was a blatant lie. It replicated the old government's strategy of delaying things until they could be quietly left undone.

The defence minister, Sardar Swaran Singh, claimed that the news that India had sent its army into Thiruvithamkoor was a lie. The land formerly known as Thiruvithamkoor was made up of places that were currently in the Indian states of Kerala and Tamil Nadu. It was India's stance that such a land did not exist any more. And the country did not need anyone's permission to send its army to any part of its own territory. India had always supported the struggles of the people of the old land of Thiruvithamkoor who wanted to become part of India. It would, he reiterated, continue to do so.

2 December

The organization Bharatiya Jana Sangham declared 2 December as Thiruvithamkoor Day. Its president Balraj Madhok claimed that Christian missionaries had been successful in their mission to turn Thiruvithamkoor into a Christian nation. The sole purpose of the recent revolt was to disrupt Murajapam, an important tradition that Hindus the world over considered sacred. Akkamma Cherian was an agent of the Vatican. There was also talk about a man named Basheer. One of the accused in the attempted assassination of the Maharaja, he had once been a resident of Karachi. 'What we had feared has come true,' he said. 'The State Congress was, all this time, nurturing anti-nationals.' Madhok appealed to the Indian prime minister Indira Gandhi to send the army into Thiruvithamkoor to restore royal rule and to protect the interests of the Hindu community.

3 December

Kumbalath Shanku Pillai, the defence minister in the interim government, declared that those who had assassinated Mahatma Gandhi need not worry themselves about affairs in Thiruvithamkoor. The struggle, thus far, was to join an India led by Gandhi and Nehru. Do not think that the people of Thiruvithamkoor would sit silently back and endure colonization, no matter who it was by, he stated – the North Indian gosai arrogance would not find purchase in this land. The future of the country would be decided by its people. Thiruvithamkoor was finally a fully independent, sovereign country. India would do well to cease its foolishness. Do not push the people of Thiruvithamkoor into cutting all ties between the countries, he warned.

5 December

The secretary of the Communist Party, K.C. George, asked that the leaders of the interim government cease making statements that provoked the neighbouring country. He defended the Party's decision to reject the invitation to join the interim government. The Party had no interest in joining a government in which it had no majority. The State Congress ingratiated itself to powers that held on to the hierarchies of caste and religion. It displayed the same behaviour as the Congress Party in India. If the government was interested in reinvestigating old atrocities, it should start with the shooting in Punnapra. It was in the house of a State Congress leader that the police, responsible for the massacre, had set up camp. When asked at a press conference whether the Communist Party would field candidates for the upcoming election, K.C. George replied that what the Party wanted was real democracy – people's democracy. And to the question whether the Communist Party wanted Thiruvithamkoor to be part of India, he said that the Party was the first to talk about self-determination in relation to nationhood. The decision, he said, would depend on the how the circumstances came together at the time.

1 January

The exiled Maharaja Sree Chithira Thirunal Balarama Varma signed an agreement that Thiruvithamkoor would become part of India. The event, which took place in Kathmandu in Nepal, was attended by the Indian prime minister, foreign minister and home minister. It was an unconditional surrender. Following this, India made an official appeal to the United Nations that Thiruvithamkoor's membership to the General Assembly be revoked.

Our country responded in strong terms to this development. Anti-India feelings were already at their highest point. It was, as described, the feeling that Thiruvithamkoor was being turned into a Brahmin settlement that spurred the people's revolt which finally ended royal rule. Until then, no matter how serious the issues they faced, the people of Thiruvithamkoor had always refrained from criticizing the Maharaja. In their minds, he was the harmless satvik always. They liked to believe that the problems in governance, the atrocities, were all due to the prime minister and the principal secretary. But this time, the sentiment changed, they felt betrayed. For the first time in history, people threw stones at the deserted palaces, attacked the establishments run by members of the royal family. An utterly incredible sight was the procession in Thiruvananthapuram that the people organized, carrying a symbolic funeral bed of the Maharaja.

2 January

Responding to the treaty, the Thiruvithamkoor government said that it was the first time in the history of the world that a king dethroned by his subjects had signed a treaty on behalf of the country. What had he been doing all these years after the country became independent? The incident clarified that the government of India was afraid of losing – indeed, feared – the will of the people.

5 January

An official order was released, declaring that all properties and temples belonging to the royal family were now under the control of the government. India responded by saying that Thiruvithamkoor had, with this order, sounded the battle call.

8 January

Thiruvithamkoor condemned India's renewed efforts to concentrate military power at the border. It demanded the involvement of the United Nations.

10 January

The government said that the defence treaty the old government had entered into with America was still valid. The foreign minister would soon meet with the US secretary of state and discuss matters, including resisting the threat posed by the neighbouring country. President Lyndon Johnson would be officially invited for a state visit. In the international political context, Thiruvithamkoor stood, unequivocally, with the democratic alliance.

The Communist Party declared that they would actively resist all involvement of America in the affairs of Thiruvithamkoor. The government seemed determined to invite the Americans in and enable the development of a dangerous situation as in Vietnam. It would not stand by and watch the undoing of the people's revolution, the country tethered in the cattle barn of imperialism. The murderer Lyndon Johnson would not be allowed to set foot in the country. It would seem that the Party's analysis of the interim government and the State Congress as classist was being proven right.

11 January

The Communist Party was yet again showing its true colours by betraying the people, said P.T. Chacko. At a time when the whole country should come together to resist the threat posed by its neighbour, they were busy creating rifts. It was to be expected that they might even attempt a coup with the support of the country's enemies.

20 January

An order was released banning the Communist Party in Thiruvithamkoor. The interim prime minister Akkamma Cherian explained that such an action was necessitated in order to avoid another bloody incident as had happened in Alappuzha two decades ago. The communists were getting ready for a revolt supported by the neighbouring country and other foreign powers. The prime minister said that the government was urgently restructuring the police, the army and other government departments. Too much of these spaces were occupied by those loyal to the old government and to the neighbouring country. The old government had filled these departments with its most trustworthy men, turned them into weapons to be used against the people. Without fundamental changes, it was impossible for the wheel of governance to turn smoothly. She appealed to the people that they should, in these times when the country was facing threats both foreign and domestic, stand firmly with the government.

3

I was living in a poky little room, writing notes on the historic events unfolding with unimaginable speed. My room was adjacent to a godown on the top floor of a building that had a printing press on the ground floor. I could sit or stretch out in the little space in the midst of papers and bundles strewn all over the place. The owner of the press had allowed me to live in the room rent-free in exchange for proofreading services. I scribbled notes about recent happenings and about old events that I recalled from my memory on the back of the papers left discarded in the room. Some events I wrote about in detail, taking my time. Writing was fun, but also painful. Recalling things from memory was difficult. But when a small detail surfaced, it opened a floodgate of memories. They did not come in an orderly manner, however, or in neat chronological arrangement. It was difficult to decide what was important, what needed to be written down, where to begin. After spending a few days stuck, I decided to go with the flow, embrace the confusion. Every now and then, I opened the window and looked at the world outside. There, too, it was confusion. No one said there should be order and chronology in writing. So, I began writing on whatever piece of paper I could find, whatever came to mind. Often, it was my only nourishment. Sometimes, when I felt tired, I would stop and look at what was on the other side of the paper I was writing on. Ah, what fun! Most were old notices, of the State Congress, the Communist Party, the old Thiruvithamkoor National Congress, of the Rajabhakta Sangham, of the Kerala Socialist Party. There were also those which had no names, like anonymous poison-pen letters, their purpose only to spread fear through society. I used up the space behind all of these papers. Writing about something that had happened, I would sometimes imagine what should have happened afterwards. I wrote this down, too, in great detail. Then wondered who decided whether something had truly happened or not. Bygone days are only stories. The one who wrote them down could also use their imagination. I began creating historical events and writing them on the back of historical notices. In a few days, this room would resemble Basheer's old room in Punkunnam. The air in that room was filled with stories and characters, whereas here it was full of historical events. I did think there was one difference. Basheer had gone mad because of his writing. In my case, it was the other way around.

One day, after trying to bring some order to my papers, I stepped out without bothering to have a bath. As I went down the stairs and across the small yard and into the lane, I began to feel that something momentous was going to happen that day. Even the main street was not too busy. Unease and anxiety pooled on the verandas of locked-up houses. Houses that belonged to those who had, for ages, ingratiated themselves to the government and lived comfortable lives. They had been distressed by the hungry hoard that had come rushing into the streets forbidden to them, causing those in power to run away. Yet they clung to the hope that their lives, their salaries, their comforts would remain unchanged. They, like everyone else, believed that nothing ever changes so fundamentally. Small, slow changes could be accommodated. Wasn't that, after all, the law of nature? They did not fear painless surgeries that did not wound, changes that were barely obvious. But the declarations about restructuring and the actions that followed terrified them. They grabbed their children and hid in holes. The wheel of power, that turned slowly to a constant, muted rhythm that they had sustained, had stopped. They did not have the courage to withstand the revolution and the uncertainty that followed. Who would want to be ejected from the straight line of their comfortable lives?

The usual police presence in the streets was also not to be seen. There seemed to be an atmosphere of divisiveness. The rare person I came across seemed not to possess even the simple joy of being able to breathe. Merchandise lay forlorn in the few shops that were open. The passing vehicles seemed to wish, like those forced to bundle up their belongings and flee, for darkness. I had left my room, and yet events – those that had happened, were to happen, and were imagined – flew around me. I walked slowly and finally reached the court complex.

Courts had remained functional, at least in name. Some clerks, who ignored everything around them and focused only on their duties, continued banging on typewriters. Regular plaintiffs or even the judges were nowhere to be seen. This was the place that would feel the impact of sudden, absolute changes. After all, justice changed as sides changed. I walked to the back of the building complex where a few living quarters were situated, a little apart from the main courthouse. On one of them was a signboard with the name and qualifications of a judge, and the inscription 'Inquiry Commission'. One of the houses for judges' accommodation had been turned into a makeshift office. The door was shut. I knocked a couple of times and stood aside, waiting. There was no sound from inside the house or from any of the nearby quarters. After a long wait, an old man cracked open the door and stuck only his head out. And before I could speak, he shut the door and went away. As I stood there not knowing what to do, he opened the door, stuck his head out again, and offered me a coin. He had assumed that I was a beggar.

'Ayyo, it's not that, sir,' I said. 'I've come to see Justice Anantharaman sir.'

He looked at me inquiringly.

'He's in charge of the new commission set up to look into the old case of the attempted assassination of the Maharaja? I saw a notice in the newspaper asking people who had information to come forward. That's what I'm here for.'

I glanced at the nameboard once again. The important degrees that Justice Anantharaman had amassed in London were written on it.

'I am he,' he said. 'Tell me what you have come to say.'

'Well, there's a lot to say, sir.'

He looked at me as though he didn't quite believe me.

'Truly, sir,' I said again.

'Come, then.'

He held the door open. I stepped into a small hall and sat on a bench. He sat on a cushioned chair and scrutinized me. My eyes were on the full-sized mirror hanging on the opposite wall. A barbaric figure with greying hair sat inside it. Body prematurely aged from lack of nourishment. Stick-thin limbs. Unruly beard. No wonder the judge had taken me to be a beggar. As though to justify himself, he caught my eye in the reflection. Our reflections, in turn, watched us.

I began to speak, and he, the retired judge, sat back disinterestedly in his chair and listened to me. I talked about Bhasi as though he was another man, and I was just someone who knew all about him. At no point did he display any interest. In fact, when I came to the parts that would have shocked any other listener, he opened his mouth and yawned. It disappointed me, made me want to somehow end my story and leave. Still, I persevered and described all the events in as much detail as I had intended. Every now and then, the judge's wife came out, stared at me and went back inside.

'Are you done?' he asked at last.

I remained quiet.

'What I don't understand is why all this old stuff needs to be dug up and examined now,' he said.

I knew his comment was directed at the current government. It surprised me that it was the person endowed with the responsibility who was saying it. Perhaps he had taken this job he had no interest in because it allowed him to continue earning some money even after retirement.

'You're a good storyteller,' he said, his voice even so that I couldn't tell if he was serious or making fun of me. 'You should write it down. It would make good reading, like the novel *Indulekha*.'

'This isn't a story, sir,' I said. 'If you were going to make fun of them, why advertise in the newspaper asking people to come forward and tell you what they know?'

'I should feel what you say is serious, shouldn't I? First of all, is this how you give evidence before an inquiry commission? You're supposed to make an appointment. And my steno has to be present. You don't just walk in on an afternoon, blurt some things out and go away. Like I said, you're better off writing about all this.'

'There's more, sir,' I said. 'An important event that happened in 1948. It is this Bhasi who supplied the gun for the deed.'

'Ha, ha, ha!' The man who had remained listless until then laughed heartily. 'And now you'll tell me he is responsible for shooting Kennedy too.'

Stumped, I sat there unable to speak.

'You tell a good story. Rational. And it is quite entertaining. But...'

He stopped and reached towards the radio on the table.

'Let's assume you're telling the truth,' he continued. 'But there's no use telling me any of this. You see, everything changed just a few minutes ago. I was listening to the news when I heard you knocking. The Inquiry Commission and everything else has ended.'

He switched on the radio and out came communist revolutionary songs broadcast from the Thiruvananthapuram station. These were interspersed with announcements urging the people to remain calm and unafraid, to obey the police. Puzzled, I looked at the judge, and he opened the door indicating that I should leave.

I left the court complex and got out into the streets. I realized that the judge was right. Ahead of me was the main road. As I watched, two army vehicles full of soldiers wielding guns went down it. Both vehicles also had people not in uniform, civilians holding aloft red flags. The road was more deserted than before. A man alone would attract attention. What if one of them felt like using the weapon in his hand? If a child got hold of a knife, does he not cut off the heads of a few plants? Not wanting to provoke anyone, I slipped into a side lane. Further ahead, it joined up with other small lanes. Why did I go to him? Was it to see if anyone would believe what I had been writing? Then again, why insist that it should be believable. Was everything that happened in a day really believable? Even the army vehicles that I saw just a minute ago seemed unreal. The lane and the backyards of the houses along it began to scare me as they had before. I was disturbed, my heart in the palm of my hand. I found a path that took me back to the main road, and walking hurriedly, wanting to get back to my room, I heard a commotion behind me. A large demonstration was coming up the road, celebrating the revolution. I wanted to run, but they had already seen me. I stood by the verge, ready to face whatever came my way. But when they got to me, they did not pay any attention. Immersed only in the slogans they were shouting with great enthusiasm, they passed me by, passed through me. I ran to my room, to my bits of papers.

The next morning, the BBC broadcast a special report on the communist revolution in Thiruvithamkoor. It described it as a serious setback to American interests in South Asia. The US had lost an important ally in the region. If they still wanted to get involved, as they had done in Vietnam, it would be without other allies that neighboured Thiruvithamkoor. The coup was a gift to the Soviet side in the Cold War. As in the South China Sea, there now was a communist base in the Indian Ocean.

In the BBC's analysis, it was the civil strife that emerged after the people's revolt toppled the royal government that paved the way for the communist revolution. The communists had wrenched power without much bloodshed. They had help from the police and the army that had been loyal to the royals. The interim government had popular support, but butting heads with India and the announcement of a complete overhaul of government departments had undone it. There was also speculation that the communists had the covert support of India. That country, partial as it was to the Soviets, did not favour a democratic government that was influenced by America in the region. It was mainly India that the BBC blamed for handling matters in an immature manner. The new, inexperienced Indian leadership was oscillating between the interests of the Soviets and those of Hindu religious fundamentalists. Members of the interim government in Thiruvithamkoor had earlier all been ardent supporters of India. It was in India that most of them spent their lives in hiding. But India had, during royal rule, silently allowed the large-scale Brahmin migration into Thiruvithamkoor, which had fuelled anti-India feelings in that country. With the end of royal rule, the country would have naturally joined the Indian Union. India's mistake was not waiting for that to happen and trying, instead, to occupy the country by military force. It was then forced to withdraw its army when it was stopped at the borders by ordinary, unarmed people. The report ended with the prediction that the formation of a communist nation at its southern end would prove to be detrimental to India's interests in the future.

The region had become similar to Korea and Vietnam. People of one language cleaved apart into two different countries.

4

10 March

The People's Republic of Thiruvithamkoor came into existence. 'The martyrdom of countless number of people has finally been honoured,' said P. Krishna Pillai, the general secretary of the Communist Party, addressing the Red Volunteer parade. The people of Thiruvithamkoor would now strive to build a socialist society. A new Marxist model would be put together to aid this. The Thiruvithamkoor Communist Party was part of the communist movement the world over. Its focus was on internationalism. It would stand with the socialist side in the battle against imperialism. All treaties entered into with America during the royal rule would now be invalid. The nation would now work towards building strong relationships based on mutual respect with its neighbours.

Almost all countries in the Soviet Bloc officially recognized the new People's Republic immediately. India made noises of protest, but they were fake and feeble.

15 March

America stopped all its economic and military aid to Thiruvithamkoor.

16 March

Poonthura and Alappuzha ports, developed with foreign capital and private investment, were nationalized. A large people's demonstration marched to the locked-up American embassy.

20 March

The Communist Party announced a fifty-member Revolutionary Council and a five-member Politburo. The members of the Politburo were P. Krishna Pillai, T.V. Thomas, M.N. Govindan Nair, K.V. Pathrose and K.R. Gauri. A surprising fact was that K.C. George, the hero of the Punnapra–Vayalar struggles, was not in either the Politburo or the Revolutionary Council. Foreign newspapers had reported that it was George who led the communist revolution in Thiruvithamkoor. A group led by him had captured the office of the prime minister and the old palace. And it was he who had first addressed the people through a radio broadcast. But no one had seen K.C. George since.

In its first message to the people, the Politburo said that the primary struggle now was against revisionism and Trotskyism. It was imperative now that we confronted and resisted these ideologies. Given that, for the last many years, the Party had to work closely with bourgeois democratic organizations like the State Congress and Aikyakeralam, people without sufficient ideological conviction had made themselves at home within it. The difficult job of identifying them had begun. The Politburo acknowledged that, towards the end of the royal rule and during the time of the interim government, beliefs and fantasies that had no bearing on objective reality had taken root among the populace. These beliefs and fantasies had no part in the people's uprising that followed. They were merely manifestations of a collective madness that had risen from a sense of utter helplessness. The world existed based on the laws of physics. People had to stop discussing and writing about things that were untrue. The actions of the man named Muhammad Basheer had contributed nothing at all to the struggle against royal rule. He was merely an ordinary worker of the State

Congress before independence. He was not a writer. There were stories circulating that were attributed to him, that contained absolutely no progressive ideas or social responsibility. It was the Politburo's position that these stories had nothing useful for a society moving rapidly towards socialism. The police had been tasked with finding out whether this man Basheer was still alive, and the origins of the stories attributed to him. The Party believed that art and literature had important roles to play in people's progress. However, what the country needed now was not fantasy, but a proletarian literature rooted in reality and aiding the formation of a socialist society.

This proclamation from the Party had a huge impact on writers. A long poem by K.N. Ramanatha Kuruppu – KNR – titled 'Dweepum Nakshatravum' (The Island and the Star) came out immediately. The crux of the poem was the message: 'Let go of fantasies and pursue the star of hope that is rising in the sky.' He had discarded the usual symbols he used in his poetry. His vocabulary had also changed. Words such as struggle, spearhead, star, horizon, labourer, fist and gold made repeated appearances. The last lines were written as though the poet himself was speaking. It was the dream of a golden dawn that he had dreamt of when he started writing, he said, and he was gratified to be still alive at a time when this dream was being fulfilled. The poem ended with the idea that society, not the individual, was the most important, and with the hope that there would be endless human advancement and success in the universe. A critique of the poem was soon published in the magazine *Comrade*, the mouthpiece of the Thiruvithamkoor Communist Party. It was written by a person identified only as 'S'. The writer called attention to the positive changes in KNR's poetry. He said that 'Dweepum Nakshatravum' was an example of a poet who had lived in a feudalist and capitalist society embracing socialist ideas following a working-class revolution. Still, there were errors in the poem that needed correction, the critic said. And so, all writing should be subjected to constant analysis by the working class.

Udayam magazine, edited by K.P. Sukumara Menon, had not been published since the revolution. The reason was that the cashew nut factory belonging to Hamsakkoya Thangal who funded the magazine had been taken over by the Youth Federation of the Communist Party. They turned it into their office. It was clear that Hamsakkoya Thangal would not be able to fund the magazine any more. KP decided to publish one last issue, funding it with his own money. On the very first page, he wrote, in his poetic language, an editorial that praised the revolution. The Soviet lands were the holy ground of writers, he wrote, and stated emphatically that the changing circumstances in Thiruvithamkoor would pave the way for a golden age of its literature. Writers on par with Mikhail Sholokhov and Vasily Grossman would emerge. English was losing its place as the global language. And yet, why were our children still studying this language of imperialism, he asked. The editorial entreated that the government look into teaching Russian in schools, at least as a secondary language. It was in this language that the best of world literature and the most recent scientific recoveries happened. The other offerings in this edition of *Udayam* included a short biography of Brezhnev, an overview of the revolutionary movement in Cambodia, a prose poem titled 'Bayonet', and a short story about a revolutionary young woman whose brother is a State Congress member and tries to thwart her. KP had also included a short note about the new novel he was going to write. It dealt with the members of an old, degenerating Nair family slowly learning about the benefits of collective farming and industrialization.

K.P. Sukumara Menon did not have to stop publishing *Udayam* with this edition that was thought to be its last. From the next edition, it began to be published as the mouthpiece of the Youth Federation, with a cover page in colour. Hamsakkoya Thangal's old cashew nut factory continued to be its office.

5

The printing press in the building where I lived was not doing much business, and after the revolution it shut down completely. The owner stopped coming to the building, but I continued living there. Like Basheer when he was at Seethi Buildings, I spent all day writing my notes. At night, I went out in the cover of darkness and skulked through the lanes. Listened to the sounds from the houses, wondering whether they were laments or laughter. Human beings like to talk to themselves once the lights are switched off. But now, for days, there had been barely any sign of life. Either they all fell into a deathlike sleep as soon as they hit the bed, or they were sitting up, awake, barely taking a breath. After a while, I reduced my nightly meanderings. Then stopped going out altogether. The fun was inside, and the joy and the fear. Not out there. Sitting inside, one could write following only the laws there. The world outside this room, be gone and die!

One day, there was a knock on the door. I sat quietly, hoping that whoever it was would go away. But when the knocking became insistent, I cracked the door open carefully, scared of the light. It was the owner of the building. He had a handkerchief wrapped around his face, covering his nose and mouth. He looked at me, surprised. And I at him. He looked nothing like his former self. His face and body had darkened as though he had walked a long way in the sun. He also seemed older.

'Don't get me wrong,' he said quickly. 'I was expecting to see you dead in here.'

He peeked inside. Pressed the handkerchief to his nose.

'What's this stench?' he asked. 'Neighbours have been complaining about it, saying it's coming from in here. They think there's something rotting in this room.'

'There's no stench,' I said confidently.

'Then what is it?' He took the cloth off his nose and inhaled. And pulled it back as though he couldn't take it.

'The stench is outside,' I said. 'Come in if you want to escape it.'

Unbelieving, he removed the cloth once again.

'Come in quick,' I said.

Still unsure, he took a tentative step inside and inhaled. Then slowly stepped fully into the room and looked around.

'Come, look, through there.'

I shut the door behind us and took him to the window. One pane was cracked open to reveal a thread-thin space. We looked out through it with great difficulty.

Sir C.P.'s trusted old acolyte DSP Vaidyanatha Iyer was speaking at a summit of the heads of all the secret agencies. Distrusting our eyes, we looked carefully again. He was dressed in the uniform of the Red Volunteers. At a glance, he looked like a fat Fidel Castro. Nothing had been heard of him since the last days of royal rule and all these days after the revolution. People said that he had been killed, or that he was in jail, or that he had left the country. But there he sat now, with a sterner expression on his face than usual, as though affirming that he had been around all this while, right here with all of us. The uniform and the cap with its star suited him perfectly. As though that was the only attire fit for him. As though he had always, ever, only worn those clothes.

'It was here that the communists had the notice printed, which declared that they'll kill this man who had shot and killed those poor souls in Alappuzha,' the press owner said. 'Look in the almirah, there's bound to be some copies left over.'

'Ey, I think you're imagining that,' I said. 'Don't you think that, of all the people sitting there, he looks the best in that uniform?'

Vaidyanatha Iyer talked about how all the agencies should work in a unified manner under the Civil Protection Group. The objective of the CPG was to protect the working-class people of Thiruvithamkoor from threats, both domestic and foreign. Working shoulder to shoulder with them, the CPG would also lead the other classes to rethinking their ideologies. He peppered his speech with friendly anecdotes and jokes. The officers sitting around laughed with him, secure in their own ideological certainty.

Struggles to confront Trotskyism, as called for by the Politburo, were under way all across the country. Arrangements had been put in place to re-educate those who suspected the influence of Trotskyism in their own thinking in correct Marxist-Leninism. It was overseen by the Youth Federation. Cultural organizations also played a part. They staged a play titled *Mudanthan* ('Cripple') wherever they could find an audience. The protagonist, a man with a limp, was named George. The moment people heard that name, they laughed gleefully and shouted, 'K.C. George, karinkaali...' The play dealt with the efforts of a few good people who tried to fix his limp. It was only halfway through the play that the audience understood that the 'limp' was a psychological issue, the effect of Trotskyism. But the cripple did not want to be cured. Taking it to be an honourable asset, he was made to utter rationalizations that sounded foolish to anyone listening. In the end, he disowned his own mother, and the comrades put a black cloth over his head and led him away into the darkness. The play ended there and the audience dispersed, calling out this slogan:

No, no, he is not our leader
This imperialist bootlicker

K.C. George, cripple crank
Be careful, watch your back

'Well, I should go,' the press owner said, inhaling a lungful of the good air inside the room in preparation for stepping outside.

'Don't. Best not to go outside,' I warned him. 'People are beating people up, flattening the whole world into chapatis. They think it is okay to break down hills to fill holes and turn human beings into cattle. They'll take your self-respect first, and then make you stand in a line for food.'

He went away, and I looked at the outside world once again. New types of harvest songs rose from the paddy fields in Kuttanad and Nanjinad. Workers appointed by the Party measured the paddy and loaded it into wagons. It seemed like this was the third or fourth harvest since the revolution. They rewrote production figures in order to prove the rightness of their philosophies. And they believed it themselves. They sang that the farmers here were like the Cossacks, and that the Pampa was the Don. A progressive writer was writing a novel titled *Pampa Shanthamaayozhukunnu* (Peaceful Flows the Pampa)...

6

On the day *Comrade* published new photos of the members of the Politburo and the Revolutionary Council, I was writing about the sound of knocking on doors of houses. At the time, there was nothing else happening. People did not pay attention to any other sounds around them. Rendered unimportant, those sounds wandered aimlessly around. During the day, woodpeckers frightened people. At night, if they fell asleep, they heard loud knocks in their dreams. Jerking awake, they felt this was the sound of their own hearts, beating out of rhythm, louder than knocks on doors.

Some photos had disappeared and others appeared in their place in the newspapers. Among the Politburo members, two photos had disappeared. In their place was a large one of DSP Vaidyanatha Iyer. But the newspapers said nothing about the names of those who had disappeared or the ones replacing them. It was as though they wanted to remind everyone that everything was as it had always been. I thought, just for fun, that the play *Mudanthan* might now be called *Mudanthanmaar*, in the plural. Two more characters suffering from Trotskyism might join K.C. George – T.V. Thomas and M.N. Govindan Nair, for instance. What would the knocks on their doors yesterday or the day before have sounded like? Would they have been bundled off to some collective farming fields in order to be educated on the fundamentals of life? Or would they have, like the Council members who had been removed, confessed all their faults?

10 December

The Month of Re-education had started. The Politburo had published a statement clarifying for the people what needed to be corrected. Primarily, it was the State Congress mentality that had rooted itself in the minds of a small section of the populace, including some communist leaders, since the time of the agitations for Utharavada Bharanam. The statement contained detailed descriptions of its symptoms. First, those affected were incapable of fully disowning Gandhi, who had only ever been an ideologist. Second, they were unable to tolerate that some people who had, in the past, aligned themselves with royal rule now embraced communist philosophy and worked alongside the proletariat. In evaluating the growth in power of the Party and people's organizations, they allowed themselves to be driven by mere personal animosities. Third, they mistook bourgeoise democracy for real democracy. Fourth, they did not confront the conflicts within the Party with a rational frame of mind, taking them, instead, to be attempts to undermine them. Fifth, they believed that there were better frameworks than class analysis to evaluate social order and hierarchies. During royal rule, there existed a feudal society, and the fight against some prominent castes was important in that context. They found it difficult to accept that this fight had now become redundant.

In the span of a month, the Youth Federation led a number of campaigns across the country. Evaluations of leaders and social activists took place in each area, the Party restructured right from the branch level. Several leaders publicly owned up to their shortcomings and voluntarily went away to re-education camps. Newspapers routinely published such confessions in their front pages. One of these that got a lot of attention was that of Gopalakkuruppu, a member of the Council from Chengannur.

He could now see, quite clearly, when exactly he had lost his ideological certainty, he said. It was when he had lived, a long time before independence, in Seethi Buildings in the old kingdom of Kochi. A place where revisionists congregated, where the odd, mysterious man named Basheer and K.C. George, who was later found out to be a Trotskyist, had ruled the roost. He had, he said, gone to that place taken in by some pamphlets Basheer had written. Basheer had also published *Ujjeevanam*, a rag that was full of articles singing the praises of Gandhi and Bhagat Singh. But he had come to his senses now, Gopalakkuruppu confessed, and could see that these writings were reactionary and cleverly choreographed. Basheer had also promoted sexual anarchy. The stories he told in those days were full of descriptions of women from the middle class. He had, in addition, also spread stories that invited conflict between communities in a way that was detrimental to working-class solidarity.

With Gopalakkuruppu's confession, the Month of Re-education was extended indefinitely. Every day, there were new confessions about the goings-on in Seethi Buildings. Who, in fact, was this Seethi? How did such an anti-communist place continue to exist in India so close to its border with Thiruvithamkoor and for so long? Was K.C. George the real brains behind it? Who had funded their activities? The Youth Federation conducted wide-ranging searches to find the old inhabitants of Seethi Buildings. Several, like Gopalakkuruppu, came forward, voluntarily confessing to their participation. A couple of months into the re-education, a member of the Council named Bhargavan from Kollam made a confession of great importance. He had been, even in those days, staunchly communist, he said, firmly Leninist in his thinking. He had realized that the Party leadership in those days was not heading in the right direction. And so, he had infiltrated Seethi Buildings under a false name and discovered, within a matter of days, that it was indeed an anti-communist centre and that several activities to destabilize the Party were taking place there. One night, he tagged along when Basheer and his friends went out on the pretext of taking a walk. They had walked only a little when he saw, to his utter shock, T.V. Thomas joining them. But he had been unsuccessful in finding out what they were planning that night because T.V. Thomas became suspicious of him. And the strong, healthy gusthikkaaran Thomas had kicked him to the ground, and he had to run away with his life. It was absolutely important to figure out who had been the instigator of the activities in Seethi Buildings, and the efforts of the Youth Federation in this regard were to be welcomed. Bhargavan reiterated his belief that revolution and the constant conflicts within the Party were necessary ongoing processes in strengthening the Party.

After almost a year of re-education, the Party endowed the Youth Federation with another responsibility. It congratulated the Federation for all it had done, the most important of which was bringing to light what had gone on in Seethi Buildings. Several people who had interacted, knowingly or unknowingly, with the anti-Party centre there had confessed, but real clarity came through the Party's own investigations. It was revealed that in those days the enemies had, under Basheer's leadership and with significant participation from K.C. George and T.V. Thomas, given shape to a blueprint, a framework for action for the post-revolution world. Copies of this had been circulated widely across the country. The Youth Federation would now put all its energy into finding it.

From the next day, large numbers of demonstrating students from schools across the country took to the streets wielding red flags. One such demonstration went past the lane outside my writing room. I watched them through my window. A band led the procession, immediately followed by the students who had earned medals for having killed the greatest number of rats, parakeets, and the rhinoceros beetle known as komban chelli, all of which had been, following the famine, declared class enemies of farmers. One child had brought along a thorappaneli, a bandicoot he had caught that morning, tied to a piece of string. Every now and then, keeping to the rhythm of the band, he spun it in the air and smashed it on the ground. And the other children cheered. Behind the medal-winners were the rest of the students and their teachers, all walking along in orderly formation. Some were holding aloft photos of Pavlik, the thirteen-year-old who had been martyred during the Soviet Union's attempt to attain food self-sufficiency. The boy had told the authorities about his parents who had, colluding with the country's enemies, secreted food supplies, and had been killed for it by his own relatives. Imitating Pavlik, some children had donned red, backward-slanting Soviet hats. When the demonstration reached the junction, they would perform the play based on Pavlik's life, but with a slightly modified storyline. In the play, Pavlik was recast as a boy from Thiruvithamkoor who discovered, to his utter disappointment, that his father had been an inhabitant of Seethi Buildings and was now stealing paddy from the farming collective where he worked.

It took a while for the demonstration to pass by my room. The sound of the band continued for some more time after it disappeared from sight. And when that too faded away, I heard the knock on the door. The hinges, which had remained still for a very long time, moved.

7

I was sorry for having held misconceptions about them. They, those three young men, behaved with such class. They were dressed in clean pairs of trousers with shirts tucked in. Had neatly shaved faces, and hair oiled, parted at the side and combed. They smelled good like they had used a mild perfume. Beautiful black shoes on feet, and gold-capped pens in pockets. When I opened the door, the regret they felt in inconveniencing me was evident on their faces. Respectfully, they stepped in.

'How is your writing going, sir?'

How did they know about my writing, I thought, puzzled.

'Do we need to be told when great things happen in the world, sir?' One of them said, exactly as Devasia had in Thiruvambady.

It occurred to me that they were, all three of them, of the same age.

'So, shall we head out, sir? No point in delaying further.'

I stood there, silently wondering where we were going.

'The government will make all arrangements, sir. Information, food, clothes, accommodation. All you have to do is write.'

Commiserating, without words, on my living conditions, they looked around the room. The bed of old sacks and bits of cloth on the floor, the cobwebs, the dead moths, centipedes, the roof tiles leaking rain and sunlight, the rags on my body. My starving, sunken stomach and dry eyes.

With great care, they sat me in the back seat of the car, with two of them sitting on either side and the third driving. A long time had passed since I had seen the outside world other than through the window of my room. The capital city looked resplendent, clean and tidy as never before. Good roads, gardens, multistorey buildings, statues of Lenin and Stalin, large martyr memorials. Some places had changed beyond recognition. People walked about as though on a stage, wide smiles on their faces. Children cavorted. Here and there were posters with the photo of a curly-haired European and words that welcomed him.

'Comrade Nicolae Ceauşescu,' said the man driving the car, watching me through the rear-view mirror.

The president of Romania. He was the state's special guest for this year's Revolution Day celebrations.

The sights on both sides of the road were blocked by huge walls. When the vehicle slowed down a little, I thought I heard something that sounded like wails from beyond those walls.

'People cheering,' said the young man sitting to my left.

They seemed to be excited to show me the sights.

Poojappura. The name had been changed to Gorky Square. But when we entered the research centre for writers, beyond the long lane and the watchtower, I felt that the inside looked the same. The same yard and blocks of rooms with iron bars on doors. As I was led away, I turned and looked at the block where Bhasi had lived with C. Keshavan, P.T. Chacko, P.T. Punnoose and Basheer. It was bathed in the afternoon sunlight. In the old days, when a new inmate was brought in, there would be cheers and slogans. But now, there was only the sound of our footsteps. I glanced at the sky. That space was still the same. When one enters this place, it is that space above that one feels like looking at.

We did not have to wait even a minute in front of the director's office. The young men who brought me went away, and a man dressed in a daffadar's uniform opened the door for me. The inside looked to me like the office of a librarian. All along the four walls were ceiling-high, glass-fronted almirahs that looked impossible to open, stuffed with books. They scared those who entered with their big names and forbidding covers. At a table along one wall, that held a telephone, a few decorative items, files and a pen stand, sat a man in the uniform of the Red Volunteers. When he saw me, as though to make room, he set the files to one side. Got up slowly, took the cap off his head and welcomed me.

'Come in, sit,' he said, pointing at the chair in front of the table.

I was surprised. It was the old jail superintendent Subrahmanya Pillah. The same man whose death I had written about in my notes – that a crowd had pulled him out of his house near Virakupura, along with his twin wives, and had beaten him to death. There was a smile on his face. But it showed no sign of familiarity, of recognition. The world had already forgotten me. I had finished my wandering days without even a shadow to keep me company. Imagine a man who had lived an unremarkable life a hundred years after his death. That was me now. He would not remember me. I was a new man now. I felt that the man in front of me was also a new man. There is no sense in thinking that people carry memories.

Producing a bottle of foreign-made liquor from under the table, he poured two glasses and slid one over to me.

'Drink,' he said. 'Don't worry about the time. This helps with having an interesting conversation.' He took a sip from his glass. 'So, how goes the writing?'

'Good. Almost finished, I think.'

'Ey, don't say that.' Pillah said this as though he wanted nothing but the best for me. 'Does writing ever finish? Especially history writing? It goes on and on, doesn't it?'

'I guess,' I agreed. 'Still, at some point one has to stop, no? When one has reached as far as one can go...'

'Ha, ha, yes. Well, who am I to argue with people such as yourself?'

He then said that sometimes he wished he too could write something. 'I've read somewhere that fishing is the best job there is. I'd say writing is like that. Doesn't require us to work under anyone. We can do it whenever the mood takes us. Night or day. And every moment in front of us is unpredictable.'

Pillah looked enviously at me.

'Look at my job, for instance,' he continued. 'Nothing remarkable about it. The only good thing is that I'm surrounded by people like you.'

Listing the difficulties he faced in his job, he poured us another drink. With his glass in his hand, he sat back and pulled out a book from the drawer of his table. His face flushed red as he held it.

'Look at this,' he said, holding it out to me. 'Just see what vulgarity and nonsense it contains.'

'What is it?' I asked without accepting it.

'Have a look,' he insisted.

I took it from him. An ordinary book of an average size. The words 'History of Thiruvithamkoor' were written on the cover, but the author's name was absent. I wondered if that was because it was a textbook for college students. Pillah denied it.

'Sorry, I didn't know such a book existed,' I said. 'I'm not a widely read person. It's only after I started writing that I began reading a little.'

'This is not a book though, is it?' Pillah was angry.

I opened the book halfway through and read a little. As he said, it was full of lies. But it was also interesting. It did not make any mention of our country gaining independence. Instead, it said that on 15 August 1947, it became part of India. It mentioned that a Sankaran Namboothiripad and an Achuthanandan, both dead men, were its chief ministers. There was a short mention of Akkamma Cherian, that after leaving the Congress, she stood for elections to the Indian parliament in 1953 and lost. Rosamma

Cherian was said to have married P.T. Punnoose, become Rosamma Punnoose, and, later, a member of the legislative assembly. N. Sreekantan Nair was said to have had an ordinary death. Most of the book was concerned with descriptions of the governments that came and went. The writer had followed the edict that verisimilitude should be established by giving extensive details about unbelievable things. And because of it, it succeeded in persuading the reader that these things had happened.

'Ha, ha, not bad at all,' I said. 'The writer has a good imagination. Even says here that K.R. Gauri and T.V. Thomas got married. I guess one could read it as a novel.'

'A novel?' The director shook with anger. His response was as though I had written the book myself. 'Call all this obscenity a novel?'

It was written with the express purpose of shaming the Party and the country, he said. It attributed the death of our eminent leader to a snakebite. Who gave him, the writer, the right to kill those who were still alive and bring back to life those who were dead? Why else, if not to ridicule, would it say that Politburo member Comrade K.V. Pathrose was expelled from the Party and had to resort to selling rope to make a living? It even said that the Communist Party took part in the elections of the bourgeois democracy!

'There's more that cannot even bear mentioning. Have a read of page thirty-two.'

He had marked several passages with a pen. The title on the page was 'The Attempted Assassination of Sir C.P.' It was only a short description. Varghese's name was not even mentioned. Instead, it was K.C.S. Mani who was said to have done it. And it was Sir C.P. Ramaswami Iyer he attacked, not the Maharaja. Sir C.P. was said to have left the country within a few days. And my country joined the kingdom of Kochi to become Thirukochi, and then with Malabar to form Kerala, which became part of India. The history that followed seemed peaceful enough. Oh God, this person, this writer, had written a history in which I had played no part. A book that was entirely the opposite of the book I was writing. Desperately, I tried not to show my perplexity on my face. Pillah told me that there was someone who was distributing copies of this book.

'Doesn't matter who wrote it, I'll get him,' he said, looking deep into my eyes.

I paid attention to the lines in the book. To the words, the repetitions, to the structure of sentences. Even after all this time, I could recognize the language of the Raktarekha letters.

'Why are your hands shaking?'

'Ey, nothing,' I said. 'Just a hereditary affliction.' Trying to smile, I handed the book back.

'Well, you are a history writer,' Pillah said. 'That's why I brought this up. There should be some honesty in writing, no? Not spew nonsense like this…'

'Well, some changes are bound to creep in, aren't they, according to the writer's thinking?'

'What changes? What thinking? Those can be cured with a sound beating. There is only one truth.'

Picking up his glass, he thought for a moment, then said, 'For instance, it is true that Thiruvithamkoor is a socialist society, isn't it?'

'Yes,' I agreed.

'It is true that Basheer, K.C. George, T.V. Thomas, and so on conspired against the revolution, isn't it?'

'Yes.'

'It is true that Thiruvithamkoor is, under the leadership of the honourable general secretary and Vaidyanatha Iyer, in constant battle against imperialism, isn't it?'

At that moment, a scream was heard. A tearing cry of unbearable pain. I looked at him, shocked.

'No need to worry,' he said. 'This place is full of writers. Someone must be shouting with joy over some new idea or metaphor.'

Pillah pointed at the liquor bottle, asking me whether I wanted some more.

'No,' I said.

'Right, then, you can start your work. No more delays. Everything has been arranged.'

'Sure. Right away.'

He got up to see me off.

'Yours is a job of great responsibility,' he said, placing his hand on my shoulder as we walked to the door. 'A writer is the engineer of the human soul.'

8

The place was still a complex of buildings that housed people. The huge old walls still separated different groups from one another. Some walls seemed as though they had become higher. A person arriving newly to this place would not know that there were others here. Their world was confined within the walls of their building. They would know that there was something beyond, but not that it went on and on, spreading over a large area.

I was in the same old place, the building that used to be known as tenth block or the solitary ward for political prisoners. Nothing much had changed except for a couple of applications of whitewash over the period. The guard who accompanied me had a pleasant face. He had my bedding, a rolled-up mat, a pillow and a sheet under his arm. And a plate and a glass in his hand. Amazingly, the room I was taken to was the same one I had shared with Basheer all those years ago. It had bars at the front and no windows. At the very top of the high back wall was a small opening for ventilation. It was evening, almost sunset. The guard apologized to me before locking the door from the outside. As it was late, there would be no supper tonight, he told me, and wishing me a peaceful, worry-free start to my work, he went away.

The night was quiet. Spreading my mat across the room and pulling the sheet up to my neck, I lay down staring into it. There was a mild chill in the air. Had Pillah recognized me? Why would he allot this specific room to me otherwise? The chances were minimal. He would not remember me. I was a different person now. My looks, gait, voice, all changed. As for age, who knows how many years have passed. He, Pillah, too was a different person. Perhaps he was not even the same person, the old jail superintendent Subrahmanya

Pillah. The real Pillah might have been killed, as I had written in my notes, many years ago. As I lay there thinking such thoughts, the night became colder, the chill crept under my sheet. I might die soon. I had such a dream in my sleep.

It is the next morning. Two people drop my dead and stiff body into a hole. They leave without filling it. If only I had someone to call mine, I cry, a son perhaps. But who would I have had that son with? Vanaja from *Diary of a Lover*? Elikkutty in Thiruvambady? I imagine that I had created a son with Elikkutty. A son I would never meet. I cry thinking of him. Of everything that I have written, of the hope that someone will read it some day.

Then I woke up, and it was still dark outside. I could hear my own sobs as though I had cried for real. In the visibility that comes when eyes adjust to the dark, I could see the blackness of the other rooms near and far. Who was now in the room C. Keshavan had occupied? In the room P.T. Chacko and P.T. Punnoose had shared?

As it had been in the old days, during the day I was allowed to walk around in the compound inside the walls. There were a few others standing in the shade of the buildings and the trees. None of them looked familiar. Perhaps because I never had any interactions with people like these. It took me a whole week to strike up a conversation with one of them. They, each and every one of them, showed a reluctance towards everything. Stepped out of their cells only to withdraw into them soon after. Some gave the impression that they would not leave this place even if they were let go. They behaved as though they had forgotten the existence of a world outside. Their faces shone with expectation only three times a day when it was time for food. Then, for a while, their gazes would be fixed on the doors of their rooms. Those were also the times when they said anything at all to one another. And they usually only spoke about food, what they were given yesterday or what they would receive today. Or about the peculiarities of the people who took turns to bring them their food, who had become familiar. A bunch of them also seemed to be engaged in some kind of betting game about who would bring their food on the day and what it might be. Like pet cats, they purred around the servers and the serving dishes, brushing against them. Until the servers shooed them lovingly away, saying, 'Ha, move aside, this is for you only.' For a while then, the inside of these walls would fill with the sound of plates and pots and fond murmurings.

It was while sitting together on the veranda, eating, that I spoke to the young-looking man who was a poet. I had, several times before that, tried to strike up a conversation with him. Broached various subjects like literature, football, women. He did not pay attention to any of it except to grunt half-heartedly on a few occasions. It was the same with all of them.

'How is the mambazha pulisseri?' I asked him that day, biding my time until almost the end of the meal.

'Excellent,' he said.

'I thought so too.'

'The mangoes are good. And the taste of the curry, mildly sour and sweet at the same time, is wonderful.'

'Yes, yes. These are also good as pacchadi, cooked with a little jaggery.'

'To be fair, I like this theeyal better. The coconut has been roasted just right. And they have added plenty of coconut oil.'

'Who cooks all this, I wonder.'

'Don't know. I'd like to meet them though.'

'Yes. Excellent they are, like Nalan, the cooking maestro from the puranas, himself.'

For the next few days, we talked like this over our meals and before our afternoon naps. As we became close, we began spending nap times in each other's rooms. One day, he told me that his name was Sukumaran and that he was a poet. His home was near

Ettumanoor. He was in the army for a while, and then worked as a schoolteacher. He had several poems published in K.P. Sukumaran Nair's *Udayam* magazine and in Malayalam magazines published in India. He then began to say something and stopped himself.

'What is it? Tell me,' I said.

'Ey, nothing important,' he said. 'You'll know what it is without me having to tell you.'

Sukumaran told me how, at first, he had not realized that his writing was rife with old ideas and aesthetic imagination and reactionary values.

'It's not your fault or mine as writers,' I said. 'It is social norms that shape our writing. You can't be blamed for that.'

'No, it is our fault. We are at fault if we don't change even after society has changed.'

The first to understand the anti-working-class sentiments and feudal values in his poems were his wife and daughter, he said. Using the love poems he had written to her before their marriage, his wife had tried to make him understand this. And his daughter told him that his new poems caused her embarrassment among her colleagues in the Youth Federation.

'But I was still unable to understand it at the time,' he said.

Finally, his wife and daughter alerted the authorities, which led to his arrival here. He was happy now, he said, to have the opportunity to correct the mistakes in his old poems and to try and write new ones. Even the director had told him, after having read them, that he was making good progress.

'So attentive he is about our welfare,' he said, turning over to face me.

I looked outside. It had begun to drizzle. Expecting a chill, I pulled my sheet over my head.

'I think we will have hot kanji for the evening meal,' Sukumaran said.

9

The director visited the tenth block once or twice a month. Just to ensure everyone's welfare. Every now and then, on these visits, he also came into my room. Sometimes, he would flick through what I had written. Leave without saying anything, or give me a quick pat on my shoulder. Once, I saw him secretly comparing what I had written with what was in the book, *The History of Thiruvithamkoor*, that he had shown me at our first meeting. My heart began to race. But he let out a long sigh and left the room with a small smile on his face.

The last time he visited, he expressed great joy. I had been writing about the protests that had taken place in Alappuzha in 1946. I wrote that the argument that it was under DSP Vaidyanatha Iyer's express command that hundreds of people were shot dead and several more subjected to custodial torture was unbelievable. And that it was a narrative created by the paid scribes of the State Congress and of India. Iyer was then, and had been ever since, a frontline soldier on the proletarian side. In fact, it was he who first recognized that Sir C.P.'s American model of governance was a creation of imperialism. The dictator of the Alappuzha revolt, K.V. Pathrose, had, in fact, acted according to directions from the DSP.

'This is most excellent,' the director said. As he continued reading, he gave me a left-handed hug.

A revolution should have taken place in Thiruvithamkoor at that time, I wrote. The revolt was the beginning, but it was scuppered from the inside by K.C. George, T.V. Thomas and their ilk. State Congress leaders such as C. Keshavan, Akkamma

Cherian and Kumbalath Shanku Pillai banded with the army and drowned it in a river of blood.

'Adi sakkey!' The director slapped his thigh and ululated.

He had great hopes for my writing, he said as he left. And that my language was also showing improvement.

After our midday meal, I walked around the compound within the walls with Sukumaran. I had begun to feel that this space was as wide as the earth itself. Like ants exploring the universe, we crawled in that space. Others like us were napping in their rooms and on the verandas. Some, with grinning faces, followed the servers to the doors as they went away with the dishes. And came back after seeing them off with the remains of the grins still on their faces. There were also some who, having recognized the reactionary nature of their writings, had chosen the path of self-harm to come out of it and find new ideas and words. One such person had tethered himself to a tree and remained there in the sun and in the rain. As days went by, the halo around his head and the shine in his eyes strengthened. Some others wrote constantly, as though it were a penance, only to sorrowfully tear it all up after reading it over and start again.

Sukumaran was also troubled. The last two or three times, the director had read his writing and gone away without commenting.

'Don't worry,' I said, trying to console him. 'Forget everything you have written so far and start again. It will be all right.'

'Doesn't matter what I try, I can only seem to summon the old words,' he said.

He told me that his wife had underlined some lines in his last letter home and sent it back. Wasn't he ashamed to write such things, she had asked.

'I'm scared,' he said.

'Ha, ha. Why?' I asked. 'Is there any place as safe as this?'

His worry was that, if his writing did not improve, he would be moved to the blocks beyond the walls.

'That might not be so bad either. Perhaps you might receive better training there.'

And to prove that he had my support, I put my arm around his shoulder.

Our walk had taken us close to a building that stood at the back of our block. Stuck between the block and the wall beyond, barely any light fell there. The ground was damp and strewn with decaying leaves that had floated in with the rainwater. Even after having been here all this long, this was the first time I was coming across it. We stopped talking and went forward with no particular intention. We were both in deep, separate thoughts. The building had rooms locked and unlocked, the floors dusty and the walls riddled with mould as though it had lain there forgotten for quite a while. As we neared, I saw a rat running away noisily along the veranda. It had come out, drenched, from one of the rooms. Sukumaran did not pay attention to it. I saw that the room was locked from the outside with a big lock. It must have been an empty room like all the rest of them. It was unusual to lock a room from the outside during the day if it were occupied. But the darkness inside made it seem like a cave where someone could hide. Were there two eyes glittering in the darkness? Was that a suppressed grunt that I heard?

'No, don't go there,' Sukumaran warned as I began to climb on to the veranda.

The bars and the lock itself were rust-ridden as though no one had touched them for a long time. I stood well away from the bars and looked inside. Inside, a human shape of substantial size moved. I could not tell if it was old or middle-aged. A dirty cloth around the waist. Skin discoloured from not having washed. He stood leaning against the far wall. He must surely have seen me.

A horrible stench emanated from the toilet inside, perhaps not cleaned properly for a very long time. I stepped back.

'Who is he? Seems familiar,' I said as we walked quickly away from there.

'He was there when I came here first,' Sukumaran said. 'Maybe he refuses to correct his writing or write in the new way. Or maybe he doesn't know how.'

'What did he write? Poems?'

'Stories and novels, mostly. I've read some. They're good. Most of it in the social realism mode. Thinking about it now, though, it had some serious reactionary stuff.'

He was considered, in the beginning at least, to have been on the side of the revolution, Sukumaran told me. But the Youth Federation had, through its people's reading, criticized his books and brought him here for re-education.

'Come to think of it...' Sukumaran stopped walking for a moment. 'How is Thakazhi Sivasankara Pillai ever going to rewrite such books as *Scavenger's Son, Two Measures* and *The Reward for Sacrifice*?'

We were at the back of that building, at one end of the block. I leaned against the stone wall. It felt so strong. The barbed wire on top had been placed in such a way that it hung down on both sides. Standing here and looking up, it felt that the sky had been fenced in. I pressed my cheek to the wall. It felt cold. And it smelled of age. I felt that I was leaning against the shoulder of a trusted friend. What if this wall was built not to stop anyone but to support them? Suddenly, I heard a scream from the other side. Louder, scarier than the one I had heard when I was in the director's room. A person could cry out like this only if they were being skinned alive.

'Ayyo! What is that noise?' Sukumaran asked, terrified.

'I didn't hear anything,' I said. 'You must have imagined it.'

The pitiful cry was repeated several times. And each time, I stood there as though it had not reached my ears.

All that night, I sat up on my mat. From my position, I could see the wall that separated our block from the seventh block. The old prison for women beyond the wall. Below the wall was the space where Basheer had nurtured his garden. There was nothing there now. I had looked to see whether even a stub of the old gandharajan plants remained. I remembered that Akkamma and Rosamma were at the women's prison. How they used to sing loudly the Bengali song 'Jana Gana Mana' every evening. I heard again the slogans that rose from this side of the wall then, and the curses that a woman called out from the other side. Where would they be now, Akkamma Cherian and all the others? They used to make mango chammanthi, pack it in coconut shells and lob them over the wall to this side. The lovers who would receive them – V.V. Varkey and P.T. Punnoose – where might they be now? All that remained was the story of their love that straddled the wall that Basheer had told me. The details of the story and the characters in it had been made out of his imagination. A story that was a huge lie made out of a little bit of truth. Sitting here now, it was his story that had come true. There was no Akkamma or Varkey, no love nor mango chammanthi.

It was that time when sleep remained elusive and the night felt never-ending. A small bird came flying in, hovered above the ground at a height of a couple of men for a few moments, and flew away. It came back and did this again. I watched it and slept with my eyes open, or slipped deep inside myself. I was woken from it by a familiar sound from a long time ago. The horse carriage of the hangman, arriving at the same time as it had then, in the same rhythm as it had then. It would have woken up the whole area within the humongous wall that contained inside it other walls around building complexes. But no lights came on. No one made a noise. After a long time, I heard the sound of the plank dropping, and I thought of Varghese. Soon, the horse carriage went away, this time with the soul of the life it had taken tied to its back. It went away at a pace slower than when it had arrived.

10

I had always been able to foretell the nights when the hangman's horse carriage would arrive. Those were the nights when I was unable to sleep. On the day after such a night, I was walking around the yard. The ground was littered with wingless eeyal, the flying termites that foretold rain. Crows hopped around, feeding on them. On the mornings after the horse carriage went back, the faces around here showed signs of relief and happiness. It was so today as well.

Sukumaran and a few others stood sunning themselves by the wall between us and the seventh block. They were exactly in the spot where Basheer's garden, which existed no more, had been. Slowly, I walked up to them. As expected, they were somewhat jubilant. We exchanged pleasantries. Given how many of us were inside, we did not have to think about the outside world much. If we were asked to leave, we would. But with reluctance, thinking about our rooms, the tasty food, the people we knew, and so on. I stood in the erstwhile garden and looked to the other end. A mango tree still stood with its branches leaning over.

'There's a real nice smell here,' Sukumaran said.

'Yes, I was thinking that myself,' said a young man who stood beside him. He was a playwright, a somewhat newish arrival.

'It's from the other side,' I said. 'They house beautiful women over there, don't they.'

I laughed as though I had made a joke. But they did not laugh with me. Instead, they stared at me. One of them tried to change the subject, talking about something entirely unrelated. They disbanded pretty quickly and went away. Sukumaran put his arm around me and pulled me to a corner.

'Other than me, you are the most senior here, yes?' he asked, prefacing the advice that was to come. 'How long has it been since you came here?'

I realized he was right. Everyone who had been there when I came, except him, had gone away elsewhere. I would also be the most senior in age.

'Don't you still know what to say and what not to say?'

'But what did I say that is so wrong?' I asked.

'Don't you know who is on the other side of that wall?'

'Women, right?'

'Women?' Sukumaran gave me a pitying look. 'Who told you this nonsense?'

'So, who is there then?'

In a low voice filled with amazement at the extent of my ignorance, Sukumaran said, 'You old fool. It is Basheer over there.'

'Basheer? Which Basheer?'

'How many Basheers do you know?'

'Have you seen him?'

'No.'

'Then? Who told you this? Someone who knows for sure?'

'No.'

Still, it turned out that everyone believed this, that it was Basheer who was on the other side of the wall. The surprising thing was that it was only I who did not know this. That block was the most secure of them all. It had the highest walls with the most barbed wire on top of them. Electrified too, perhaps.

'Is he alone there?'

'Must be.'

'Why have they put him there alone?'

'What else would they do with such a man?'

He must have been put there long before, Sukumaran said. Even before the revolution, perhaps even before independence. When I said that was impossible, he looked at me like the faithful look at a rationalist. What else was there to do with a man who had done so much harm, he asked again.

'Well, one of the things you say must surely be wrong,' I said. 'If, as you say, he has been in there all this time, how will he have done all the harm he's said to have done? Besides, I have seen him, like, see, like this.'

Looking fearfully around him, Sukumaran too left me and walked quickly away. For the next two days, he avoided me. On the third day, as I lay in my room after the midday meal, he came and lay down next to me.

'Do you need to see a doctor?' he asked me. 'I've watched you sitting up all night with no sleep.'

He fell silent for a while, and then continued, 'I'm not sure if you know, but you've been talking to yourself. People are laughing at you.'

I did not respond.

'What you said – that you've met him. Is that true?' he asked.

'Yes,' I said. 'We've slept like this, side by side. Wrestled with one another.'

'Something else, you are. With a man like that ... You've told me this. Now make sure you don't say this to anyone else.'

Then I told them the story Basheer had told me, 'Viddhikalude Swargam' – Fools' Paradise. Every now and then, he raised his head and looked around to see if someone else was listening to it.

'Well, it does feel a bit sad,' he said with a yawn when I finished. 'But it is a story that disrespects the working class and their poverty. And in the end, it tries to establish him as some great, kind man.'

Ignoring him, I began telling the story 'Mother and Son'.

It begins like this: 'With a sorrowful heart and exhausted body, I sat under a tree.' The experience of a man who had spent the night among the most downtrodden of human beings.

By the time I finished the first sentence, Sukumaran was asleep. Careful not to make a sound, I got up. Stepped outside. Tired from the searing heat, everyone else had fallen asleep too. The servers had left with the empty dishes from our meal. No wind, no birds. No movement in the trees. That the earth rotated at speed was a mere story that someone had made up. Look, here everything was motionless. I walked towards the entrance to our block. I felt that the wall there was the outer wall to the entire building complex. For a long time, I stood there, pressing my ear to it, listening as I had never listened before. Could I hear what was happening outside, the conversations there? They must be coming in, filtering in slowly through the granite. I pressed myself closer to the wall. Yes, I could hear them, like the faint broadcast from a faraway radio station. I had to concentrate. Only then would I hear the sounds.

I could hear the sounds of human beings, unable to feed themselves, clearing forests and cultivating the land. The sounds of collective farming fields catching fire in the summer sun. The Youth Federation, even after all these years, still searching for the secret blueprint Basheer and his friends had prepared. The screams of those they were interrogating. Gunshots. The changing photographs of Politburo members. There were also the sounds of people being herded to the work centres and industries created by the government. Sounds of scientists breaking granite, intellectuals butchering animals, doctors hoeing fields, dancers operating machines. The breathing of those standing in queues for rations. But the sound of people talking was low. Even under their sheets, they spoke quietly. The lizards and moths on the walls, and the rats in the attic paid attention to what they said.

Even their own children would take what they say and deliver it elsewhere.

Vaidyanatha Iyer said that there was new information about Seethi Buildings. It was still functioning. Basheer, K.C. George and T.V. Thomas were still at its helm. They had been joined by a few new people. And they had access to the limitless funds flowing in from America. Iyer said that the Party's investigations had revealed a shocking truth. There was another who played a significant role in preparing the blueprint aimed at defeating the revolution. He had been identified. 'We need to march to the highest centre of power right now,' he said, 'because the person sitting there is responsible for betraying the Party.'

Finally, I also heard a poem, titled 'Cement', being read, written by a progressive writer. It praised the industrial revolution that was taking place through the work centres. It described the sweat drops of the hard-working labourers flowing across their bodies like the sacred thread.

That evening, the poet KNR was brought to our block. He was advanced in age. His eyes were puffed up and sticky, and his feet swollen. He looked as though he would fall asleep in the middle of a sentence. It was just before the rooms were locked for the night, so I had the opportunity to spend a few minutes with him. As his legs were too frail to carry him, he had been made to sit on a wooden chair. I went to him, bent down, and tried to get his attention. He was looking around, wondering where he was and why he had been brought there. The white film of cataract in his eyes made it seem that he could see nothing. I told him that, despite not being an avid reader, I had read his poems including 'The Island and the Stars', but there was no change in the expression on his face. He had, in the intervening period, corrected and rewritten his old poems several times as suited the new times. Even the new ones he had corrected, realizing the inherent class character of his words. Had written an essay criticizing his own poems and sent it to *Comrade*. Still dissatisfied, KNR had finally disowned everything he had ever written. As though he did not know what more he could do, and taking me to be someone in a position of power, he pressed his palms together and bowed to me. Said something in an unclear voice that sounded like a plea.

KNR passed away two days later. Much later, a couple of men arrived and took his body away, showing no signs of respect. I went to the wall and pressed my ear to it again. I did not hear a gun salute or any other sounds marking his funeral.

II

When the morning brightened after yet another night, Sukumaran was nowhere to be seen. Had he been transferred to another block as he had worried, or had he left for the outside world? I walked to the building at the back, the one I had gone to with him the other day. Everything looked the same there. The room locked from the outside remained the same. But it was empty. I walked to the back of that building and stood near the rear wall. The sound, the cry I had heard that day had come from beyond that wall. Would Sukumaran have been moved there? I cocked my ears, but there was nothing to hear. Were there no buildings beyond the wall after all? Was it only some overgrown plot or wasteland? What if I had only imagined that there were other blocks beyond the four walls of our own? Was our block the only reality?

The next day, too, I came to the spot. Now, in the intervals between silences, I could hear something. Something like the chopping of firewood or digging. Whatever it was, it was not being done with much energy or enthusiasm.

I looked around me and then called out twice, 'Oi ... Oi...'

There was no reply.

'Oi ... Is that you, Sukumaran?' I tried again.

The sound stopped.

'Is that Sukumaran over there?'

'No,' said a male voice, not very deep. 'Who are you?'

'I'm one of those who live here. And you?'

'Whose name were you calling out?'

'My friend. Sukumaran. He's been missing for two days now. I called out to see if he's there by any chance.'

'Right. I don't know him.'

'Who are you, you didn't say.'

'Like you, I live here, on this side. Name's Zacharia.'

'Where are you from?'

'Near Pala.'

'I had an old friend there. A Devasia. He migrated to Malabar.'

'O.'

'Anyway. So, what do you do?'

'I was under the impression that I was a story writer. But here they've given me the job of digging holes.'

'Holes? What holes?'

'That I also don't know. I am to dig a hole at one end of this block and carry the mud to the other end. Tomorrow, I have to carry the mud back and fill the hole. Day after tomorrow, I must dig in another place. It goes on like this.'

'Excellent. Just the job for story writers.'

'Ha, ha, yes. Like making jokes, do you? So, what do you do?'

'I'm not a writer like you. But I'm trying to write history.'

'That's good. That means you can write whatever you like.'

We fell silent for a while. I heard him dig once or twice.

'Since you're writing history, let me ask you,' he said, 'do you know anything about what's happening outside?'

I told him about pressing my ear to the wall and capturing the news from the outside world.

'That sounds good,' he said. 'I don't have that ability. So, what did you hear?'

I told him all the information I had. When I finished, I suspected he was laughing.

'What?' I asked.

'No, nothing.'

He went back to his digging.

That same evening, the director came rushing into my room, worried. He looked different from his usual self. Unkempt hair, crumpled uniform, shoes covered in mud. I was crouched on my mat, writing furiously.

'Stop,' he said. 'Stop.'

He wanted only me to hear what he said, but in his excitement his voice had risen.

'Throw away everything you've written so far. And start again from the beginning.'

I smiled at the director.

'What are you smiling at, you dog? Better get on with it.'

It was the first time he was speaking badly to me like this. Never mind, I thought, something must be really worrying him. Still smiling, I held out what I was writing to him. It was a biographical note about the new general secretary, Vaidyanatha Iyer.

Vaidyanatha Iyer's parents were confirmed socialists. He was born in an agraharam, the residential quarters of Brahmins, where all the houses were of equal proportions. By the time he was four, the social consciousness that he had imbibed from his surroundings had settled deep within him. Studying the Vedas at a young age strengthened his intellect. He realized that, unlike everyone else, his destiny lay not in social service but in secret service. Even as a schoolboy, he became active in the underground activities of the students' organization. Much later, when the communists had their first meeting near some rocks in the village of Pinarayi in Kannur in India, he was secretly present in the vicinity.

When Vaidyanatha Iyer was fourteen years old, his family moved to Thiruvithamkoor. It was a feudal society, but the royal family ran dining rooms in the service of Brahmins across the country. A laudatory activity in the socialist model. After completing his education, he decided to continue his secret service by joining the police, the torture device of the government. It was the time when the organization called the State Congress, colluding with bourgeois leaders including Gandhi of India and supported by British and American imperialist forces, was strengthening its activities in Thiruvithamkoor. He recognized that the primary duty of a communist was to confront them. He was successful in his activities to stop their growth. Around this time, Vaidyanatha Iyer, along with a handful of communist leaders, secretly boarded a Soviet submarine that had arrived at Thiruvithamkoor's shores and went to Moscow for a meeting with Comrade Stalin. Locking themselves away in a room, the two great leaders discussed the future of Thiruvithamkoor and the international communist movement for hours. After returning to his country, it was his influence that paved the way for Thiruvithamkoor taking a firm stance against fascism during the Second World War.

After the war, Vaidyanatha Iyer immersed himself in the work to liberate Thiruvithamkoor and end royal rule. It was he who had planned and executed the Punnapra–Vayalar revolt. Its failure was the result of the work of the State Congress and the few imperialist spies who had infiltrated the Party...

'The rest is yet to be written,' I said, shyly.

Excited, the director embraced me. 'Forgive me, sir,' he said, 'for using bad language earlier...'

After a few minutes of pleasantries, he said goodbye and left the room. Then he came right back and said, 'If you need anything at all, just ask. There have been some complaints about you. They say you leave the room forgetting to put on clothes. That in the night you talk loudly in different voices like two people having a conversation. And you've been seen standing at the wall pressing your ear to it. They also say that you behave as if you were invisible. Do you need to see a doctor?'

It took me two or four years to finish writing the biography of the general secretary. This writing business is hard. Sometimes one can write only one meaningful word a day. The day I finally finished, I stepped into the yard and rolled around. Grabbed handfuls of sand and threw it in the air. Shouted.

The guards and other inmates came running. 'What's the matter?' they asked. 'What happened?'

'I've finished writing it,' I said. 'Took me years!'

'You only started two days ago,' they said.

I had to laugh. 'I think my time and your time are different.'

When I ran out of paper, I began to write on the walls and on the iron bars. And when there was no more space left, I wrote in the plate in which I ate my food. Someone came and grabbed it out of my hand, so I wrote in the mud. When people walked over it and erased it, I began to write in the air. The wind and the sun made it invisible, so I wrote on the trees in the yard. And when I ran out of bark and leaves, I sat on a tender leaf on the topmost branch and looked around me. There it was, the humongous wall that would not run out of space no matter how much one wrote. Like two large, blank books opened at right angles and facing inwards to create a square, it was trying to trap me in and make me write. All that is to be written should be written on walls. No wonder the kings carved all their news on stones. Why didn't Basheer think of that? Using my fingernails, I scratched on the wall. When, after a few days, they were worn down, I picked up stones off the floor and used them. And as I went on, there were no more stones to be found. I looked everywhere. But there was nothing to use as a writing tool. Then I used my saliva and my blood. And when I had used up everything that was there to use, I used my own shit and wrote the history of my country on that enormous wall.

12

'Writers need solitude, don't they?' the director asked me, looking me straight in the face.

'Yes,' I agreed.

He had made me sit on a chair in his room. My hands and legs were tied with belts. Like that first time I was in this room, he had a glass of foreign liquor in his hand. Or perhaps it was the same one. And I had only just got here. Those three lovely young men had only now brought me here from my room above the printing press. There they were now, standing behind me with their arms folded. On his table was the book of history, written without my involvement.

13

There was only darkness in the room of solitude. Darkness with no beginning or end, from before the world was formed. I touched its cold floor and walls. And realized that it was not a room but a corridor. Lying on the floor, I began to crawl towards one end. Days passed, and I could not reach it, so I crawled back. Stood up and jumped. But could not reach the roof either. After a while, I decided to wait for those who had brought me here to come back. What if they never came back? When I felt like I would petrify, I began crawling to one end again. There must be some end. Were these never-ending corridors? There were no sounds. Only the slight rustle of my body rubbing against the floor.

I wanted to press my ear to the wall. Something might be received from the outside? I pressed myself against the floor and listened. Nothing. Only the echo of silence. Again I listened. And again. Told the most effective of my senses to try harder once again. Amazing! Some things were coming in. Feeble. Thin, very thin, particles of sounds. When my ear captured them, I tried to detach it.

It was Vaidyanatha Iyer. Murajapam was an event that exalted internationalism, he said. People came to it unmindful of national borders. It would be reinstituted, he said, after restructuring it to suit a socialist Thiruvithamkoor. One of the powerful conduits of the working class was the intellectual. In the old society, it was the Brahmins who had undertaken such roles. A role that was still relevant. I felt that Vaidyanatha Iyer was a man who would never die. It would have been years since he came into power. What would it be like if there was to be a ruler who was immortal?

How far into the years would he be able to see? Generations would come and die away as he watched. Once again, I tried listening to the outside.

And then I heard footsteps from the inside. They came nearer and nearer. I had not heard them until now because I was busy listening to the outside. I knew who it was from the way the feet rubbed against the floor. The fragrance of medicinal herbs confirmed my thought. I was overcome with the urge to cry. Where had he been all this while? Had he not known that the mind of this hapless man had fractured? That he had fallen all the way to the floor? That he was crawling in his own bodily secretions? The warmth and smell of his body was now right next to me. I reached out and grabbed him. Those strong arms lifted me off the floor. In that moment, I weighed only as much as a kitten. He slung me across his shoulder and began to walk slowly. My body pressed against his back, my head and arms hanging down. A while later, he slowly lowered me. I recognized that bed by touch.

A big handful of cold oil slapped into the crown of my head. As it sunk to the roots of my hair, I felt sleepy. Then he raised my legs. Moved my head into a position where it hung down from the railings of the bed. I understood that the world would now begin to shudder and end. Calling out to God Almighty, I shut my eyes. He picked up the medicine in the jackfruit leaf cup and blew it into my nostrils. All was peaceful. Good. My world exploded into particles.

Many years later, I opened my eyes and ears to the sound of things turning upside down. Sounds rushing into soundless spaces. Endless sounds of things falling apart. I jumped up. The earth quaked with the impact of something big falling. Sounds of cheering, running away, chasing. Gunshots and screams. Wailing. My dark corridor was also breaking apart. I ran towards the light at its end.

The sights outside were astonishing. The old jail blocks where we had lived and the walls around them had fallen. Guards and other officers were nowhere to be seen. Some people were dancing with joy, standing on top of the rubble in the dust that had not settled. I could not see anyone I knew. A large group of people ran off outside. After a moment's uncertainty, I too ventured out. It had been a long time, so I was finding it difficult to walk and to see. My legs were unsteady, like those of someone just disembarked from a ship. My eyes wrestled with the light. The first sight I saw was people toppling over a statue, as tall as a multistorey building, with a raised finger pointing to the distance. I did not know whose statue it was. At least a few people must have died, crushed under it as it fell. A large crowd rushed past, setting fire to government and party offices. My legs had steadied, so I too ran. And as I ran, I saw people kicking, spitting and urinating on statues of many sizes that had been pulled down. No one paid any attention to me as I ran in my barbaric clothes. I could hear them shout that statues were toppling over and walls breaking down not just here but the world over. These were the same roads that I had used daily once upon a time. Yet they, everything, looked unfamiliar. New types of clothes. New buildings. Newly laid paths. People were taking down the walls that blocked the view on both sides of the main street. And from beyond them, emaciated humans entered the city.

When I finally stopped running, I was in front of the building with the printing press which, although old, still stood. Other than the waist-high clumps of plants they called communist pacha and pothachedi, a few stunted trees that had grown out of its walls, and the bits that had fallen off its back, nothing much had changed. Trampling over the plants, I reached the veranda. Old papers lay discarded on the wooden stairs to the upper floor. Stamping on them, I climbed up. Termites had turned the wood-panelled upper veranda into their work centre. The door to my room stood as it always had. No one seemed to have opened it after I had left with those three lovely young men. A few effortless pushes and it opened, and I went in.

Although covered in a thick layer of dust, my papers were still there. A few pages were damaged by the rain. Termites seemed to have left them alone. I began dusting them off and gathering them. Lovely young men, thank you for not taking these when you took me away, I said in my mind.

As I collected them, I read through some parts. Oh God, what had I done to my country? I sobbed. These were indictments against me. Papers filled with the results of my doings. Wiping my eyes and face on hands coated with black dust, I read some more. And as I read, I thought about rewriting some parts. At that moment, I heard the sound of something travelling down the road, something hard like iron chains. It came closer and closer. Once again, I looked out of the window.

This time, the view outside the window was that of the future. My country would thrive. Representatives elected by the people would come into power. All that had happened so far was the preparation, the forging in fire, for this future. People who spoke my language and those who had run away from here would try to join us.

And in the neighbouring country, the seeds sown by K.K. Nair would mature, ready for harvest. Basheer had said that stories were dangerous weapons. That country would be ruled by those who fed stories to their people. They would hoist the flag that my country had abandoned. They would install the bespectacled man I had accompanied from Rameswaram on the highest pedestal. Those who had lived quieter lives for a short while would resurrect themselves and make their voices heard over all others. As the screeching sound came closer, I picked up my papers and left the room.

The street of the future was deserted. I saw what was making that screeching noise. Armoured military vehicles of the neighbouring country were rushing towards mine, ploughing up the streets with their tracked treads. Would they reduce my country to a mere line of blood in the southern end of the subcontinent? Once again, I thought about all that I had done to my country. I saw, before my eyes, Varghese, Mani and the old man dressed in the single mundu. Thought about Vanaja, Elikkutty and Devasia. Where might they all be right now? Would Devasia and Elikkutty still be alive in the house in Thiruvambady to talk about me at least once a day, to remember me? What was being cultivated in their beautifully terraced compounds on the side of the hill? I imagined the face of my son who could have been born to Elikkutty. I called him by his name. Imagined sitting with Devasia, drinking charayam. And finally, I thought of Basheer.

Oh Basheer, you trapped me inside a story. Listening to the stories you did not write, imagining the stories you might have created, I pursued you. All I am is a shadowless man who followed you like a shadow. What is my real name? What is my country? How old am I? Gently, I touched the crown of my head. The coldness of Vallappuzha Vaidyan's oil was still there. The huge, armoured vehicles from the future were almost near. They came bearing all that my country had thrown away along the way. I walked slowly forward. The indictment against me was still in my hand. As though making a small effort to block their way, I stood directly in front of the tanks. In the next second, they would pass over me. And I would lie on this road. A line drawn in blood. A raktarekha.

Descriptions of Key and Recurring Characters

S. HAREESH AND JAYASREE KALATHIL

P.S.

Insights,
Interviews
&
More ...

Maharaja Sree Chithira Thirunal Balarama Varma: The last king of Thiruvithamkoor. Considered a weak king compared to his ancestors, it is said that his mother Amma Maharani and his diwan Sir C.P. Ramaswami Iyer had him under their control. It was in Thiruvithamkoor under his rule that people of the lower castes were allowed to enter temples for the first time in Indian history. After Independence, he became the rajapramukh of the newly formed state of Thirukochi. He passed away in 1991.

Sir C.P. Ramaswami Iyer: Sir C.P. was born in a Tamil Brahmin family in the Madras Presidency in British India. An erudite man, he was an expert in law and served as advocate general in the Madras Presidency. He had close relationships with people in key positions in the British government. He was also a close friend of Gopal Krishna Gokhale and Annie Besant, and was at one time the secretary of the Indian National Congress. But his enmity with Gandhi and Nehru made him distance himself from the Congress. It was because of Sir C.P. that Sree Chithira Thirunal, a minor at the time of the death of Maharaja Moolam Thirunal, became the maharaja of Thiruvithamkoor which was under regency rule. Sir C.P. served as adviser to the king at first and then, from 1936 to 1947, became the diwan of Thiruvithamkoor.

A great administrator, Sir C.P. was also an autocratic ruler. The inexperienced, weak king and Amma Maharani, the queen mother, were under his control. He had the reputation of being a womanizer, and it is believed that he was in a questionable relationship with Amma Maharani. Significant sociopolitical events such as the Punnapra–Vayalar uprising and the agitation for Utharavada Bharanam – responsible government – were suppressed with much cruelty under his stewardship. It is believed that he was the architect of Thiruvithamkoor's decision to remain independent and not join the Indian Union when the British left. In July 1947, there was an attempt to assassinate him. (In the novel, he hatches a skilful plan to portray this as an attempt on the life of the maharaja, much beloved to his people.) He sustained stab wounds to his face. After this, he left the country, and Thiruvithamkoor decided to join the Indian Union.

After Independence, Sir C.P. served as visiting professor in several foreign universities. He became the vice chancellor of Banaras Hindu University in 1954 and served for two years. Sir C.P. passed away in 1966 in London at the age of eighty-six.

Vaikom Muhammad Basheer: Basheer (1908–94) was a Malayali writer who has a mythical stature in Kerala. Fondly called 'Beypore Sultan', stories about Basheer are as popular as the stories he wrote. At a young age, he had the opportunity to meet Mahatma Gandhi when he came to the Vaikom Satyagraha, an episode that wrought great changes in his life. Another person who influenced him politically was Bhagat Singh. Basheer is said to have travelled all around undivided India and experienced many bizarre life events. Author of several novels and short stories, Basheer was known for using a simple, conversational style of Malayalam in his writing as well as for his unique sense of humour, and his writing mixed up fact and fiction with abandon. *August 17* references many of these stories. Some of his works are set in a bhavanaadesham, a world he created out of his imagination, named Kaduvakkuzhi, which he also called Sthalam – the Place. In the novel, the protagonist makes a trip to this place. Basheer experienced madness and was treated by an Ayurvedic healer Vallappuzha Govindan Nair (who appears in the novel as Vallappuzha Vaidyan). It is perhaps accurate to say that his real life and the imagined worlds in his stories seeped into each other. He is still one of the most read writers in Malayalam. In 1982, the government of India honoured him with the Padma Shri. Basheer passed away in 1994.

Some of Basheer's books are available in English translation: *The Love Letter and Other Stories* (translated by V. Abdulla), *Me Grandad 'ad an Elephant!, Childhood Friend, Pathumma's Goat* (all three translated by Ronald E. Asher and Achamma Coilparampil Chandrasekaran), *The Walls* (translated by V. Abdulla), *Magic Cat* (translated by N. Kunju) and *Poovan Banana and Other Stories* (translated by V. Abdulla).

Akkamma Cherian: Akkamma Cherian was a freedom fighter and a teacher by profession. She gave up her job to lead the agitation for responsible government against royal rule. She was twenty-nine years old when she, along with her sister Rosamma Cherian and Rosamma's future husband P.T. Punnoose, travelled under dangerous circumstances from the Madras Presidency to Thiruvananthapuram to lead a march to the royal palace. History records that the British police, about to shoot at the crowd, withdrew when faced with Akkamma Cherian's challenge to shoot at her first. At a time when women, especially Suriyani Christian women, were utterly dominated by men, Akkamma Cherian led a life that was of legendary proportions, because of which she was referred to as the Jhansi Rani of Kerala. After Independence, she was neglected by political leadership and went into obscurity. Akkamma Cherian passed away in 1982.

K.C.S. Mani: Mani was born in a Tamil Brahmin family in Ambalapuzha in Thiruvithamkoor. It was the socialist leader N. Sreekantan Nair who brought him into political activism. Although unknown at the time, it was later revealed that Mani was the person responsible for the real-life assassination attempt on Sir C.P. Ramaswami Iyer. After Independence, Mani remained largely inactive in politics. He passed away in 1987.

Varghese: It is believed that there was a man named Varghese who was brought in on the plan to assassinate Sir C.P. in case K.C.S. Mani failed in his mission. Further details are unavailable.

DSP Vaidyanatha Iyer: Vaidyanatha Iyer was the district superintendent of police who was responsible for the brutal suppression of the Punnapra–Vayalar uprising. No details are available about his personal life.

K.K. Nair: Born in the Kuttanad region of Thiruvithamkoor, K.K. Nair finished his education in London. He joined the Indian Civil Service and worked as district collector in several places in present-day Uttar Pradesh before and after Independence. It is widely believed that he was a corrupt official. It was while he was the district magistrate that the idol of Ram Lalla was illegally placed in the Babri Masjid, which was situated within the area under his control. K.K. Nair and his wife Shakuntala Nair are said to have played a part in the conspiracy. He was elected to the Uttar Pradesh assembly and to the Lok Sabha under the banner of the Bharatiya Jana Sangh, an early avatar of the Bharatiya Janata Party. Shakuntala Nair also became a member of the Lok

Sabha with the support of the Hindu Mahasabha and the Jana Sangh. It is possible to imagine that, without the support of K.K. Nair in his powerful office, the Babri Masjid–Ram Janmabhoomi altercation would have turned out differently, perhaps also changing the course of India's history. K.K. Nair passed away in 1977.

Pattom Thanu Pillah: Freedom fighter and one of the main leaders of the agitation for responsible government. He did not quite get on with Sir C.P. but was compliant to royal rule. After Independence, for a brief period, he was the prime minister of Thiruvithamkoor. When the state of Thirukochi was formed he became its chief minister, and later the chief minister of the newly formed state of Kerala. He has served as the governor of Punjab and Andhra Pradesh. He was the leader of the State Congress, and after Independence, of the Indian National Congress. Later, he formed his own party called the Praja Socialist Party.

K.C. George: K.C. George was one of the founding leaders of the communist movement in Thiruvithamkoor. He played a major part in the armed revolt in Punnapra–Vayalar. He was a member of the first legislative assembly after the formation of Kerala. K.C. George wrote a book about the uprisings against royal rule titled *Immortal Punnapra Vayalar* which has been an important reference in the writing of *August 17*.

Annie Mascarene: A leader of the State Congress and a freedom fighter. Mascarene worked with Gandhi briefly in the ashram in Wardha. She was the first woman minister in Kerala's legislative assembly after Independence and the first woman from Kerala to be elected to the Rajya Sabha. She stood for the elections as an independent candidate.

T.V. Thomas: Thomas was a leader of the Communist Party. When the state of Kerala was formed, Thomas became the minister of labour and transport. He married K.R. Gauriyamma, a fellow communist leader and a minister in the same cabinet. Following the split in the Communist Party, Thomas and Gauriyamma found themselves in different factions. Their political and personal lives have inspired several Malayalam movies.

P. Krishnapillah: A founding leader of the Communist Party who has a legendary status in Kerala. Known simply as 'Comrade', he is described as the first communist in the state. During his early political career, he was a Congress activist and participated in the Salt Satyagraha and the Guruvayoor Satyagraha that demanded temple entry for people from the lower castes. It is thought that he was the person who inspired and instigated the Punnapra–Vayalar uprising. Comrade Krishnapillah died of a snakebite while in hiding after the Communist Party of India was banned in 1948. He was forty-two years old at the time of his death.

Franco Raghavan Pillah: Puthiyaveettil Raghavan Pillah was the man who led a small village named Kadakkal in Thiruvithamkoor to independence – although only for nine days – much before India gained independence. The rebellion, known as the Kadakkal Revolt of 1938, a civil disobedience movement against Sir C.P. and his tax collection policies, began in the village of Kadakkal and was affiliated with the agitation for responsible government. The agitators liberated Kadakkal, and Raghavan Pillah is said to have ruled the place as its king with others appointed as ministers. Sir C.P. is said to have instigated the media to deem Raghavan Pillah's activities 'fascist' and name him 'Franco' after the Spanish dictator General Franco. After the revolt was squashed, Raghavan Pillah went into hiding for a long time. There are several stories about his life in hiding. Raghavan Pillah was only marginally involved in politics in his later years and died a natural death.

Ponnara Sridhar: Freedom fighter and a leader of the State Congress who was influential in bringing socialist ideas into the party. Sridhar became a member of the Kerala legislative assembly after Independence.

A.J. Simson: Simson was a mysterious individual who was said to have had close associations with the Thiruvithamkoor government. He had formed his own 'pada' – an army of miscreants known as the 'Simson Pada' – to suppress political action against royal rule and to terrorize the agitators. For this work, he was rewarded well by the diwan and enjoyed many privileges from the royal family.

E.M.S. Namboothiripad: An important leader of the Kerala communist movement and the state's first chief minister. He was not a native of Thiruvithamkoor but was born in British Malabar.

A.K. Gopalan: A native of Malabar, AKG was a freedom fighter and the leader of the Communist Party, perhaps its most popular face. He was the first opposition leader in independent India.

V.S. Achuthanandan: A member of the Communist Party during the Punnapra–Vayalar revolt, Achuthanandan was the leader of the opposition during several governments. He became the chief minister of Kerala in 2006 – the state's oldest chief minister, assuming office at the age of eighty-two – and served until 2011. In the novel, Achuthanandan dies as a young man, but his real-life death took place on 21 July 2025.

K.M. Chummar: Freedom fighter and historian, K.M. Chummar is mentioned in the novel only in one place and in a single line. His book dealing with the history of Thiruvithamkoor, *Thiruvithamkoor State Congress*, has been helpful in writing this novel.

P.T. Punnoose: An early leader of the Communist Party. After Independence, Punnoose was twice elected to the Lok Sabha. He married Rosamma Cherian, the sister of Akkamma Cherian, who was also elected to the Kerala legislative assembly several times.

Mannath Padmanabhan: One of Kerala's prominent community reformers and the founder of the caste-community organization Nair Service Society.

Kumbalath Shanku Pillai: A freedom fighter and leader of the State Congress, Kumbalath Shanku Pillai rose to the rank of president of the Kerala Pradesh Congress Committee. His autobiography, *Ente Kanzhinjakaala Smaranakal*, has been useful in writing this novel.

N. Sreekantan Nair: A charismatic politician, Sreekantan Nair was a socialist and the founder of the Kerala Socialist Party. He was elected to the Lok Sabha in 1952 from Kollam. He was also known as a writer, and was the translator of Thakazhi Sivasankara Pillai's magnum opus *Kayar* (Coir) into English.

Thakazhi Sivasankara Pillai: One of Kerala's most important writers, Thakazhi Sivasankara Pillai was known for realist depictions of ordinary lives in his novels and short stories. He received the Jnanpith Award in 1984 and the Padma Bhushan in 1985.

Zacharia: Paul Zacharia is a prominent contemporary writer in Malayalam. Known primarily for his short stories, he received the Kerala Sahitya Akademi Award in 1979 and the Kendra Sahitya Akademi Award in 2004.

*

In addition to the people described above, several other historically important figures make their appearance in the novel. It must be reiterated, however, that they do not behave in the novel as they did in their real lives, nor are their personal and political histories depicted as they were in real life. In imagining an important historical event unfolding differently, their destinies too have changed and become something else.

ABOUT THE AUTHOR

S. Hareesh has published three novels – *Meesha, August 17* and *Pattunoolpuzhu* – and three short-story collections – *Adam, Appan* and *Rasavidyayude Charithram.* He has won the Kerala Sahitya Akademi Award twice – for *Meesha* and for *Adam*. The English translation of *Meesha* by Jayasree Kalathil, *Moustache,* won the 2020 JCB Prize for Literature. Hareesh has received many other accolades including the Geetha Hiranyan Endowment, the P. Padmarajan Award, the Basheer Sahitya Puraskaram, the Thomas Mundassery Prize and the V.P. Sivakumar Memorial Prize. He is also an award-winning writer of screenplays, and his credits include the 2019 film *Jallikattu,* which was India's official entry for the Best International Feature Film at the 93rd Academy Awards, and *Nanpakalnerathu Mayakkam,* which won the Rajatha Chakoram Award at the 2022 International Film Festival of Kerala. Hareesh lives in Neendoor in Kottayam district, Kerala.

ABOUT THE TRANSLATOR

Jayasree Kalathil is a bilingual writer and translator, and the author of *The Sackclothman,* a children's book that has been translated into Malayalam, Telugu, Hindi and Urdu. Her translations have won the Crossword Book Award for Indian Language Translations (twice), the JCB Prize for Literature, the V. Abdulla Memorial Translation Award, the Mathrubhumi Book of the Year Award and the Muse India–G.S.P. Rao Translation Prize Jury Commendation. Jayasree has also been shortlisted for the ALTA National Translation Award in Prose. Currently, she is the managing editor of translated fiction at *The Bombay Literary Magazine* and a mentor on the ALTA Emerging Translators Mentorship Programme. She has received the 2025 Camargo Foundation Fellowship, Cassis, France, and was the translator-in-residence at the British Centre for Literary Translation, University of East Anglia, UK, in 2023.

HarperCollins *Publishers* India

At HarperCollins India, we believe in telling the best stories and finding the widest readership for our books in every format possible. We started publishing in 1992; a great deal has changed since then, but what has remained constant is the passion with which our authors write their books, the love with which readers receive them, and the sheer joy and excitement that we as publishers feel in being a part of the publishing process.

Over the years, we've had the pleasure of publishing some of the finest writing from the subcontinent and around the world, including several award-winning titles and some of the biggest bestsellers in India's publishing history. But nothing has meant more to us than the fact that millions of people have read the books we published, and that somewhere, a book of ours might have made a difference.

As we look to the future, we go back to that one word—a word which has been a driving force for us all these years.

Read.